UNLADYLIKE RULES OF ATTRACTION

AMITA MURRAY

UNLADYLIKE
RULES
OF
ATTRACTION

A Marleigh Sisters Novel

AVON

An Imprint of HarperCollinsPublishers

UNLADYLIKE RULES OF ATTRACTION. Copyright © 2024 by Amita Murray. All rights reserved. Printed in the United States of America. No part of this book may be used or reproduced in any manner whatsoever without written permission except in the case of brief quotations embodied in critical articles and reviews. For information, address HarperCollins Publishers, 195 Broadway, New York, NY 10007.

HarperCollins books may be purchased for educational, business, or sales promotional use. For information, please email the Special Markets Department at SPsales@harpercollins.com.

FIRST EDITION

Designed by Jackie Alvarado

Library of Congress Cataloging-in-Publication Data has been applied for.

ISBN 978-0-06-329652-7

24 25 26 27 28 LBC 5 4 3 2 1

To Sam
For teaching me about creativity, for always making things better,
and for giving me my first real inkling of home

UNLADYLIKE
RULES
OF
ATTRACTION

1

The cork ball came at her like a pistol shot.

Most people would duck to save their heads from such a delivery, but Anya Marleigh calmly swung her bat and whacked the ball half a mile down the field. She may be a mere singer in the Queen's court, but she had learned to play cricket on the streets of Delhi, and no one was going to say she didn't know how to handle a bat.

Her partner at the other end of the pitch started pelting down to take the run, muslin skirt in hand, but Anya stood by her wicket, one fist on her hip, jauntily leaning on her bat. "Hold your fire, Trixie," she said. "That's going for a six."

She was right. The next few balls also didn't tax Trixie Cleaver, Anya's sixteen-year-old protégé, all that much, going for fours and sixes across the many acres of the Budleigh estate. Trixie, who had straw-colored hair tied in a prosaic knot and pretty hazel eyes, was whooping at Anya's every crack at the ball.

It was Anya's annual trip to the Budleigh estate, though she was surprised to be here this year. Dowager Countess Budleigh, who normally invited her, had died at Christmas, and Anya had expected the winter gathering to be canceled. What was more surprising was that she was not here to play music. She was here because the Budleigh lawyer, Mr. Prism, had asked her to come to the reading of the dowager's will.

Normally, she lived at court, like some of the other ladies-in-waiting. And though she didn't have duties of the bedchamber or companionship as the other ladies did, and she was hardly the Queen's chief source of society gossip, the Queen liked to have her at hand for impromptu musical evenings.

Not that she had anywhere else she could afford to live. These spots of travel for her extra jobs, like the annual trip down to the Budleigh estate in Folkestone, always felt like little treats. Not this year, though.

Anya frowned as she waited for the cricket ball to be found. It was strange to come all the way down to Folkestone just for the reading of a will. But the dowager had been generous, and perhaps she had left Anya a little memento—an oak chest or an armoire or something that would be the devil to transport back to London. The lawyer's letter had conveyed an urgency, or maybe it was the serious tone. *I hope you will come, even if there are objections to it.* Objections, what objections?

She and Trixie were playing three-a-side cricket with the Budleigh grandchildren while they waited for the lawyer to turn up. Anya couldn't help thinking that the four scamps, one girl and three boys, ranging in age from six to thirteen, were a much nicer bunch than any of their parents or uncles and aunts. While Dowager Countess Budleigh had always treated her with respect and openly enjoyed her music and her company, and the Budleigh grandchildren loved to play with her, the dowager's children, the middle generation, were condescending at best. They were the kind of people who looked down their noses at her for being a court singer and treated her with such frozen politeness that it was all Anya could do not to stalk off in a huff. Even the thought made her bristle like a cat.

"We missed you, Anya!" the six-year-old girl, Laura, shouted, jumping up and down from the side, her red braids, tied with periwinkle ribbon, bouncing all about her. She broke into Anya's thoughts and made her smile. Yes, much nicer, the younger Budleighs. Less puffed up.

They were playing boys versus girls, and Laura had been run out after two runs. Anya replaced her, and she was now touching sixty-five runs. The boys didn't seem too happy about this.

"Have you been practicing?" the oldest one, Toby, said with a pout. He had a tendency to go red when he was playing some sport or annoyed—right now, he was both. "I suppose they play at the palace? You know, you could *try* not to look like you're enjoying thrashing the life out of us."

"But that would be a lie, darling!" Anya shouted. "Because I'm enjoying it *very much*."

It was winter, and frost curled the ostrich fern around the pond and feathered the edges of the outbuildings. Anya waited for Toby, Trevor, and Brendan to find the ball and bring it back. As she stood there, whistling and leaning on her bat and boasting to Trixie that the ball was probably in Calais by now, a man dressed in dark clothes walked up the lane.

The man looked bored, like he was wandering past the house and decided to saunter in, in case it was mildly entertaining. Anya looked at him in surprise; she had not heard any sounds of a carriage or a horse.

Anya was about six inches over five feet, and the man was probably no more than an inch or two taller than her. He was wearing breeches and a black overcoat that was flapping carelessly open. His Hessians were smart but not shining. He had untidy black hair and brown eyes, the color of wildflower honey, and they looked amused and cynical and bored, all at the same time. He stopped at the edge of the garden and looked critically at Anya.

Anya lifted her chin. He must be Mr. Prism, the lawyer. He was looking insolently at her, and she flushed, knowing that with no greatcoat on, the cuffs of her dress rolled up, and her hems muddy—*and* she had been whistling in a very unladylike way—she looked like a scarecrow.

He glanced at the tally on the chalkboard. It showed sixty-seven runs. Laura was keeping the board meticulously marked in large, slightly crooked numbers, but right now she had run off after her cousins to look for the missing ball.

"It would be good to see what you make of a real delivery," the man said. "Though not a bad swing. For an amateur."

She gasped. She quickly schooled her face, though she knew her eyes were flashing. "Thank you, sir. And if I ever need unasked-for opinions from a *complete stranger*, I suppose I know just where to find them."

Now his other hand was in his pocket too, and he was smiling. This made her feel like a prim old miss who never spoke to strangers—which was blatantly untrue, since at court all she did was talk to people she didn't know—and this only annoyed her more. She was trying to think of a cutting remark when the Budleigh children came running up to the man, calling out, "Cousin Damian, Cousin Damian!"

Who the devil was Cousin Damian? She shot a look at Trixie, who shrugged. Trixie was pulling her coat on, and since she hadn't had to do much other than stand around and watch her partner swing a bat, her hair was in much better shape than Anya's. Anya's tight ringlets were coming loose from her bun and skimming her shoulders, her face was shiny with sweat, and her clothes were rumpled and grubby. Come to think of it, most scarecrows looked like they were going to high tea with a duchess compared to her.

The children were milling about the man, and though he wasn't exactly warm with them, he was pulling Laura's braids and telling Trevor, who was eleven, to be less of an urchin and button up his shirt. Laura was shouting over all of the boys and explaining to "Cousin Damian" that the girls were winning because Anya had already got a total of sixty-five and the best the boys had ever come up with in previous games was thirty-six. "And sixty-five is *much* higher than thirty-six! It's higher than thirty-seven, and thirty-eight, and thirty-nine, and forty! Wait, *is* it higher than forty, Cousin Damian?"

The man shot a look at Anya. "I'm sure Miss—uh—Anya is a very good sportswoman. But your bowling, Toby, needs a bit more practice. Now, if *I* tried one of my deliveries—" He looked inquiringly—challengingly—at Anya.

Anya pursed her mouth. "No, thank you, sir," she said coolly. "I need to tidy myself up before Mr. Prism gets here." Because whoever this man was, he wasn't the lawyer, since it was unlikely the children called the lawyer *Cousin Damian*. She gestured to Trixie to head in to the house.

The children were protesting loudly and physically (children seemed incapable of shouting without also jumping up and down at the same time, it seemed), but Anya was ready to walk away, when the man said, "Running craven, Miss—"

Her nostrils flared. "Anya Marleigh," she said shortly.

Though why she was introducing herself when the man hadn't bothered to mention his name, she didn't know. She stole a glance at Trixie, who gave her a tiny smile. Trixie knew

Anya would find it impossible to back down from such an open dare. Such a *rude* challenge. It would be good to teach the man a lesson. Anya firmed her hands around the bat. She took her place at the wicket again and looked challengingly at him.

He smiled and took the ball from Toby, who whooped. To which Cousin Damian said that he'd never seen anyone who sounded so much like a baboon and would the boys please get out of his way and could Laura stand where she couldn't be hit by the ball? He took his position. He rubbed the ball carelessly on his coat, came running up to the pitch, and with a neat bowling arm tossed the ball. Straight into Anya's stump.

Anya gasped. But she had no time to complain that she'd not been ready. Because the delivery was high enough that after crashing into the wicket and knocking it clean over, it kept on flying, then bounced once, which strangely made it go flying up again and all the way to the morning room window. Where it smashed into the window, breaking it into smithereens.

There was breathtaking silence around the pitch.

Anya broke it. She said, "The devil!" before she could mind her language. She dropped the bat and cupped her mouth with her hands. Where there were whoops, shouts, and laughter a minute ago, now there was deathly quiet. If the ball had broken one of the conservatory windows, it wouldn't be such a problem. They would have got told off, but it would be mended right away. But the ball had crashed into the irreplaceable sixteenth-century stained glass that lined the morning room French windows. The Budleigh estate was a rambling one, and some parts of it dated even further back than the sixteenth century.

The housekeeper, Mrs. Winsome, appeared in the now-jagged window frame.

She was a small and desperately scrawny woman, and every

employee in the house was afraid of her. "That glass is never getting repaired," she announced dispassionately.

Behind her was Clara, Lady Budleigh. She was the late Dowager Countess Budleigh's daughter-in-law, and Toby, Trevor, and Brendan's mother. Her husband, Lord Preston Budleigh, was the dowager's oldest child. Her mouth was opening and closing like a fish.

"Lady Budleigh!" Anya finally found her voice.

Lady Budleigh found hers. "Miss Marleigh, I don't know how they expect their women to behave at the palace. But being that you are a guest here, you could have perhaps found it in yourself to show a modicum of breeding. Or if that is not possible, at least common politeness." Clara Budleigh stopped abruptly and blotted her lips. She was a tall, thin woman, her face long, her eyes a very pale blue, her brown hair pulled back in a sharp bun out of which a strand of hair never dared escape. The sleeves of her dress covered every inch of arm flesh, and if the neckline were any higher it would cover her mouth. She seemed to be struggling with herself. She hardly ever bent enough to talk to a mere employee at length, and Anya had never seen her surface crack. Lady Budleigh took deep breaths. She swallowed. She opened and closed her mouth, and then opened it again, a bit like a fish. "Boys, if you can only behave like street children, you need to go to the nursery at once. And no tea for you today."

"No tea today," said Mrs. Winsome, in the same way a judge pronounces a death sentence.

There were gasps of outrage and protest.

Anya said quickly, "Oh no, it wasn't the boys! It was . . ." She turned wildly around.

The man—Cousin Damian—had disappeared.

She stared at the empty space near the far wicket. She stared at the Budleigh children. But none of them were saying anything. She turned back to Lady Budleigh.

But Lady Budleigh wasn't looking at her. "Boys, I said off to the nursery. And take Cousin Laura with you. Miss Marleigh, I suppose you couldn't help it, and I can hardly expect *you* to have any reverence for our old artifacts and traditions," she said in a way that made Anya wish the woman were yelling at her instead. "Luckily, it was only a pane of the harbor and not— not the cliffs . . ." Words failed her. Her breasts, stiff, high and important, were quivering.

Anya swallowed. The pane had been exquisite. Not one of the more imposing ones of the white Folkestone cliffs, but a deep blue-and-green underwater scene with two fishing boats nestled at the bottom, and sandstone sea cottages in the background. She looked guiltily at Lady Budleigh.

Lady Budleigh pressed her lips with a plain white handkerchief. "Mr. Prism will be here shortly." She looked at Anya's muddy skirt like she'd never seen anything like it before. "Please use the basin upstairs to freshen up."

"That mud is never coming off," Mrs. Winsome pronounced.

2

Anya was seething all the way up to a spare bedchamber that the Budleighs had put at her disposal for the duration of her and Trixie's stay in Folkestone. She was followed closely by Trixie. "It was a corker of a delivery, you *have* to give him that," Trixie was saying.

Anya thrust her hands into the washbasin, splashing water everywhere. "I wasn't ready! Anyone could see I was distracted!"

"Distracted by what?"

"An owl."

"An owl?"

"Or a pigeon! It's impossible to tell the birds apart in the countryside. Haven't you noticed it?"

"Not especially," Trixie said, frowning like she was really thinking about it.

Anya growled and tried not to bite her protégé's head off. She muttered about uppity young women, which made Trixie grin. Trixie was an orphan, a daughter—technically an illegitimate daughter—of a lower lady-in-waiting who had died some years ago and an unknown gentleman. She didn't fit with the royal staff, or with the ladies-in-waiting because of her illegit-imacy and her lack of name or fortune. Anya, though she had very little to give Trixie in a material sense, had tried to take the girl under her wing and educate her. And she couldn't help thinking that she in turn had come to depend on Trixie's friendship. Though why Trixie had to take the man's side, Anya couldn't fathom. The dressing-down from Lady Budleigh was pinching her. She knew Clara Budleigh had little time for her social inferiors and had only tolerated Anya because she had been the dowager's guest. Anya didn't want to be rude to Lady Budleigh now, but to get a telling off like that! And it was all that man's fault.

Since Trixie looked smart as a button anyway, in her white floral muslin, she helped Anya fix herself. This was easier said than done. Anya washed her face and smoothed her hair—which instantly sprang about her face again in tight coils. She straightened her dress—a fine muslin, the color of effervescent pink champagne, with blue roses embroidered at the hem—but the muddy stains and creases were hopeless.

And it wasn't helping that she was fuming and kept batting Trixie's hands away. "What a strange man! What a *rude* man! Who on earth is Cousin Damian? I bet you he isn't a cousin at all but some impoverished tenant on the estate who the children feel sorry for and kindly call 'cousin.' To disappear like that and not admit what he did! Oh, I'm so sorry, Trixie, did I hurt you? Just keep your hands away because I don't know what I'm doing."

It took a good twenty minutes to try to get some order into her dress and hair, but the same could not be said of her head. "If I *ever* see him again!"

"He's hardly likely to have slipped away," Trixie said practically. "So whatever you'd like to do to him, I'm sure you'll get the chance to."

"You know, Trixie, this prosaic air you have, this air of being right all the time, it isn't at all pretty for a sixteen-year-old."

Trixie smiled and teased Anya's curls between her fingers. She didn't say anything, which, Anya thought, people only did when they wanted to fan the flames and be especially aggravating. She told Trixie so. They finally made their way down the stairs, arranging paisley shawls about their shoulders.

But now that the appointment with the lawyer was here and she had to confront the Budleigh family—without the watchful eye of the dowager, who never allowed her children to be rude to their guests or employees—she suddenly felt paralyzed. She hovered outside the front parlor.

Why was she here? She was never in her element when she was surrounded by people—unless she was singing or playing her sitar. Sometimes she thought the only time she felt like herself was when she felt those hard strings on the pads of her fingers. She hung outside the Drawing Room, fighting the impulse to run. Trixie was busy pinning up her paisley shawl.

The dowager had liked Anya, it was true. The dowager despised her three children and their two spouses (she had often liked to wonder out loud which one she despised more than the others). She once said to Anya, "You're the only one around who is not after my money. Tell me, m'dear, what were you telling me about Caroline Herschel's findings of a new comet?"

Anya knew a little about a lot of things and had chatted with Dowager Countess Budleigh on many topics, including court gossip, an astronomer's interest in comets, and the deadly habits of the Venus flytrap, and the dowager liked that. She had little time or patience for her children. The oldest was Lord Preston Budleigh, and he had inherited the title after his father's death. His wife was Clara, Lady Budleigh. Amelia Canningford was the middle child, and Charlie Budleigh the youngest. "You don't bore me to death with your nervous complaints like my Amelia does," the dowager had complained. "Nor get browbeaten the minute anyone blinks at him, like Preston does. And of Charlie, let's not say a word about my youngest, nor about Preston's horsy wife. I can't stomach any of them," she said, eviscerating her children with a quick and effective summary.

But, whatever said and done, the dowager's children had not been openly rude to Anya when the dowager was alive. Perhaps she should have behaved with more decorum now that her chief supporter in the household was gone.

Finally, Trixie was done with her shawl, and Anya braced herself. They entered the drawing room.

The *man* was still there.

Her eyes landed on him right away. He was looking as cool as you please. It was on the tip of her tongue to yell, *There he is, he broke the window!* but she bit her tongue and swallowed her words. The poor children—very unfairly—were nowhere in sight and were probably starving.

The lawyer had arrived. He was young and lanky and serious-looking and gravely shook Anya's hand when Preston Budleigh introduced them. Lord Budleigh then introduced Lord Damian Ashton, a distant cousin of the family's, who was also invited for the reading of the will.

Lord Damian Ashton!

Anya inclined her head graciously in the man's direction, then pointedly turned her shoulder and spoke to the lawyer. Half her mind (more than half) was wondering who *Lord* Damian

Ashton was, why he was here, and why Preston Budleigh had glanced nervously at his wife, Lady Budleigh, when he introduced the man to Anya. Anya was pretty sure Lady Budleigh was looking at the man with frigid politeness. Mrs. Amelia Canningford, the dowager's middle child, was openly bristling and fretting. And Charlie Budleigh, the youngest, was sitting on the windowsill, his leg anxiously beating. He was ignoring everyone, but especially Damian Ashton. Had they not expected him? Had the man come here uninvited? It sounded like him.

Tea was served.

Charlie Budleigh's leg was still beating, and now he said, "You know, Anya, I wasn't expecting to see *you* here." Charlie had light brown hair and overbright blue eyes and would have looked younger than his twenty-seven years if his face weren't red and blotchy and he didn't look like he regularly drank himself into the gutter. "Though it's good you're here. You're much more entertaining than the rest of this dismal lot."

"Were you expecting to be entertained at the reading of your mother's will?" said a voice.

Anya started. She had been talking court politics with Mr. Prism and hadn't realized that *that man* was perched right behind her, on a side table, ankles crossed, eating a slice of fruitcake.

Charlie went even redder. "What are *you* doing here, *Cousin Damian?* Have you not inherited enough of the family money already?"

"You missed out the word 'wrongfully,'" Damian Ashton said. He sipped his tea and impartially smiled at everyone.

"Charlie." Amelia Canningford nervously frowned at her brother.

"Now, now," Lord Budleigh said, wiping his brow on the

back of his hand and glancing nervously at his wife. "What must Anya think of us?" He was medium height, in his midforties, and going soft in the middle.

"What *does* Miss Marleigh think of us?" Lord Ashton responded like he was mildly interested in this point.

"She is not so ill-bred as to think anything," Lady Budleigh was goaded into retorting.

"What, ever?" Lord Ashton inquired.

"*I* think that—" Lady Budleigh started.

"Oh, but I was only asking what Miss Marleigh thought," Lord Ashton said politely, sipping his tea.

Anya bristled, not willing to be a shuttlecock in whatever this game was. "I will try to think of *you* as little as possible, sir," she said to Lord Damian Ashton.

Charlie gave a bark of laughter.

"I didn't know you would have to make an effort, Miss Marleigh," Lord Ashton said.

"I won't," she said shortly. She turned her shoulder again, though she could feel his eyes on her back.

Unfortunately, the lawyer was now talking to Lord Budleigh. Amelia turned to talk to her sister-in-law about the number of times she had wondered if she had the typhus, and going into copious detail about her symptoms. This left Charlie to make half-smiling conversation with Trixie.

Anya uneasily watched them. They were standing on the other side of the room, and it would be marked if she walked up to them, but Trixie looked uncomfortable. At her age, Trixie was fair game for the court drunkards, and apparently it was no different here. This was a big part of the reason Anya had taken her under her wing in the first place and took her with her when she traveled for her work. Though how you were supposed to watch out for a sixteen-year-old all the time was beyond Anya. It was not an easy task.

She was wondering how she could intervene when a voice startled her.

"What *are* you doing here, Miss Marleigh?" said Lord Damian Ashton.

3

She turned to face him. "What do you care, my lord?" Anya said, her voice as cordial as his but there was a dangerous glint in her eye.

"Please call me Damian. You call a few of the others by their first names. Like Amelia and Charlie."

"Oh, but I know them," Anya said. She didn't add that Amelia hadn't invited her to call her by her given name, but in fact it was the dowager who had insisted that Anya do so. Anya had never been able to bring herself to call Lord and Lady Budleigh by their names.

The man smiled appreciatively. A real smile that crinkled the skin around his eyes and his mouth, so that his whole face lit up suddenly, instead of the half-mocking smile she'd seen so far. "A leveler, Miss Marleigh. And I'm sad to hear that you think you don't know me. You've had a full hour to quiz the children about me. I'm hurt."

"I have no interest in you or the details of your life."

He was watching her with that half-mocking look. "Still, we aren't that different, you know."

She gritted her teeth. There was something incredibly annoying about the man. "We're completely different. *I* wouldn't have let other people take the blame for something *I* did."

"Oh, does that still rankle? I'm sorry. But like you said, I don't know you. So it was neither here nor there if you took the blame. Why should that concern me?"

She was glaring at him. "A *gentleman's* approach to things, my lord?"

"Damian. And who said I was a gentleman? Ask the people in this room. I grew up no better than a street urchin in the Caribbean. Lived there until I was thirteen. Was shipped here to boarding school to mend my ways—which I didn't. Then when people I barely knew—I don't remember most of their names—died of a wide and surprising variety of illnesses and accidents, I became earl of a crumbling estate about two years ago. Which no one should have envied me, except it came with a title, and *everyone* grudges me that. If I—and my brother—didn't stand in the way, the estate—which borders this one—would have added to the Budleigh acres and the title would have gone to Preston Budleigh."

So this explained the frosty way in which the family had introduced Damian Ashton to her. And in fact, it rang a bell now. She hadn't met this man before. But didn't someone—Lady Budleigh?—say something about some upstart cousin who had inherited land that should have melted seamlessly into the Budleigh acres, someone whom she described—Anya remembered it now—as an *urchin thief* who grew up on the streets of Jamaica? Wait, didn't Lady Budleigh imply that there was something dodgy about the way the man had inherited the Ashton estate?

She studied him. The slim nose, the neat jaw, the level eyebrows that met faintly in the middle, the mocking brown eyes.

The features should have made the man look delicate, yet she had the strange thought that she'd rarely met anyone with so much raw animal masculinity.

"I don't see how this makes us at all alike, my lord."

"Oh, doesn't it? An urchin who the family had never heard of before, with a Jamaican native for a grandmother, a man with no claim to anything, snatches the title away from the family under their noses."

"I still don't understand."

"I have no claim on the Budleigh family titles or estates, yet I seem to be infernally lucky and have got everything the rest of the family wanted. And *you* have no claim to anything under my great-aunt's will, Miss Marleigh. But you have the charm to get yourself what you need. It must come in handy at court, and it clearly came in handy with my great-aunt."

She clanked her teacup hard on the saucer.

Conversation paused. Anya felt herself flushing. Lady Budleigh looked like she was too polite to notice the clumsiness, though there was a dangerous glint in her eyes. *She* no doubt thought it was Anya's breeding again. Amelia looked vaguely surprised. Anya turned to glare at Lord Ashton. "Used my charm to get an *oak chest* out of the dowager?" she snapped.

"An oak chest. Is that so? It might be a bit more than that, don't you think, for her to invite you here when there's only family here?"

"Now, now, Lord Ashton, that is too much," she said, fluttering her hand. "*You* can't really call yourself family, and *you're* here."

He smiled appreciatively again. But didn't say anything.

She placed her saucer and cup to one side. She kept her voice as steady as she could. "If you're implying that I ingratiated myself with the dowager to see what I could get from her—"

"Implying? No, no, now, *that* is too much, Miss Marleigh. I thought I was saying it quite clearly and directly."

Her eyes flashed and she moved an inch closer. "An urchin *thief* from the streets of Jamaica would expect everyone else to be cut from the same cloth."

He watched her with those hooded eyes of his. "You *have* been asking about me—and the details of my life—after all, Miss Marleigh. I'm flattered."

She nearly launched herself at the man. Her hands were clenched like she'd like to put them around his throat. She did in fact growl under her breath, but luckily for all, at this moment, Lady Budleigh whispered something to Lord Budleigh, who said, "Yes, yes, m'dear, just as you say." He drew himself together and suggested that perhaps it was time to hear what Mr. Prism had to say.

"Oh, how I hate this kind of thing," Amelia said, fanning herself with her hands. "It is threatening to bring on a migraine any moment now. I can feel it hovering on the edges of my vision. And my pulse is racing! Don't you feel that females are not cut out for such things as wills and jointures?"

No one had anything to say to this. Just then, Sir Canningford, Amelia's husband, came into the room, with a strong smell of cigar smoke hanging about him. He clapped Amelia so hard on the shoulder that she nearly tottered over. "Buck up, old chap," the man said to his wife. "No point crumbling at the last defense, eh?" He looked around. He was broad-shouldered and broad-chested, in fact big all around. The man started when he saw Lord Ashton. "You here? Why?"

Amelia whimpered at this plain speaking. Lady Budleigh looked pained. Lord Ashton was still smiling, and Anya had to grip her skirt in her fists so she didn't punch the man.

People sat down around the fireplace, and Anya inched away

from Lord Ashton so she didn't have to sit next to him. Trixie gracefully excused herself. Anya ended up at the end, with Amelia next to her, and Amelia's husband on the other side of Amelia. The rest of the family sat down too. Damian Ashton wasn't part of the semicircle they made around Mr. Prism, who was sitting at the coffee table, facing them. Lord Ashton was no longer perched on the side table, but he was still leaning against it, ankles crossed, looking mildly interested in what was going on.

Mr. Prism, looking even more serious now, read out a long list of bequests to employees, tenants, and relatives. He said now that the will was being read, he would let the relevant people know about these. The estate was entailed, along with the title, and had already passed to the oldest child, Lord Preston Budleigh, when the old earl died.

The bequests were going on so long that Anya was widening her eyes to keep them open. Sir Canningford was openly yawning. Lady Budleigh significantly cleared her throat.

"Yes, yes," Lord Budleigh said. "Quite so." He looked at the lawyer. "We know all that, man. Can't we speed things along? My father left my mother with a lifetime interest in the money. Now that can revert to me, and I can spend some of it on this infernal estate that's always bleeding money. Is that not so?"

Mr. Prism gave a noncommittal incline of the head. "Not exactly, my lord. You see, you are right about your father's income from the estates. He left your mother with a lifetime interest in these monies, and they will now revert to you. However, the bulk of the money we are discussing today belonged to the dowager herself. She inherited this wealth from her now-deceased uncle, and it came to her after your father was already dead. And hence the dowager could do with this money what she chose."

Lord Budleigh was looking a little wide-eyed. Charlie openly looked impatient and kept tapping his eyeglass on his leg. Lady Budleigh cleared her throat even more significantly.

"Come now, man," Lord Budleigh said quickly. "Let's get on with it. So, what's Mama gone and done? Eh? I wager she's done something eccentric. Divided it all between the three of us? Is that why you're hedging, man? Unusual, you'd say, and I can't say it won't be inconvenient, because the estate needs the cash, let me make no bones about it. The roof is falling about our ears. What am I supposed to do to save the family seat if I have no cash—"

"Live in a smaller place," murmured Lord Ashton helpfully.

"Really, can't we just get to the point?" Lady Budleigh snapped. "It would be a miracle if Lord Ashton understood the meaning of blood or legacy."

"Quite so," Lord Ashton said. "But you would, Clara. I really bet you would."

Lady Budleigh did not respond, but her jaw tightened.

Amelia was taking deep breaths and fanning herself with her hands.

"*Is* it divided amongst us? Is that why the hoo-ha?" Lord Budleigh said.

"I doubt that *that's* why there's a hoo-ha," Lord Ashton said.

Everyone turned to look at him. Anya couldn't help thinking he knew something about the way the money was left. She watched him curiously. The Budleighs were palpably impatient. Lady Budleigh was openly sneering at his every word. But he was relaxed. Of course, he didn't have a stake in it like they did. But yet, he looked *too* relaxed.

"What do you mean, Damian? Really, it is impossible to decipher your cryptic sayings," Lord Budleigh said with admirable self-control.

Lord Ashton smiled. "Has anyone noticed that we've been sitting here for an hour listening to a list of tedious bequests, yet Miss Marleigh's name has not come up?"

Anya started. She'd been bored with the long list too and impatient at the bickering of the Budleighs. But now she stared fixedly at Lord Ashton.

"Don't be ridiculous," Lady Budleigh said, her eyes narrowed. "What can poor Anya have to do with Mama's wealth? She is just a singer. Hardly more than a servant. Mama must have been in a gracious mood to leave her some little thing, that is all."

The lawyer inclined his head. "The dowager's wealth has not in fact been split amongst you and your two siblings, my lord. *Half* of the dowager's wealth has been split amongst her four grandchildren, which adds to the salaries they have already inherited from their grandfather. The other half has been left for Miss Anya Marleigh."

Anya nearly fell off her chair.

4

The Budleighs were all gaping. Lord Damian Ashton was laughing. Lady Budleigh was on her feet. "You are joking. She is nothing but a singer! Hardly even respectable!" She pressed her lips together.

Mr. Prism did not answer.

"That's that, then," Charlie said. He was unusually pale. His eyeglass was frozen. "So much for a forlorn hope."

"Preston!" This was Amelia. "It can't be true, can it, Preston?"

"She isn't family. She isn't anyone," Lady Budleigh said, staring wildly. "It is our duty to look after the Budleigh estate, and Mama knew it."

"Clara," Lord Budleigh mildly admonished. He too looked pale.

"Oh dear, oh dear, I'm sorry, Anya." Amelia was dabbing her mouth with a handkerchief. "I like you, I do. I have never minded your background, no matter what anyone says, but it seems so strange, even for Mama."

"Strange? It's preposterous!" Lady Budleigh said. She was looking at Anya. "You work in the court! Your mother was no better than a common . . ." She placed her trembling fingers against her lips.

"Come on, man, is this some kind of joke? Even my eccentric mother-in-law wouldn't—*couldn't*—have lost her mind to this extent?" Geoffrey Canningford was looking at the lawyer.

"Those are the terms of the will, my lord," Mr. Prism said. He was the other calm member of this odd group. His hair was neatly combed back, and not a strand had strayed since he started reading.

"But surely Mama couldn't leave the money as she chose," Lord Budleigh said. "Surely, it belonged to my father, the money, and rightfully comes to me." He looked pale and horrified.

Mr. Prism inclined his head. "But, as I mentioned, the money came to the dowager after your father was already dead and so the dowager could, indeed, leave it as she chose."

Lady Budleigh sat heavily down. "It can't be. It just can't be. Preston is her oldest child. Budleigh was her home." She couldn't help turning and staring at Anya. "I suppose you knew about this, Miss Marleigh? It must be your doing. Why else would Mama have lost her mind so completely?"

Anya was gripping her hands in her lap. She gave her head a sudden shake. This had suddenly turned into a nightmare. The money—there *must* be some confusion about that, but right now everyone was looking at her like they hadn't known they were nursing a viper in their bosom. The veiled insinuation that Anya was a singer in the court and that made her no better than a whore was always there, perhaps, but Lady Budleigh had never dared speak to her like that when the dowager was alive. And to mention Anya's mother! Anya's heart was thumping.

"Let's be calm, everyone," Lord Budleigh said. "It is obvious to me that there's been some mistake. Or that Mama was more senile than we thought." He looked at Mr. Prism. "Is that it?

She'd lost her mind and we have to go about proving it? That's the ticket with these things, isn't it?"

"I'm afraid the dowager took precautions against it, my lord," Mr. Prism said. "She had Dr. Tremble do a thorough examination and declare that she was sound of mind when she made the will. Everything has been properly witnessed and signed. And verified. The doctor's and witnesses' signatures are all here if anyone would like to see them."

Apparently, no one wanted to see them. Anya was looking at each of the Budleighs. But she saw now that one person didn't look outraged. Her eyes narrowed. "You knew about this, Lord Ashton."

Everyone turned to stare.

"Not the extent of it. But my great-aunt mentioned something like it to me," he replied calmly.

"You knew and encouraged it," Lady Budleigh suddenly burst out. "You must have loved getting the better of us. You perhaps planned it together with Miss Marleigh. What a famous story! The upstart thief and the wh . . ." She pressed her lips together again, her bosom heaving.

"Me? Of course not. I encouraged her to leave the money to Preston, of course," Lord Ashton said.

Lady Budleigh frowned. "You did?"

"No," answered Lord Ashton.

Lady Budleigh looked like the top of her head was about to blow off.

"I can't understand. Maybe I'm stupid, but—" Amelia started.

"There's no 'maybe' about it, old chap," her husband said.

Everyone was talking. Amelia was fanning herself and saying that she felt faint. Her husband was thumping her loudly on the back and telling her to buck up. Charlie was saying that he should have known Mama would pull such a trick when the family was desperate for money and staring a debtors' prison in the face. Anya's head was humming.

The lawyer's even tone finally broke the din. "Miss Marleigh may have an income from it now, but the bulk of it will be held in trust until the day of her wedding."

Heads spun toward the lawyer again.

"I assume my husband is the trustee?" Lady Budleigh said, somewhat violently.

"Yes, yes," Lord Budleigh said, soothingly patting her hand. "Who else would it be? I am the head of the family."

Mr. Prism calmly continued, "Miss Marleigh will receive the bulk on her wedding day, as long as that should take place on or before her twenty-fifth birthday. Her trustee will need to consent to her marriage."

Everyone turned to stare at Anya again. "How old are you, Anya?" Amelia asked.

"Twenty-four," Anya said with as much dignity as she could find. "I'll be twenty-five in four months."

"And are you betrothed or likely to be?" Amelia asked.

"She works as a court singer. She plays the sitar," Lady Budleigh said, rhyming "sitar" with "cheetah" like it was a dangerous thing. "Her parents were not even wed when they had her. Who would marry a—"

"Clara," Lord Budleigh said feebly.

Anya's hands were working in her lap. Her limbs seemed to have gone into shock. As had her mind.

"If Miss Marleigh is not married by her twenty-fifth birthday, then the money will go to her trustee."

Heads and eyes snapped toward the lawyer. He gazed back calmly.

There was a sudden, palpable softening in Lady Budleigh. "Well, that is something, then. At least Mama had *some* sense left. Though why she put us through this rigmarole at all, I cannot imagine. That should make things simple. I'm sure even Anya sees the rightness in it. The money *should* revert to her trustee in four months' time. And I'm sure the family would like her to enjoy a respectable salary from the estate for the remainder of her life. That would be fair." She nodded graciously at Anya. "We could do that, couldn't we, Preston?"

But Preston Budleigh was looking at the lawyer. The lawyer cleared his throat. Lady Budleigh's eyes shot to his face.

"Get on with it, Prism! I am Miss Marleigh's trustee, am I not?" Lord Budleigh said.

"No, my lord. That would be Lord Ashton."

5

There was a thundering silence. Anya was the first to break it. She hadn't realized she was on her feet. "What!"

"I don't understand," Lady Budleigh said, looking pale and addressing the lawyer. "What has Lord Ashton to say to any of it?"

"Mama has gone too far," Lord Budleigh said. "Too far!"

"Yes, by jove, completely dotty, by the looks of it," said his brother-in-law.

Charlie stood up and started pacing the room.

Lady Budleigh whirled about and stared at Damian Ashton. "*You* knew about this!"

He was frowning for the first time. Anya was trembling. She grasped at the shawl that had fallen to the back of her chair. She picked it up and pulled it about her. Lord Ashton was watching her, frown still in place. She gave him stare for stare. "Lord Ashton said he knew about it," she said through clenched teeth.

He jerked his head. "I knew that I was your trustee. But I had no idea of the terms." The words were abrupt. He looked shaken by the latest revelation.

"You don't know me," Anya said. "Why should I ask for *your* consent? What can you possibly have to say about my marriage?"

"Nothing at all," Lord Ashton said. "I can have nothing to say. I have no idea why my great-aunt would put us in this impossible position."

Lady Budleigh was looking scathingly at him. "Oh, there is no need to look so green. I have no idea if you knew the terms or not. But I don't see how *you* can have a problem with this situation. All you have to do is withhold consent to Anya's marriage and the money is yours!"

A tinge of color mounted Lord Ashton's cheeks. "I don't want the Budleigh money."

"Ha! I am experiencing a strange sense of déjà vu," Lady Budleigh said. "Is anyone else? You never want anything, Damian, but it all comes to you anyway. People fall ill all of a sudden, they get murdered, they—they . . ." She placed the back of her hand on her trembling mouth.

Lord Ashton's jaw was clenched. Anya was watching him. He apparently had nothing to say about the accusations Lady Budleigh was hurling at him.

Charlie abruptly stopped pacing. "Marry me," he said suddenly, looking straight at Anya, who was still standing there, hands clenched on her shawl.

She flushed. "Of all the—"

He quickly walked to her. He looked like he was going to grip her arms, but then he stopped himself. "It's the best solution. Then *he* can't have the money. And you and I, we can split it between us. It is the *only* solution! And I have to say, I've always liked you, Anya. You're beautiful, clever, well-informed. I've often thought we understood each other—"

Lady Budleigh put a hand to her face and sank into a chair. "Dear god, Charlie."

"What, you think I can't marry her?" Charlie said. "Or are you implying that I *shouldn't* marry someone of her birth?"

"Oh, I am sure *you* can marry Anya. If *she* would marry someone with so little address is another question altogether."

Charlie flushed. "You come up with something better, then. If you're any less sunk in debt than I am, I'll cut off my arm and feed it to the family dog." Saying this, he left the room.

"You—Anya—you could give up the money, couldn't you? Even someone like you can see that it would be fair." Lady Budleigh was looking at Anya, not with her usual severity but with such an unusual note of beseeching in her face that Anya was rattled.

Now that the first shock was over, her first impulse was to give the money up. It was never meant to be hers. She had no idea why the dowager made up such a mad plan. She didn't *want* the money. Yet, even within a few seconds, she realized the money would give her what she had never had and what she desperately wanted, not only for herself but for Trixie: To get away from the palace, with its court politics and the constant need to watch what she said and did. To decide if she wanted to work there or not. To sing and earn a living where and when she chose. To have not only independence, but security for an old age she was almost sure she would be spending alone. Lady Budleigh wasn't wrong. Who would want to marry her? Someone with her birth. How could she give up a chance at independence?

"Miss Marleigh can choose to give it up *after* it is hers." Mr. Prism cut into everyone's thoughts. "But it cannot be hers until she marries."

Lady Budleigh covered her face with her hands. "We're sunk, wholly sunk."

Lord Budleigh placed a hand on her shoulder. "It isn't as bad as that," he tried.

"How can you say that, Preston? We don't have a feather to fly with! The debts, the mortgage, after everything we've done to try to keep things together . . ."

Over Lady Budleigh's head, Anya's eyes met Damian Ashton's. They stared at each other. His stare was hard, but that aloofness of his, that was still there. She wondered if he cared about anything or anyone. Truly cared.

In that moment, Anya knew one thing at least. Whether she would have given up the money to the Budleighs or at least shared it with them, she didn't know. What she did know was that Damian Ashton should not see a farthing of it.

6

Damian had no idea what his great-aunt had been thinking. To put him in such an intolerable position! She had told Damian she wanted to leave some money to the penniless court singer Anya Marleigh. When he'd asked her why she wanted to leave anything to Anya Marleigh, she'd replied, "So my hopeless family doesn't see all of it, of course, why else? Who do *you* think should inherit, Damian?" she demanded. "Charlie, who'll fritter it away in less than five years on drink and gambling hells? Amelia, whose hysterics make me want to throttle her? Or the simpering old auntie that is my eldest born? *Who* do you think I should leave it to? Not Preston, my dear, never Preston, because you can bank on it, he won't see a penny of it. It's Clara that holds the purse strings."

The dowager gave him a long list of reasons why she didn't want her children and their spouses to inherit her money, but Damian Ashton privately thought that Anya Marleigh must be the kind of person who knew how to play her cards right. She had clearly been able to get exactly what she wanted from the dowager.

He thought about this now as he hammered a nail into

the fence that protected his goat pen. He pulled up the other end of the panel, evened it out with sure hands and eyes, and hammered it in with a few steady thrusts.

When he asked the dowager why Anya Marleigh, why not someone else, she gave no clear answer. She liked her. The girl had a divine voice. She was a straight talker, not missish. She spoke her mind and knew things. She was the bastard daughter of an earl, and his Indian mistress, Naira Devi. (Rumor had it the woman had been a court dancer, would you believe it?) Anya was transported to England at the age of six when her parents died. Transported to London to live with her stepmother, the Earl of Beddington's first wife—in fact, his *only* wife—and his firstborn child, Jonathan Marleigh, the current Earl of Beddington. "Can you imagine?" his great-aunt said. "Poor child!" And once she was old and couldn't sing any longer, who would want her, what would she do? She needed money to have some independence.

Of course, none of this really explained why Anya Marleigh. But the dowager said in an exasperated voice, "She doesn't want my money! That's why!"

Damian Ashton had not believed her. Anya Marleigh was a penniless singer. Of course she would want and need money. She maybe didn't grovel at the dowager's feet, and she gave the *impression* that she didn't want her money, but the idea that Anya Marleigh didn't want it, that was a bit rich.

Life at court must be comfortable, but living like that, always on display, your every move watched, every penny you earned dependent on what you said and did, how you looked and didn't look, whose game you played and whose you didn't, with loss of favor always around the corner, couldn't be comfortable for anyone. She must be easy game for the men. People saw ladies-in-waiting as willing mistresses. And what when the royals tired of her voice or she lost it or she wasn't pretty enough or young anymore? She'd have nowhere to go.

No, it was too much to ask anyone to believe that the woman wouldn't snatch the opportunity to be independent.

The hairy pygmy goat—the gray one with the shaggy tail, Sally—was balefully watching him as he picked up another panel. Her mate, Prinny, the black-and-white one with the beard, named after none other than the Prince, of course, wasn't even bothering to watch him. He had turned his arse to Damian and was chewing on some winter hellebores.

"Don't look at me, then," Damian said now. "Act like I'm not here." Sally bleated, but Prinny did nothing but flick his ear. The goat was aptly named for his royal attitude to everyone he thought was his inferior. Damian put the next panel in place and started hammering it in.

Just the fact that Miss Marleigh didn't grovel showed how clever she was. She must have known that the dowager, his great-aunt Griselda, hated toadeaters. It was why she liked Damian, because he didn't suck up to her. In fact, it was the main reason the dowager had hated Clara Budleigh, her daughter-in-law. However cold she was to anyone else, Clara had always been on her best behavior when Great-Aunt Griselda was around, solicitous, forbearing when her mother-in-law was impatient, never talking back, hiding her own quick temper. The dowager would have done anything to put Clara Budleigh's nose out of joint. What a masterstroke, in fact, not leaving the Budleigh children any money at all. He gave a short sharp bark of laughter.

Sally bleated.

He looked at her. "Don't ask me, I have nothing to feed you. Except the clothes and boots I'm standing in." She looked at him with interest. "Well, you can't have 'em!" He stopped to check the angle of a panel, then carried on with his task.

His great-aunt had forgotten to mention the tiny matter of the terms of the trusteeship. Anya Marleigh had to find a willing bridegroom within four months, and he, Damian Ashton, had to consent to Anya Marleigh's choice or the money would all revert to him.

The whole thing was revolting! He scowled. Sally sauntered over and headbutted him in his leg. "That's the way to ask for what you want, is it?" he demanded.

She blew a raspberry at him.

He sighed at her bad manners, fished an apple out of his workbag, which lay on the ground, and gave it to her. He picked up another fence post and held it in place.

He couldn't help chuckling at the memory of Clara's shocked face when the lawyer had explained the terms of the trusteeship. She wasn't wrong. He was a thief from the streets of Jamaica.

Damian's grandfather Archibald Ashton had been the son of a plantation owner. He had fallen for a native Jamaican woman, Kalisa, who was the daughter of a schoolteacher and widely read herself, and had married her. She had changed his mind about slavery to such an extent that he had broken away from his family and their way of life and made a life for himself and his wife. He had bought a small farm that he ran all his life without enslaved people. He had never risen to the height of wealth and status of the local enslavers, but to his dying day, he had kept to his principles. Kalisa had made it a life mission to educate the local children.

Damian's father, Jonas, was Archibald and Kalisa's son. He and Damian's mother, Miriam, had lived in Jamaica, and Jonas had been a staunch opposer of slavery too and everything that went with it, teaching his sons that slavery was never acceptable, not in any form, not between any people. But Damian hardly had any time to get to know his father.

At the age of thirty, when his older son was just six, Jonas had died. When Damian was eight, his mother, Miriam, married again. Damian was not large, but he was muscly and fit and hard now. At the age of eight, Damian was tiny. But he was fast. The first time his stepfather beat him, he got away with it, and the lash of the belt stung on Damian's back for days.

But never again.

The second time his stepfather lifted his fist, Damian grabbed the first missile he could find—a dinner plate—and flung it straight in his stepfather's face, where it split open his nose and left a deep gash (a permanent mark, it turned out). His stepfather never beat him again, but Damian spent the next several years trying to protect his younger brother, Jeremy (who was taller and bigger but slower and kinder and more trusting of humanity than Damian), from his stepfather's drunken wrath. His mother waited until Jeremy was eleven and then shipped both boys off to boarding school in England. After five long years dodging their stepfather's blows, they'd finally escaped him. But they never saw their mother again. Miriam died a few years later, a long way away from her sons.

Damian grew up making his own way, looking after himself and his younger brother and no one else. And as an adult, he saw no reason to change his ways. He had built a fortune of his own through sound investments and trade. Of course, he put some of it into saving the crumbling Ashton estate.

Damian was twenty-eight, his brother two years younger and already a captain in the army. He was recently injured in Portugal and would be heading back home any day. Other than Jeremy, Damian cared for no one. He relied entirely on himself, not on the whims of other people. And that was the way he liked it.

He didn't see why he should have to worry about Anya Marleigh.

He straightened and frowned into the distance. All she had to do was find a husband. It *should* be dead simple. She was beautiful, with all those spinning dark ringlets that seemed as if lightning were passing through them. The eyes were wide open, almost black, and she had this way of looking at you like she could see right through you. And then her eyes would flash suddenly and pierce your flesh.

She didn't have long, but she *could* find herself a husband in four months.

Then he could wash his hands of the affair.

He didn't want the Budleigh money. The sooner Anya found someone to marry, the better. If she didn't, by god, everyone would say that *he'd* made it impossible for her to marry, that he'd held back his consent to whichever poor sod she picked for a husband, and it had been so that *he* could get his hands on any money he hadn't already stolen from the Budleighs when he became Lord Ashton.

He savagely hammered the next nail in, nearly bashing his thumb off. "Ow!" he wailed.

Sally lifted her head and brayed. Even Prinny turned around and stared in a *ha, you poor idiot* kind of way. Damian held his throbbing thumb for some minutes, trying to make the pain stop.

Rumors of foul play had been clinging to him for years. Though how he could have done away with seven or eight relatives that stood between him and the earldom, he had no idea. But the last Ashton—Arnold Ashton—had died under suspicious circumstances, shot by a masked highwayman, yet not robbed.

Suspicion stubbornly clung to Damian over Arnold Ashton's sudden death. There were still rumors, two years later. It didn't help that he kept himself aloof, he didn't attend *ton* parties, he didn't play the game of the marriage mart. If he did, everyone would forgive him. As it was . . . no, it would be unbearable if Anya Marleigh couldn't find herself a husband. Everyone would say he'd held on to the dowager's wealth by hook or by crook. That he'd murdered the last Ashton to get a title and now he'd got himself Griselda Budleigh's money too.

Could he help her find a husband?

He growled impatiently. This, this was exactly what he had avoided all his life. To get embroiled in other people's affairs. He cared about Jeremy and Jeremy's welfare, and if he was completely honest with himself, Jeremy was the only one he allowed himself to fully trust. And now to have to worry about whether or not some conniving and mercenary court singer could find herself a husband was too much.

Apple demolished, Sally was on her feet and staring at him again.

He put down his tools, crouched down next to her and tickled her under her chin and smoothed her funny velvet ears. "*I* don't see why *I* should care if Miss Anya Marleigh can look after herself." Sally looked up from his hand and brayed in his face. "In fact, so far she's done an admirable job of looking after herself. Who would have thought anyone could con my incorrigible great-aunt into leaving them an arse-load of money?"

It wasn't for nothing that Damian grew up on the streets of Jamaica. His neck prickled, and he whirled around and came to standing in one motion. But it wasn't a highwayman or stray poacher with a rifle standing on the other side of his fence. It was a young woman, her hands in the pockets of her greatcoat, her eyes digging straight into his brain. Standing just outside the goat pen.

He placed his hands on his hips and ruefully shook his head. "Miss Marleigh."

"Lord Ashton," she said coolly.

It had been two days since he had last seen her. In fact, he hadn't thought he'd ever see her again. They could communicate by letter about the trust. Why was she still in Folkestone? And why was she *here*?

She looked cool and composed. *His* shirtsleeves were rolled up, and he was streaked with sweat.

"A friendly morning visit?" he inquired.

"We aren't friends," she said sweetly.

"Now, now, Miss Marleigh, what a spiteful thing to say. It's almost like you don't like m—" But he didn't get any further. Because he was rudely headbutted straight in his arse. He blinked. Turned around. It was Prinny. He gave the goat a hard glare, then turned to Miss Marleigh again.

"An intelligent creature," she said. "There's always a chance he could be more intelligent than he looks."

He nodded slowly. "He is."

"I was talking about you."

He couldn't help grinning. She gave him a polite smile back. Prinny headbutted him again. He let out a resigned sigh. He got another apple out of his workbag. Turned and handed it with a bad grace to his bad goat. Sally bleated crossly and started angrily toward his crotch. He didn't argue—a man has to know when he can't win—and hastily gave her a carrot. He turned around and faced Miss Marleigh again.

"I like them," she said.

"I will cook them at the earliest opportunity."

"Heartless."

"Sadly."

"I am leaving tomorrow. It is the Queen's birthday next week, and I must be at the palace for the celebrations."

"How can I help you, Miss Marleigh?"

God, she was beautiful. The curve of her neck. The feathery green of her fine muslin dress, with the tiny red embroidered roses on the neckline. The hair that was blowing all about her in the breeze in angry coils.

"I wanted to let you know that I have asked Mr. Prism to act as my lawyer."

"I didn't know you needed one."

"I mean that he's the one to contact when it's time to hand over my inheritance."

"Yes, of course. That suits me." He wouldn't have to see her and she wouldn't have to see him. "I see that you're reconciled to finding yourself a husband."

Her eyes flashed. "It's funny how quickly one can become reconciled."

"I expect you're very good at looking out for your best interests, Miss Marleigh."

A pulse was beating in her neck now. She had been—or at least looked—cool as a cucumber a minute ago, but he was annoying her. He was staring at the beat of that pulse. He had the strange and sudden impulse to put his lips to it.

The very idea. It brought blood rushing to parts of his body that he would much rather not think about right now.

"You can despise me as much as you like, Lord Ashton. Your opinion doesn't matter to me."

He looked up and their eyes met. He found his own pulse beating faster. Now he was staring at her mouth. His eyes lifted, and their eyes met again.

"Why should I despise you?" he said. "I've made my own way in the world. I don't despise you for doing the same."

She gritted her teeth, and now she was clenching at her coat. "You think I insinuated myself! You think I'm the kind of woman who—"

He jerked his head and in a few quick strides walked closer. She almost jerked backward, but then she steadied herself and stood her ground. He was standing close to her now, but they were on opposite sides of the fence. She was still glaring at him. She was almost as tall as he was. He couldn't stop looking at her. The eyes, the thoughtful eyes that seemed to look through you. He couldn't help it. He reached out for her hand. He held it almost like this was a social evening and he was going to bend low and kiss it.

He felt for a second the wild beating of the pulse in her wrist with his thumb. The veins under the thin skin. The curve of the mound of Venus. The hollow of her hand. She looked breathless. And he could see the dampness of the tendrils around her neck. She had walked here, not slowly, not meandering, but at a fast pace. He turned her hand palm up. He leaned forward and placed his mouth on the veins of her wrist. When he let go and looked up at her face, it was as cool as ever. But he had heard it, the sharp intake of breath when his lips found her wrist. They stared at each other.

"What happened to your thumb?"

"What?"

"Your thumb, Lord Ashton."

He looked down at his thumb. He'd forgotten that he'd nearly crushed it with his hammer. Now that he thought of it, it was throbbing and swollen.

"It's nothing," he said.

She was staring at it. And he had the time to study her. The deep, intelligent eyes. The soft curve of the lashes. The little scar at the base of an eyebrow. The slightly snub nose. The hint of stubbornness in the mouth. She was staring at his thumb for so long, it was like she'd bent forward and placed her mouth on it. For some strange reason—his head was clearly fevered—he felt like the pain receded.

"You should put it in ice," she said.

"I didn't know you cared."

"I don't."

"I'll wait with bated breath to hear of your betrothal, Miss Marleigh. How long will it take you? A few weeks should be enough, shouldn't it?"

Oh, she wasn't angry. And she was no longer staring at his thumb. She was pulling the open lapels of her greatcoat together. "Believe me, Mr. Ashton," she said. "I will do *anything* to keep *you* from touching a farthing of the dowager's money." She spun around and was walking away.

"What happened to your wrist? There was a cut," he said behind her.

She reluctantly turned around. "There was some oil spilled at the top of the stairs this morning."

His eyes narrowed. "Outside your bedchamber? At Budleigh?"

"Trixie bore the brunt of it. Though no bones broken."

"Miss Cleaver comes out in the morning before you do?"

"Not usually. I've been restless. I get up and go for a walk early. Trixie was with me this morning. I only flailed about, quite gracelessly. She fell a few steps."

"Do you know how the oil came to be there?" He was watching her face.

"Lady Budleigh seemed to think it was one of the house-maids." She turned away again.

"Miss Marleigh?"

She looked exasperated this time when she stopped.

"Take care of yourself."

Her eyes flashed. "I didn't know you cared."

"Miss Marleigh, you've heard of me—the urchin from Jamaica—from the Budleighs. Perhaps from Clara. So you have probably also heard that I care for no one other than my brother, Jeremy. He is a captain in the army and doesn't need me to care for him, but you must have heard that his and my comfort are the only things important to me. They are right. I am selfish. But . . ." He paused, then carried on. "I think it's a very good thing you're heading back to the palace and will no longer be at the Budleigh estate."

She looked at him consideringly. He wondered what Prism would say if he asked the lawyer what would happen to the Budleigh money if Anya Marleigh died before she had the chance to marry.

"Goodbye, my lord," she said and, turning around, walked away.

"Damian," he said behind her.

7

There were a few men who wanted to marry her. Anya knew it. It would be easy enough to choose one.

There was Mr. Greenwood, a charming and handsome man, a second son of a baron, who would need to marry into money. He was tall. He was big. He was good-hearted. And, most importantly, he didn't talk to goats.

And then there was Lord Pennyworth. Granted, the man was forty-five at least, which wasn't old, but older than her by more than twenty years. He thought she was a gift to mortals, her voice was angelic, her disposition flawless, her temper eternally sweet. He also did not talk to goats. *He* had already offered for her, months ago. He was a widower and told her that though he knew she didn't return his worship (how could she do that, he said, when he was a mere mortal and she a goddess . . .), he was sure she would find him nothing but an adoring husband.

A few men had asked her to be their mistress over the years. Being a singer at court, that was about par for the course. If you worked at court and lived at court with some of the other ladies-in-waiting, people assumed that you would be someone's kept mistress. If not the King's or Prince's, then at least someone high up in court. Many men in fact assumed that she'd jump at the chance. That wouldn't help her now. But one or two of them might be brought up to scratch if they knew about her inheritance. A penniless but desirable woman could be your mistress. A wealthy and desirable woman could perhaps be taken to the altar. She would bet *none* of them talked to their goats.

"It would be nice to be wanted for *me*, for once, and not because of my voice," she complained.

Trixie turned to look at her. "It's so sweet and clear, and in a way, so perfectly self-contained that I suppose men can't help wanting to possess it."

Anya looked at her protégé. Insightful. And shockingly cynical. Not to mention that Trixie looked wan—more than usual. Anya grimaced with guilt. Was she so obsessed with her own problems that she was neglecting Trixie? Anya often wondered if she had made a mistake in taking up the young girl—only eight years younger than Anya herself—helping Trixie get better at reading and writing, and expanding her knowledge of geography and history. It wasn't as if the girl could become a governess. She was the daughter of a lady-in-waiting, and her father was unknown. Most people assumed that she would end up, at best, a lady's maid, so why raise her ambitions?

Trixie had a nervous, helpless air. Anya had tried hard to teach Trixie to stand up for herself, to protect herself if she had to. But she had a sweet and accommodating disposition, and it made her easy prey.

If yet another man pawed at the young girl's breasts, Anya felt like she might punch him. Yet what could she do? She didn't have enough money to take Trixie away and rent a small cottage like she wanted to. She had no independent means at all, despite trying to scrimp and save almost everything she earned. The trouble was she ended up spending every farthing she earned just to *look* like she belonged in court. She was the Queen's musician. She could hardly dress in rags.

"Trixie?" she said gently.

Trixie started. She turned and looked wide-eyed at Anya, then quickly shook her head. "I'm woolgathering."

The grounds were crisp and cool this afternoon, and fog was clinging to the leaves. The palace was shrouded in freckles of mist. It was quiet on this side, in the grounds at the back, though on the other side carriages would be clamoring to get their passengers out in good time for the afternoon's presentations in the Queen's Drawing Room.

It was an interesting time for the royal family. King George III had been ill for a long time, but despite his illness, he was a popular king. He had not only lived through the revolution in France and led the war effort there in the Seven Years' War, but he had always supported progressive politics and been a staunch supporter of the prime minister Mr. William Pitt, who had famously been a reformer and an abolitionist. Not only were the King's politics progressive, but he was also famously faithful to his wife and loyal to his family. Perhaps because of the King's many episodes of illness, Queen Charlotte led society and was very popular amongst the *ton*. Now, rumor had it that the King was too ill to govern and perhaps his son would become Prince Regent. Today was the Queen's birthday Drawing Room, and Anya couldn't help wondering how many more of these there would be once they had a Prince Regent. She couldn't help hoping that Queen Charlotte, known for her dignity and forthrightness, would remain a social leader.

Under the damp silence, Anya thought she could hear a frenetic cry and jostle, coming from across the palace grounds.

Trixie had wanted to head straight to the royal presentation, but Anya had dragged her out for a brisk walk. She wondered if her cheeks were as pink as Trixie's. She looked at the young woman and couldn't help thinking that Trixie looked pale.

"Anyone bothering you, Trixie?" she asked.

Trixie bit her lip. There was a frown playing hide-and-seek on her brow. "No, miss."

Anya studied the girl's face. Anya had known the girl since she was thirteen, and it had taken a year to rid the girl of the habit of calling her "Miss Anya." But now and again, when she was troubled, she slipped back.

Trixie looked up at her, her eyelashes curled with dew. "It's nothing new. It's just Mr. Terence Rimball."

Anya gritted her teeth. "The man is fifty if he's a day! Old enough to be your grandfather."

He was a frequent visitor, as he was one of the many gentlemen who did business for the palace. He was not a peer, but wealthy enough to think that even at the age of fifty he could do what he liked with a sixteen-year-old. "Did he hurt you?"

Instead of the sharp jerk of the head she expected from Trixie, the girl hesitated. "No." She colored a harsh red. "It's just he caught me in a hallway yesterday and—"

"Spell it out," Anya said. Her voice was more curt than she meant it to be.

There was a shake in Trixie's lip. "I always think I'll stand up to him like you've taught me. I always think, *Next time . . .* He had me backed up against a wall before I could run past or say anything. And next thing his hand was down my—he was squeezing—" She stopped abruptly. Her hazel eyes looked less green than usual.

Anya grabbed her hand. "The bastard!" When Trixie wouldn't

look at her, Anya propelled her chin around. "It isn't your fault, do you hear me? The reason he does it *isn't* because you're weak or you encourage it, Trixie, it's because he knows you are defenseless. For a man like that, if you had wealth or birth, or—or—even a stupid git of a man who farted and belched all day, even *that* would count for something in Mr. Rimball's mind!"

The girl's eyes filled with tears. "They don't bother *you* so much."

Anya made an impatient sound. How could she explain to Trixie that it wasn't that she wasn't groped and prodded by men who lived at the palace or visited there? She was. It's just that—she thought with some horror—she was inured to it. It was just another lecherous man to bat away. "When I was new in the palace, I was hardly more than twenty, Trixie. Fresh out of a seminary and imagining that to come to the palace was the best, most glamorous thing that had ever happened to me." She couldn't help reflecting now that the years she had spent being educated in a select seminary for girls in Bath that taught languages, music, deportment, geography, were perhaps some of the best years of her life, away from her stepmother's influence and independent in a way. Palace life had seemed glamorous after those years at school, but the constant frantic bustle, the gossip, the competition to be the Queen's favorite, and the social life did tend to wear on her. "It wasn't only that I wasn't good at keeping men in their place in those early days. Give me a handsome face and I fancied myself in love or imagined that the man saw *me* and not just my cursed voice or the fact that I was friendless. I was a much bigger gormless idiot than you can ever be. It took me a long time to figure out that men either put me on a pedestal—or they look at me and imagine my ankles crossed behind their ears."

Trixie flushed again but giggled too.

Anya dragged Trixie's hand through the curve of her arm. "We will get away from here," she said firmly. "You wouldn't have this problem if you didn't have to live here, as exposed as we are, with no one to turn to. I know how difficult your position is. People know that your father is unknown. That your mother passed away. They know you don't have a dowry. But we can get away from it. All I have to do is marry. And it will solve the problem for both of us. Believe me, I am spending *all* my time making a list in my head of suitable men." She frowned uncertainly. "I just hope—four months isn't long."

She bit her lip guiltily, because the sad truth was she was spending only half her time making a list in her head. She was spending the other half thinking about a man who talked to goats. Who was in fact the last man she wanted to marry. Why her stupid head couldn't keep things straight was a mystery.

"You can't sacrifice yourself for me, Miss—I mean, Anya. You said you'd marry for love or not at all. I've heard you say it a thousand times."

They were walking again. "This is no time to be maudlin. The time to fall in love is gone. I need to be businesslike about it. Mr. Greenwood is the best bet. But I'm worried—there is no one in his family to present to the Queen or King, and so he might not show up today. And *then* I would have to think about Lord Pennyworth, and I can't help thinking that so much worship at breakfast will make me nauseous. Still, never mind that. In the dark, maybe he will feel no different from Mr. Greenwood."

Trixie giggled again and they walked on.

Mr. Greenwood was amiable. He even listened to her overexcited chat about Mary Wollstonecraft's writings about women's rights and then at the end said, "It is noble of you to want to expand your mind." *That* made her want to hit him. And the thought of kissing him made her feel a little dead, which was a big problem, but those things could be sorted out.

The dong of the chapel bell—two dongs!—made the two women shriek. *Two!* They stared at each other in dismay. Skidding and scrabbling and nearly falling on their faces on the slushy cobbles, they started running, skirts in hand, toward the palace doors. How could it already be two dongs, and how could they have completely lost track of time?

8

They crashed in through the nearest door, nearly upsetting the cleaners, who would have cleaned the front rooms for the presentation hours ago but were now doing the rooms and hallways at the back. Janet Longworthy, who supervised all the cleaners, yelled at them for being the curse on her life, told them to stay away from her suds or else, and shook her mop at them.

The chapel bell had long stopped dinging. How the devil had Anya missed the time? Hadn't they come out into the grounds not long after noon? Her tummy was growling too. They'd forgotten all about lunch. As they skidded past a long-suffering cook, Anya grabbed a bread roll off a tray. She broke off half and stuffed it in Trixie's hand as they ran.

It took them fifteen minutes to run through the hallways, out to the courtyard, then across to the other wing, down the long stone hallways again, and to the court where the presentation was to take place. Even with all the running, past stray staff who looked disapprovingly at the pair, past the odd courting couple peeled against a wall, heaving and moaning like there was no tomorrow, snatching a moment in a dark hallway when the rest of the court was, well, in court, it still took them that long. It looked like the Drawing Room had started a little late anyway, but Anya and Trixie still didn't make it to the start.

It was only when she was nearly outside the door that Anya realized that she was still wearing her sturdy black boots and they were muddy and wet. There was no time to run to her bedchamber and change into her satin slippers. She groaned. Thankfully, she would only stand in the wings and watch from a distance. Later on, in the evening, she was—or her singing and sitar were—part of the entertainment, but for now, she was just an onlooker. While the higher ladies-in-waiting and the women of the bedchamber would be in court this morning to attend on the royal couple, Anya and other musicians would only be needed in the evening. Her dress was wool, and she was still wearing her greatcoat. Not suitable for the Queen's birthday Drawing Room at all. But that would have to do too.

They crashed in. They ran around the gallery and then, finding a hopeful opening, elbowed past some of the onlookers. There were gasps and dark mutterings about their terrible manners, but they managed to find a decent view, even if the woman next to Anya smelled of stale sweat and she was afraid the man on the other side of Trixie was so tipsy from his ale that he would hurtle headfirst off the balcony and down into the court below.

The presentations had started, but the clamoring and shoving between the ticketed and unticketed onlookers carried on. Anya looked down from the balcony into the room. The long saloon glittered. Not only with the silks and laces of the guests, the velvets embroidered in silver and gold, and the thousands and thousands of jewels and beads, but the sunshine streaming in through the windows. The King and Queen sat at the top of the room, surrounded by courtiers, and the hopefuls were announced through one of the doorways.

The Queen had her usual reserved and elegant look about her, yet Anya couldn't help thinking that she also looked a little strained this afternoon, the lines of worry perhaps more prominent around her eyes than in recent years. Next to her, the King looked less elegant and regal, a little out of place, and Anya wondered if he was going through another one of his episodes. Because it was the Queen's birthday Drawing Room, the royal couple were dressed quite plainly, though it still made them stand out amidst everyone else's finery.

There were many presentations this afternoon. A long list of young women entering the marriage mart, soldiers returning from war, men coming into their fortunes or their titles, politicians who'd made a mark in Parliament, and who knew who else. The crowd on the balcony commented on every enormous hooped dress studded with rubies and diamonds and curled with ribbons, every powdered and patched face, satin breeches that were too tight, women pushing their daughters to the front, girls nearly swooning, and every last pompous, red-faced baron. Though the fashion in this era was for high waists and narrow, sleek skirts for the women, court dress was still fashioned with large hoops and heavily embroidered, and it was all eye-smacking to behold.

The Queen made it a point to exchange some words with everyone presented to her, but Anya could see that many answered her in monosyllables, perhaps feeling too awestruck to say more. The Queen often complained that the onus of conversation remained fully on her and that people didn't always do their bit.

The guests had also been instructed never to a) cough

(choking was allowed, but not coughing), b) sneeze (it had to be held in at any cost), or c) fidget (even if they were in pain). And indeed, Anya couldn't help noticing that while some people looked red in the face, it was impossible to know if this was because they were hot, shy, or in fact trying desperately to stop themselves from coughing and sneezing.

It was just as well, Anya thought after the first hour, that she wasn't in satin slippers and was wearing her sturdy boots, not to mention that there was such a crowd of giggling, murmuring people around her that she hardly had to stand up straight and was simply propped up by the throng.

The Queen was making a valiant effort to nod at every presentation, say a gracious word or two, and kiss the peers' daughters on the cheeks, but even she looked like she was starting to flag after nearly two hours. Her hooded eyes seemed more hooded, and her long and narrow face pulled in. The cinnamon hair was curled and powdered. After two hours, the Queen was starting to tug at her diamond choker, and the King, who at the best of times seemed a little young for the job and a little lost, his eyes dreamy and faraway, was getting more and more fidgety.

Anya's chin was propped on her hand and she was nearly nodding off when the Budleigh family was announced. Anya woke herself up and looked curiously at Lord and Lady Budleigh, who were presenting someone, a niece or a young cousin, to the Queen. The young girl was wearing a white dress and a white ribbon in her flaxen curls. She was quite pretty, though had inherited Lord Budleigh's nervous air. She looked breathless and had already tripped once when she came out of her deep curtsy.

Anya hadn't known that the Budleighs would be here this

afternoon. Lady Budleigh had sent her a note the day before, and it was the first she had heard from Lady Budleigh since coming back from Folkestone.

My dear Anya,

I am writing to offer my profound apologies for the way I lost my poise when you were with us. I trust that you will forgive me. The will was a shock to me, as I trust it was to you. I would like to see you and apologize in person. We are staying in London for only a short while for the Queen's birthday festivities. I wonder if you will allow me a brief visit tomorrow; we will be at the palace for the evening celebrations. I know you will be busy, but if you can send me a quick scrawl back to name a time and place, I would be grateful.

Your servant,
Clara, Lady Budleigh

Not only was the note written and franked in haste, but the Budleighs' messenger hadn't had the time to stable his horse. He was holding on to the horse's reins as Anya read the note, and the horse was nervous and skittish. The messenger with the enormous sideburns and drooping left cheek said, "Miss, just a quick note to say time and place. I'm already late." The man looked harassed and the horse restless, and Anya, who had come out to see him, said she had no paper or quill. One-handed, the man came up with a tiny scrap of paper torn from something else, and a quill. He was so anxious to be off again and the scrap of paper so tiny that Anya just had time to scrawl the destination of a conservatory near the chapel entrance and the time of one in the morning, before the man tore it from her, touched his hat, and was off on his nervous horse.

Anya didn't see the point of a chat with Lady Budleigh. She had half a mind to hand the Budleighs the whole fortune and be done with it. Except for two things: One, the fortune wasn't hers to give. She would have to marry to get her hands on it. And two, she *needed* the money so that she and Trixie could set themselves up comfortably, not only right now, but in the future, when they were old and no one wanted them.

Why had Lady Budleigh written to her at all? She had been cold, and truth be told, she had been rude to Anya at Budleigh. Why the apology now? Why the note? Anya couldn't help thinking that Lady Budleigh would only condescend to apologize to someone as lowly as Anya Marleigh if she wanted something out of it.

A frown played on her brow. There was the accident with the oil at Budleigh that morning. One of the maids at Budleigh, whose name was Jane Simmonds, had apparently spilled the oil from an oil lamp. Or at least there was oil spilled on top of the stairs and when Anya and Trixie slipped on it, Lady Budleigh made a big deal of calling the housemaid and asking her to explain herself. Jane Simmonds, a comely and efficient woman with neat brown hair and pretty freckles, who Anya knew was a young mother, had maintained her innocence throughout, saying with dignity that she would never be so clumsy as to hurt a guest, that she took her duties seriously. When Lady Budleigh had looked disbelieving, Jane had looked briefly at Anya—it was obvious that the woman was determined not to cry—and said, "I care about my work, miss. I'd never hurt a guest." Anya had tried to intervene and say that it had been an accident and to not make a big deal of it. That she had already let the matter go and perhaps the Budleighs could too. But Lady Budleigh had said that whatever Miss Marleigh was used to, she wouldn't tolerate such low standards from her staff, and had dismissed Jane Simmonds that very morning.

Anya had got away easy, but Trixie had bruised her ribs and banged her head on the banister. Anya hadn't made too much of it at the time, hoping that Lady Budleigh might be persuaded to rehire Jane Simmonds. But then later on, when Anya had got back from her chat with Damian Ashton at the goat pen, and she went out for a horse ride with Charlie Budleigh, the horse had run off with her and tossed her into a ditch.

Anya was a decent rider. Nothing in comparison to her older sister, Lila Marleigh—or actually, now Lila Tristram. Lila was the rider in the family. She was as good as any man, and better than most, both on the back of a horse and driving a curricle, or even a high-perch phaeton. But Anya was not such a numpty as to be thrown willy-nilly into a ditch. It was lucky that she only ruined a riding jacket and badly bruised her thigh, instead of breaking her neck.

Surely, both of those things were accidents. Surely, she was only perturbed because of the way Damian Ashton had reacted when he heard of the incident with the oil. Surely, neither of those incidents could have been intended to harm her.

Yet Lord Ashton had planted the seed of doubt, and when she came back to the palace, she wrote to Mr. Prism to ask him what would happen to the dowager's wealth if Anya died unmarried. The man wrote back, saying that Lord Ashton had asked him the same question, and he thought the answer was that since the dowager made no provision for Anya's death in her will, the money would revert to the dowager's next of kin, that is, to Lord Preston Budleigh. But, the lawyer conscientiously added, he wasn't sure on this point. He would look into it and get back to her.

Anya's eyes had glinted at Mr. Prism's disclosure. Not about what would happen to the money if she died, but the fact that Anya's kind executor, Lord Damian Ashton, had asked the lawyer the same question. *He* was interested in what would happen to the money if she died, was he? Well, wasn't that interesting.

She peered down into the gallery, where Lady Budleigh had just done the deepest curtsy in the history of curtsying. By this point, the Queen was barely keeping her eyes open. She shooed the family on their way. Lady Budleigh nodded graciously and then chivvied her husband and young charge out of the space.

"She looks constipated," Anya murmured.

"It's all the gammon she eats," Trixie answered.

Anya snorted. The woman next to her, powdered, pomaded, and patched to the nines, yet still smelling of stale armpit sweat, frowned her down. Anya smiled sweetly, then turned back to watch the presentations.

Had the dowager really wanted Anya to have her inheritance? Why Anya? And why in such a strange way, all at the mercy and goodwill of a certain Lord Ashton and his consent to her marriage? It felt like the dowager had set Anya up to fail. When Lady Budleigh had originally told Anya about him, she had mentioned his brother, Jeremy Ashton, saying that given that Damian Ashton was wealthy and Jeremy Ashton an officer in the army, surely neither man needed the Ashton estate. And then, more recently, Damian Ashton himself had verified that his brother was the only one he ever cared about, had as good as said that he would have no care to spare on a virtual stranger like Anya.

So why had the dowager made him Anya's trustee? Anya and

the dowager had certainly enjoyed each other's company. Anya admired how the dowager did not seem to care what anyone thought of her. And the dowager respected Anya's independence, her musical skill, and her wide knowledge.

Had the dowager only left Anya her wealth to annoy her family? Maybe that was it. Anya couldn't help a chuckle. That sounded a lot like Dowager Countess Griselda Budleigh. After all, what would annoy the Budleighs more than not getting their hands on the dowager's wealth? The threat of a penniless bastard like Anya, who was not even distantly connected to the family, inheriting the money, and Lord Ashton, whom they all patently hated, having control of the whole thing.

The easiest—and most cowardly—thing would be to do nothing at all and let the whole sorry business play out. It would be over in four months, after all, when she turned twenty-five. She could sit on her haunches and do nothing. Yet she found that she couldn't. To meekly hand over the money to the already wealthy Lord Damian Ashton, to not even try to keep some of it for herself and Trixie, to hand it over! No, that was the problem. She couldn't see herself being such a fool.

The man was insufferable. That mocking look! It was like he believed he was heaven's gifts to mortals.

A gurgle escaped Anya as she thought of the two goats. They at least had his true measure.

"Lord Damian Ashton and Captain Jeremy Ashton!" the lord chamberlain announced.

9

Anya nearly fell off the balcony when she heard the announcement.

Trixie elbowed her hard in the ribs.

There he was. Anya blinked, wondering if her thoughts had conjured him up. Why her heart was racing was a complete mystery.

He was dressed in beautifully tailored though not ostentatious court dress. Silk breeches, a velvet jacket, his hair still a little untidy. She examined him critically. There was something incredibly masculine about him. She couldn't tell if it was the muscular thighs, shoulders, and chest; the direct, yet aloof way he had of looking at you; the careless disregard for others' opinions. Yes, that was definitely part of his appeal. Others around him were darting glances at the royals, even sometimes at the onlookers from the gallery, to see their own effect on other people, to check who was there, who'd been invited, who'd had to buy tickets, who was being presented. Lord Ashton wasn't looking around, not darting looks, not conscious or caring if anyone was looking at him, if anyone found him appealing or not.

Stupid, *stupid* man.

With him was Captain Jeremy Ashton, who must be Lord Ashton's brother. She didn't know anything about the captain, other than what Lady Budleigh had mentioned. And of course the brief words Lord Ashton had said at the goat pen. The captain was also dark in coloring, but not as dark as Lord Ashton. He must have just returned from abroad, and that was why he was being presented at court. Taller, bigger, more easygoing, and kinder-looking. No, not exactly that. It was something else. Anya couldn't help staring at Lord Ashton's brother. It was hard to put a finger on, but it was like he truly, deep in his core, believed in and wanted peace. It was something about his kind eyes. Different from his brother's aloof ones.

Poor man, she thought in sudden and unexpected sympathy. He looked like he believed in peace. To have to go to war when you believed in peace. Why did he go, then? Did his brother not share his wealth with him and he'd had no choice but to join the army? That must be it. It sounded like Damian Ashton. Anya's eyes flashed. A very irritating man. No, he should definitely not see any of the dowager's wealth.

When, an hour later, the presentations were finally over, and Anya mingled with the hordes of people downstairs in the enormous glittering foyer, there was no sign of Lord or Captain Ashton. Not that she was looking.

Trixie had gone off to ask if she could help in the kitchens for the celebrations that night. Anya didn't know what she was doing there in the large foyer, surrounded by chattering people. What she needed was a quick rest. Later she would have to take some time to dress and do her vocal exercises before the celebrations began.

There was a hand at her elbow, and her heart sprang into her throat. She turned slowly, her heart inexplicably pounding.

It was Charlie Budleigh.

"Mr. Budleigh," she said, sounding frostier than she meant to. "Charlie, I mean."

He looked flushed. There was wine and burgundy going around, and he had probably already had a few glasses. He was dressed in a yellow velvet jacket and a deep pink silk waistcoat, and his cravat had probably taken an hour to tie, though it was now askew.

"Anya, it's so good to see you." He leaned closer in a way that made her want to bat him away. "I made a hash of things back at Budleigh, didn't I?" His voice was meant to be caressing and rueful but sounded more like a thick whisper.

She looked coolly at him. "Did you?"

"You're so appealing, I lost my head." He awkwardly placed a hand on her shoulder and rubbed his thumb in the hollow there. She firmly removed his hand. He pouted at her. "Don't be prim. I see how you look at me. I just made a mess of how I proposed to you."

She looked at his face. It was fleshy and flushed. There was something boyish and awkward about him, but also hedonistic, like he was drowning in his own pleasure, like he was wasting away inside. Yet was it pleasure he was drowning in? With Charlie Budleigh, she had the feeling that he did things out of compulsion. That something was eating away inside him.

"Are you saying you were going to propose to me anyway?" she asked, sounding as skeptical as she felt.

"You're beautiful. You're accomplished. The dignity of you. It's incredibly appealing, you must know it is, men want to drown in it. You can't be short of offers—some kinds of offers. Your voice—"

"Are you telling me you've secretly been in love with me—what is it now?—nearly two years since we've known each other, Charlie?"

"Is that so hard to believe?" His voice was like overcooked caramel.

"Yes."

"One of the things I admire about you, Anya, this forthrightness. But let me be forthright too. I think you're wonderful. And no, I didn't have any clear idea of marriage until now. But I can't imagine that you want to scrounge around for a bridegroom for four months, and I can't imagine that you would want your inheritance to go to Damian of all people. And I don't either. So, if we make a match of it . . ." His eyes were overbright. Yet she couldn't help thinking he also looked hounded. Whether by drink, his creditors, or something else altogether, it was hard to say. She wondered if this proposal was his idea or Lady Budleigh's.

Oddly, the thought that this was a definite way out, that she actually had a concrete offer, that Charlie Budleigh could indeed solve her problem and his own, didn't occur to her. "No, Charlie. Thank you, but we wouldn't suit."

He flung a desperate hand out and grabbed her arm. She gritted her teeth, but she didn't flinch. She placed her other hand firmly on his to remove it. But he gripped her harder and moved closer.

"Charlie—"

"I'm not asking you to love me," he said, his words slurred, but under it there was a hint of aggression now. "We could give each other independence. We would have wealth, and we wouldn't need to be tied to each other's apron strings. I am hardly a ladies' man, I wouldn't embarrass you, and I would let you have every freedom. You are an incredibly sensuous woman. I would be very understanding."

"What a delightful picture, Charlie. Every woman's dream of marriage. I'm blown away. But no, thank you."

She was rattled by the look on his face. She was about to turn away when he said, "I will change your mind, you know. Or time will. Four months is not long. How many offers of marriage are you expecting to get?"

The voice wasn't pleasant. She narrowed her eyes.

"An earl's bastard daughter, Anya. *I* don't mind it, but are you expecting you'll get another respectable offer? Because people mind about blood, you know. And even if people don't mind bastards, they mind native blood. They care about their bloodlines. What do you think they see when they look at you—a native slut."

Her nostrils flared. "If I'm ever desperate, Charlie, and in the mood for some healthy self-loathing, *then* I'm sure I'll come to you."

A flash of anger or hatred in his eyes that he wasn't quick enough to hide. She turned away, shaken by the loathing in his words and in his face. She had wondered if the Budleighs would show their true colors after the restraining influence of their mother, the dowager, passed. After all, someone like Lady Budleigh would only ever see Anya as a lowly employee. But this level of disdain was still unexpected, and it rattled her.

If she thought about it, someone young and helpless like Trixie would be much more Charlie Budleigh's cup of tea. She shuddered. The vein of aggression she'd seen in him just now had felt like it wasn't directed just at her, but at women in general. Yes, that was it. Charlie, just then, looked like he despised women. Had she sensed that in him before, or was it his desperation for money and the idea that Anya could solve the problem for him bringing it out in him?

She would have to steer clear of him, and make sure Trixie did too. Not that there was any real danger of seeing that much of him. He was only here today because of the young cousin who was presented at court, or in fact, the young cousin was an excuse, and Lady Budleigh had bulldozed him into making Anya another offer.

She was heading out of the foyer, lost in thought, and she practically banged into Darren Greenwood, the suitor for her hand who was on top of her list and who she had almost given up hope of seeing today.

"Mr. Greenwood!"

"Anya." He was eyeing someone behind her. "Was that man bothering you? I didn't like the look of him, to be honest."

She smiled. A baron's second son or not, the man had a stolid farmer air about him that was appealing. She could almost imagine turning to him for comfort. If she held her breath, maybe she could even imagine kissing him. Her stomach hardened at the idea. Damnation. She wished her body would behave. "That's Charles Budleigh. He's harmless. More bark than bite. How are you, Mr. Greenwood? I was hoping we'd see you here today."

"I'm glad to hear it, Anya." He looked down and noticed her completely incongruous boots. His eyes twinkled. "How like you. You are so devoted to exercise, both of the mind and body."

Lordy. "I would rather sit by myself and read a book, it's true. Or go for a long walk. I'm hopeless."

"You want to broaden your mind and better your position, what is wrong with that? Most people are content with their lot. *You* always want to improve."

Her brows snapped. Really, she was *never* going to want to kiss him if he kept up this tedious prattle. She looked at the narrow, angular face; the green eyes; the pale, almost cadaverous complexion. His hair was sandy, and he was very tall. He was not unattractive. There were young women at court who tried to throw their caps at him. Yet the thought of kissing him. If she could get past that. Maybe she would have to find him in a corner one evening . . . maybe tonight. She was sure he was exactly the kind of self-righteous man who would instantly propose if you kissed him.

"Anya, there's something I want to talk to you about. It's just that I find myself so unworthy. You know my position. I've tried and tried to get you out of my mind, but I can't."

She was staring at him. Good god. Here it was. He was about to ask her to marry him. Just like that. She didn't even need to kiss him. She spoke quickly. "Mr. Greenwood, will you be around tonight? Maybe we can talk then? I've just remembered I promised to help Trixie—uh—to help her do her—to help her! I'm late."

Disappointment washed over his face, but he was quick to hide it. "Not at all. I am rushing you. Tonight is plenty of time. Don't let me keep you from your duties. I know how devoted you are to everything you do."

"Dear god, I'm really not!" she burst out. He looked astonished at the outburst. She breathed deeply. "I'm sorry, so many people—it's exhausting. I hope I will see you later."

She rushed off before he could say anything more, cursing herself for not jumping at the offer. When it was the answer to everything. A simple, clear, and not entirely unappealing solution. Here it was, right in front of her face, and as usual, contrary woman, she turned away from it. No, not just turned away, but she didn't even let him come out with it. If she had done that, she could simply have delayed the answer, not stalled the question. What was the matter with her?

Tonight, she would say yes. Tonight.

Stupid, stupid woman.

10

Anya dressed with care for the evening. There were other musicians that would accompany her. Serena Mercurio on the violin and Mary Drummond on the pianoforte. But all eyes would inevitably end up on Anya Marleigh when she sang. Anya liked to think that in those moments, even court politics ceased. Even her haters and detractors forgot to hate her.

For Anya, in those moments, when she was singing and playing her sitar, time stopped. The throng of people, three hundred guests, faded, and she found an inner place where only she existed. A place of peace, yes, but also desire and need. A place where all the rivers that flowed from her—pain and pleasure, longing and satiation, all her threads and stories, some of them contradictory, others stubborn, all merged and became one. The only place where she felt whole.

And if there was a longing there, a longing to find that oneness *with* someone and not just by herself, well, there was no time for that. And often, she wondered if it was even a real thing, this idea of oneness with another, or if it was the outcome of a fevered imagination, a wisp of an answer that was always only around the corner and never real. The craving she had for union with another soul, to give parts of her soul over to another and for them to give her theirs, maybe it was a fantasy.

Her dress was gold gauze, fine and gossamer. The skirt was threaded finely with stripes of bronze sequins. The neckline was low, the narrow skirt and high waist fit her perfectly, and the little gold lace sleeves fluttered. Her eyes seemed even darker than usual, and her curls were tight, some escaping from where she'd gathered them high at the back of her head. She didn't wear much jewelry, but she had a thin tiara that rested lightly on her head. One of the ladies of the chamber had given it to her once when Anya had helped her out of a spot of bother with a lover. It was a simple thing, two skinny bands of bronze gold. She had the tiara, and she had her mother Naira Devi's turquoise ring, the only thing she had of her mother.

She looked down at the ring now. A little turquoise egg.

She was only six when she moved to London. And she had her sisters with her: Lila, older by a year, and Mira, a year younger. She should have had some sense of belonging, some sense of family, even after her parents died. But the sisters had, it seemed, made a pact with the devil. They had given up their younger triplet sisters, left them behind in Delhi, and chosen to come to London. To live with the devil, Anya thought.

Sarah Marleigh, their stepmother, and Jonathan Marleigh, half brother, had taken them in. For all that Anya was surrounded by love in her first six years, the years she spent in the Marleigh house in Grosvenor Square were her loneliest. It was where she learned to hide. Where she went quiet. Where she learned that to protect the deepest part of herself, she had to build an impenetrable wall. Lila was strong and fierce, and she would fight injustice to her dying breath; Mira wanted only to be independent, to make a life for herself that no one else could rupture. But Anya hid herself away, looked out at the world from far away, where no one could touch her.

They survived. Each in her own way survived. Replaced Delhi heat with London fog. Crisp fried jalebi and roti cooked hot on the tandoor with cold, indifferently cooked food in the Marleigh house. The glitter and bustle and laughter of the parties hosted by her parents with the tomb-like quiet of their stepfamily. But each survived.

Anya thought there were bits and pieces of her missing, bits and pieces that she may never recover. Not just what she had lost as a child, nor just the missing triplets, but in fact Lila and Mira too. With the shared guilt of leaving behind the triplets, with the games that Sarah and Jonathan played to keep them apart, with their separate schools in separate parts of the country, the sisters had grown further and further apart. And yet half the time Anya didn't know why they still remained cut off from one another. Lila and Mira were an ache in her heart. Yet she had protected her soul from invasion for so long, she no longer knew how to let the sisters back in.

When she made her way down to the heaving ballroom in which the celebrations would take place, she spent the first half hour or so working with the other musicians. She was surrounded by people and the instruments, but somehow the uncomfortable thoughts about her sisters clung to her. She tried to shake them off by focusing on what was going on around her.

Serena, the violinist, was dressed from head to toe in black. There were black feathers in her headband, her dress was cut in unrelieved black, and even her satin slippers were black. She had startling, very light blue eyes and had little to say to anyone who wasn't as obsessed with music as she was. Anya knew that despite the haughty look, Serena was painfully uncomfortable in social situations.

Unlike Serena, who was tall and skeletal, Mary, on the pianoforte, was small and round and jolly. She was wearing a bright floral dress of her favorite yellow color. Serena and Anya didn't dress in the obligatory enormous hoops for court like the guests did, needing to be able to breathe to do their work, but Mary wore eye-smacking hoops and always looked cheerful. She was older than the other two women and treated them like her charges. "Come now," she was chivvying, "you both look thin. Are you sleeping, Anya, and Serena, do you ever come out of your chambers? You're wasting away, both of you." Both Mary and Serena lived outside of court. Unlike Anya, they had families they could live with. And family homes. Anya often envied them that.

Anya looked down at herself and gurgled when she heard Mary's comment. She had inherited from their mother the deep bosom that her sisters inherited too. Her sister Lila was muscular and sporty, and Mira had deep, sensuous curves that she hid under severely cut dresses. Anya was tall and willowy. But they did share the bosom.

"I don't see how you can call me thin," she said ruefully.

"Your bosom isn't the only thing I'm looking at," Mary said. "Unlike all the men here. Who is that eyeing you through his eyeglass?"

"Which one?" Serena asked, sounding bored and making minute changes to the tuning of her violin, alternately tucking it under her chin, then taking it down again, then tucking it snugly in again. "They are all ogling us."

Mary settled down at her piano. "They see *me* as a mother to their future—or in some cases, their present—children. But the two of you, they imagine you flat on your back, legs in the air like dead chickens."

They stifled giggles.

Anya knew she was attracting attention, having already spied Charlie Budleigh and Darren Greenwood looking at her. Charlie looked anxious. He was already in the ballroom when she came in and now kept darting glances at her. Darren Greenwood arrived soon after, made his way across the room, made her an elegant bow, said he knew she was busy but hoped that she would have time to chat later. She gave him what she hoped was an encouraging smile; she was afraid it was a sinking one.

"Miss Marleigh."

Her heart sank as she turned around. It was Lord Pennyworth. Her oldest and wealthiest suitor, who didn't need her wealth. He didn't have the staid and stable demeanor of Darren Greenwood. But he did have a worshipping look. "Miss Marleigh," he said, "I have seen a vision."

"I hope it's gone now, Lord Pennyworth," she said. "It sounds uncomfortable."

"You are so droll, Miss Marleigh. I cannot tell you how much I've been longing to hear your voice. Do you know it enters one and remains embedded in one's heart—no, one's soul—for eternity?"

"How painful, my lord," she murmured, conscious that Mary and Serena could hear every word and would tease the life out of her later.

Lord Pennyworth hoped he would have the pleasure of a comfortable conversation with her later on, though, he added, you couldn't look at the very picture of the divine and then hope for something as prosaic as a comfortable chat. You could only hope for nature's wonder to fully reveal itself to you.

Anya turned around after he left and glared at the other two musicians. Mary was openly chuckling. "He's hot and bothered for you, that's for sure."

"Yes, but one cannot look at an angel and be so base and carnal," Serena said majestically. "One can only kiss the hems of her dress."

Anya spluttered. Mary laughed. Even Serena managed an ironic smile. Through her laughter, Anya was conscious, for the first time, of a new set of eyes on her.

It was Damian Ashton. In black silk knee breeches and beautiful stockings.

She abruptly stopped laughing.

And was only vaguely aware of his dress and bearing. She was mostly conscious of his sardonic look, the mock bow he made her from a distance, but also something else in his eyes. Some new stillness as his eyes rested on her, that made her heart beat wilder and quicker. She couldn't help remembering, suddenly and viscerally, the feel of his lips on the thin skin of her inner wrist. It was like she could feel them now. She gave him just as cool an incline of the head, wondering what she gave away with her eyes. She turned away, hoping that Serena and Mary had not noticed this little exchange.

As she tried to get her focus back on her music, a summons came from Queen Charlotte, who was sitting at the top of the ballroom. The King was making tentative conversation with some gentlemen at the other side of the room. Anya followed the courtier and made a deep curtsy to the Queen, offering felicitations to the Queen on her birthday.

Queen Charlotte surveyed her head to foot. "A pleasing figure, Miss Marleigh. Never have children. And if you do, perhaps stop at one or two."

Anya's lip quivered. The Queen had borne fifteen children. "I have no plans to at the moment, Your Majesty."

"*I* never had plans," the Queen said in her ironic way. "Plans only exist to give us an *illusion* that we have control, never forget that."

Anya's eyes drifted involuntarily to the King, who was vacantly smiling at someone, a courtier he had seen a hundred times before, but whom the King thought was a stranger.

"Are you going to offer me pity or effusive praise?" the Queen demanded.

Anya quickly brought her eyes back to the Queen. "You would have my head on a platter if I dared give you either, Your Majesty," she said and was thankful to see a small smile on the Queen's face. "I was merely thinking that given the enormous weight of responsibility on your shoulders, that you should be allowed to escape it on your birthday."

The Queen snorted. "I *am* bored. What does a woman have to do to find some entertainment in this palace? Do you have any idea how tedious most people are? Most people have no conversation *and* no address. Do you have a suitor?"

"No, Your Majesty."

The Queen unpinned a bronze rose, a brooch, from her bodice. "Keep it that way, Miss Marleigh. Never marry a man unless he knows where he keeps his heart." She handed the rose to Anya. "Pin this on your tiara. It is too plain. It is a bribe so that you'll regale me with your music, instead of simpering at me like everyone else does. Now, off you go."

Anya went a little pink as she pinned the rose on her tiara, next to her ear.

The people in the court were watching her as she left the Queen, some indulgently, but many with bitter looks, possibly plotting how to be the Queen's next favorite.

Mary beamed at her when she got back to her place and Serena gave her what could be a half wink. "Mind that rose,"

Mary whispered. "Everyone will be ogling it and trying to get it off you."

Anya turned to her sitar. She felt self-conscious. When people saw how she played the sitar—not sitting on a stool like Mary with the piano, not standing like Serena with the violin, but sitting on the ground, legs bent to one side, the long stem of the sitar across her thighs—there was a lot of gawking and whispering. On a memorable occasion, a dowager fainted and had to be fanned back to life. But over time, people had got used to it, and Anya inured herself to that first buzz when she sat on the rug on the floor, backed by thick sausage cushions. But today she was aware—even though she wasn't looking at him—of a new set of eyes. Which seemed, inexplicably, to make everything different. She was conscious of every one of her movements, everything felt like it was in sharp relief. And she felt like she hadn't felt in a long time. Like she was in danger of doing something stupid. Twanging a string too loud. Dropping the sitar altogether. Or doing something unforgivable like sneezing.

In the next hour and a half, the musicians entertained the company, sometimes just the instruments, sometimes just Anya with her singing or her sitar, and sometimes all together.

When she started singing and playing her sitar, the familiar hush fell on the ballroom. Her voice, not loud, nor high, but clear as a mountain stream, halted conversation, but also halted thought. She was normally only hazily aware of these things, because once she started singing, the ballroom receded and she entered a deep, inner space that was hers alone. The twang of the sitar seemed to be her gateway to her soul.

This wasn't working today.

She was irritatingly aware of Damian Ashton. She caught

glimpses of him once or twice, but it felt like she was conscious of him all the time. She didn't have to see him to know where he was.

This, she thought, as she took a break and let Serena do a solo on her violin, was the outside of enough. Nothing and no one disturbed her when she was singing. Nothing broke her connection with herself. No one broke that gossamer thread that she craved so badly. Yet here it was today. It was as if the awareness that he was in the room, that he was watching her with that strangely still look, like he was struck by something, a thought or a thunderbolt, *that* was mingled with her singing.

It only reiterated the one thing she was sure of: the quicker she could rid herself of Damian Ashton, the better.

11

Anya Marleigh had been singing off and on for an hour and a half, and Damian was damned if he could take his eyes off her.

It wasn't so much that she was a good singer. It wasn't that her voice was all emotion, a conveyance for everything she thought and felt. It wasn't those things. It was that the music seemed to pass *through* her. Even more breathtaking was the way she dealt with her sitar. (He found himself making pains to discover how it was correctly pronounced—it turned out it rhymed with "guitar.") The way she sometimes closed her eyes, the way she was so comfortable on the floor—a thing one never saw in this country, let alone in the palace, of all places.

This was her third encore and would probably be the last one. He felt a pang for her that surprised him, because he was not used to thinking of anyone's well-being other than his brother's and his own. She must be tired. Her eyes were closed, and he was almost hating himself for looking at her, it looked so deeply intimate, this connection she had with her music.

He envied her. Was there anything in his life that he connected with or cherished that much? He would do anything for Jeremy. And he was dedicated to his business, interested in developing fairer practices with traders in the Caribbean in a way that most people weren't. As a peer, now that he had a voice in Parliament, he was vocal in speaking out against slavery in the empire. Slavery on British soil was declared illegal three years ago, but it still existed across the empire. He was committed to helping change that, carry on something that his father and grandfather had been deeply passionate about but that his father, certainly, had hardly had any time to pursue because he had died so young. And, strangely, the Ashton land that was now his, that had become important to him too.

But half the time he felt like he was drifting, doing things automatically because they seemed like the thing to do. That there was no passion there. No deep connection. That if he wasn't doing those things, he'd be doing something else that occupied his time.

Yet it was more than that. He envied her the connection she had with the sitar, of a lost part of herself that she must have picked up in India when she was little. He had no such connection with Jamaica. No connection with the streets and the food that were his home until he came to boarding school. And what if he could get his hands on some fried plantain? Or invite someone over to play the djembe? It would be out of place here. And he didn't want that connection. He even hid it at times. Not because of what people would think of it, but more because it was a schism with himself, the cauterization of what had been his life, his being. He sometimes thought he was a foreigner to himself.

He was losing his mind.

And all because a woman was sitting on the floor and playing the sitar.

Miss Marleigh's music, it made your soul ache.

Which was patently ridiculous.

The song came to an end. There was dead silence in the ballroom. It was like no one was breathing.

And then Anya Marleigh opened her eyes and looked straight at him. And time stopped. And he felt his heartbeat. He had the strange thought that he couldn't remember the last time he felt his own heartbeat.

Noise returned gradually, and he was conscious that he was staring at her. She turned away first.

He drifted about the room, achingly aware of her. She had stopped singing now, and the musicians were done. The fireworks would start in half an hour or a bit longer, after people ate and drank. He should leave. But instead he was painfully aware of an ache down his spine, the ache *not* to turn around. It was making him cross. He would find his brother and leave. He had done his duty, presented Jeremy. What more was he supposed to do?

He frowned. Jeremy had been doing so well in Portugal. He genuinely liked being in the cavalry. It was astonishing because he was the most peaceful man Damian knew. So peaceful that it made those near him and around him lose their angst too. It was so obvious in his face and eyes that it was the first thing people noticed about him, the deep desire to find peace. But Jeremy liked feeling useful. He had a rigorous, active nature, and he liked feeling part of a team; he liked camaraderie, feeling part of a cause. But now that he was back from Portugal, something had changed. He was talking about staying in England. Damian couldn't put his finger on it, but something was wrong. Some cloud hung over him.

Did Jeremy leave the cavalry willingly, or had he been asked to leave? Damian wanted to know but couldn't bear to probe, and the thought lingered in his mind—if Jeremy needed him, he would turn to him. Surely, he would. Yet Damian had the sneaking suspicion that though Jeremy might turn to him for practical or material support, to bare his heart to his older brother was another thing altogether. The thought troubled him.

A tap on his shoulder. He turned around. It was Preston Budleigh. Damian hadn't seen him since that fateful afternoon earlier this month, when Great-Aunt Griselda's will had been read and all hell had broken loose.

Preston was sliding an uncomfortable finger into the neckline of his shirt and tugging at it. He looked like he had been unwillingly thrust in the direction of his distant cousin Damian Ashton. Damian could easily guess who had done the pushing. He caught Clara Budleigh's eye at the far end of the ballroom. She quickly turned away.

Here was Preston, sweaty, his trousers uncomfortably tight, looking like he didn't want to be here. "Well, well, a squeeze, isn't it? Full to bursting."

"As usual, Preston, a champion of stating the obvious," Damian murmured.

"Give a chap a moment to breathe, Damian," Preston said querulously. "You'd like nothing but for a man to come straight to the point, no doubt, and not even bother being polite."

Damian sipped his wine. "I wouldn't like you to come to the point at all, Preston. I have a feeling it would bore me."

"I told Clara there would be no point speaking to you!"

"And did she listen? No."

"No, she didn't! That is to say, no, she thinks conversation the best way to solve problems. The best of natures, my wife. Most noble. Most obliging. No one like her."

"Oh, sorry, Preston, for a moment I thought we were speaking of Clara. Who *are* we speaking of?"

Preston's nostrils flared. "I've never found another man as rude as you!"

"Why, were you looking very hard?"

The man was spluttering. "To tell you the truth, I'd rather not be here at all. Still in mourning for Mama; isn't the thing to seem too hasty. But Clara said to strike while the . . . I mean, we had to present Emily, my niece, to the Queen. Have to do the right thing. Family duty and all that. Nothing is more important to Clara." He glowered at Damian. He spluttered some more and then finally arrived at the point as if dragged there by a runaway horse. "But I won't beat about the bush, Damian. You know you're mighty smug and always have been. There's many in the family who felt that showing some humility at your good fortune may have been a better way to go. Might have won us over. Not me. Others. You can't say *I* haven't tried to befriend you."

"Can't I?" Damian raised an eyebrow.

"What are you planning to do about Anya Marleigh? That is the only question I have for you," Preston Budleigh was goaded into saying. "And then I will leave you in peace."

"Promises, promises, Preston," Damian murmured. "As for your question, what do you expect me to do? I will consent to her marriage if she comes up with a bridegroom—which I hope she will."

"You won't stand in her way?"

Damian looked down his nose at Preston.

"Fine, fine," Preston said hastily. "No need to take that tone. One would think you had nothing to be grateful to the Budleigh family for. If you hadn't feathered your nest—"

Damian, trying to hold on to his cool, looked disdainfully at Preston. "The Ashton land," Damian said through a clipped mouth, "came to me by chance. I did not ask for it. I used my earnings to save it. This money, your mother's wealth, will only come to me because *you* are such a peevish rotter, Preston, that your own mother couldn't bring herself to leave you anything. And that too, only if Miss Marleigh cannot find a bridegroom. It will not be *my* doing." He ground his teeth. He was about to turn away. How ridiculous to lose his cool for someone like Preston Budleigh.

But Preston stopped him, with a hand on his arm. Damian stared down at his hand, and Preston withdrew it.

"We—I wondered if you'd think about handing over the trusteeship to me." Preston said the words quickly, like he didn't believe them himself. "Can't imagine that you want to be saddled with a business like that; you have other things to do. And you have enough to fly with, Damian, and we don't. Don't want to go into it, but we're on the brink of disaster. House mortgaged to the hilt, in debt all around. And the money rightfully belongs to us; even you must see it. I've never grudged you the Ashton estate." He stopped abruptly, tottered a little, and then, seeing the contemptuous look on Damian's face, amended his statement. "I've never *said* you shouldn't have it." Another, even less believing look. "For god's sake, man! I've accepted that you inherited it! But Mama's money—that's too much to ask! If you hand over the trusteeship, I could give you a little something. We could come to an agreement." A look of extreme boredom crossed Damian's face now, and Preston looked more and more flustered. "If you don't hand over the trusteeship, all I can say is, Miss Anya Marleigh should be careful. She should watch her back—"

For the first time, both the amusement and the contempt were wiped from Damian's face. He took a step closer to Preston, and Preston backed off a little, looking warily at Damian. Damian said in a soft, affable voice, "If you threaten Miss Marleigh again, Preston, you'll regret the day you were born." He took a step back and smiled. "Now, if that's all, Preston . . ."

Preston looked rattled. And a little confused because Damian was back to being cool.

Damian was always cool. He had no idea why he had let Preston rile him up like that. It must be that he didn't like people who preyed on helpless beings. Not that Anya Marleigh was helpless.

She was alone, though. She didn't have anyone to look out for her.

He couldn't help glancing in her direction. She was surrounded by the other two musicians and a thick huddle of men (Darren Greenwood and Lord Pennyworth amongst them, but also several others).

Not so alone, then.

Fine, she was not alone. And she was certainly not his problem. Or she wouldn't be for much longer. This trusteeship, that was what was making him so tetchy. How stupid to get so rattled. He looked crossly at Preston. "Are you still here?" he said. "I have to give it to you, Preston. You're not one to take a hint, are you?"

"All I have to say is this, Damian," Preston blustered. "You have your day in Parliament coming. You're a high and mighty peer now, with a say in everything, whether you deserve it or not. Whether it's your rightful place or not! But I'll say this: you don't want any more blots on your name."

Now Damian was confused. What on earth was the man going on about now?

"'That's right!" Preston said. "That's right! People already whisper that it's all a bit convenient what happened to a load of Budleighs and Ashtons before *you* got your hands on the Ashton place and title." Preston leaned closer, so that Damian could feel his warm breath. "Your hand in Arnold Ashton's death. People might be interested in that, don't you think?"

Damian's eyes narrowed. Not this again. Not Arnold Ashton, who had died at the hands of a highwayman two years ago, which had led to the Ashton estate coming to Damian. Would the rumors ever go away, or would they cling to him forever? Before Damian could punch the man, Preston turned on his heel. Damian was frowning so hard, he was practically scowling. It was one thing to make out that he'd done everything he could to get his hands on the Ashton title and land. But to openly say that he had killed one specific Ashton . . .

Mostly Damian was good at shrugging off the rumors. But there was something different today. Different in the direct way Preston had confronted him with it. For some reason, Damian couldn't shrug it off as easily. It was only when he felt someone next to him that he dragged himself back into the room.

"You look like thunder," Jeremy said.

Something lightened in Damian at the sight of his younger brother. And he felt a guilty pang. Jeremy had so much easy love inside him. All Damian had was cold detachment. A strange indifference. "I wonder if I care for anyone," he found himself saying.

Even Jeremy looked surprised at the wistful note. "You care for me, for one."

"And for two?"

Jeremy was quiet. Apparently, he really needed to think about this one. Damian's eyes veered to where Miss Marleigh was standing with her court of admirers.

"She's exactly as you described her."

Damian abstractedly turned to Jeremy and looked a question.

"Miss Marleigh, I mean," Jeremy said, his face innocent. "Calculating. Mercenary. Average in looks."

"I never said she was av—" The devil take Jeremy.

"Oh no, wait, you said you didn't notice what she looked like." Jeremy took a sip of his drink. "I can understand that. I mean, the woman's hardly noticeable. Drab. Plain. What color are her eyes again?"

"Take care no one breaks your other arm," said Damian Ashton.

At this very moment, of all things, Miss Marleigh broke away from her group and walked up to the brothers. Damian couldn't help freezing. Or heating up inside like a fire was lit under him. Dear god. Miss Marleigh gave them a little curtsy. The men bowed to her. Jeremy was grinning. Damian introduced his—damned scoundrel of a—brother to Miss Marleigh.

"Miss Marleigh, I've heard a lot about you from my brother," Jeremy said, taking Miss Marleigh's hand and bowing over it.

Damn him, he was much too charming. Even more so with his broken arm in a sling.

"Oh," Miss Marleigh said. "That's a shame. What shall I do to change your first impressions of me?"

Jeremy was so startled he gave a bark of laughter, and the two of them were laughing together now like they were bosom buddies, blood-bonded at birth. Jeremy was wiping a tear. Miss Marleigh, flushed after a couple of glasses of champagne, was laughing in a carefree way that Damian had never heard before.

"Funny," Damian said. "Very funny, both of you."

She looked coolly at him, the gurgling laughter gone from

her face. "I can see you're not denying it, Lord Ashton. I suppose you said hideous things about me. Let's see now. Cold, venal, groveling?"

"Only enraging, Miss Marleigh," Damian said.

"Oh. Oh no, Lord Ashton." Her eyes were looking at him in a way that made him want to haul her over his shoulder and carry her out of the room there and then. "The last thing I want to do is enrage you. I have to do all I can to stay on your good side." She smiled. "How are your goats? They were delightful."

"I mean to fatten them up as soon as possible. Have you picked a bridegroom yet? Or is it too hard to know whom to pick out of your long list of suitors?"

Her eyes flashed. Touché to Lord Damian Ashton. Damian grinned. Miss Marleigh's gold dress caught the light from a thousand candles and made her sparkle. She wasn't like a shooting star, which was, after all, just a rock. But instead, she was like the luminescence at the heart of the ocean. God almighty. He was losing his mind.

"It's only a matter of time, Lord Ashton," she answered, thankfully addressing his question and not able to read his mind. "My suitors are all so kind, so nice, it's hard to choose."

"They sound tedious as hell."

She looked innocently at him. "But you don't mind whom I choose, do you, Lord Ashton?"

"I couldn't care less. They all look like boring old sods to me. But you must please yourself."

"Oh no, Lord Ashton," she said, the witch. "I only want to please *you*."

To his great annoyance, even though the little wretch was talking about *pleasing him* to get his consent to her betrothal, or in actual fact, was only trying to goad him, he felt himself flush at her words.

But before he could think of a suitable retort, she turned to his brother. Whose eyes—devil take him—were twinkling. "I like you," Jeremy said to her, Brutus that he was.

"And I like *you*."

Jeremy glanced at Damian, but then turned back to Miss Marleigh. "My brother isn't used to being teased. Sadly, being an older brother and having a lot thrust on him at an early age has made him—"

"Autocratic?" she said.

"I was going to say—"

"Dictatorial?"

Jeremy grinned.

"Puffed up in his own consequence. Arrogant. Full of himself? A cockerel, in fact?"

Jeremy actually laughed. "I was going to say, 'a little aloof.'" He gave her his charming smile. "Though there's no one who loves you more deeply if he does love you."

Damian was so shocked that he nearly fell over. Did his brother really think that? He turned to Miss Marleigh to see how she was taking this. At Jeremy's words, there was a flicker of something on her face. Something that was gone so quickly he almost missed it. Something almost like—longing. No, it couldn't be longing. He watched her face like a hawk. A hungry hawk. He wanted to see it again, that look, whatever the hell it was.

"That must be nice." The mischief was completely gone from her face now. And that inward look replaced it. The way she made you realize there were deep wells there that she let no one into. "How lucky you are," she said lightly to Jeremy.

"Your voice and your playing are heaven, Miss Marleigh," said his stupid brother poetically.

Oddly, she suddenly looked reserved.

"Did I say something annoying, Miss Marleigh?" Jeremy asked.

"No, not at all. You said something lovely. I just hate being liked for my voice, that is all."

Jeremy grinned. "I can assure you, I like a hundred other things about you. Were you trained?"

Her face lightened. She waved a hand. "I used to do some singing with an Indian master in Delhi. But I was very young at the time. He taught me the sitar too. Then at the seminary in Bath where I was educated, oddly they had an Indian music teacher for a short while. He helped me with my singing and gave me tips to keep up my instrumental training. Wonder of wonders, my schoolmistress at the seminary let me have a sitar with me. And the harpsichordist gave me lessons."

Jeremy was all questions and wanted to know more. They chatted about it, now completely ignoring Damian. Well, wasn't that nice. They were apparently the best of friends.

Miss Marleigh suddenly said, "What a wonderful listener you are, Captain Ashton. Most people aren't, you know."

"You must call me Jeremy. And I'm not 'Captain' for much longer. Plain old mister."

She looked concerned. "Oh, are you all right?"

And much to Damian's shock, a forlorn look flittered across Jeremy's face. Damian stared at his brother.

"Oh, please tell me all about it, won't you?" she said. "You have such a deep look of peace about you. I noticed it right away and wondered why you were in the army at all. Do you not like it?"

Someone claimed Damian's attention—one of the investors he did business with. He turned to speak to the man, but he couldn't take his eyes off his brother and Miss Marleigh, who were now talking like they had shared a cradle. Jeremy, it looked like, was pouring out his troubles to her—blast it, she was a stranger!—and she was looking sympathetically at him. They were practically clasping hands. Had no eyes or thought for anyone else. What was bothering Jeremy, and why the bloody hell was he not talking to his own brother about it? He couldn't hear all of what Jeremy was saying to her. But she was listening deeply, lightly touching Jeremy's arm with her fingertips. And from the stray word or two Damian could hear, Jeremy was apparently telling her about what it was like to be in the cavalry.

His acquaintance finally wandered off, and Damian drifted back to his brother and Miss Marleigh. She made him a cool little curtsy and walked off too, and Jeremy turned to him, looking like he had successfully unburdened his troubled soul and felt much better for it. If Jeremy chose to confide in a complete stranger over his own brother, he washed his hands of him. Damian tried not to glare at him.

"I love her," Jeremy said.

"Unbearable woman," Damian said, unable to take his eyes off her now that she was conversing with—of all people!—Charlie Budleigh. Couldn't she see what a loser he was?

"That bad, is it?" Jeremy murmured.

Damian turned a face of supreme indifference to his brother. "I have no idea what you mean." And then he was goaded into saying more. "Has it ever occurred to you that if you are in trouble, you can talk to me about it?"

Jeremy looked at him in that open-eyed sheepdog way of his. "Has it ever occurred to you, brother, that you come across as so—invulnerable—that it's almost impossible to open up to you, even when I really want to?"

That was a leveler, if ever there was one. A good time for the ground to open up and swallow a man. Damn it, did no one understand him? At all?

12

There was a reek of alcohol coming off Charlie Budleigh. And he was swaying slightly, though the anxious look was still there too. No, not just an anxious look. A fevered, desperate look. Anya couldn't help wondering why he drank so much if it didn't make him feel better.

"Why not make things easy for yourself, Anya?" Charlie was saying. "Think of it: wealth, independence—you can get away from here. And I wouldn't trouble you, you know, after you were married. I wouldn't have a single thing to say about how you lived your life. You're a sensual woman. You'll want to live your life."

Anya sighed. She was suddenly exhausted. She was always tired after a musical evening. She felt she had nothing more to give afterward. She had felt all her senses ping sharply awake when she was sparring with Damian Ashton, but now she was deflated and she wanted her bed and darkness. And to forget about marriage and inheritances and wills. And goats. Definitely goats.

Couldn't she escape? Who would notice? She remembered she had promised Trixie she'd find her on the grounds for the fireworks. She squeezed her eyes shut for a moment, but then tried to focus on what Charlie Budleigh was saying. Not the marriage thing again.

"Charlie, I said no." She sounded as weary as she felt.

"Come now, Anya. We would suit admirably."

"We would not suit at all."

"I like how you speak your mind."

"No," she said tiredly, "no, Charlie, you don't."

A desperate look crossed his face. "The family is on the brink of ruin. I—I don't have a feather to fly with. The creditors are threatening me with debtors' prison."

She couldn't help thinking that this was a better tack. This approach might work better with her. But how on earth anyone could marry Charlie Budleigh, she couldn't fathom. Could she marry someone else and then give the Budleighs half the money? It would be fair, perhaps, and would get Charlie off her back. Not to mention Lady Budleigh. She was about to say it when he lurched toward her. Anya couldn't help it, a look of revulsion crossed her face.

Charlie saw it and his lip curled. "You think you're too good for me. With your silks and laces and life in court. But I suppose we'll see how good you really are."

She searched his flushed face, his overfull lips, his sandy hair. "Are you threatening me, Charlie?" Though with what exactly? He was looking at her with so much knowing and contempt that it made her feel sick. She realized it was because it reminded her of Jonathan Marleigh, her half brother.

How, she asked herself, how was it possible to survive being loathed when you were a child? How was it possible to come out the other end intact? There was something so broken inside her, she was sure of it, that she couldn't be close to anyone. She didn't even know how to be close to her sisters.

"Leave me alone, Charlie," she said, sounding lonely and wretched.

She was on the brink of telling him again that she would share the money with the Budleighs, but just at this second, even that was too much effort. She turned away, half expecting Charlie to stop her. But he didn't. He was standing there, looking more knowing than ever, like he knew something she didn't, and for some reason, even though he was like a child, a bullying child, it made her even more uneasy.

She was heading blindly to a door. Trixie would find someone else to see the fireworks with. Surely, surrounded by so many people, she would be safe enough.

But now someone else was stopping her.

She saw with dismay that it was Darren Greenwood. Panic rose, even more than at the sight of Charlie Budleigh. This was simple. So simple. He was ready. You could see it in his face. It was determined, a little nervous, diffident, yet hopeful all at the same time.

"Miss Marleigh," he said breathlessly.

She put up a hand, a sudden, urgent hand to ward him away.

For a second, her eye caught Damian Ashton's. He was speaking to an acquaintance. But he was looking at her. He had a hard look on his face. His eyes veered to Darren Greenwood. Then he looked back at her. He almost started in their direction. But then he stopped himself. As if he had come to his senses.

"Miss Marleigh, you know what I want to say to you."

"Please, please don't, Mr. Greenwood," she found herself saying. There was almost a sob that cracked her voice. Dear god, why was she crumbling? And *what* was she saying? She had spent all day making up her mind to accept Greenwood. *Mr. Greenwood, of course I will.* The words weren't forming.

But he was looking concerned. "Do you have a headache, Miss Marleigh?" he asked, his face full of sympathy.

"Yes, yes, I do."

"You must be exhausted. What a bore I am to press you. Is there any way you can give me some of your time tomorrow afternoon?"

She lifted that hand again, as if to say no. She caught herself in time. She briefly nodded, then turned away. She had to leave the ballroom, all the people, everything. What was the matter with her? She felt like she couldn't bear to be here, surrounded by all the people, for another second.

The exits all seemed to be blocked. Lord Pennyworth was standing at one. Charlie Budleigh near another. And at the third, Lady Budleigh was making rigid conversation with someone.

Was there no getting away? She pressed her hands to her face. Her cheeks were burning. She turned blindly and fled instead to the outer doors. The ones out to the grounds. She would have to make her way to her bedchamber the longer way. She took a second to grab her coat from the antechamber. Moss velvet with pink embroidered roses. She slipped it on and escaped into the night. At the door, she stood for a second and turned. There he was: Damian Ashton, deep in conversation now with a beautiful young woman with bright green eyes, long red curls, and the creamiest complexion Anya had ever seen. Someone of his own class. The sight of the pair made her feel more forlorn than ever.

Outside, it was so cool, the stars were so bright, and there was a full moon, and it all seemed to touch her heated skin so that she uncurled her hands from her coat and let it fall open. She meant to circle back inside and head to her room, but, drawn as if by magic, she made her way to the rose garden. The fountain with the wide, low parapet that ran around it called to her. But she ignored it, and it was only when she got to the sundial that she stopped, gripped the stone edge, and hung her head.

She stood there for some time, eyes sharply closed. For seconds, all she could feel was the pain in the pads of her fingers where she had pressed them into the sitar strings.

She heard a rustle behind her. She turned. *Damnation.* "Can't you leave me alone? Do you have to be everywhere?"

"What's wrong?" he said, searching her face. "Tell me."

She made an impatient noise. She stalked toward him, intending to brush past and run up to her room, but then strangely, she didn't know how, but she was in his arms. Her lips found his.

She wasn't sure if she was pushing against him or drawing him closer. His hands were steady. And solid. There was a sureness to them. Like if she leaned into them, he wouldn't let her fall, wouldn't let her dither at the edge of uncertainty. The coolness of his lips cooled her. Was his brow as furrowed as hers? Was his hunger as great as hers? Was he slaking her hunger or stirring it up? She broke away.

"I have no idea what you think you're doing, Lord Ashton," she said breathlessly.

"Damian," he said.

She moaned as she kissed him again. She drew closer, if that were possible, pushed against him, felt his chest with her hands, the slight roughness of his cheeks, the dark hair entwining in her fingers. She could feel his hardness through all their layers, and she rubbed against it like a cat, and he stifled a curse.

"Were those men bothering you?" he asked, searching her face.

Right at this second, she couldn't remember the men. What men? "The men?" she said breathlessly.

He kissed the corner of her mouth. She gasped.

"Were they?" he murmured.

"I—I can't remember."

He kissed the other corner. It was nothing as intense as the first kiss, yet it felt like the feel of his lips, lightly, like that, was making her arch, making her want so much more.

"Can't you tell them to get lost?"

"Who?" she said breathlessly.

"The men," he murmured. He moved the hair away from her neck. Found a spot just behind her ear and kissed it.

She gasped. "Jealous?" she asked, barely breathing.

"Who, me? Never," he said. He turned her face a little. Found the identical spot at the other ear and kissed that too.

He walked her farther into the garden, and now something nudged the backs of her knees. It was the parapet that ran around the fountain. He was looking at her with those soft brown eyes of his, like everything she said and did, everything, was important and must be seen. Like he was hungry for it. Aching like she was. His lips were warm at the base of her throat, at her collarbone, at the hollow of her neck. His mouth warm and open.

He laid her down on the parapet. And then he sat next to her. She felt strangely exposed and vulnerable and so out of her mind with desire all at the same time that she whimpered. She reached out her hands and grasped his face, and though he bent down and kissed her, he moved her hands away, laid them on either side of her, moved down to the V of her dress, and pushed it aside, letting the cold January air pucker her skin, before wrapping his mouth around her breast. She gasped and arched, her legs instinctively opening. He was doing something that was going to drive her mad, lightly squeezing her breast as he lapped at her nipple. She was panting and moaning and who knew what else she was saying?

He lifted his head for a moment. "I wish you didn't have to worry about being here on your own, the long hours, the men of the court, the inheritance, any of it."

His face was serious. She desperately wished he would stop talking and put his mouth on her breast again. But he was looking so seriously at her.

"You don't think I can look after myself?" she said.

"Can you? Is it hard to let someone else look out for you?"

She grasped his face. "You tell me, Lord Ashton. Is it?"

His eyes were dark now. She kissed him hard.

He moved down again, placed his lips between her breasts for a moment, and it was like she could feel them deep down in her belly. He moved his mouth again, planted kisses on the swell of her breast, and moved back to the nipple.

For many minutes, he stayed there, lapping at her with an endless hunger. And when she was practically crying, he moved farther down her body. Her skirts were lifted and the cool air feathered and touched her flesh, and to her intense surprise she felt his mouth on her.

She gasped. Said, "Oh no, please don't!"

He quickly looked up from between her legs. "Am I hurting you? I'll stop."

She almost laughed. "No, no, of course not. It's just . . ." She bit her lip.

"What is it?"

He looked so concerned that she couldn't help gurgling. Now he looked bewildered, which only made her laugh more. "It makes me feel self-conscious." Her face burned as she said it, and she felt more exposed than ever.

"Can I try again?" he asked, almost diffidently.

It took her such a long time to relax that she was sure he would get bored and give up. But he stayed there, finding her crevices, listening to her and responding to her noises, changing tacks if she didn't respond, staying with something when she made noises of pleasure. It was strange, but he seemed in no hurry to stop; he didn't look up impatiently, he didn't rush her, he didn't move on to something else. He wasn't moving away, wasn't getting bored or tired; he wasn't in a hurry, not demanding, not asking her for anything.

And then to her intense surprise, she opened more than she had ever opened—everything opened, heat spread through her body like a fire, and something seemed to uncoil in her that she hadn't even known had been coiled. She gasped.

He made a sound, as if her pleasure felt good to him. And she felt as he bent to her again that she became one not only with the midnight sky above her and the swath of stars but also with the steady trickle of water from the fountain that seemed to enter her body and give her its song.

13

He stayed there for many more endless minutes, uncoiling her again and again until she was nearly crying. It was not as if she was completely inexperienced. And she hadn't lied to Trixie. She had had her infatuations. But this, this leisure, the lack of hurry, the care and attention he gave her, this was something novel.

But then they had to get up in a hurry because suddenly there were noises. The doors had obviously opened, and out poured many if not all of the guests. Damian and Anya were tucked away in the little nook of the rose garden, but anyone could venture in at any time, to explore the grounds before the fireworks started. Other couples might have the same idea. She was shaking a little, and to her surprise, he was too. He was looking at her intently. She, a little shyly. He helped her straighten her clothes. He gave her a quick, unexpected kiss on her temple.

"I—I didn't get to—" she said, reaching a hand to him in longing.

He gave her a quick smile. "Later." He kissed her hard on her mouth.

They were heading to the mouth of the little rose garden, and reality was settling in further. She said, "Perhaps it would be better if we didn't leave together."

He looked at her a little questioningly. But it was hard to explain. She didn't want him to feel he owed her anything because of what they had just done. But then his mouth curled in his familiar look. "Oh yes, of course, Miss Marleigh, we wouldn't want your many suitors to back off, would we?" And he became Lord Ashton again, touched by no one, bothered about no one.

The coolness of the tone, so soon after what he'd done and what he'd made her feel, made her recoil. She steadied herself with a deliberate effort. "We wouldn't want that, would we?" And if her voice sounded small and forlorn, he didn't seem to notice.

They left the rose garden, not together.

She stood far away from him. Lost him in the crowd. And felt more alone and colder than ever. And yet, and yet, there was a hum between her legs, and her body felt at the same time almost sedated yet wider awake than ever, almost as if she were floating away with the ash and smoke of the fireworks. Like she wasn't in her body at all. She closed her eyes as the fireworks started and exploded overhead.

For many minutes, she stood there, alone, though surrounded by people. She saw Trixie once and was happy to see that she had found two other girls who looked to be about her age. Anya let herself stand there and forget, forget what exactly she couldn't say. Everything, or just herself. She couldn't tell if Damian Ashton had slaked a thirst, a deep parched thing that she didn't even know was inside her, or in fact, if he had stirred something, a hungry demon that would never be able to rest again. Sometimes it was better not to even have a taste of something. Not to have memories.

When the fireworks finally came to an end after a profusion of oohs and aahs, the crowd was fizzing more than ever. The clock struck one, and Anya realized with dismay that it was time for her meeting with Clara Budleigh. She had forgotten all about it. When she'd hastily scribbled the unlikely hour on that note to Lady Budleigh, she hadn't thought that that hour would come. But here it was. She didn't want to go to the conservatory. Lady Budleigh only wanted to see her to find a way to convince Anya to give up the money. Nothing more than that. It was certainly in no way an apology for her behavior at Budleigh. She shook her head, half annoyed and half dismayed. She wished she never had to see Lady Budleigh or Charlie Budleigh ever again.

She squared her shoulders and turned in the direction of the conservatory. It was best to get it over with. The woman would keep at it until she got this meeting. The sooner she could speak to her, the sooner she could be in her bed and forget about this evening. Forget it or relive some parts of it, she wasn't sure which. If she ever managed to get Lord Damian Ashton's eyes out of her head, she'd call it a big success.

She circled the palace wing and reached the conservatory, and it was dark and cold after the fireworks. It was empty. She and Trixie used this place when it was a sunny day, and so there were some candles strewn about, and she lit a few like she was waiting for a lover. She couldn't help laughing. A romantic tryst. Lady Budleigh had as much romance in her as a peanut shell. And as for Anya, maybe she had already, just in one night, had as much romance as she was ever going to get.

She shivered and reached for one of Trixie's shawls that was hanging on a hook and wrapped it around her. Footsteps approached, and she couldn't help feeling a sliver of irritation.

Maybe she shouldn't have minded being rude and should have forgotten this appointment. Lady Budleigh could be cold and frigid and condescending. And yet Anya had, after all, inherited money that should have rightly gone to the Budleighs. Perhaps one conversation, she could give the Budleighs that.

She turned as the door opened, conscious suddenly of the lit candles and the inviting smell of the orangery.

It was Charlie Budleigh. She recoiled in shock. He came in, his face knowing, his eyes bright, the pupils sharply dilated.

"I have no idea what you're doing here, Mr. Budleigh. I was expecting your sister-in-law."

He walked forward and grasped her arm; his hand was hard. "Come now, Anya," he said in a caressing voice. "It is romance and passion you want, isn't it, and I have been too hasty and mercenary. Let me show you that we *would* suit."

Before she could stop him, his wet, hard mouth was on hers and he was ruthlessly kissing her. If something so harsh and blind could be called "kissing."

She gave him a stinging slap. He recoiled, and the caressing look was gone, to be replaced with an ugly one. "I will show you passion, Anya, since that is what you are looking for. One way or another."

The heat rose to her face. She realized that she was utterly alone. No one would hear her if she screamed. The fireworks had stopped, but the crowd was chattering and laughing too much to hear anything. If she wouldn't agree to marry Charlie Budleigh, she was going to be made to. The rage rose in her. She looked at him with revulsion. "This is your idea of passion, is it, Mr. Budleigh? If I won't open my legs to you, you will open them for yourself?"

"What a nasty little mouth you have, Anya. Come now. If you come to me willingly, it'll hurt less."

He reached out with both hands and grabbed her waist. Before she could think of any kind of plan, anything that would get her out of here, she was fighting him with everything she had, and at the same time, acutely and suddenly aware that a drunken lush though he was, he was stronger, a lot stronger, than her. They were fighting; she was pushing against him, spitting at him, and he had her backed against a wall near the door of the conservatory. Her skirts were already bunched up at her hips, and he was at the same time fidgeting with his clothing. His hardness was pressing into her stomach, digging into it.

A wild panic. A sudden, sharp fear. She gathered up every last ounce of strength and punched with both hands. He staggered a little—it was by far not enough—but then strangely, he was on the floor, on his back.

She looked in shock. It was—of all people—Jeremy Ashton who had pulled Charlie away at the same time as she pushed. Her voice broke on a sob, but before she could say anything, thank Jeremy, Charlie Budleigh was on his feet and the men were fighting.

And Jeremy had a broken arm! And she could see Charlie Budleigh viciously pressing on it. Jeremy managed to punch the man. But Charlie jabbed at the bad arm. Now he was squeezing it hard. Jeremy was in pain. Sharp, horrible pain.

She ran forward. She grabbed Charlie Budleigh from behind and pulled hard. At the same time, Jeremy pushed. Between them they managed to disengage Charlie Budleigh from Jeremy and his broken arm. Charlie staggered backward and fell, but as he did, a shot rang out.

And Jeremy Ashton stood there, looking down in surprise at his shoulder, a hand clamped there, a hand that was suffused in red within seconds. Dear god, Jeremy had been shot. She ran to him, helped him to the ground. She quickly unwound

Trixie's shawl from around her shoulders, bunched it up, made a hard little wad, and pressed down on the wound on Jeremy's shoulder. "It's all right," she was saying, "it's all right, Jeremy. I won't leave you, I promise."

"I'm fine," he was saying, even though he was pale. "Make sure that blighter isn't going to reload that damned pistol." His voice was strained, weakening, and no matter how much she was pressing down with the shawl, the wound was bleeding. Dear god, what was she going to do? How was she going to get help? She couldn't stop the pressure on the wound.

She glanced at Charlie Budleigh. But he was still lying there. Where he had fallen. She got a shock because, though he was still and white as the tomb, his eyes were wide open. His head had hit a hard and very heavy iron plant pot. Was he dead? He had no grip on his pistol now. It lay next to his hand.

She looked back at Jeremy. Her breath broke on a sob because he had fainted. "What am I going to do?" she said desperately.

And then by some miracle, the door to the conservatory opened. She turned, and it was Damian Ashton. "Jeremy's been shot," she said. "I can't leave him. He'll bleed to death. I—I—it was my fault—"

He was beside her, looking almost as pale as Jeremy, but steady too, infinitely steady. "He won't," he said, in a sure voice. "We need to bind his wound. Do you know anywhere I can get more cloth?"

"I saw Trixie—you know my protégé? In the grounds."

He looked seriously at her. "I'm not sure I can leave you here. If someone comes in . . . Charlie Budleigh looks like he's dead. What did he die of? A head wound? There'll be the devil of a row."

"It was me, it was my fault. Not Jeremy's. And he can't—he *can't* take the blame, not right now, not the way things are for him in his regiment."

He searched her face. "I will ask you to explain that later. I saw a shed outside. I was following Jeremy, wondering if he was ready to go home. I think we have to move my brother, before I go to find Trixie. We'll think about what to do later."

Just at that moment, Jeremy came to. "At least it was the same arm," he said. "Imagine both arms out of commission."

Lord Ashton pressed his good shoulder. "Stay with us, little brother. Can you walk if we support you?"

Jeremy was pale, almost green, and he was biting his lip but he nodded. With difficulty, with Anya still pressing hard on the gushing blood, between them they managed to make it to a shed not far from the conservatory. It seemed to take forever to get there.

It took Lord Ashton almost fifteen minutes to come back with Trixie, but at least they came laden with strips of cloth and cotton wadding. Trixie, who could be a mouse if she encountered bullies, was no mouse in the sickroom. She knew exactly what to do, and between the three of them they managed to bind the wound, and mercifully Jeremy had fainted again. The bullet was still wedged in his shoulder, but at least they had stemmed the bleeding for now.

When they were done and all three looked exhausted, Lord Ashton turned to her. "Tell me what happened."

She explained. His face was like thunder when she mentioned the scuffle she had with Charlie Budleigh before Jeremy came into the orangery. "I tried to push him off me, and I don't think I was strong enough, but Jeremy pulled at the same time. But then Jeremy, with his broken arm, wasn't—he . . ." She swallowed. "He wasn't strong enough and he pushed as I tried to pull Charlie off him. Charlie fell. But by this time he may have had—he *must* have had—the pistol in his hand. I heard the shot but thought it must have been fired into the air. But it was Jeremy. The bullet, I mean. It was in Jeremy's shoulder. And then—and then, I think when Charlie Budleigh fell, his head hit the iron plant pot. I don't know if he died of the head wound—or—or his neck broke." She stopped abruptly, her chin shaking.

Lord Ashton's face was grim. Jeremy stirred right at that moment. "It was me. It was my fault. What happened to Charlie, I mean. I pushed him."

"No, it was me!" Anya said quickly. "*You* can't take the blame, and you know it!"

"It wasn't your fault, either of you, but I don't know if the law will see it that way," Lord Ashton said. "They will not take your side, Anya. And Jeremy." He looked steadily at his brother.

"I'll take the blame," Jeremy said again.

"No!" Anya cried.

No one spoke for some moments. "We need to think this through," Damian said finally. "And Jeremy needs a doctor. And for the bullet to be taken out. Urgently. We need to get out of here."

14

The rest of the night passed without sleep. How long would it take them to find Charlie's body? She paced about her room. She had wanted desperately to go with Damian and Jeremy, to help. She was terrified Jeremy would die. Would bleed to death before he could be taken to a doctor. He would bleed to death, all because of her. He was so kind, so peaceful. That he should die in this horrible, violent way! She could picture it like she had seen it happen, seen his last breath leave his body. Seen the kind light in his eyes die. All because of her.

She couldn't stop shuddering at the thought of what had nearly happened. What would have happened if Jeremy hadn't come into the conservatory and helped her fight Charlie Budleigh off? Charlie Budleigh had had one thing on his mind. She didn't think she would ever get it out of her head, the ugly look on his face moments before he died, the feeling of his erection pressing into her belly. The hatred not just for her, but for women. And he had that pistol. He'd meant to use it. He *had* used it. It had even found Jeremy Ashton.

How long before they found Charlie's body? Trixie and

Anya used the conservatory on wintry or wet days, to sit in, to take rounds of exercise in, to find some heat in. The gardeners worked in there too. But it could still be a day or two before someone went in there and found the body. How would she get through a whole day or two of waiting? She imagined herself going in there and screaming, pretending to find the body. She pictured it step by step, clearly, in her mind. But she couldn't bring herself to do it. It was like the more vividly she could picture it, the more she was paralyzed.

She had begged Damian Ashton to let her go with them, so she could help with Jeremy. But he said it was safer if she didn't. That once the body was found, if she wasn't anywhere to be found in the palace, it might look suspicious. She was one of the few people in the palace who knew the Budleighs. She had spent some days in their home very recently. Not only that, but any number of people would have seen her talking to Charlie Budleigh in the ballroom. Charlie had looked drunk and she had looked disturbed. She couldn't afford to be missing. She had to stand her ground.

Just before she and Trixie parted from the brothers, Damian Ashton pressed her hand, with a look in his face she hadn't seen before. If anything, she might have expected gratitude. And she would not have wanted it. But this wasn't gratitude. It was almost an apology for leaving her there, or worry that she would be there alone and he was leaving her. Something new that she didn't think she had ever seen before. Not only from Damian Ashton, but from anyone. It burned a hole in her belly at first, that look, but then as the night wore on, she questioned if she had seen it. She thought she must have misinterpreted it. Damian Ashton, caring for her welfare, or showing a glimpse of some feeling, a strong feeling, for *her*. She must have imagined it.

It was only now when she was pacing her room that she came to an abrupt standstill, her hands at her throat. The note.

It was only now she remembered the note she had written to tell Clara Budleigh where to find her. In the conservatory, at one in the morning. How, how had she forgotten? There was only one way Charlie had turned up there. Lady Budleigh must have told him where to go. Was the whole thing a setup? The note from Lady Budleigh asking for a meeting. The skittish horse. The groom, anxious to be off. The scrap of paper he handed her, to write down a time and destination, but no names, not addressed to Lady Budleigh. Was it a setup from the start? To make it look like she was inviting Charlie to the conservatory, for a romantic tryst maybe?

How did she fall for it? She was a fool. Because she believed Clara Budleigh's note of apology. Or at least, she had wondered why Lady Budleigh wrote it, had known perhaps that it wasn't an apology but a way to ingratiate herself with Anya and influence her decision about her marriage, but she hadn't thought it sinister. Naïve, so naïve.

She remembered that knowing look on Charlie's face. Like he knew something she didn't. If she didn't say yes to his marriage proposal, then he'd find another way—the Budleighs would find another way—to convince her. Yet what way? Had they thought that assaulting her would make her marry Charlie? No, the assault must have been Charlie's idea. Drunk that he was. And he hated women. She'd seen that in him. Clara Budleigh must have wanted him to seduce her, not rape her. For someone like Charlie, maybe there was no difference between the two. She realized that now. Lady Budleigh might have meant Charlie to seduce her and to make it look like she had invited him for a tryst. Assaulting her was likely Charlie's idea.

She was shaking. Badly. She dragged a shawl around herself. Stoked the fire. She couldn't get near enough to the flames. She needed them to enter her and warm her. She was freezing, shivering uncontrollably now. She sat there, as close to the hearth as she could, for a long time, until the shaking started to pass, though shudders still ran through her.

Hers was a small room. Not exactly a servant, she lived in the same region of the palace where some of the lesser ladies of the chamber stayed. A small but comfortable room, with very simple furniture—a four-poster, an armoire, a dresser. The palace did lots of trade with the colonies, and she had over the years decorated the room with scraps of Indian silk with a gold border, a rosewood plant pot, some small musical instruments—a bansuri that she played indifferently, a mouth organ, a set of dilapidated bagpipes, a set of tabla drums.

Yet today it didn't feel like home. Today she felt like a prisoner. She felt like she had been living a borrowed life. If anyone connected her with Charlie's death . . .

Suddenly, she knew it. Of course, there was no reason for anyone to make that leap. Except for Clara Budleigh and maybe Preston Budleigh. They would be the ones who sent Charlie to the conservatory in the first place. *Of course*, they would connect her with his death. There was no other conclusion.

She could hardly breathe. What at first seemed an unlikely outcome now seemed to be the *only* one. Of course, they would connect her. In fact, she had to confess. Not to murdering the man, but to pushing him in self-defense. She had to do it before the body was found. If she did it, if she raised a hue and cry about the body, then there was a greater chance of people believing it was an accident. Or that she was defending herself.

She stood in a fever of anxiety. *Would* anyone believe her? She was just a court singer. A mere employee. Not a guest.

Not even quite a lady of the chamber. She had no standing. No reputation. No one to support her.

But she couldn't let Jeremy be connected to this scandal. No, she had to say what had happened, but leave his name out of it. He hadn't been dishonorably discharged from the army. But he said it could happen at any moment. There was suspicion that surrounded him. Because of his friendship with someone. A man. Kenneth Laudsley. In fact, Anya knew the man. It was her sister Lila's friend Kenneth. Jeremy had been asked to leave the army or risk exposure, risk a dishonorable discharge. Just because of his relationship with Kenneth Laudsley. She would be damned if she would make this harder for him. He was heartbroken at what had happened. That he'd had to leave a profession he enjoyed, a group of men he felt he belonged in, because of who he was, because of who he loved. It was like all along he had been accepted on false pretenses.

He told her in the palace ballroom when she asked him what was wrong. He was not only upset about what happened in his regiment, he was also worried that he and Kenneth didn't know each other that well. That they were just feeling their way. He wasn't sure how Kenneth felt about him. A lot was unsaid. What if he had burned and destroyed the one thing he was good at—being in the cavalry—for something that was a myth, not real? He was upset by it, of course he was, and he hadn't told Damian Ashton about it—it was hardly surprising; "empathy" was not Damian Ashton's middle name—but she felt she had soothed him a little. Comforted him by listening and not judging. He had only told her reluctantly, at first only in half-formed sentences. And only because she was asking him and because he saw that she wouldn't judge him, but she thought that he had felt the better for it.

Anya didn't get any sleep that night. She was so exhausted

from pacing by five in the morning that she fell on her bed, fully clothed, and into a half-awake stupor. When Trixie jolted her awake, it was only two hours later, and she felt more exhausted than ever. Trixie looked pale and tired too, but Anya still wanted to complain about the early hour. Couldn't Trixie have waited to wake her?

"They found him," Trixie said.

Anya gasped and sat bolt upright. "Already? How?"

"How do you think?"

"Lady Budleigh."

Trixie nodded.

"I must get up." Anya was already flinging off the gold gossamer dress—something she should have done last night. She didn't know if she could ever bear to look at it again.

"No," Trixie said. "Your name hasn't come up."

Anya stopped tearing off her clothes. "What?"

"Lady Budleigh hasn't said anything. She raised a hue and cry about Mr. Budleigh being missing. That's how they found him in the orangery, after a big search. I came to tell you because the palace is in an uproar. But you have to wait. She hasn't said anything about you. I didn't want you to wake up not knowing what had gone on, and then do something rash."

She saw Trixie's calm, practical face. Trixie was pale, yes, but Anya couldn't help noticing that in a crisis, there was steel in Trixie's backbone. She reached out and squeezed Trixie's hand, for once not to reassure Trixie but because she herself needed reassurance. The girl was young, so young! And here she was trying to be pragmatic and resourceful for Anya. Anya felt guilty for having embroiled her in this mess. Perhaps she shouldn't have taken her up at all, should never have pretended that she was strong enough to take on a protégé.

"Trixie," she said helplessly.

Trixie firmly pressed her hand. "Don't work yourself up. Keep a calm head and it'll be fine."

Anya couldn't help wondering how Trixie looked so capable all of sudden. So capable, when Anya felt so weak and helpless. "How can you look so calm?"

"I'm not," Trixie said, and indeed she was pale and her face was pinched. "But it won't do to lose our heads."

Anya sat on her bed in agony. She had left it too late. She should have been the one to wake the palace about Charlie's death. She should have told her story—just leaving Jeremy out of it. Now it was too late. She had to wait for what Clara Budleigh would do next.

"I have to talk to Lord Ashton," she found herself saying. She had to make sure their stories matched. Not that anyone would necessarily connect Jeremy with it. Clara Budleigh didn't know he'd been there. As far as Lady Budleigh knew, it was only Charlie and Anya in the conservatory. But the anxiety that Jeremy was dead was flooding back too now that she was awake, her body exhausted after the sleepless night. What if Jeremy was dead? If it had seemed like a likely outcome two hours ago, now it seemed a certainty.

"He'll come," Trixie said, before leaving the room.

Anya had no idea how Trixie could sound so sure. Lord Ashton cared for no one but himself. She remembered his pale face last night. Maybe he cared for his brother. Yes, it was obvious that he did. The gentle way he had spoken to his brother, the way he had steadily worked with Trixie and Anya to bind the shoulder. He cared about Jeremy. But certainly not her. She remembered the way he had held her hand before he left. No, that was concern for his brother too. She'd been half out of her mind at the time. She'd exaggerated or misinterpreted the look. In fact, it had probably been more warning than concern.

An involuntary shiver ran all the way through her as she suddenly and viscerally remembered the rose garden.

She couldn't believe she had forgotten. It was hardly something to forget. Yet after everything that happened with Charlie Budleigh and with Jeremy's shoulder, she *had* forgotten it. But it seemed her body remembered because after that first violent shiver, she felt a treacherous trickle of wetness. It couldn't have meant anything to him. Of course, it couldn't have. It was only searing through her own brain and body. He would likely never think of it again. Especially not after the night they had had.

She resumed her pacing. She couldn't think about that now. If Jeremy was dead, then there was nothing else to think about, nothing to remember. She'd never be able to think about the rose garden without thinking about what had happened to Jeremy so soon after.

Strangely, after Trixie came, no one else did. She paced about her room, alternately falling down on her bed and falling into a dreamless, almost violent sleep, and then restlessly pacing again. But no one came. No one came looking for her. She finally dressed in her day clothes and left the room in the early afternoon.

The palace was in an uproar. There was bustle and frantic bursts of energy everywhere. Outbursts, crashes of things falling to the ground. Yet the staff were going about their daily business. Whatever scandalous thing had happened in the palace, whatever fever everyone was in, the daily chores had to go on. The palace was a behemoth, almost a city. Nothing short of a fire could bring it to a standstill.

She caught snippets of conversation. Charlie Budleigh had

been found dead. The Bow Street Runners, whose job it was to police the city, to keep the peace and find criminals, were all over the palace. The death could have been an accident; the man could have fallen and hit his head on the plant pot. There were signs and evidence that Charlie Budleigh had been heavily drinking, that he was a habitual heavy drinker. There was the small matter of the pistol. The man had a pistol lying next to his hand when he was found, and it had been discharged. Yet there was no bullet wedged anywhere.

Where was the bullet? Did anyone in the palace have an unexplained injury? No one seemed to. No doctor had been called. There was no blood (Trixie had made sure there was none). Of course, there had been hundreds of guests. One of them could have an injury. Could have a bullet wedged in them. But that would take time to investigate.

No one came for Anya. She was dreading it. She was wandering about the palace and at times staying in her room. But no one came. She found it unbearably sinister. Clara Budleigh knew why Charlie was in the conservatory at that time. She knew. So why wasn't she saying anything?

Anya had worked herself into a fever by the time the summons came. And when it came, it wasn't the Runners, like she'd dreaded, but Clara Budleigh herself. It was evening. Clara Budleigh was in one of the small rooms off the long gallery that were not used by the royals, but sometimes used by the ladies of the chamber to entertain a guest. Clara Budleigh asked to see Anya. Anya fixed herself in the mirror. She breathed deeply as she walked the long walk to the parlor room. She was shaking by the time she knocked and entered.

Lady Budleigh did not stand to greet her. She was dressed in black. In mourning for the dowager but also presumably for her brother-in-law. Her back was rigid, her face tight. She indicated for Anya to sit, like this was her house in Folkestone and not a royal palace.

Anya watched her warily as she sat on a deeply upholstered chair across from her. It was old and soft, and she sank into it and immediately wished she hadn't. She felt vulnerable. She made herself get up, replace the chair with a straight-backed hard one, and sit down on it. But she felt just as exposed as before.

"We both know what happened last night," Lady Budleigh said.

"Do we?" Anya was surprised to hear how calm her voice was. She was gripping her hands in her lap. "I'm sorry for your loss, Lady Budleigh. It must have come as a shock."

"Not really," Lady Budleigh said to Anya's surprise. "He was always going to end that way. A drunken brawl, drowned drunk in a puddle, or forcing himself on a woman. Is that what he tried to do?"

Burning anger flashed through Anya. "Isn't that what you told him to do?" She'd meant to pretend that she didn't know what Lady Budleigh was talking about. Meant to say she wasn't in the conservatory, had not kept the appointment. Lady Budleigh could prove Anya had made the appointment, but not that she'd kept it. The line was thin, but still, no one could prove she was in the conservatory. But the anger that flashed through her was still rumbling there like ominous thunder. The feel of Charlie's breath on her face. The look on his face. And this woman had sent him there, to the conservatory.

"No, as it happens, I did not. I asked him to use his charm. I forgot that he didn't have any." Lady Budleigh's mouth curled in disgust.

Anya knew without a shadow of a doubt that Lady Budleigh didn't feel any remorse. Not that Charlie had tried to force himself on Anya and not that he was dead. She may have asked Charlie to be charming, to seduce Anya, to push his marriage proposal, get Anya to see the mutual benefits. That could be true. But if Charlie *had* forced himself on Anya, and if Charlie hadn't died, Lady Budleigh would have put that down to what—a minor irritant?

"Charlie fired his pistol. But you do not look hurt," Lady Budleigh said, scanning Anya's body as if expecting to see a pistol wound.

"I wasn't there," Anya said. Though she had no conviction in her voice. She realized she didn't want to lie to Lady Budleigh. She wanted to throw it in Lady Budleigh's face. That she knew what Lady Budleigh was up to. Knew what she was like.

"I have your note," Lady Budleigh said, laying her cards on the table. "All I have to do is give it to the Runners, and you will be the prime suspect. Everyone will say that your native blood showed in the end. That no matter how many years you've spent in the palace, your breeding won."

There it was again. This sneering at Anya's Indian blood. And Lady Budleigh was right; this was the problem. Anya would be a convenient person to hang a murder on.

"I can say that he was forcing himself on me. That I defended myself."

"It's much too late for that, Anya. You should have done that right after it happened, and you know, people might have believed you, even if they thought you must have been asking for it. A court singer. The way you sit on the floor and close your eyes and sing. Every man in the room stares at you—and I can assure you, they are all thinking of only one thing. It was a matter of time before some man lost his head."

Anya stood up in a rage. "I have nothing more to say to

you." She was shaking again. There was no point saying to Lady Budleigh that she was exactly the kind of woman who would say something like that, blame a woman for being savagely attacked by a man. There was no point. It would be like trying to speak French to an orangutan.

"I, however, have something more to say. I have your note, Anya, like I said. I also have the bronze rose from your tiara. It was in Charlie's hand when he fell. I took it from his hand when I found his body."

Anya sat down in numb shock. It took her some minutes to find her voice. "Why did you do that? Why not let them get me? If they hang me for Charlie's death, then you'll get what you want. If I die unmarried, your husband gets the money."

Lady Budleigh gave a tight little shrug. "That is what the lawyer thought at first. That if you die then the money will revert to next of kin, that is, to Preston. But Mr. Prism made some inquiries, and it seems that your death would amount to the same thing as if you didn't marry in time. The money would go to Damian."

A bark of laughter escaped Anya.

But then she couldn't stop herself and she went off into a peal of laughter. She was suddenly laughing hard, all the pent-up emotions of the evening before and the terrible restless night swooping through her. She was wiping her eyes, and Lady Budleigh was sitting frigidly on her chair. "Oh, I see." She was gasping, trying to breathe. "That's why—that's why no more attempts on my life. That's why it's not so—not so—convenient to hand me over to the Runners. You wouldn't get what you want, now, would you? That's why the attempts on my life have stopped."

Lady Budleigh scoffed. "What, the oil and the runaway

horse? That was Charlie all over. Clumsy and ineffective. Believe me, I have no wish to resort to such crude measures. I merely wanted Charlie to use some gentle persuasion so that we could have what is rightfully ours. I trusted the wrong man, that is all. Though it wouldn't be the first time," she added bitterly. "I have always maintained that if a woman wants something done well, she must do it herself. Be that as it may, I have no wish for you to die. Perhaps someone like you cannot understand it, but all I want is what is rightfully ours. And not just for me or even for my husband. We have a duty, a responsibility to make sure we preserve our estate. You cannot do that on a pittance, and to tell you frankly, we no longer even have a pittance left. We have been spending freely—on the estate—for years, believing that we would come into Mama's money when she died and we could pay off our creditors. The money rightfully belongs to the Budleigh estate. Not to you." Her eyes were hard as flint, but Anya could see she believed what she was saying, every word.

"Not to a bastard," Anya said.

"You cannot shock me, Miss Marleigh." Lady Budleigh's lip curled. "But whoever you are, whatever your background, I have no wish for you to die or even be hurt."

"No. You didn't. Not now that the money would go to Damian Ashton." Anya wondered if Lord Ashton knew this little fact. She remembered now that a letter had arrived from Mr. Prism yesterday and she hadn't opened it, and had then forgotten about it. It probably told her the same as what the lawyer had told Lady Budleigh. That if she died, the money would, after all, be Damian Ashton's, and not Preston Budleigh's. She had to bite the inside of her cheek so she didn't laugh again. But she still couldn't help wondering if Damian Ashton knew how much he had to gain from handing her over to the Runners. Maybe that's why he wasn't here today. Hadn't sent even a note. The thought hurt more than anything Lady Budleigh was saying.

"I have no wish for you to die," Lady Budleigh said again. "I want you to consider marrying."

"Who? Charlie—your unwilling sacrifice—is dead."

"We can find another Budleigh. Someone more to your taste. Or if not, someone—someone—"

"Old, perhaps? Someone about to die?"

"It can be arranged."

Anya stared at the cold, frigid face. She knew Lady Budleigh was obsessed with the Budleigh estate and name. She knew the family was on the brink of ruin. All their possessions could be taken away by creditors at any moment. She knew the woman was cold. But this dispassionate scheming—this was astounding. It was like now that she was desperate and worried about being thwarted all bets were off. Here was the true Lady Budleigh.

"And then what happens? If I marry some old Budleigh cousin?" She was asking, almost in fascination, like Lady Budleigh was a strange and unusual insect.

"Then you get a handsome settlement for your pains. And you sign the money to us. It's simple. You're fair, Anya. You must see that this is the right way. The money isn't yours."

"And if I don't do it?"

"Then we can't get the money in any case. And I will feel no reluctance in handing you over to the Runners. I have your note. I have the flower from your tiara, a tiara everyone saw on your head last night. Everyone knows this rose was a special gift from the Queen."

Anya clutched her hands tight. Lady Budleigh was right. She was in a very dangerous spot. If Lady Budleigh couldn't get her hands on the money one way or another, she would hand Anya over to the Runners out of spite.

And in one way, what did she have to lose in marrying some old Budleigh? She would have a settlement, the Budleighs would get what they wanted, she and Trixie could make a life. Would it be so bad? She couldn't bring herself to marry Darren Greenwood, it seemed, no matter how much she knew she should. A Budleigh on his deathbed could be a good solution. A marriage that was loveless from both sides, in which there was no pretense. People did it all the time. She came to her feet.

Lady Budleigh stood up too. "Think about it, Anya. Don't be an idealistic fool. I know you are resourceful. If you weren't, how would you have made a life for yourself so successfully, given your background? I will give you a few days. Please let me know your decision. If I don't have your decision soon, I will take *that* as a decision."

Anya walked back to her room, numb from tiredness and worry. There was no news from Damian Ashton. She had no idea if Jeremy had lived or died. No one had thought to tell her even that. She felt resentment against Damian Ashton shoot through her, for forgetting all about her. Not telling her what happened to Jeremy. Not wondering what was happening to her in the palace. Maybe letting her hang for Charlie's death would be the neatest solution for him too.

The next morning, a note finally arrived from Damian Ashton. It was the briefest note possible, Anya saw with chagrin. After another sleepless night, she had woken up cross, anxious, exhausted, and nearly ready to give herself up to the first Runner that crossed her path.

The note from Damian Ashton simply said, *This is my temporary address in London. We are fine and I hope you are too.* These brief lines were followed by the address of rented lodgings in Mayfair.

"'We are fine!'" she screeched. "'We are *fine!*'"

Trixie, who'd brought her the note, said soothingly, "He can't say more, can he? Not in a note that anyone could read. He can't say anything about his brother's injury."

Anya was furious. She had tossed and turned all night, imagining that Jeremy was dead and that that was why she hadn't seen Damian Ashton or had a note from him. She had been worried sick. "I have no idea why he has given me his address. It's not like he's inviting me to go there to speak to him. And he hasn't bothered to come here to speak to me."

She read the note again. Did the man care at all about the agonizing minutes they'd shared when they were binding Jeremy's shoulder? And what of the rose garden? She flushed, avoiding Trixie's eyes. Of course he didn't care about that. Well, that was just fine. She was a woman of the world. A court singer. She wouldn't care either. It was clear it had been nothing to him. It needn't be anything to her either.

She was pacing her room again. Trixie took up some darning and settled herself down in a large chair. "It's simple," Anya said, coming to a halt. "If I can get the note and the flower from my tiara back from Lady Budleigh, then she has no evidence I was in the conservatory when Charlie died. That's the only answer. Without those two things, she has nothing. She has no evidence."

It was blindingly simple. She could pretend to Lady Budleigh that she had chosen to accept her terms, and get her note and flower back that way. Though she had a feeling Lady Budleigh wouldn't give those things up—there was no way—before Anya was well and truly married to some decrepit old Budleigh.

Now that Jeremy Ashton was all right—or so his brother's stupid note implied—she needed to get on with her own plans. There was no time to be lost. She no longer needed to worry about either Ashton brother. They were happy looking after their own. She would look after herself. Like she always did.

"And then what? Marry Mr. Greenwood?" Trixie asked, breaking into her thoughts.

"I will have to. I'll be damned if I go to the trouble of getting out of Lady Budleigh's trap, and then meekly hand over the dowager's money to *Lord* Ashton. But I will worry about that later. First I must pay a call on Jeremy Ashton."

Trixie looked at her from under her fair eyelashes. "And why must you do that?"

"*I'm* not uncivil. Whatever Lord Ashton is like. Jeremy was nearly killed. I have to pay him a call. He's my—friend."

"Didn't you just meet him?"

Anya nearly screamed. "So what? He nearly died!"

"That's very thoughtful."

Anya quickly looked to see if Trixie was being ironic. Her protégé was looking blandly at her. Anya narrowed her eyes but didn't pursue it. There was a streak in Trixie, an uppity know-it-all streak. Not at all becoming. She must speak to her about it when they had more time. For the moment, it was merely enough to lift her chin and be dignified. And ignore Trixie's little smile as she bit off her thread.

She dressed in a frothy morning dress the color of the sea, studded with rhinestones at the hem, and a pelisse, warm but that fitted her to perfection. Her ringlets—they were a little hopeless after the night she had had, but Trixie helped her get some bounce in them, twirling them again and again in her long fingers and wondering out loud if it *really* mattered what she looked like if she was visiting a man who was injured. Anya forbore comment.

It was not far and it was a dry morning, and so she walked

to Damian Ashton's lodgings in Mayfair. It was an elegant town house, but not ostentatious. Small, really, given Lord Ashton's wealth and the kinds of houses people of the *ton* normally rented when they were in town. But Damian Ashton wasn't known to be an active member of the *ton*. Maybe he didn't care what anyone else thought of him or his lodgings.

She pursed her mouth. It sounded exactly like him.

Someone who didn't look like a butler opened the front door. The man looked more like a valet, and not that much of a valet either. He was probably about Damian Ashton's age, but tall, skinny, and hard-looking. He had a vicious scar that ran all the way down his face from left eyebrow to jaw. The eyes were hard as flint. And though his hair was light, his eyes were even lighter and seemed like they could look out but you couldn't look into them, no matter how hard you tried. He was thin, even skeletal, though not unhealthy-looking for all that. He introduced himself as Linus Temperance. "I'm Lord Ashton's man, ma'am. His lordship might not be available."

He didn't look like he was going to let her in. But she insisted that he at least tell Lord Ashton that she was at the door. He reluctantly showed her into a drawing room and repeated that it was unlikely that his lordship would be available.

She stood there, feeling like she was going to jump out of her skin. She was at the same time overexhausted yet agitated. Was he simply going to deny her? His man seemed to think so. The thought stuck in her chest. She tried to remind herself she was here to see Jeremy. Would Lord Ashton have asked his man to deny her, her specifically? She heard brisk footsteps outside the room, and to her annoyance, her heart sped up. She'd been standing as she waited for him. At the sound of his footsteps, she quickly sat down, picked up a periodical, and started looking through it like it was the most interesting thing she'd ever seen.

Lord Ashton stopped at the threshold.

She casually lifted her face. There was something in his face, something she couldn't name. Maybe it was just annoyance at seeing her. Her heart was beating painfully. She remembered the cold note he had written. Why was she here? The note had made it clear he didn't want her. How stupid of her to have come. But it was too late for that now.

"Lord Ashton, forgive me," she said coolly. "I hope I'm not disturbing you. I only wanted to pay a call on Jeremy. To see how he is doing. I told your man that that's who I wanted to see. I really have no idea why he disturbed *you.*"

15

Damian couldn't understand how someone could look so beautiful and at the same time be so infernally aggravating. It was a mystery. He had sent her the note to tell her his address in London. He'd written and rewritten the note several times, getting more and more annoyed with himself. The first note he wrote followed his address with the words *Do you think you could visit me?* He changed that to *visit us*, then *visit Jeremy*, then back to *visit us*, and then he added *at your convenience*. All of those notes had ended in the hearth.

He tried variations on the theme. But in the end couldn't figure out *why* he was asking her to visit. There was no good reason. It wasn't like he had any reason to ask her. She might not even want to see him.

He couldn't bear leaving her at the palace. Felt like he had betrayed her somehow. She looked small when he left. And defenseless. He had pressed her hand at the time, tried to convey—he didn't know what he had wanted to convey. If there were words to say whatever it was, he didn't know what they were. Did she think he was betraying her when he left her there? Shouldn't he have asked her to come with them instead of pressing her to stay at the palace? She and Trixie. Both of them worked tirelessly to save Jeremy's life. The doctor said that without that timely intervention Jeremy would have bled to death. Without a doubt.

He finally, in exasperation, wrote down his address, and left it at that. Now, here she was, in a velvet pelisse and one of her effervescent dresses—a blue-green indescribable color today. He realized when he saw her face that he hadn't for one moment stopped thinking about it since he last saw it. It was like she was living inside his brain now. Had taken residence and was refusing to leave. Stubborn. How very like her. She, on the other hand, looked completely nonchalant. Some might even say indifferent.

"Do you usually read periodicals about investments, Miss Marleigh?"

She didn't glance down at what she was holding. "I love them. They are so entertaining. A guilty pleasure."

"Especially when read upside down."

She calmly placed the periodical on the coffee table. Not ruffled at all.

"I wanted to come to see you at the palace. But I wasn't sure it was a good idea." The words came out all abrupt. Why did he say that? First all the needy notes he'd tried to write, and now this. She looked utterly unmoved by him. Damn it. Why did he care about that? He never had before, not with anyone. She was used to men falling all over her. He was acting like he was one of them.

"I can't imagine why you would do that." She looked innocently at him. "Why would you? Can I see Jeremy? And then I will leave you in peace. I'm sorry for showing up like this, unannounced. I know you didn't mean me to. Or you would have invited me." She sat elegantly straight-backed, calm as a daisy, one hand placed over the other, on her lap.

So that was the problem. He hadn't invited her. (Was that the problem? He was so confused. Something was definitely the problem.) "I didn't want you to feel like you had to—" He stopped abruptly. With no idea what to say. Or how to finish the sentence.

Next second, Jeremy walked into the room. She instantly transformed. She quickly stood up, took a few steps forward, and stretched her arms out to Jeremy. She lit up—a complete transformation from her coolness one second before. Jeremy's peaceful face—deathly pale and drawn as it was—lit up too and he walked forward and took her hands in his, and then bent to place a kiss on each cheek. She was flushed with pleasure.

Wasn't that fine and dandy. How happy they were to see each other. A picture of happiness. "I suppose your arm and shoulder aren't troubling you now?" Damian couldn't help saying to his brother. "They only hurt you when you need to do something—pass me a rack of toast or cut your meat or pull your boots on?"

Jeremy grinned. The pair of them were still looking at each other and in fact, both were grinning. Damian wasn't sure he'd ever seen Miss Marleigh grin before. Teeth and everything. Her entire face transformed. She lost that inward look.

A blighting image passed in front of Damian's eyes. Miss Marleigh in a wedding dress, made of the finest pale blue lace that brought out her eyes, and a long veil. And her groom, dressed in regimentals and looking very handsome, the handsomest man in the room. Captain Jeremy Ashton, who had decided to go back to the cavalry after all, since his new bride had brought the spring back in his step.

Damian glared at the pair of them. Though since neither was paying him any attention, the look was wasted. His stomach was churning at the vision. Anyone could see the pair wasn't suited. They were children. Neither one would know how to look after themselves, let alone the other. They'd be riding horses and singing all the time. How would that work? The answer was plain for everyone to see. It *wouldn't* work!

"Are you okay, Jeremy? I've been worried sick. Couldn't you at least have sent me a note? I imagined you dead about a hundred times. Do you know I haven't slept in two nights?"

Jeremy! Not only was she addressing him by his first name, she also didn't mind showing him that she was hurt at his— Jeremy's!—lack of note. That she had been worried sick about him. Private as she was about her feelings, she didn't mind letting Jeremy see them. Wasn't that nice! Did she realize that it wasn't Jeremy who'd sent her that note telling her his address?

"I desperately wanted to. I asked about you again and again. But we weren't sure if it was safe to. We thought it might compromise your situation in the palace, Anya. You saved my life. I owe you forever."

Did Jeremy have to look quite so tall and congenial? The man had too much charm for his own good. Had Damian noticed how puppy-dog his brother's eyes were? And now he was taking Miss Marleigh's hand and kissing it. Not kissing it like men perfunctorily kissed a woman's hand, but really kissing it and holding on to it. And looking at her with his soul in his eyes. Like he was handing the damn thing to her for her asking. Dear god. He could hear wedding bells.

She blushed prettily. "You owe me nothing, Jeremy. I owe *you*—everything."

A look passed between them.

And Damian couldn't help remembering what Charlie Budleigh had tried to do to Anya Marleigh, what Jeremy's intervention had helped prevent. If the man weren't already dead, Damian would have taken matters in his own hands. All he felt when he thought of the dead man was murderous rage.

And Jeremy and Miss Marleigh weren't smiling at each other now. They were looking seriously into each other's eyes. Something churned darkly in Damian's belly. No, of course, it was not hatred toward his own brother. It was simply that he didn't think he could stomach Miss Marleigh as his sister-in-law. That was all.

"I'd kill him now if he weren't already dead."

Now Jeremy was stealing Damian's thoughts! He thought he would be sick if he had to look at the pair of them for much longer. Or shoot himself. "Are you both quite done?" he said, sounding a lot more irritable than he intended.

"Of course, Lord Ashton," Miss Marleigh said calmly. "If *you're* asking us to be done, we *must* be so."

Jeremy—damn his eyes—grinned cheekily at his brother. "I love this woman."

Damian gritted his teeth. But luckily for all, Linus entered once more and said, "Mr. Kenneth Laudsley, sir. I'll bring him in, shall I?"

He was about to ask who the devil Kenneth Laudsley was and what was wrong with Linus that he couldn't just send the man about his way. It was clear the man wasn't wanted. Hadn't he given explicit orders to refuse admittance to random people who showed up at the door?

Except Jeremy's grin disappeared. He nodded jerkily at Linus and thanked him. His face was drawn and he darted a look in Damian's direction. Damian wondered what that was all about.

Was the man at the door a friend of Jeremy's? The pair—Jeremy and Miss Marleigh—were now exchanging speaking looks that Damian couldn't interpret at all. What was the matter with this Kenneth Laudsley? Was he a criminal? A baboon? A criminal baboon? Would anyone explain to him what was going on? And anyway, how did Miss Marleigh know about this Kenneth man?

And then, before anyone could say or do anything more, a vision entered the parlor.

There was no other way to describe it. Damian stared. It was a man, that much was clear. In beautiful silk satin trousers and a coat that was the color of champagne. A waistcoat of a deep chocolate silk. Boots that some men would kill for. He would look like a dandy, except it was also easy to see his powerful arms and thighs.

But the expression on his face wasn't one of a dandy either. His face was pulled tight, and Damian was startled to see a glint of what looked like unshed tears in the man's eyes. Every cell in his body was on edge. The man was looking—urgently—at Jeremy.

The vision—the man—came striding into the room and stopped next to Jeremy. It looked almost like the man would have embraced Jeremy—the tension of holding himself in was there in his body; it was palpable.

"If you die on me, Jem, I'll kill you," he said, his voice strangled.

And Jeremy. Jeremy had been watching Laudsley like he wasn't sure what the man was going to do or say. Like he didn't know how Laudsley felt. But now, at the man's strangled words, Jeremy's eyes lit up—like they were lit from within. All the more powerful for being understated. Jeremy held out a shaking hand. He looked—all of a sudden—even more vulnerable than before. The men were clutching each other's hands so hard, it was likely Jeremy would have another hand out of commission soon. They were staring into each other's eyes. Neither saying anything now.

"I'm so sorry," the vision—Kenneth Laudsley, that was the name—was saying. "I'm so sorry, Jem. I wasn't in London. I couldn't be here a minute earlier. I rode straight from Hailsham when I got your note. Will you forgive me?"

They were still gripping hands.

"You're here now," Jeremy—*Jem!*—said. His voice could hardly be strung tighter.

There it was, then. Miss Marleigh didn't look in the least surprised. She looked happy, relieved even. And things that had been irking Damian fell into place. Here was the explanation for why Jeremy had had to leave his regiment. Here was the reason. And here was the reason Miss Marleigh had insisted that no shadow of blame could stick to Jeremy over Charlie Budleigh's death.

There you go. Damian Ashton. Always the last to know. He'd have some things to say to his brother about this. But more annoying was the way they were sneaking glances at him now. Not only was Jeremy looking at him like a puppy dog, like he was worried how Damian would react. But even Miss Marleigh was looking at him from under her eyelashes. Apparently, *she* wanted to know how he would react too.

He looked at his brother. Found to his annoyance that Jeremy had little pink spots on his cheeks and was still looking at Damian. "This is Kenneth, brother."

"So I see," Damian said.

They were all still watching him.

Laudsley held out his hand. They were now watching him even more intently. What the devil did they think he was going to do? Refuse to shake the man's hand? Challenge him to a duel on Hampstead Heath at dawn for taking his brother's—his brother's—good god.

Damian took a step or two forward, held out his hand, and shook Laudsley's. When he let it go, he saw that the man instantly renewed his death grip on Jeremy's hand.

"Try not to break his other arm," Damian said mildly. "Or only if he really deserves it."

He didn't know if he was happy to see the palpable relief on Jeremy's face or enraged. Did his brother have so little faith in him? Did he think that Damian was so craven that he couldn't accept his own brother as he was? For the love of all that was good! Jeremy knew how to make you feel really, really small. Damian glanced at Miss Marleigh. "Would you like a cup of coffee in the study, Miss Marleigh? It is only indifferently furnished, but comfortable enough." And then he realized something else. At least now he didn't have to worry about the sickening eventuality of Miss Marleigh becoming his sister-in-law. He smiled brightly at Kenneth Laudsley. "And I will have coffee sent in for you too," he said graciously. He was sure he would grow to like Kenneth Laudsley.

Anya Marleigh inclined her head, sent a saucy grin at Jeremy, said she was very pleased to see Mr. Laudsley, that it had been too many years. Laudsley instantly told her she was as ravishing as her sister, but had always seemed much less exhausting, which was a big positive in his mind. He also invited her to call him Kenneth. "I pray I shall have the pleasure of getting to know you better, Miss Marleigh. I always wanted to know you better, but what with one thing or another, it never came about. One cannot have too many beautiful people in one's life. It is soothing to the eyes."

"Do call me Anya, Kenneth," she said before following Damian out of the front parlor.

Kenneth! How many times had he asked her to call him Damian? And Anya! Of course, she hadn't invited Damian to call her that ever, not once.

And that look that crossed her face when her sister was mentioned. A look of yearning, *and* she chuckled at the same time. She and Laudsley looked complicit then, like people do when they poke fun at someone they both know and love. Why couldn't she share those looks with Damian? Not that he wanted her to. He was merely curious as to why.

"Nicely done, my lord," Anya said as he escorted her to the study.

As he entered the study, he was suddenly conscious that these rented lodgings *were* indifferently furnished. Strangely it hadn't mattered to him before Anya stepped inside the house. Now all he could see was fading wallpaper and paintings on the wall that were chosen by someone who didn't care. The books were all perfectly symmetrical, like they'd never been touched. They were probably in terrible taste. He hoped she wouldn't think he'd bought them. He was casting a quick eye around the room. Why did everything look faded and indifferent?

She didn't sit down, but instead stood by a side cabinet and touched this or that ornament. The woman wasn't in the least restful. She had him in a rage half the time, and as for the other half . . . "You know Kenneth Laudsley?"

"He is my sister Lila Tristram's friend. I don't know him very well. It's many years since I last saw him."

He fought with himself but then couldn't help it. "I suppose *you* knew?" he said in irritation. "Didn't you meet my brother the day before yesterday? And spent—what?—twenty minutes with him? And yet you seem to know everything that is the most fundamental about him. Whereas I've only known him all his life." He knew he sounded querulous and annoyed, like a child.

She didn't say anything for a few moments. She was touching a cast-iron paperweight with thoughtful fingers. "People don't give you parts of their soul if you keep yours safely tucked away, Lord Ashton. Now if you will excuse me, I won't keep you—"

"Sit," he said abruptly.

She gave him one of her cool looks.

He jerked his head. "That was rude. Would you sit for a few moments? I think we should talk about what happened."

"Surely, if you thought we should talk, you would have come to the palace or asked me to come here?" She wasn't moving a muscle to sit down.

He made an impatient noise. How could he explain to her? He didn't visit her at first because it was touch-and-go with Jeremy. His brother nearly died. The doctor looked grim, he worked quietly and urgently to get the bullet out, he warned Damian afterward that it could still go one way or the other. That Jeremy wouldn't recover his full strength for a while. That he could get an infection in the wound.

By the time the doctor finished tending to Jeremy, it was midmorning and he meant to go to the palace then, but then wondered if she normally received any visitors like him and if it would seem suspicious so soon after Charlie Budleigh's death if he went up to the palace and asked to see her. He meant to ask her to come to his lodgings and then convinced himself he couldn't ask a woman to do that. Not even someone as un-usual as Anya Marleigh. Not even in these strange and pressing circumstances. And anyway, he never did that. He never asked people for things they might not want to give.

Instead of trying to explain any of this to her, he said, "My apologies. But we should talk about what happened now that you are here, don't you think?"

Annoyance flashed across her face. But she graciously gave him the tiniest nod possible and sat down at the edge of a chair, hands crossed composedly on her lap, her posture perfect. He sat down too.

"Lady Budleigh has incriminating evidence against me," were her first surprising words.

He wasn't expecting her to say that. He asked her to elaborate and she did. He sat back at the end of the story and let out a breath. He'd had no idea it was this bad. He had worried that because of her connection with the Budleighs, suspicion could fall on her. He asked her to remain in the palace that night so it didn't look like she might have run away from the scene of the crime. But he'd had no idea that Clara Budleigh could have evidence. A note naming the conservatory and a time, in Miss Marleigh's handwriting. And the bronze rose from her tiara. A rose that even he, who wasn't exactly au fait with female clothing or accessories, would recognize distinctly as hers, a present from the Queen. Those were hugely damning. "We must get those things back from her."

She widened her eyes. "There is no 'we,' Lord Ashton, though how very kind of you. I can do it myself. I was merely filling you in since you wished to talk about it."

"I will help you. If we can't get them back, then *I* will take the blame for what happened. I can say it was an accident. And I'm a peer. However much I hate the laws of this land, they might win me clemency."

She looked shocked. That was good to see. At least her cool composure could be shaken. Oh, he'd like to shake her composure some more.

"Why would you do that?" she asked. For the first time, she wasn't looking quite as cool. He had surprised her. There was that thing lurking at the back of her eyes, that he sometimes saw there, that he didn't think she was aware of. A need to be seen. A need to be wanted, to be important to someone. A sort of yearning for something she didn't think she could rightfully have. It made a pang ring through him, which surprised him.

"Jeremy can't take the blame. So I will, in his place," he said.

It was apparently the wrong thing to say.

The veil dropped over her eyes again. "Oh yes, of course. I see. For Jeremy. Considerate of you. But if anyone must take the blame, it's me. I will make sure everyone knows you weren't there. So there is nothing more to say." She came to standing.

"Please," he said, his voice curt. Could the woman not sit down for one minute? He knew puppies that were more restful. She reluctantly sat down again. "I'm hoping it won't come to that. Like you say, all we need to do is get your note and the rose from Clara. All we need to do," he said firmly, "is figure out how to do that. Can you give me a little bit of time to think about it?"

She looked like she was going to say no. She was struggling with herself. He was sure she was going to object again, especially to the "we." She could probably come up with a long list of objections. To his plans, but mostly to him. But then she finally and reluctantly nodded.

He was walking out of the study with her when Linus came up to them and asked if Damian could speak to the housekeeper for a moment. Damian excused himself, conferred with the housekeeper, Mrs. Garner, on various household matters that apparently couldn't wait—the leaking roof, no fresh eggs, the London fog. He looked at her, slightly bemused, and asked if her list of complaints could wait. She looked affronted at the question.

When he came back to the parlor, Miss Marleigh was still there, and she and the two men were laughing like they had grown up together playing hide-and-seek and frolicking in the English countryside alongside the damned sheep. He sighed.

But the two men sobered up when Jeremy asked her how things were in the palace after Charlie Budleigh's death and Miss Marleigh filled them in on Clara Budleigh's ultimatum. Jeremy, who was pale and weak now that the momentary excitement of visitors had passed, looked grim. He was sitting in one of the slouchy chairs, sinking into it like he never meant to get up from it.

"We have to get those things back from Clara," Jeremy said at once. He looked at Damian. Damian, leaning back against a side cabinet, arms crossed over his chest, nodded shortly.

"You know, you should marry as soon as you can. Put the woman's nose out of joint." This from Kenneth Laudsley. "She sounds like the kind of woman that would put one in a coma just with a look."

"We need to make sure Clara can't saddle you with murder," Damian mildly intervened. "Before we think of marriage."

She looked at him through hooded eyes. "Oh, but I *must* think of it. There's no time to be lost, my lord."

He looked at her in resignation. "I'm glad to hear you so reconciled. Have you found someone suitable?"

"I was thinking Darren Greenwood," she murmured, still looking at him from under those long and curly eyelashes of hers.

"A prosy bore."

"There's always Lord Pennyworth."

"Simpering fool."

"There was a young man hovering around Serena, the violinist, the other night," Miss Marleigh said. "If she is not interested in him, you never know, he might divert his attentions to me."

"A red-faced child."

Suddenly, Jeremy straightened. Damian still look bored. Really, could she not come up with one suitable man? Disappointing. He didn't want the Budleigh money. She should get a move on if she was going to achieve a marriage before her twenty-fifth. At this rate . . .

"You should marry me."

Something froze in Damian's heart. At Jeremy's words. Had he just heard his brother say those words?

Miss Marleigh laughed. "A noble sacrifice, Jeremy."

Jeremy blushed. "It's just that you know. You *know*, Anya. It's not like I will ever marry."

Jeremy and Laudsley exchanged quick glances, but neither said anything to the other. That was the thing. Damian had a feeling the relationship between the men was relatively new and not on a sure footing yet. Whatever a sure footing would be for them. Jeremy was right. Whatever it was, it wouldn't be marriage.

"We are already such good friends," Jeremy was saying now. "You would have wealth and independence from my great-aunt's inheritance. We would be the best of friends. What do you all think?" Jeremy said, looking at each of them in turn.

Laudsley spoke. "It would give Anya what she needs— independence. Which is not something to sneer at. And the strange thing is, it would give you respectability, Jem. It wouldn't be a real marriage, but it would have a lot going for it. Marriages are built on less than friendship and mutual liking. One shudders to think what they *are* built on most of the time."

Jeremy nodded. "That's right. Exactly."

Damian frowned deeply. He was fast revising his opinion of Laudsley, who he had thought was a sensible man. Clearly, his head was full of fluff. Jeremy was now looking at Miss Marleigh.

Miss Marleigh laughed again. "We *are* friends. I do like you so much." She sounded playful, but she wasn't saying an outright no.

Jeremy was looking at Damian now. "Don't you think it would work all around? It would solve a lot of problems. After we get the note and the rose back, it could be a neat solution to Anya's problems. My problems too."

"It is the worst idea I've ever heard," Damian said.

They were all talking at him now. No, wait. Miss Marleigh wasn't. Jeremy was. He was pointing out all the advantages of his brilliant idea. Laudsley had such a meandering way of talking that it wasn't clear if he was arguing for or against. But, on the whole, probably for. But Miss Marleigh wasn't talking to him. She was looking at him. In that way of hers that looked like she could read his mind. He stared back. His blood was still running cold at the thought of Jeremy and Miss Marleigh marrying.

As he was wondering if he had entered a nightmare, the door knocker went off again. A third time.

Who was it this time? Did everyone have the idea of visiting Damian today? Could they not get a break from visitors? It was like it wasn't his own house anymore. What was the point of having a staff if they couldn't protect him from invasion?

They didn't have to wait long. Before Linus could announce

whoever it was, a woman magically appeared in the parlor. There was such a vitality in her face and such energy in her body that you didn't see that she was quite small.

Anya Marleigh was on her feet and staring at the woman. The woman was staring back. The depth of conflicting emotions running through both faces was hard to see. Like watching something painful and deeply intimate and old as the sea. That no one was supposed to witness.

The two women—one willowy, her blue-black curls tight ringlets that skimmed her shoulders, those black eyes deep as ocean water; the other shorter, vivacious, and athletic, all fire to Anya's water—stared at each other.

"Lila." Anya's voice cracked open on the name.

16

Anya was only six when she moved from Delhi to London. Her sister Lila was a year older and Mira a year younger. The sisters were close when they lived in Delhi. They stuck together to sneak samosas and jalebi from the sizzling wok when their parents held parties in their diya-lit garden for the East India Company nabobs and the Indian nobility. They'd learned to ride early and astride, in their jodhpurs, because their mother was adamant that they be treated equal to men. They played cricket together in the street, dived in scummy ponds, and tried on jewels in the mirror when no one was looking.

Then all of that changed.

It changed when their mother disappeared for months and their father nearly lost his mind. A few months later, she came back, and soon after, she nearly died giving birth to triplets, who were no bigger, it seemed, than gutter mice.

Their father hated the scrawny little things on sight, and so did the three older sisters. The little mice, as they privately called them, had nearly killed their mother. And there was something else about them, something hard to put their finger on, but something that hung like a dark thread between their father and mother, something that was never spoken about. Whatever it was, it ruptured the family, broke it into fragments.

And then, when the triplets were toddlers, and there was a chance the family might heal given time, their parents died, drowned in a river in the storm. It appeared that the rupture caused by the little mice wasn't the worst thing to happen to the Marleigh family, after all.

As the older girls and the triplet toddlers were still frozen with shock and fear in this new life without their parents, it turned out that not only had their father had another wife in London, but the girls also had a half brother.

Sarah Marleigh did not do anything as far gone as taking a voyage all the way from London to India. That was not her way and wouldn't have suited her at all. Instead, she sent an emissary to collect her husband's belongings. And to bring back three of the children. She asked for her husband's sons to be sent to London and the daughters to be left behind.

But Sarah Marleigh did not have that choice. All six of the offspring were girls; there were no boys. So Sarah Marleigh asked Mr. Pinkwhistle—a misnamed man, who didn't have a whimsical cell in his spare, tight, pious little body, a prosy man who told the girls that even god could not cleanse the scourge of such a birth as theirs—to send the lighter-skinned girls to London and leave the darker-skinned ones in India. Mr. Pinkwhistle picked the three oldest girls.

But Sarah Marleigh didn't stop there. There was another trick up her sleeve. Mr. Pinkwhistle, carrying out her instructions, gave each of the older girls a choice. She could go to London and be part of a family, her father's *real* family, or instead, she could choose to give up her place to one of her darker-skinned younger sisters.

Each older sister chose to go to London. Each one chose to go and to leave behind the toddlers.

And they carried with them the guilt of what they had done. Across the ocean and across the many endless weeks of traveling. Through the introduction to their new life and the rapid realization that it was more like a nightmare than the dream of a new family that each had created on their voyage. This guilt grew stronger and more mammoth over the years they spent in the Marleigh household in Grosvenor Square, as Sarah Marleigh preyed on their insecurities and pitted them against one another, and Jonathan Marleigh told on them and got them into endless trouble.

Recently, it had come to light that not long after the girls moved to London, the triplets were also adopted by English families, though by three different families. As a cruel masterstroke, Sarah Marleigh had chosen to separate the triplets, not only from their older sisters, but from one another.

Each of the older daughters was educated in select seminaries. But different ones, so that they couldn't even find the time to bond when they were at school. Oh, Sarah Marleigh had been skilled at keeping the sisters apart. For years before each sister adopted a way of life, made a life for herself, they had already been living apart.

Each sister had chosen a way to earn a living. Each had known that making a life with Sarah and Jonathan was not an option, was unthinkable. That each would have to forge her own way.

Anya's younger sister Mira wrote society gossip columns, though anonymously. They were wildly popular and in demand. Anya read every single one, holding it like a secret in her hands, never letting on, not even to Trixie, that she knew the author. She admired how Mira not only wrote society goings-on, but she had a stance. She defended the poor. She made fun of the rich. She upheld and argued for women's rights. But she was witty, and society loved her. Anya had never written to Mira to congratulate her on her columns, though she saved each one.

Anya's older sister, Lila, had opened a gaming salon. Before she had married some months ago, she had been one of the most successful society hostesses in London, hosting musical evenings, setting up faro and piquet tables and maintaining one of the most sought-after salons in London. Lila had always been the audacious one. The one who chose never to hide who and what she was. The one who would throw her background, her name, her upbringing in your face if you dared sneer at her for it. She was the courageous one.

A few months ago, Lila had asked her sisters to her wedding, and to Anya's eternal shame, neither Anya nor Mira had accepted the invitation. Mira had said no without hesitation. Anya had said a troubled no at the time but had then agonized over the decision for weeks. She had spent the day of the wedding shut up in her room at the palace, windows shuttered, curtains drawn against any infiltration of light.

All she had wanted for years was to reconcile with her sisters, for them to atone for what they had done to their younger sisters, but to atone together, not apart. For them to talk about what Sarah and Jonathan Marleigh had done to them. It was all she had wanted for a long time. But she had never had the courage. Lila seemed too independent and Mira too impenetrable. Anya had believed for a long time that she was the only one who wanted to reconcile, to unite. That her sisters didn't. Yet when Lila had reached out, had invited her to her wedding, what had she done about it? Nothing. Habits of a lifetime had prevented her. Even then, she couldn't believe that Lila really wanted her. Wanted her, Anya, and that she wasn't just doing the right, proper thing by inviting her sisters to her wedding. What was it like to feel wanted? Anya thought now. Truly wanted, deep in your core, in your bones, for who you really were. It was something she thought she would never know.

"What are you doing here?" Anya asked her sister. With a funny crack in her voice.

"My fault," Kenneth said, to Anya's intense surprise. He was grimacing.

"*Your* fault?"

"I hope I haven't blighted this friendship before it has begun." Now that his anxiety for Jeremy was allayed, he was lounging limblessly on a recliner. "I had the idea in a flash. When you and Lord Ashton were in the study, I'm afraid I sent her a note. You see, Lila doesn't live that far away." He was looking apologetic. "I couldn't *not* tell her."

"I would have murdered you if you hadn't," Lila said.

"You see what I mean?" Kenneth was saying. "One is helpless in the face of so much passion. I have learned to ride with it. There is no point fighting it."

"I'm not here to fight," Lila said.

And as usual, even though there was so much in Lila's face—pain, love, loss—there was still that stubbornness. She was *saying* she wasn't here to fight. What she was really saying was that if there was a fight, it would be Anya's doing, not hers. Anya didn't know if she wanted to laugh or cry. Was a reconciliation even possible?

She had the strange impulse, the unbelievable impulse, to look to Damian Ashton. For comfort. For reassurance. For understanding.

How stupid.

That was definitely the stupidest thought she had had all morning. Almost anyone in the room—in fact, *anyone* in the room—would give her more comfort and reassurance than Damian Ashton. Take your pick. Each of the others could give her more. Jeremy's friendship would count for more. Kenneth would have some cryptic but not unkind things to say. And even Lila could be ferociously protective if she wanted to be. Yet, her treacherous, *treacherous* body—and she knew exactly what part of her body she must be thinking with—wanted desperately to look at Lord Ashton for comfort. So much so that she was finding it hard *not* to look in his direction.

"I suppose it didn't occur to you that this is my house before you invited people to it." Mild words uttered in a mild voice. It was Damian Ashton. Anya hadn't realized he was so close. Had he moved? He was still standing, leaning against something, in his habitual pose that made it seem he didn't care for anything or anyone. Like he was mildly bored. She almost laughed. Exactly the way he was standing during that fateful reading of Dowager Countess Budleigh's will. It felt like a long time ago. He was standing right behind her. She was sure he hadn't been there just seconds ago. She was wondering what to do or say when Kenneth spoke.

"I had better make myself scarce. I am testing your brother's goodwill," he said to Jeremy. "This invitation to Lila, I fear, has taken him over the edge. And I am convinced that *that* wouldn't do at all. He seems like one of those men whose goodwill should not be tested. Curious, because in some ways he is not at all frightening." He peeled himself off the recliner and, pressing Jeremy's hand and giving him a speaking look, headed out of the room.

"It *is* your house," Lila said, her eyes blazing as she looked at Lord Ashton. "So if you're going to ask me to leave, you may as well do it now."

Anya almost laughed again. Not a conciliating bone in her sister's body. Some things never changed. In fact, the more vulnerable she felt, the more she'd try to chew your head off.

"Anya?" It was Lord Ashton. She finally allowed herself to look at him, just a few inches behind her and to her left, leaning against that cabinet. His calm face. Even the aloofness was strangely calming. The eyes were palm fronds. "What would you like to do?"

She was startled at the question, at the tone. He didn't look mocking or sardonic. Or irritated. And he was saying he would do anything she asked. Whatever she needed. She wanted reassurance, and here it was. He was saying she could do what she pleased, be as reasonable or unreasonable as she chose, and he would back her. She felt somehow—magically—infinitely reassured. Maybe she could deal with this, after all. She looked back at Lila. "Why did you come?"

"Kenneth said in his note that you were in trouble." The voice was still stubborn. Tenderness was not Lila's way. Fierce love, yes. Tenderness, no. "I want to help."

"Why, why do you want to help?"

"You're my sister. Isn't that reason enough? Or can't you bear to tell me about your troubles?" Lila looked at Jeremy and more speakingly at Lord Ashton. "Or do you have so many supporters that you don't need me?"

"I never said I had supporters," Anya said.

"Anya has supporters," Ashton said in that calm voice of his. "She can choose if she needs—or wants—more."

It was strange. It was like she could feel his cool hand on her back. It wasn't there. And she couldn't feel it. But it felt like she could. This, she thought, this must be what it was like to feel protected and loved.

"I still don't completely understand why you're here," she found herself saying to Lila. She reflected that she was, perhaps, not unlike Lila. It was a startling thought. For months, she had been telling herself that if another opportunity came to reconcile with Lila, she would take it. She wouldn't spurn it again, like she had the wedding invitation. But here it was. And could she accept it gracefully if not with open arms? Apparently not.

Lila was looking steadily at her. "I have wanted for years to reconcile. For us to talk. About everything. I invited you to my wedding. You didn't come."

"You invited me—and Mira—because it was the proper thing to do." Now she sounded stubborn. She knew she did.

Lila made an impatient noise that was as familiar as her own breath. "Since when have I ever done anything just because it was proper? You know me better than that, Anya."

Anya hovered on the edge for what felt like an eternity. Why she was dithering she couldn't have explained, even to herself. Why was it easy to love her sisters when they weren't there and yet when one was here, like this, miraculously, all there was was this hard shard wedged in her chest. A sort of paralysis. Made of the weight of years and memory and hollowness and pain.

"I'll tell you what's happened," she finally found herself saying to Lila. "So that you have the facts. It's . . . ." She swallowed. "It's nice of you to come." She turned to Damian Ashton. "I'd like my sister to stay."

He nodded. Said no more. But it was enough.

And strangely Anya felt like she could bear anything if he would just stand there like that, leaning against the damned cabinet, so near her, yet not touching, arms and ankles crossed, and nod like that at whatever she wanted him to do.

17

Once again, Anya laid bare the facts. She told the same story again. In a measured way. Calmly, almost like it was someone else's story.

Lila was pacing the room. Jeremy looked almost green now, and had settled himself down on the recliner recently vacated by Kenneth. Under protest, he had allowed his brother to give him a blanket for his legs. Anya hadn't managed to sit down. She was too agitated. And Damian Ashton was back to leaning against the cabinet, not far from her.

She went over the whole thing. The dowager's will. The terms of it that made Damian Ashton the executor. Clara Budleigh's note that Anya had received at the palace and the appointment in the conservatory. How she hadn't meant to keep the appointment with Lady Budleigh but had done so anyway. She meant to keep it brief, had lighted candles in the orangery to make it warmer and lighter. She faltered at the part where Charlie attacked her. But she kept that part brief too, as brief as she could get away with.

Lila's eyes were blazing, but she didn't say anything. Then came the part where Jeremy was injured and Charlie Budleigh fell backward, hand on his pistol, and died of a head injury, Charlie's bullet lodging itself in Jeremy's shoulder. And the last part, the threat of exposure from Clara Budleigh. The need to get the note and the bronze rose back from her before she handed both over to the Runners.

"I should have confessed right away," Anya was saying. "If I'd done that—"

"Confessed to what?" Lila said sharply. "You didn't do anything."

"No, I know it was in self-defense, but—"

Lila made that characteristic impatient noise again, so familiar, yet heard so long ago, that Anya almost cried. She was looking at Anya in her usual blazing way. "No, you fool. You tried your best not to be raped. *That* was in self-defense. He didn't die because of that. He died because when you managed to get him off you, the idiot fired his gun, lost his balance, fell backward, and hit his head on a metal plant pot. It seems clear to me what happened. *You* need to get it clear in your head. And you need to get it clear now. Or you will act on whatever guilt you think you should feel, when it is clear that you have no reason to feel any. The man had his gun in his hand, Anya. He meant to injure or kill. He did injure Jeremy. And then he fell."

Anya let out a breath. How was it possible that Lila, of all people, understood something that Anya had not even articulated to herself? That she'd wanted to give herself up for causing Charlie Budleigh's death. She knew she didn't murder him. Didn't even push him to hurt him. She only meant to save first herself and then Jeremy. But he died there in the orangery. Because *she* was there. Because she said no to him.

Something lightened in her. She exchanged glances with Jeremy, who also looked relieved. Perhaps he too had been feeling guilty, even though he too had only been trying to save Anya and then himself. Trust Lila—and her lioness nature—to point out in a flash what should have been clear all along.

"I can throttle the rose and the note out of this Clara Budleigh if you like," Lila said.

There was silence for a few seconds, and then Anya gurgled.

And then everyone was laughing. Even Damian Ashton when she managed to turn her head a little and look at him. Even his face was lighter and all lit up and their eyes met for a second. And there was that smile on his face, the one from the goat pen, that she'd been stupid enough to think was just hers. Did he smile like that at anyone else? She quickly looked away.

She was weary all of a sudden, the sleepless nights catching up with her, and she turned and found another place, a couple of feet to the right of Damian Ashton, on the cabinet next to his, and leaned thankfully back against it. She liked his nearness— that must be the tiredness. It was cooling, like being suspended in delicious water when you were boiling inside. There was calm there, a place she didn't have to hide or pretend.

It was clear she was losing her mind. She risked a glance in his direction. She was startled to see that he was looking at her. "We could talk about this another time. Maybe you should get some sleep."

Now she was even more startled. The voice was still aloof, but that he should say something like that was a shock to the system. "Are you feeling feverish?" she found herself blurting out.

Jeremy laughed. Nothing changed on Lord Ashton's face, but a smile lurked in his eyes.

"I *am* tired. But I want to talk about it now," she said. "I won't get any sleep until we know what we need to do next." *We.* That slipped out. Yet it wasn't their problem. It was only her problem. When had it become *their* problem?

He searched her eyes for a second, then nodded. "Then let's get it over with. So we know what we're doing."

"So we find a way to get your note and rose back," Lila said. "And then you find someone to marry so you can claim your inheritance and thwart this Clara Budleigh, who sounds like exactly the kind of woman designed to put you in a rage." Lila was watching her face.

"Oh, Anya has already found someone to marry," Jeremy said.

"Has she now?" Lila murmured, still watching Anya's face.

"She and I will get married," Jeremy declared. He was pale and his voice was weak, but the declaration was sweet for all that.

Lila's eyebrows rose a little as she stared fixedly at Anya. Her eyes then—seemingly involuntarily—flickered toward Damian Ashton, and then back to Anya's face. Her face was expressionless. She looked from Anya to Jeremy now, and then back to Anya again. "Oh, I see. Of course. That should have been plain. Why ever didn't I notice your—uh—feelings for each other?" she said politely.

Here was another problem with Lila. Vivacious and energetic as she was, it would be a mistake to imagine that she wasn't acutely sensitive, sharp as a tack.

"Of course we're not in love," Anya said impatiently. "*You* know about Jeremy and Kenneth. Jeremy is helping me out."

"Yes, of course." Lila smoothed her skirt. "*That* is the most obvious way out of your predicament. No other solution jumps to mind." She suddenly looked sweetly at Lord Ashton. "What do you think about this solution to the problem, my lord?"

Cat. My god. Lila. Anya could murder her. Or laugh. She wasn't sure which. The woman was a witch.

"It's nothing to do with me," Lord Ashton said.

Lila nodded slowly. "I can see that you don't have any feelings on the matter. None whatsoever. It would be obvious to anyone in a flash. Let us plan, then," she said, her brisk voice back. "Where do we think Clara Budleigh might keep such important things like Anya's note and this rose? Is she the kind to trust people—her family, her staff, anyone else?"

Damian Ashton scoffed. "Not for a second. She wouldn't trust a single soul."

"No, she wouldn't," Anya said thoughtfully, giving her full attention to the matter now, but planning to throttle her sister at a later and more convenient time. "She wouldn't trust anyone. I don't even think Lord Budleigh—her husband—would know where she kept anything important, do you?" She turned to Lord Ashton.

"I agree with you. Preston is more of a—lackey, really, one can't help feeling. Something as important as the note and the rose—which she thinks are tickets to get exactly what she wants—I think she would keep them close to her chest. Reveal them to no one. She would think that Preston could give the whole game away. And she isn't wrong. He can be a blundering fool. Not exactly the brains in that partnership."

"Let me find out for you if she has been to a bank yesterday or today," Lila said.

Anya looked at her. "Can you do that?"

"Of course. It's simple. Ivor—my husband—has an extraordinary valet. His name is Hector. He is a force of nature. He really should be employed by the foreign service. If Clara Budleigh or anyone from her house—family or staff—has been to a bank, or any such place, Hector will find out. That way we'll know if she has the items in her keeping or not."

"She could be keeping them locked in an armoire or a drawer or something," Jeremy said.

Anya suddenly shook her head. "No. I mean, yes, she could. But I would bet anything she has them in her—"

"Reticule," Lord Ashton said.

Anya nodded. "That's what I think. I don't think she'd want them out of her sight. She wouldn't risk it. Think of it. They are the ticket—her *only* ticket at the moment—to get her hands on what she thinks is rightfully hers, or at least the Budleigh family's, and she doesn't mind what means she employs. She can't risk losing the note and the rose."

"I wonder if we can make sure of it." Lord Ashton seemed to be thinking.

Anya turned to look at him.

"Do you remember the Budleigh housemaid who was dismissed for spilling the oil?" he said to Anya.

"Jane Simmonds," Anya said. "Though Lady Budleigh as good as admitted to me yesterday when she came to the palace that the oil and the horse were Charlie's ideas."

"She still dismissed Jane."

"Yes," Anya said. "I know. I didn't want her to."

"I hired her after she was let go."

Anya's brows rose. "You did what?"

"I hired her. First, I questioned her because I wanted to know about the oil. I thought maybe one of the family might have asked her to spill it. But I was wrong. She had nothing to do with the oil at all. She was sure she couldn't even have done it by accident. She hadn't done any lamps yet. I believed her. She is very reliable. I hired her because she was wrongfully dismissed, but I also had a sort of instinct that she might come in useful."

Anya was half certain her brain was addled. "You questioned her about the oil spill?" she said stupidly. She'd barely heard the rest of it. Wasn't he aloof? Didn't he always make sure you knew he didn't care for anyone? At least no one but Jeremy? Yet he'd tried to find out how Anya got hurt, and who wanted to hurt her. "You know *you* get the money if I die," she said.

Lord Ashton looked steadily at her. "Thanks for letting me know. I'll keep that in mind next time I find my hands—inadvertently—around your throat."

Anya was staring at him like she'd never seen him before. She must be really, *really* tired. Anyway, he wasn't looking at her. He was looking at Lila and Jeremy again. "Jane knows the staff in the Budleigh house. I could ask her to post up to London and speak to the Budleighs' London staff. Or even be allowed in to search Clara Budleigh's room. That way we're sure we're right and the rose and note are not in the house."

"Would she do that just because you asked her?" Anya couldn't help asking.

"She might, I suppose," Lord Ashton replied. "Because I helped her. But mostly she'd do it for you."

"Why on earth?"

"She told me you stuck up for her. Asked Clara not to dismiss her."

"Anyone would do that!" Anya said.

"Hardly anyone would," Lord Ashton replied.

She stared at him again. He looked calmly back. That calm look was making her knees weak.

"If the things are in Clara's reticule . . ." Jeremy started. "The only way we can get at Clara's reticule is to have someone steal it off her."

"Stage a robbery," Lord Ashton said.

"Yes," Anya said eagerly. "There's no other way she would put it down in a public place."

"They're in mourning. How would we even get Clara somewhere we can corner her?" Jeremy asked.

"Let me work it out," Lila said. "I can get her invited to something. Something sedate."

The plan evolved from there. It seemed to take hours. Finally, they had the bare bones of it. Long before they were done, Jeremy fell asleep where he lay, on the recliner. Lila—without any tender words or a hug, nothing remotely sisterly—gave Anya a fierce look, told her she was welcome in Berkeley Square at any time, and left.

Anya stood in the foyer after seeing her sister to the door. Lord Ashton was there too. She wanted to say goodbye and then leave. Perhaps go straight back to the palace, collapse on her bed, and sleep like the dead. That's what she wanted. Yet she didn't. She turned to him. And walked into his arms.

He was surprised at first, and his breath left him. But she wrapped herself around him. She moved closer until her lips were a whisper away from his. She didn't kiss him but looked up at him questioningly. He swore, then bent his head and fitted his mouth to hers.

He kissed her like his life depended on it. Maybe he always kissed her like that. Or maybe it was her life that depended on it. Maybe it always felt like that to her. An agony of a kiss. But there was something different about this one. It wasn't sensual. It wasn't the slaking of a thirst. It wasn't an invitation. She just wanted to tell him what it meant to her, his looking out for her. Noticing her and seeing what she needed and offering it to her in case she wanted it. In his quiet way, without making a big deal of it.

When he finally broke the kiss, his breathing jagged, he buried his face in her neck and was breathing her in. His lips were on her collarbone. They traced the neckline of her dress. He pressed them closed on the swell of her breast. There was a frown on his brow. She lifted his head and looked into his eyes.

"Can't we—can we—" she said.

She stepped closer still, her hands on his chest, her cheek on his, her eyes closed. He was hard and she rubbed herself against his erection. He groaned. He was breathing hard, his body taut. She opened her legs a little. An invitation. She found his mouth again. They clung to each other with a desperation that was an ache.

He finally pulled away. "Soon, Anya. I promise. But you have to get some rest. And I have to make sure we have Jane Simmonds here."

She protested.

He kissed her on the forehead, holding her close for a second. "Will you go home now? We have to set this in motion. We have to be ready as soon as we can. We don't have long. Your sister—my god, she's a tornado, isn't she?—I'm sure will try to arrange things as soon as she can. We have to be ready too. Clara won't let us dally, if I know her at all." He held her close. "Soon," he promised.

18

She did collapse on her bed and sleep like the dead. When she woke up, if anything, she was wearier than ever.

Everything ached, like she had spent the last few days running. Running from what, she wasn't sure. A Runner or two was still around in the palace, making a show of trying to find out what happened to Charlie Budleigh. Rumor had it that the Runners believed that one of Charlie Budleigh's many debtors or loan sharks had caught up with him at last and killed him or at least caused him to fall and die. And Anya was half surprised that no one came for her, that Clara Budleigh didn't hand in the evidence.

She told herself this was the last thing Lady Budleigh wanted. She wouldn't want Anya to be jailed and unable to marry. She wouldn't want Anya to hang either. In either circumstance, the money would revert to Damian Ashton. Lady Budleigh's only hope was that Anya would marry and then give the money to the Budleighs or at least share it with them. And if Anya didn't do that, then Lady Budleigh would hand over her note and her rose to the Runners. She would feel no guilt.

Trixie woke her up in the afternoon, knowing she had an

evening engagement. "I want to die," Anya complained, lying arms and legs open, staring up at the ceiling.

Trixie cajoled her to get up and figure out what she was going to wear in the evening. "Wear something nice," she said, "so you look pretty and someone will ask you to marry them, right there and then."

"Why, why must I marry?" Anya said with a long sigh, reluctantly peeling herself off the bed and staring unseeingly at the contents of her wardrobe. She eyed Trixie, who looked pretty and neat in yellow muslin, one of her many notebooks tucked under her arm. She placed it now on a side table so she could look more thoroughly through Anya's wardrobe, since Anya didn't look like she was giving the matter any attention.

Anya yawned widely, ignored the wardrobe and Trixie's questions about the various dresses she could wear, and picked up Trixie's leatherbound notebook. Trixie had been taking meticulous notes on a book she was reading on Georgian buildings. Anya couldn't help a swell of pride at Trixie's diagrams. She flicked through them. Page after page of neat lines, meticulous notes, and even further questions that the book hadn't answered but that Trixie wanted to read more about.

"Here is a very good example of when the student far outstrips the teacher in their learning." She traced the precise lines and angles with her fingers. If she herself showed any aptitude in engineering, it would be a miracle. But she could see that Trixie understood what she was reading. Goodness! She looked guiltily at her protégé. "I am so selfish, Trixie." She put the notebook down again. Trixie was half looking at her dresses and half giving her attention. "The dowager's wealth would give us independence, Trixie. It would give me a pension for my old age. It would allow me to escape living all alone, here, always waiting on someone's pleasure, after my voice and face are gone and I'm a hag. But you." She looked contritely at Trixie. "Because I am an earl's daughter—even though a bastard daughter—I at least have a smidgen of standing in the palace. Not much. But more than you. If we don't escape the palace, you will have no choice but to become a servant here. And all your wonderful knowledge! What a crying waste it would be, Trixie."

Trixie gave her a prosaic look. "What's brought this on?" She had picked out a silver dress and laid it on the back of a chair. She was looking inquiringly at Anya but also starting to think about accessories. She was picking up jeweled hairpins, a brooch, a thin chain.

"I didn't let Darren Greenwood come to the point the other day. He was about to. I haven't said yes to Jeremy Ashton."

"Jeremy Ashton wants to marry you now?" Trixie said, turning to look at Anya, her eyebrows raised. She blinked at Anya. "And his lordship, does he have anything to say about that?"

The question was so casually uttered Anya wanted to bat her protégé on her head. She was clearly as bad as Lila with her questions. "Of course not. Why would he? Anyway, I was saying that I must not be selfish and must find someone to marry, that is all."

"Or you could find someone to love and that would neatly solve the problem too," Trixie said. "But right now, stop fidgeting and fretting and let me do your hair. You're making a mess of it on your own."

Anya gave herself into Trixie's capable hands, silently chiding herself to stop being so selfish and get a move on the marriage question.

That evening, Anya was employed to sing at a masked ball. It wasn't the kind of ball people would give once the season started properly in the spring. It was a small affair—only about thirty or so couples—and she was only employed for the first part of the evening. Her part of the evening had already come to an end. Once the dancing began, she would be free to leave.

But even though she sparkled in a luminous silver cloud of a dress that skimmed off her shoulders, with a matching silver mask that covered the upper half of her face, and even though people complimented her heavily on the singing and plied her with thanks, food, and drink when it was over, half her head, or most of it, was elsewhere.

She stood at the edges of the ballroom. It was after nine. Her bit was over, and she meant to leave as soon as she had had a drink. The dancing was slowly starting around her, and she watched in a haze as the adrenaline of her performance left her.

It was true that she had been thinking about Damian Ashton since she met him at the Budleigh estate. Since that conversation at the goat pen. But something had changed now. She was thinking about him in a different way. An inner shift that was hard to put a finger on. Jeremy was right. When Damian Ashton cared about someone, it was something else again.

She caught her breath at the memory of the way he had moved closer to her earlier that day, sensed that the meeting with Lila brought with it old and complicated feelings that were painful. The way he told her—with Lila and Jeremy there in the room—that he would do whatever she wanted and needed, that it was up to her to decide what she wanted to do.

She wasn't naïve enough to think he cared. It couldn't be that. He didn't even take her to his bed when she offered herself up on a platter. She blushed as she watched the first couples take their place on the dance floor. She practically *begged* him, and he refused. On some paltry excuse about needing to send a message to Jane Simmonds, the Budleighs' former housemaid, and something about Anya needing to get some sleep. He couldn't possibly want her like she wanted him if *that* was his excuse, or if he needed to make an excuse at all.

The couples started moving gracefully about the room. They were only doing a country dance or two to start with, but given that it was a masked ball, and there were already whispers and giggles about the candlelit ballroom, she was sure it wouldn't be long before a waltz was struck. She stood there a little wistfully—unexpectedly wistfully—wondering when she had last danced. It was hard to remember.

There was dancing at her parents' parties in Delhi when she was little, which she and her sisters—long after they should have been in bed—watched from between the banisters. Sarah Marleigh rarely gave anything like a party. At the Bath seminary where Anya was educated, she learned to dance and the strict schoolmistresses sometimes gave the girls a treat and invited young men to what they called a *discreet evening of quiet enjoyment*. But she was an employee at court now, and in the parties and balls where she found herself, she wasn't a guest. She was working, and you didn't give employees the opportunity to dance. She sighed louder than she intended, but luckily the masked couples were too engrossed in one another to notice.

The ballroom was dimly lit now. The couples had taken the trouble to dress as if it were the height of the season, instead of a relatively quiet evening. While most of the company was made of married couples, it was also a chance for some mamas to try out their young daughters before they were formally presented in their first ball. Anya watched the couples dip and twirl and curtsy, the shy smiles and the giggles, the couples who were dancing with one another but scanning the room for more appealing partners.

She couldn't deny the look in Damian Ashton's eyes when she'd offered him her lips, or the way he'd kissed her.

She shivered at the memory, felt a treacherous clenching between her legs at the way he'd paid attention to her, not just the noises she made and her sighs and kisses but also to what mattered to her and what hurt. That, she realized, was the most important thing of all. She envied Jeremy suddenly. Because he had it all the time. That kind of silent protectiveness that Damian Ashton gave those he truly cared for. She had it only for now, and even now it was intermittent, when something stirred him or caught his attention. Or perhaps he felt responsible, as her trustee. Jeremy had it all the time.

Her thoughts stirred a nameless longing that she felt was buried so deep inside her it couldn't be plucked out, could perhaps never be satisfied. A hungry sea.

Before she realized what she was doing, she had drunk two glasses of ratafia. She was so thirsty after all the singing and the three encores that she hadn't realized she was gulping down the drink. Slightly unsteadily, she placed her empty glass on the table behind her. She had drunk those glasses too fast.

She was wondering how to skirt the edges of the dancing couples and take her leave from her host. The lighting was dim, much dimmer than when she was singing. Some of the candles had been put out, and only a few still hung in sconces around the room. There was a medieval look to the ballroom, an air of mystery and intrigue, instead of the usual overbright look that was more common in *ton* parties.

She was drifting away from the table when a hand tugged at hers and she found herself being pulled through the sea of couples and into the melee. It happened so quickly that she could hardly catch her breath before she was standing there facing her masked partner.

He was dressed in black satin breeches and a coat of a deep burgundy, and his mask, which covered the upper half of his face, was charcoal silk. Her heart was beating so hard, she felt a little faint. She stood there and stared at him, wondering if her thoughts had conjured him up. Or if she was asleep and dreaming.

The band struck up a waltz, she felt his arm go around her waist, and it was like she couldn't breathe at all. She laid her hand in his, and they started moving across the room. They felt their way for a few seconds.

"What are you doing here?" she managed to ask after he twirled her and then fitted her back in his arm. They were moving more surely now. And she felt like she was floating, skimming the floor, and it was so perfectly what she had been silently longing for that her face broke into a smile. She laughed.

He grinned back. "No one will recognize me. I don't come to *ton* parties."

"They'll recognize me. And I'm not supposed to be dancing, my lord. I'm working."

He was so close, it was like their lips were touching, even though they weren't. "You can tell them you're dancing with an earl and they can go to the devil if they don't like it." He was talking, but it wasn't in his usual aloof way. It was with a smile playing on his lips.

"And you like being an earl, my lord, do you?"

"Only if it means anything to you, Anya. Most of the time, the title can go hang."

"You think it means something to me?"

He drew her closer as they moved across the floor. She wouldn't be surprised if everyone was staring, wondering how the singer employed to entertain them dared to be dancing with a stranger—she doubted many people would recognize Lord Ashton in his mask and in the dim lighting. But she had no mind to look around her. She wanted this moment to last a little bit longer before it ended.

"No, Anya. I think it means nothing to you."

She pressed herself closer and heard him suck in his breath. She smiled a little smile. "And me being a court singer, what does it mean to you, my lord?"

She said it in a teasing voice, but then held her breath, wishing she hadn't said it, hadn't asked the question, even as a joke, because if he did what every other man did and sang her praises, said how divine her voice was, how perfect she was in every way, she would cringe from him. She wanted to take the question back. She could see him thinking about the answer. But now he was already opening his mouth to answer, and she braced herself like she did with every other man who saw her as an unreachable nightingale.

"Do you know what I like about you the most?" he said softly. "It's the way you seem to think things you don't say. Feel things you don't tell people about. Need things you'll never articulate."

She stared at him.

He grinned to break the spell. "What do you need right this second, Anya?" His voice was teasing now.

"Right this second?" she said lightly. "I have everything I need, my lord."

She seemed to become one with the music the band was playing. Perhaps she often did that with music, but this was different. It was like he was a part of it too. As the waltz came to an end, he bowed to her.

She knew he wouldn't risk dancing with her a second time. It was bad enough to have done it once—she was no guest. But to dance with any woman twice would cause gossip and people would start wondering who he was. It was possible they were already trying to guess, possible that someone or another would have recognized him. And if they did, they would hold it against him that he was only dancing with her and leaving the other women to fend for themselves. She looked at him in panic.

He pressed her hand reassuringly, walked her quickly to the side of the room, bowed again, and then before she could speak to him, ask him when she would see him again, he left the ballroom. She stared forlornly at the door.

There were people around her now, looking for refreshments, and she didn't want to linger. It was better to slip out now, before anyone asked her what on earth she was doing dancing like a guest. She had packed her sitar away earlier on. She picked it up now as she left the ballroom.

Thankfully, her host was busy and didn't see her. She pulled her coat closer about her as she stepped out. The house was off Oxford Street, an easy walking distance from the palace, and she had said no to being driven home in a carriage, hoping that a walk would cool her. It was not long after ten. But now she wished she hadn't refused the offer of a ride. It was cold, and a misty rain clung damply around her.

A carriage suddenly pulled up as she walked away from the house.

She stared at it, hoping it was only someone looking for directions and not someone seeing a lone woman and seeing it as an opportunity. That happened often enough, and she thought her stubborn independence would get her into trouble one day. She kept a sharp blade in her reticule, and though it was sheathed and she couldn't feel its sharpness, she hugged the reticule closer. She quickened her pace, but the carriage had come to a complete halt. The door opened and Damian Ashton stepped out.

The breath left her body in a whoosh. "Lord Ashton," she said breathlessly.

"Damian," he said and made her chuckle. He took her sitar case. "I forgot to mention it just now, but Jane Simmonds is already in London."

"You came back to tell me that?" she asked, her heart still beating painfully hard. He was here, he was *here*, he didn't leave her there in that ballroom.

He was staring at her, a strange stillness in his eyes. "I've done some of what I needed to do." He hesitated, and she could hardly breathe now. "I don't suppose you'd come home with me now, Anya?"

She felt herself underwater, suspended, hardly breathing. There was a deep pool in the back lawn at her parents' house in Delhi when she was little. Lila and Mira splashed around in it, but Anya liked to suspend herself in it and stay there as long as she could, not moving, arms adrift on either side of her, hair floating like tentacles. The others thought there was something ghoulish about it, and Mama once asked her, with a crease of concern, if she thought about death when she was down there. But she didn't. She did it because it was the most peaceful place in the world. Where everything else, including thought, ceased.

"What is it?" Damian Ashton asked her now as he looked at her face.

"I feel like I'm underwater."

But he held her face and kissed her hard. "Are you coming with me?"

"Do you need to ask?"

"What happened earlier on when you were at my house? What did I do?"

"What do you mean?" Though she thought she knew.

"Something's different. You're looking at me different."

"You noticed. You cared. You looked out for me."

"Other people must do that. Don't they?" There was a note in his voice. A hopeful note, or something hard to define.

"No. There's no one." How could she explain? There was Trixie. Trixie looked out for her, a lot more than Anya gave her credit for. Yet Trixie was so young, Anya felt responsible for her. She didn't feel responsible for Lord Ashton. She didn't feel like she had to be the grown-up one.

He grasped her hand. He placed her sitar carefully in the carriage, and then handed her in. He clasped her hand in his, fingers entwined, surely and strongly. As the carriage drove off, he didn't say a word. She didn't either.

It was a short ride. Neither one spoke. They turned heads to look at each other once or twice, and it was with that same stillness, like the air between them hardly existed, had turned to water, elemental water that connected and nourished and fed and was a timeline, and Anya felt that parts of her were already softening—or maybe that had already started when they were dancing. Nipples puckering. Moisture between her legs. A pulse beating somewhere in the deepest part of her. Every part of her body wanted to taste him and feel him.

She hardly registered when she got out of the carriage, walked into his house, walked up the stairs and into his room.

A fire was blazing there. He closed the door of the chamber. Their breathing was jagged, though they had only touched hands so far. He closed the distance between them, his hands reaching for her coat. He took it off. Now she stood in her sparkling silver dress. She and the fire were ablaze. Her heart was going to explode. And the pulse between her legs was going to drive her mad. He bent toward her, to kiss her, but she shook her head.

He instantly moved back, looking searchingly at her. "If you don't want to, it's fine. We don't have to."

She almost laughed. There was no time to explain that she didn't want kisses right now. She didn't want whatever slow way he had in mind. Later, maybe. Not right now. She moved closer to him. The gap between the bed and the fire seemed too great, and she didn't want to leave its warmth. She pulled a rug from the nearest chair as he watched her. She spread it quickly and efficiently on the thick carpet in front of the fire. Not too far from it. She was staring at him, like she wanted him to read her mind.

He seemed to understand. Some of it, anyway. He walked to her again and placed his hands on her arms. But she shook her head, impatiently shook his hands away. She placed one hand on his chest and the pressure made it clear. She wanted him to lie down on the rug. He was looking questioningly at her, but his body was catching on before his head, and his breath quickened again. Her own felt like it might make her chest explode. He took off his coat and waistcoat. She slipped out of her embroidered shoes and he took his boots off. They were moving fast now, yet everything was slow, too slow.

When he was finally lying down, she straddled him. Awareness filled his face, and his eyes became even more still, even darker and more focused on her. When he tried to reach out again, she held his arms, placed them on either side of him. She quickly undid his shirt so that she could feel his chest, the dark springy hair there. Then she undid his trousers and at the sight of him, smooth, hard, and made of silk, she let out a sigh of great longing. He was watching her, her face, her eyes, and a look of longing was in his eyes when he heard her sigh.

Still straddling him, she shrugged her dress off, quickly as she could. Now in her chemise, she couldn't wait any longer. Her thighs were bare. She impatiently undid the laces in front of her chemise so that her breasts could spring loose. He was trying to reach for her. But she pressed his arms down again.

Then she took one hand downward and found him. He gasped as her cool hand touched him, encircled him, and guided him exactly where she wanted him.

As he entered her, he gasped again. This time she couldn't move his hands away. As she took him in deeper, lowered her hips farther, she bent forward, and he placed a hand around her breast. "Yes, please," she murmured, lowering herself farther. As she started moving on top of him, hardly breathing, eyes hardly open, he lifted his head and wrapped his mouth around her nipple.

The first convulsions began almost instantly, like she was waiting for just that, the feel of his warm mouth on her. As he circled her breast with his tongue and she felt the entire length of him inside her, she exploded all around him, until it wasn't clear if the flames in the fireplace were outside her or lighting her from within.

She clung to him so hard, she could feel him pulsing. He stilled her hips for a few moments, breathed deeply, then let go. She moved more slowly now, taking her time. Both his hands were at her breasts now, playing them, she thought, skillfully like a musical instrument. She purred. She braced herself, found the exact spot and rubbed harder at him, and convulsed around him again. This time he claimed her mouth, held her close, and breathed her in as she rode him.

19

The pieces of their plan were falling into place.

Damian had asked for Jane Simmonds to come to London, and she was settled with his small London staff, made up of the cook, Mrs. Garner, who also served as housekeeper; a housemaid called Tuppence who was only too happy to have Jane's company; and, of course, his man, Linus. Lila Tristram was good as her word, and the day after she'd come to his place—unannounced and uninvited, but he couldn't complain; she was a little frightening—she sent word that her husband Ivor Tristram's man, Hector, had already made inquiries and, no, it was confirmed that Clara Budleigh had not made any trips to a bank or anywhere else where she could store things, and neither had any of her staff.

Preston Budleigh had already returned to Folkestone with his brother's body and was making preparations for the funeral. Clara Budleigh was soon to follow him, but it was spread about that she was staying in town for a few extra days to make alternative arrangements for their niece Emily's chaperonage. Emily was the Budleigh cousin the family had presented at court.

Of course, Clara wasn't staying in town because of some

simpering cousin. Damian knew that. She was staying so she could make sure of Anya's answer. She was there so Anya couldn't forget that Clara Budleigh would hand her over to the Runners if Anya didn't do exactly what Clara wanted. Damian had no illusions about dear cousin Clara.

Lila Tristram also arranged for one of her friends, a Dowager Crowther, who famously numbered a cockatoo and a spider monkey amongst her many pets, to have a little intimate musical evening at her house, at which Anya was invited to play, and Clara Budleigh was invited as a guest. The soiree was in five days. Lila made sure that *all* of the dowager's guests knew that Anya would be there. They couldn't take the risk of Clara Budleigh using her recent bereavement as an excuse not to go. Damian was sure that she would come if she knew it might give her a chance for another conversation with Anya. At least he hoped she would.

It was strange. The plan was put in motion for just five days away. And in some ways, he wanted to get it over with. For Anya's sake. And so they could all get on with their lives and not have Charlie Budleigh's death hanging over their heads. He had a day in Parliament two days after the soiree at Dowager Crowther's, and he wanted to be completely clearheaded and make his speech about slavery in the empire.

Yet he didn't want the five days to be over. In Anya's arms, other things, other realities, plans, threats, work, all seemed to be too far away to worry about. Nothing else mattered.

"You are sure of Linus's loyalty?" Anya murmured into his chest hair.

He was half falling asleep, but the feel of her lips laying kisses around his nipple and down his rib cage, and then her straddling him, as he lay on his bed, pinged all his senses awake.

He placed an arm around her, tossed her over, laid her back down on the bed, and lifted himself between her legs. She was already reaching a hand down for him. And he was ready and willing, but she was way too impatient. He knew one way to slow her down. Only one. He grabbed both her hands and placed them above her head on the bed and then bent his mouth to her nipple. She gasped and instantly arched. And then there was no rushing, no words, no impatience to have him inside her. It was like a little switch you could turn on. He smiled at her breast and lapped at her.

"Always in a hurry," he murmured.

But she wasn't answering. Not now that he was playing her like a harp—her analogy, not his. It was only two nights since she first came to his room, but already he felt he was getting to know her sounds and smells and her arching and wriggling. He was getting to know them, and yet was in awe of them, like he'd found a gift that he had dreamed about but hadn't been sure existed.

She was appealing all the time. Her connection with her music was awe-inspiring. Her forthrightness, the direct way she looked at you, the layers and layers that seemed to lurk inside her—all of these were deeply attractive. Then that surprising thing that happened—how much it meant to her that he noticed what she felt and stood up for her and her feelings. That took him by surprise. That it meant that much to her. And it humbled him. And he wanted to feel it again. That thing she made him feel. He wanted to keep standing up for her. No one. There's no one. That's what she had said.

But in bed, she was something else again. Deep as her waters ran when she played music or when she simply stared at him—even when she was annoyed at him, *especially* when she was annoyed at him, which was often—in bed it was like being transported along with her, anchored by her waves of feeling so that everything else ended. He thought being with her gave him a connection to something eternal that he had no other access to. But that eternal thing wasn't just the world, wasn't just her, it was also a connection with the deepest, most hidden part of himself. Like in being with her he finally found himself.

He was going mad.

And it just went to show. Show what exactly, he wasn't sure. It went to show something.

He felt himself hardening further. Her ridges and valleys, the intense warmth inside her, the way she clenched desperately at him. When she straddled him, she sometimes told him— ordered him—to stop moving his hips so that she could feel him exactly where she needed him. It made him laugh and cry at the same time.

Even when he was inside her, on top of her, even then he played with her breasts and it made her open deep inside and she cried out. And he made sure to do that, to feel that, as many times as she wanted. Delaying his own pleasure. But somehow that only made it more intense when he finally came. This he hadn't realized before. Her pleasure made his more intense. How simple, how elemental. How shockingly profound.

Afterward, when they both lay side by side on the bed, and he was drifting off into sleep—or maybe he was in a coma—he remembered her question. It woke him. "I trust him."

"Hmm?"

"Linus. He's been with me ten years. I know him."

She was awake now. How she could be so wide awake so soon after what he hoped he'd just done to her, the number of *times* he'd done it, was a marvel. A moment of doubt—maybe he wasn't as good as he thought he was. He looked at her. He wanted to ask her if it mattered to her, how they were together, mattered as much as it mattered to him. But then he couldn't bring himself to ask.

"It's a big thing to ask him to do," she mused. "How do you know you can trust him?"

He lay on his back and looked up at the ceiling. He dragged his mind from Anya—it was nearly impossible to do—and tried to think about his man, Linus. He tried to focus on what Anya was asking him. Linus. Could he trust Linus?

Ten years ago, Linus was close to starving to death. Damian was eighteen when he met Linus. But Linus was not much over fourteen. He was tall and scrawny and hungry, and though he was too big to clean chimneys like he had when he was little, he was not too little to get really, really good at picking pockets. He was regularly punched and slapped, but rarely caught. Except then he tried to pick Damian's pocket. Damian, who hadn't grown up on the streets of Jamaica for nothing, caught him at once, told him off, and took him home to be cleaned.

Home was just simple lodgings in those days. It was long before he became Lord Ashton. Jeremy was still in school. Damian was done with school and was heading down to Oxford soon and needed a valet. And he had no time for the usual gentleman's gentleman. He wasn't a gentleman, not really, and he couldn't be bothered with the usual fripperies. A man who wanted him to tie elaborate cravats or polish his boots with champagne would drive him mad.

Why not Linus? Damian doubted Linus cared about such things as cravats and cleaning boots.

No one treated Linus with kindness or concern. Damian didn't either. He chided him, told him off, scolded him, and made him clean himself and eat a proper meal three times a day. Linus at once channeled his skills and all his loyalty to his new employer. His new employer didn't beat him or threaten him with jail. And didn't think he was beyond hope. It was a distinct improvement on his lot in life. Linus didn't look back.

No one except Jeremy knew of Linus's past as a pickpocket and a thief, and even Jeremy didn't know everything. Damian told Anya about it now. She listened with her usual attention. Wide-eyed, rapt, the way she always listened. He told her about Linus and his past, how they had met, how Linus had become steadfastly loyal to Damian. Linus had had a careless disregard for the law when they met, it was true. He didn't think it mattered stealing from someone who had too much and who didn't share. Even hurting someone who would have hurt him. Damian had had to teach him a firmer sense of what was right and wrong. Even though Linus still had his own code of conduct, Damian said, and it wasn't altogether easy to take the pickpocket out of him, he still trusted his loyalty. He told Anya all about it. She didn't look altogether convinced. After all, what they were asking Linus to do was a big task, and Anya wanted to be sure he could be trusted, that they weren't being naïve. Damian told her everything because he wanted her to see why he trusted Linus.

It was only when she had gone back to the palace an hour or so later that Damian suddenly felt something he hadn't felt before. He felt exposed.

He never felt exposed because he never let himself feel that way, never since he had moved away from his stepfather. With his stepfather, he'd learned how to protect himself. He'd learned how not to trust. How to look for signs of building rage. But also signs of how small someone else—Jeremy—felt when confronted with a bully. His stepfather had taught him a lot. He and Jeremy escaped their stepfather, but Damian never forgot the lessons he learned. He never needed to feel small and exposed again because he never let anyone close enough to make him feel that way.

Except now.

When Anya left, Damian lay there staring at the pebbled ceiling of his bedroom. It was just Anya, a part of his brain was saying. Yet the uncomfortable feeling wouldn't go away. It was Linus's secret, his past, not Damian's. He shouldn't have told anyone. Why had he told Anya something he had never told anyone before? He hadn't even told Jeremy as much as he had told Anya.

The unease lingered. It was mingled with his feelings for Anya. It felt like the unease and the desire—if he was honest, the *need*—he felt for her were mingled, almost the same thing. He couldn't feel one without also feeling the other.

This he wasn't at all sure he liked.

When she came back later that night, she made him forget that unease. When she came to him, he thought they would talk or eat or drink, but she wanted to go to bed first. Bed first, food and drink after. He was happy to oblige.

After, they lay awake in bed and talked. And he always felt that those hours were even more magical, more untouched by the world than when they had sex. Maybe she could help him forget the way he felt uneasy and exposed. When she was with him, he did forget those things.

Some nights, when she came to him like that, he found himself telling her about Jamaica. And that was something he never spoke about, not even to Jeremy. Speaking about it to Jeremy would bring up pain that he couldn't visit. Maybe

Jeremy felt the same. There was no chat about their stepfather or even their mother, but there was also no recollection of the Jamaican markets with their enormous fruit that was bursting with flavor. Of the sweet breads he had sometimes stolen off a cart and shared with Jeremy. The colorful houses or the smoked fish. He found himself telling her of that. Almost like it had all happened to someone else. And maybe that was the only way to tell her.

He did that tonight. They talked for hours. After they made love. The unease receded, and he realized he only felt uneasy when she wasn't there. That was it. He just needed to keep her close. Surely, everything would be all right then.

20

A few days later, Anya found herself singing in Dowager Crowther's Drawing Room. Lila hadn't exaggerated. The dowager was a colorful character. The house, or what she had seen of it, was jangling with light and color. There were enormous chandeliers with candles trying to jostle others out of the way. If those weren't enough light, then wall sconces added to the brightness. The wallpaper at the top of each wall had a large panel of gold swirls that framed snow-white swans facing inward toward a chalice. Beneath this panel was a teeming woodland scene, complete with birds flying in and out through dense foliage. There were large bowls of colorful fruit on every available surface, and glasses of ratafia and lemonade.

She was singing, yes, but not with her usual absorption. Her connection with herself was missing today. She was mouthing the words but not feeling the music. She was surprised the guests weren't ignoring her or carrying on with their conversations. Lady Budleigh wasn't there.

Anya kept looking to the front door of Dowager Crowther's house. She couldn't see it from the front parlor, where the small company—all women—was gathered, but that wasn't stopping her eyes from darting in the right direction. She felt twitchy. She kept wishing that they weren't doing this tonight. What had made her think that it was a remotely good idea? The number of things that could go wrong was enormous. Yet at the same time, all she wanted was to get it over with. To carry out the plan and put the whole thing to rest. But that could only happen if Lady Budleigh actually showed up.

She, Lila, and Damian had each at different times wondered out loud what would happen if Lady Budleigh didn't show up. But Anya at least hadn't taken the possibility seriously. She'd pictured the evening so many times, what would be an undoubtedly stiff conversation with Lady Budleigh and the walk out of the house at the end of the evening, that she couldn't believe right now that Lady Budleigh wouldn't show up and none of what she had imagined would come about.

The uneasy questions about Linus's part in the plan lingered too. Damian was sure he could trust the man. He had saved him when Linus was a boy. Damian could sense her doubts and he had told her all about Linus's past as a pickpocket, Linus's distrust of humanity, his unique code of right and wrong. Instead of reassuring her, as she knew Damian intended, it only made her more uneasy. She could believe Linus meant well, perhaps, but what if he was careless? And his loyalty didn't stretch to Anya, after all. What if his part of the evening went wrong? She had tried to bring it up once or twice with Damian, but she could see he didn't like her doubts about Linus, and she had tried to drop it.

She tried to focus on the parlor. Dowager Crowther was someone who caught everyone's attention, and it wasn't just her color-clashing house. She was dressed in a spring-green silk gown with rows and rows of fat purple beads, gold chains, sparkling jewels, around her neck and trailing down to her belly, and a gold turban on her head. She was ignoring the fashion for high waists and simple skirts, dress lines that showed off breasts and hid uncomfortable lines around the belly, and instead was wearing hoops and what looked to be a heavily boned corset. But that wasn't the most remarkable thing about the dowager. The spider monkey sitting on her shoulder and working its way through a pear was causing a sensation. It was tiny and so utterly black that it may as well have been strung together with balls of charcoal. The tail was long and curly, the limbs agile. The monkey was chattering nonstop in between nibbling at the pear, and its eyes were startlingly intelligent. The women were in turns shrieking and desperate to stroke its fuzzy head. The dowager called the monkey Lancelot, and she seemed to have an endless supply of nuts that he was picking directly from her fingers. Even the chattering of the monkey was making Anya nervous.

Anya didn't know if this soiree was already planned or if Lila had asked the dowager to do it especially. Either way, the dowager had gone all out. There were cucumber and watercress and salmon sandwiches for tea, chunks of freshly baked bread and pots of golden butter, clotted cream, brambleberry jam, scones that melted in your mouth, a variety of cakes, salted almonds, and trifles frothy with cream. Anya didn't have an appetite and was too anxious to do more than make a show of eating after her music came to an end. Since Lady Budleigh wasn't there, she thought she may as well head home after her part of the evening was over, but the dowager wanted her to stay and eat.

Anya stood there nibbling at a cake and nervously twirling her turquoise ring. Her mother had given it to her before leaving for the journey, which had turned out to be her last. Anya had asked her why she was giving it to her, and Naira Devi had said that the deep blue reminded her of Anya. It was like the sea, thrashing and calm and deep and troubled and peaceful all at the same time. "I want you to have it one day. But for now it's just a loan," she said.

Anya had heaved a great appreciative sigh at getting something that she loved playing with on the rare occasions she got to sit in Naira Devi's lap since the triplets had arrived and ruined everything. She said something like that to Naira Devi, and her mother frowned and said the triplets were Anya's sisters and she should love them like she loved Mira and Lila. But Anya shrugged and said that they looked like rats, not sisters, and anyway they didn't really look like their three older sisters at all. Her mother seemed like she was in pain, like she wanted to say more, but then she just gave Anya an absent kiss on her forehead before she left.

This flashed incongruously through her brain as she twirled her ring. What was she doing here? She suddenly couldn't bear to stand there, waiting for she didn't know what.

But before she could make her excuses, a party game started. A young woman who had been recently married, and who was wearing a pretty ivory dress and pink sash, had to mew like a kitten and crawl on her hands and knees from one woman to another, and the guests had to keep a straight face and say, "Poor pussy." If a guest laughed or even grinned, the guest became the kitten, and it was her turn to crawl to each of the other guests.

Anya pressed her hands together and wondered if she was going mad and imagining that a woman was crawling around on her hands and knees from guest to guest. The woman had pretty brown ringlets dressed around her ears, and she was wearing a ribbon threaded into her hair. She had a pert mouth and round breasts that were straining out of her dress as she crawled. It was bizarre, and it made Anya cower into the curtains so that no one would pick her for the game. She was already on the verge of hysteria.

Trixie had helped her dress for the evening, in shimmering turquoise. Anya felt guilty. She was spending so much time at Damian's. Wasn't she leaving Trixie alone for too long? But Trixie assured her that she had other supporters. And when Anya spent more and more hours at Damian's, Trixie didn't question her. Anya had caught her watching her sometimes in the last few days, but Trixie didn't say anything. At least not often. She asked as Anya was getting dressed if she had given any further thought to marrying Darren Greenwood. Mr. Greenwood had been so far from her thoughts for so many days that Anya had hardly recognized the name. She hadn't seen him since the Queen's Drawing Room.

"Who?" she'd said absently to Trixie.

Trixie had silently watched her with those round eyes of hers. Then said, "Mr. Greenwood. Have you thought what you might say to him if he proposes? Is he due in the palace soon?"

Anya had turned away to do her hair, even though Trixie had already helped her do it perfectly. No one could get as much curl in it as Trixie could, yet help it stay in place. "No one does my hair like you do. I mean, I know *I* can't. What do you think about this little string of beads? Shall I wear them or are they too glaring?"

Trixie, as usual, had not pressed it.

Her marriage seemed like a distant, almost impossible idea to fathom.

Vying with thoughts of Trixie and everything else that was on her mind was something Anya didn't really want to think about. Not yet. Lila. Lila had helped find out Lady Budleigh's movements. She had organized this soiree so that Anya would have the opportunity to set Lady Budleigh up for their plan. It seemed by mutual and silent accord, both sisters had agreed not to talk about anything else until Anya had managed to extricate herself from Lady Budleigh's clutches. But Anya felt like she was holding her breath. Perhaps Lila was too. Lila certainly watched her, as if waiting for Anya to do—what exactly? Throw Lila out? Confront her and all of the years that they had ignored what lay between them?

And what would Anya do when she and Lila did confront all that lay between them? The truth was she didn't know. She had seen Lila once or twice since that first day when Kenneth Laudsley had sent Lila a message. But it was always to plot and plan, always with at least Damian or Jeremy around. The truth was Lila's presence was at once a glowing, secret, hopeful thing, and the thing that made Anya feel wretched. How would they deal with all the unspoken things that stretched tightly between them?

She looked restlessly about, tossing her head to rid herself of uncomfortable thoughts. She was wondering how soon she could leave when Lady Budleigh was announced.

And there she was, just like that. Anya stared at her.

Lady Budleigh was standing at the threshold of the parlor and staring at the guest that was crawling on her hands and knees like she couldn't believe her eyes. She clutched at her throat with her sepulcherous fingers and said in a voice of doom, "How very droll." Her thin face looked thinner, there were deep circles under her eyes, and she seemed to be all brittle angles.

Anya froze at the sight of her, but Lady Budleigh's severe black clothes seemed to paralyze the rest of the company too.

The guests tried to keep the party game going, but it fizzled. Lady Budleigh saw Anya at once, but she didn't acknowledge her. Anya wondered if that was so she didn't seem too eager for a conversation with Anya or if she thought that it was beneath her to notice a mere singer.

It turned out it was the latter. Someone happened to remark that Lady Budleigh had just missed the most pleasurable part of the evening and gestured at Anya, but Lady Budleigh said, "Oh, goodness, I didn't see you there, Miss Marleigh." She gave Anya the tiniest nod and turned away.

Irritation flashed through Anya. But this was Lady Budleigh all over. Dowager Countess Budleigh had snapped at any child of hers who was discourteous, and Lady Budleigh had kept herself in check when the dowager was around. But now the dowager was dead and there was no one to teach Lady Budleigh not to be rude to her social inferiors.

But Anya wasn't here to be her friend. In fact, a picture of what she was planning to do, as soon as Lady Budleigh was ready to leave, rose sharply in her mind, and she felt suddenly nauseous.

They were playing Blind Man's Buff now, and one guest at a time was blindfolded and had to feel their way around and guess who they were touching. It was leading to a lot of hilarity. Lady Budleigh looked pained—either at the inanity or maybe because she thought she *should* look pained at such silliness. With her, it was hard to know what she actually felt. And no one could accuse Lady Budleigh of having a sense of humor.

Anya excused herself from playing. Lady Budleigh apparently had the same idea. Her back was rigid and she stood on one side of the room. Somehow she managed to edge closer to Anya as if she hadn't noticed Anya at all and had stopped in that exact spot near the food table (she hadn't eaten a single crumb of anything) completely by accident.

"I was hoping to see you here, Anya," she said, her eyes fixed on the game, her back stiff. "It's a week since we last spoke, and honestly, I expected your answer before today. I don't know how long you expect me to wait."

Lady Budleigh was wearing black, but her reticule, made of velvet and strung a few times around her wrist, was a dark gray. Jane Simmonds had managed within two days of arriving in London to speak to Lady Budleigh's dresser and search Lady Budleigh's room in her house in Chelsea. Jane had reported that no bronze rose or note was anywhere to be found.

Of course, those things could be anywhere. Lord Budleigh could have taken them with him, or they could be in his study in the London house. Lady Budleigh could have handed them to someone—a friend or confidante—for safekeeping. But neither Anya nor Damian thought that this was a real possibility. Lady Budleigh wouldn't give up something so precious, not even to her husband. And Anya hadn't been able to stifle a bark of laughter at the idea of Lady Budleigh having a friend or confidante.

Anya tried her best not to let her eyes flicker to Lady Budleigh's reticule.

Her brain was busy. She wondered if there was any way she could get access to the reticule. Could she get Lady Budleigh to put it down and then search it? That way Anya wouldn't have to go through with the rest of the plan. The thought of going through with it was making her dizzy. What if things went wrong? What if things went too far?

"I have an answer," Anya said. "But please, don't ask me to talk about it here. When you leave, perhaps I could walk out with you?" It sounded flimsy. Her voice faltered.

Lady Budleigh looked impatient. "I don't see what there is to talk about. It's either a yes, you'll do it, or a no, you won't. Surely."

Anya couldn't help thinking that in a way Lady Budleigh was right. "I'd like to know—I'd like to know who—" She stopped. Wondering if this sounded even lamer.

Lady Budleigh looked at her with derision. "You have said you would prefer someone on their deathbed. I have said I'll find someone. Does it matter who it is beyond that? If it comes to that, it doesn't really need to be a Budleigh. Charlie would have been ideal. And you never know, he might have fallen down drunk in a puddle and taken himself out of your way. After you married him."

Anya's insides curled in distaste. She knew Lady Budleigh didn't have any love lost for her late brother-in-law. She knew she felt no grief at his death. But to speak of him in this cold, almost brutal way . . . She couldn't hide her disgust.

Lady Budleigh looked at her scornfully. "You managed to convince my mother-in-law to leave you half her wealth. My mother-in-law did not like or trust anyone. You had no hesitation in manipulating her. How else could you have got her to give up her famous suspicious ways and trust someone to the extent of leaving them her wealth? At the expense of her children and poor grandchildren!"

Anya gritted her teeth. "The grandchildren are taken care of."

"I see you have taken some time to acquaint yourself with the terms of the will. What of her children? What of poor Preston and Amelia?"

Anya couldn't help thinking that Lord Budleigh, Amelia, and Charlie had brought the dowager's disapproval onto themselves, Amelia with her personality, Charlie with his lifestyle, and Lord Budleigh simply because of whom he had married. But alongside these thoughts she also felt a quiver of guilt. Wasn't Lady Budleigh right to some extent? "The dowager had the right to leave the money however she chose. She earned the right to do so."

Lady Budleigh scoffed. "Wealth and estates are inherited by birthright, not earned, Anya. I suppose you would have any pauper claim that they have *earned* their way into wealth and property? And what next, into nobility as well?"

Anya stared at Lady Budleigh in wonder at the woman's complete self-belief. "Are you not asking me to earn a share of the dowager's property by marrying someone or the other?" She felt like the two women were speaking different languages.

Lady Budleigh jerked her head impatiently. "Are you trying to tell me you have qualms about whom to marry?"

"You know, Lady Budleigh, as a matter of fact, I do have some interest in who you come up with."

"Come, then. If we must talk, then I am ready to leave. I am in mourning and shouldn't be out in company but felt that it was important that we speak. Let us leave. But it would look odd if I left with you."

There wasn't contempt in the "you," or at least no more than usual. But Anya almost laughed. Lady Budleigh was plotting for Anya to marry some dying old man so that she could then share the dowager's wealth with the Budleighs, but she was still aware enough of her social standing that she didn't want to be seen leaving the house with a mere court singer.

Anya thanked Dowager Crowther and accepted thanks from a number of guests. She left. She walked slowly down the street, her senses wide awake, her nerves taut.

Footsteps behind her. It was Lady Budleigh. She caught up

with Anya and the two women walked together. Now Anya could barely talk at all. Her eyes were darting. She was murmuring nonsense in response to whatever Lady Budleigh was saying. Was Lady Budleigh listing a few men of her acquaintance and their pros and cons? One was old, but not ill. Another was ill, but not old. One was completely trustworthy, especially if the Budleighs promised assistance for his sister after he was gone. And so on. Anya would have had trouble believing someone could talk in this cold way if she was paying attention to what was being said. As it was, she was finding it hard to focus. Every cell in her body seemed to be on high alert, knowing what was to come. Now Lady Budleigh was asking her a question.

"Well, out with it, then. Do you have a preference? Someone aging who would leave you a widow—widows have tremendous freedom compared to what you have right now. Or I could produce someone young and eligible who wouldn't turn down a comfortable independence, and could perhaps overlook your birth and way of life—"

When the shadow loomed in front of the women in the dark residential road, Anya's scream was no less real than Lady Budleigh's.

Lady Budleigh was clutching her hand to her throat, her eyes wide and staring. Anya's heart was racing. But it wasn't just the looming shadow that startled her, or the suddenness. She had been expecting a stranger to stop them and steal their possessions. Someone gruff, perhaps, someone who looked the part. Linus Temperance had promised he would hire someone to do the job. He had seemed confident that he would be able to do so. But this, this man looming in front of them in the dark, he was no hired man. The man pointing his pistol at them was Linus himself. Anya's heart was thudding.

He was disguised cleverly. He'd managed to hunch forward in a way that made him look shorter and perhaps older. His coat was a few sizes too big and quite shabby, and it made him look less skeletal. The mask that covered the lower half of his face and the low hat pulled down over his eyes kept his face in darkness. His voice was unrecognizable; even his customary northern accent seemed different, his voice more guttural and rough. Surely, it was unlikely that Lady Budleigh would recognize the man, even if Damian lived on the neighboring estate? Even if she had encountered Linus before, he was practically unrecognizable now. Surely, it was unlikely that she was looking at anything other than the pistol in the man's hand. Anya's breathing was ragged. The man spoke gruffly.

"Hand over them purses of yours. And all your jewels."

Lady Budleigh struggled with her reticule, and the man was trying to snatch it away with one hand while wildly waving the pistol straight in Lady Budleigh's face with the other, and even though Anya knew who it was, she couldn't help feeling sick with fear. What if the pistol went off by mistake? What if a bullet hit Lady Budleigh? Did Linus know what he was doing? Was Damian sure he could trust this man? He was a thief. And he had already strayed from the plan. He could even be drunk, for all Anya knew. Why was he here and not a hired man, a stranger who Lady Budleigh couldn't have recognized? Damian himself had said that his code of honor sometimes didn't match other people's.

Anya handed over her near-empty reticule. She wasn't carrying her sitar today. She had nothing else on her. Finally giving up the fruitless struggle, Lady Budleigh handed over her reticule to the man too. But the man wanted more. He wanted Lady Budleigh's pearls and Anya's ring. He gestured with his hands and said the words, "Come now. This is taking me way longer than it should. Hand 'em over, and quick."

Even though Anya knew it was Linus, she couldn't bear to hand over her mother's turquoise ring. She took it off her finger, and the hand felt bereft. Too light and all wrong.

Her breath caught in her throat. She said, oddly, "Please don't lose it."

It was an odd thing to say to a thief. She hoped Lady Budleigh didn't notice the slip. But Lady Budleigh seemed too shaken perhaps to notice what Anya was saying.

The man waved the pistol some more, warned the women not to do something stupid, like following him, and he was off now. He seemed to evaporate into the darkness, and Anya doubted that they could have found him, even if they had followed him. Neither tried to. The two women stood forlornly in the middle of the dark street, rain that they had not been aware of dripping down their necks.

21

Damian wasn't always sure how he felt about his title. He didn't think it belonged to him. He felt like an imposter. But he also didn't believe in it. He had witnessed slavery and its consequences at close proximity in Jamaica, and he didn't like the feeling that there was blood money under his name now. That he had suddenly become entitled, and simply because by accident of birth and circumstance, he now had a "Lord" in front of his name. He hadn't earned this status, or at least he had worked hard at his business interests, and so perhaps he had earned the comfortable life he led. But a title, an estate? In the circle of life, where did these belong? Who could possibly have the right to the privilege they brought? An automatic right, a birthright. No, he couldn't bring himself to understand it.

But there was one thing to be said about the title. Being Lord Ashton gave him a standing in Parliament, deserved or not, and when he got the opportunity, he made sure to add his voice to the antislavery speakers. Wilberforce was the loudest voice and had been key in having slavery abolished in Britain. Now it was up to men like Wilberforce, and to a lesser extent his supporters like Damian Ashton, to make sure slavery was abolished, and not just in Britain but in the colonies. In Parliament, he had his supporters, and he was coming to think that even the ones that didn't support his cause at least respected him enough to listen when he spoke. After all, he had real experience of what slavery could do to people.

In today's speech, he spoke again of how many Englishmen continued to benefit from slavery, even if slavery was illegal in this country. That just abolishing it in Britain was not enough. That it must be stopped everywhere that Britain did trade. He spoke passionately, yet in his usual understated way, about the treatment of enslaved people, about the rights slavery curtailed, about the wrongful sense of entitlement people felt when they owned other human beings. When he sat down, on the whole, he was satisfied with his speech. Some people had not responded, but several had nodded, and there had been a few "Hear, hears." It was excruciatingly slow work, drowning in speeches and paperwork and who knew who in a social sense, but nevertheless, he felt he had managed to overcome his natural impatience with the system and add his voice.

He was surprised to see Preston Budleigh in Parliament today and was even more surprised to see when Preston stood up to speak. If Preston had anything to say about slavery, Damian would like to hear it.

It looked like he was about to. Preston was getting ready to take the floor.

Two nights ago, Linus had handed over not only Anya's turquoise ring back to her but also—thankfully—the bronze rose and Anya's note, which had been, as predicted, in Clara's reticule. They had got off easy. And if in the last two days, it had seemed like Anya and he were both on edge, both feeling like they had got off *too* easy, he dismissed it, thinking that it was just nerves.

Anya kept saying that she was worried that Clara would have recognized Linus. Linus had meant to find a stranger to hold Clara and Anya up, but the hired man had not shown up, and Linus had improvised. Damian insisted that Clara was too superior to have noticed what his valet looked like, and anyway, Linus had only been to the Budleigh estate once or twice. But Anya wasn't convinced. They had both been jumpy and nervy and prone to minor, but self-conscious, arguments. They didn't know each other that well yet. He at once felt like he had never been so close to anyone in his life, and yet that they barely knew each other. They were both skirting around trying to get to know each other, yet feeling their way to trusting each other. It was certainly not what Damian was comfortable with, yet the yearning for it couldn't be denied either. For someone he could trust and who could take away years of loneliness and hurt.

Damian tried to pull away from his thoughts and give his attention to Preston. As Preston cleared his throat and held the lapels of his coat, suddenly Damian felt a sense of doom.

"It is good to see Lord Ashton so comfortable giving his speech," Preston said. As usual, Preston was sweating from nerves. Damian's foreboding deepened. "One would think you were bred to the peerage, Lord Ashton."

One or two of the lords present sniggered, but a few asked Preston to get a move on. It was late afternoon, and the lords were ready for their gammon pie and potatoes and looking forward to a deep sherry with their meal. Some would undoubtedly be off to Almack's for the evening's entertainment if this were the height of the social season. Right now, with town thin of company, they still had quieter social evenings and theatrical entertainment on offer.

"Though it was through a series of fortunate accidents that you became a peer, Lord Ashton, was it not?" Preston was uncomfortably picking at his lapels.

Damian had a horrible inkling he knew where this was going. He had a sudden—and slightly hysterical—vision of Preston practicing this speech with his exacting wife. "Shall we take this outside, Preston?" he said, his voice soft and ironic. Though his heart was thudding. "I doubt that the lords present here today have any interest in the typhus that carried away one Budleigh and the tiger that mauled another. Pie and sherry await. Shall we not hold them up more than we need to?" He hoped he sounded calm. He suddenly did not feel calm at all. He and Anya had perhaps been right to be jittery.

A few of the lords sniggered again at his comment, and a few others said, "Hear, hear," and there was some shuffling as people became restless. Parliament wasn't voting on anything for the rest of the day, and people were eager for the speeches to be over so they could be off. Damian shuffled his notes as he made preparations to leave. He didn't look at Preston. His heart was still thudding.

"Not Arnold Ashton's death, though, Lord Ashton," Preston said now. He was rushing now, trying to get his words out before the peers actually stood up and left the room. He was speaking over the rustling of papers and gowns. "*That* was not the typhus or a tiger. He was a distant relative of yours and mine. The last man standing between you and the Ashton estate and title. He died under very suspicious circumstances. Not long after he was seen drinking in a tavern with *you*. Mere hours after, in fact."

Damian had been making moves to leave, along with a few other peers, and there was an increasing amount of murmuring and shuffling, but at these last words, suddenly there was silence in the room.

Damian stared at Preston. The man's face was pimpled with sweat now. And he was mopping his brow. How, *how* did the man know about that drink in the tavern? This hadn't come to light before. There were always rumors surrounding Damian's ascent to the peerage. Rumors always stuck to Arnold Ashton's death at the hands of a highwayman who had never been caught, who had not in fact stolen anything from Arnold Ashton at all but had just murdered him. Some repeated the rumor and others dismissed it, saying that it was far-fetched and, moreover, Damian Ashton had never even met Arnold Ashton.

Except it wasn't true. Damian had met Arnold Ashton. He had seen him hours before the man died. And it seemed now, all of a sudden, that Preston knew this fact. How long had he known it and been sitting on it?

Noise resumed in the room, though some of the men were throwing curious looks in Damian's direction. There was a murmur, but it was hard to know if it was about Damian or not. Damian carried on gathering his papers. The speeches were finally brought to a close.

The lords shuffled out of the room, many discussing the evening's entertainment. It was early February, and Parliament had been in session only since late January, but there were soirees and musical evenings for those who wanted to find them. Most of the men were not looking at Damian, but some were giving him odd looks as they left. Damian couldn't bring himself to turn tail and leave.

He caught up with Preston under the arches outside. "What the devil are you playing at, Preston?"

The man stopped. His face was red, though it was quite cold outside. He looked hot. He was scratching at his throat. "Told you, Damian, didn't I? Told you I could make things hot for you. Told you not to get too high and mighty in Parliament, didn't I? Told you I could bring you down."

"How exactly?" Damian demanded. The initial shock was giving way to rage. He hadn't murdered Arnold Ashton, so Preston could hardly prove it. But it looked like Preston didn't care what he could prove. He only wanted to make things uncomfortable for Damian.

"Told you to keep your nose out of the business with Anya Marleigh. Don't know why you'd bother, I have to say, given she's the court slut—"

Before Damian could stop himself, he had Preston pressed against a wall, and his hand was around Preston's throat. The man wasn't in any danger of suffocating but was sputtering and going redder. He was clutching at Damian's hand.

Damian didn't loosen his grip but took a step closer. "What has this—the business with Arnold Ashton—got to do with Anya Marleigh?"

The man couldn't speak, not with Damian nearly choking him. Damian roughly pushed him against the wall before he let him go. He didn't back off, though. He was still staring at the man. A man related to him by blood. He wanted to spit in his face, like that could get rid of the distant blood connection between them. He satisfied himself with looking as disgusted as he felt.

"What," he repeated, "does the Arnold Ashton business have to do with Anya Marleigh?"

"You think you'll get away with having my wife robbed in the street, Ashton? You think I don't know who was behind that and why you did it? Stupid to get your man to do it. Did you think my wife wouldn't recognize him? She didn't at first, but then she thought about it after. Clara can't be hoodwinked so easily. Has a brain between her ears. But I suppose you wanted to rub our noses in it. If I were you, I'd watch your back."

Despite himself, Damian's blood ran cold. Of course Preston knew about that. Of course he—and Clara—knew who was behind the theft of the reticule. Anya had been right all along. Damian had tried to reassure her, say that it would be fine, that Clara wouldn't have deigned to notice what his valet looked like and wouldn't have recognized Linus as the man who'd stolen her reticule. Anya had been right to be nervous about it. But it was something else, something else that was making Damian feel cold. Some kind of prescience of what Preston was going to say next.

"I'll get you," Preston said, still rubbing at his throat. "I'll get you for Arnold Ashton's murder."

"How do you intend to do that, Preston?"

"We don't want to get Miss Marleigh in trouble—"

Damian's mouth curled. "Of course not. That wouldn't suit your purposes at all."

"As I said, we don't want to get her in trouble. We just want her to do what's fair. But if we can't get her to do that, then the only course is to discredit you."

There it was. He had to hand it to Preston—in fact, to Clara. It was clever. If Preston and Clara couldn't convince Anya to marry some old Budleigh—through coaxing or blackmail—they would have Damian discredited. Worse, accused of murder. Which could rob him of his peerage, and if not, put everyone against him. Cast enough suspicion so that he could no longer be the executor of Dowager Countess Budleigh's fortune. If he wasn't the executor, then it was likely that Preston himself would be. And it was then for Preston to give or withhold his consent to Anya's marriage, it was to Preston that the money would revert if Anya wasn't married by the time she was twenty-five. It was a clever plan.

"You'll never make your accusations stick, Preston," he said, sounding a little weary already, the rage leaving as suddenly as it came.

"Oh, can't I?" Preston blustered. "Let's just wait and see, shall we? I expect if I dig a little, there are all kinds of things I'll uncover about you, Damian. What *were* you doing meeting up with Arnold Ashton in a pub hours before he died? Caught you by surprise that I knew that, didn't it?"

That said, he cast one more nervous glance at Damian, in case Damian was going to lunge at him again, and then made himself scarce.

22

Anya stood at the window looking out into the square, waiting for Damian to return from his afternoon in Parliament.

It was late afternoon. There were nannies and toddlers wrapped up to their eyes in their winter woolens, lingering in the square, even though it was dark. It was February, but the worst of the winter was holding firm. There were some late street callers lingering on doorsteps, one trying to get rid of some leftover sprigs of lavender and another selling hot buns. The buns were leading to a bit of a tussle between the children toddling on the grass in the square and their nannies. Some nannies were reaching into their bustles and coming up with a few reluctant coins. Anya was half looking at them and half daydreaming. It was dusk, but the streetlamps gave the square a warm glow.

The stress of two nights ago, when Linus burgled her and Lady Budleigh, had left her drained, and she felt boneless. Not only was the theft itself something dark and dangerous in her mind, but the risk Linus had taken by showing up himself instead of sending a stranger was something she couldn't be complacent about. Damian was sure she had nothing to worry about there, but she couldn't rest easy. What if Lady Budleigh had recognized Linus? How could Damian be sure that she wouldn't have done?

Or maybe it was Damian who was leaving her feeling like that. Like her bones and muscles had turned to treacle. She sighed and placed her forehead on the windowpane.

His aloofness hadn't left him. He was still Damian. Capable and sure, but in a quiet way, not in a way that had to be lauded from the rooftops or bragged about. He had a quiet air of assurance that was deeply attractive and strangely reassuring, even though it seemed so insular, yet she knew right now she was seeing a side of him that other people didn't get to see. Maybe no one had ever seen it. In bed, he lost his aloofness. His eyes didn't leave hers, he listened to all her sounds and responded to them, yet there was a vulnerability to him, like he had found something he had always been looking for but had never expected to find.

It scared her.

There was a wound at her core. A wound left in her when her parents died, when she was uprooted from her home and left to live in someone's cold, cold house. A wound for abandoning her baby sisters and then not being able to reconcile with Lila and Mira either. But sometimes when they were in bed and she saw the hope in Damian's eyes, the way he watched her, she worried that his wound was even greater. That he needed her to be perfect to fill it, to heal it. Maybe her wound, though it wasn't close to healing, was partly filled by her music, her connection with her sitar, her guardianship of Trixie, and maybe now, tentatively, the scratchy, tetchy relationship that she might be developing with Lila. But Damian, though he had Jeremy, had never let anyone close again. She was scared that she'd never be perfect enough to help heal that wound.

She sat there at the window, her breath frosting it. A child was running after a pigeon now and trying to feed it its bun—not in a series of manageable crumbs, but the whole thing at once. The child's animated face reminded Anya somehow of Lila, and the thought of Lila punctured her daydreams and anxieties about Damian.

A chuckle escaped her, and at the same time that nameless anxiety that always accompanied thoughts of Lila.

Of course, over the last few days, Anya had seen Lila once or twice. Lila seemed to come to visit Anya—here in Damian's house—armed. Armed not with weapons, but Lila's own special weapon: a sort of wild vivacity that was ready to explode out of her and set things on fire. She had come by yesterday to find out what happened with Linus and the stolen reticule. She looked wildly at Anya when she found out that Anya's rose and note were now back in safe hands. She gave Anya the briefest hug in the history of hugs.

"I owe you," Anya said, her throat tight, "for what you did for me."

"How dare you say that—you owe me nothing!"

"I'm only trying to thank you," Anya said, even then on the brink of laughing, or crying, or both at once, that fierce look of Lila's was so familiar.

"Well! Don't!" Lila answered. And then she wavered, her chin lifted, her eyelashes flickering, not looking at Anya. Anya watched and waited. "You're my sister. I would sell my soul for you."

Anya had been expecting some declaration; that was Lila all over. It would be delivered in her usual punchy way, like she was trying to shoot you, and not saying something loving. But even she was startled by what Lila said. Tears filled her eyes. Her throat was hurting too much to say anything, and in any case, it wasn't like Lila to wait. Lila was already at the door and stepping out of the house by the time Anya managed to whisper, "And I you." But it was too late. Lila didn't hear.

Anya sighed now. Lila was barely back in her life. Her tentative toehold in Anya's life was barely there, and Anya was scared to touch it or even look at it too long in case she hurt it. After all, what if Lila left now that Anya was not in Lady Budleigh's clutches?

She knew they had to talk. Anya wanted to know what Lila wanted from her. Why she was in her life. She expected that Lila would want to ask the same question. For years the sisters had skirted each other. For years they had been sent to different boarding schools. In the last few years they had maintained separate lives and separate households. Anya didn't think that would be possible now, not that level of separation, not between her and Lila at least. And part of her wanted desperately to skim over the difficulties, forget about the past, simply move forward. But she knew she and Lila wouldn't be able to avoid the issue. They would have to deal with it.

"Not yet," she said now, closing her eyes for a moment. "Soon. I'll deal with it soon."

She sometimes found Lila watching her face, waiting to see how she would react to something or the other. And while she had wanted for years to have a relationship with her sisters, to feel and be seen, that kind of scrutiny was hard to bear. And she kept her eyes resolutely turned away.

Anya was counting the pigeons in the square when she finally saw the sight she was waiting for. It was Damian.

She sprang up from the window seat and was at the door long before he managed to walk up the steps to the house. She held the door wide for him. As he walked in, she engulfed him in her arms, surprised at herself, because she didn't think of herself as the demonstrative kind. He, if anything, held her tighter than she was holding him, and a qualm rang through her.

It was only when she stepped back that she caught sight of his face. It looked grim. Not the way he'd looked when he left. He'd been anxious about his speech, but not like this. "It didn't go well?" she said quickly. "You know those lords will do anything to maintain their standing in the world."

He turned away from her and took off his coat and laid aside his gloves. Linus came into the foyer. Anya felt that quiver in her stomach that she felt when she unexpectedly encountered Linus. She couldn't be so superficial that she cared about a scar or two, she often chided herself, but somehow, even after his actions had helped her out of her predicament, she still couldn't warm to him. When Damian had told her about Linus's past, and then had said that they could trust Linus to find someone to rob Lady Budleigh, Anya had asked if Damian trusted him. After all, Damian himself had said that Linus had a checkered past. And Anya had felt uncomfortable trusting him with a big job like the robbery of Lady Budleigh's reticule. But she also knew that Damian didn't like it when she questioned if Linus could be trusted. She had complained the day after the robbery that Lady Budleigh might have recognized Linus, that Linus shouldn't have taken such a big risk, that he should have made sure to send someone else to carry out the robbery. But he had shooed the thought away. If Linus was loyal to Damian, it seemed Damian was just as loyal to Linus. She couldn't help watching Linus's lean face as he spoke to Damian.

Linus asked Damian if there was anything he could get him. Damian shook his head. Anya noticed Linus looking at Damian's face. Was the man as sensitive to every flicker in Damian's face as she was herself? His loyalty to Damian ran deeper than hers; it was of much longer duration, after all. She tried to let go of the jealous thoughts, but they clung.

She walked uneasily into the front parlor with Damian. "What's wrong?" she asked.

Damian told her. Told her what happened in Parliament. She gasped when he started his story and then sat there listening to him, her heart in her throat. It took her some minutes to even start to comprehend what he was saying. She had to get her mind around who Arnold Ashton was. She knew that Damian had only inherited the Ashton title and estate because a series of unfortunate accidents and illnesses had killed off a few Budleighs and Ashtons. The man who had inherited the title before Damian was this man, this cousin, called Arnold Ashton. She reminded herself of this fact. After Arnold Ashton, Damian inherited. But of course, if anything happened to Damian, then the Ashton estate would next pass to Preston Budleigh.

"It doesn't mean anything!" she said as soon as he finished telling her the things Lord Budleigh said about him. "It's not like he can prove anything. What difference does it make what rumors he spreads?"

"It does matter what rumors he spreads. You know how society works, Anya. You live in court; you know better than anyone the price of rumors. And I've never endeared myself to the other lords or to society. People will be only too happy to have a scandalous rumor to while away the rest of the winter."

"But you didn't even know Arnold Ashton! How could you have had anything to do with his death?"

"I had a few drinks with the man a few hours before he died."

She had started pacing the room, a little like Lila might, but now she sat heavily down on a chair across from him. "What?"

"I'd never met him before. He was, after all, a very distant cousin. I knew that the Ashton estate might come to me—my lawyer had acquainted me with the facts. But it was such a remote possibility, I had never really given it much thought. And granted, a load of relatives had died, but I still never imagined anything would happen to Arnold Ashton and the estate would pass to me. As far as I knew, he was young and fit enough. But to tell you the truth, I hadn't thought much about it. I was successful in my business ventures. I had no need to hold my breath to inherit some crumbling estate. And I had already seen what titles and a sense of entitlement could do in the colonies, what beasts they could make of people." Damian let out a long breath. He was looking down at his joined hands. "Arnold Ashton invited me to join him for a drink in a hostelry near Hampstead Heath. He was wary of me at first when we met. He was surprised he had come in a roundabout way to inherit the Ashton title. Remember that a few other distant relatives had to die for Arnold to inherit the title and estate. And he knew that I was next in line. He had done his research. He knew if anything happened to him, I'd be the next to inherit." Damian rubbed his face. "He told me he'd never thought of himself as an earl. I asked him bluntly why he wanted to meet me. He said he wanted to tell me in plain words how little the Ashton estate was worth, how it was crumbling and he didn't have the money to restore it. He said he wanted me to know in case I had any interest in doing away with him and inheriting next. He was only half joking." Damian sighed and shook his head. "To tell you the truth, it surprised me that he even knew that I was the heir. I didn't think anyone knew; our branch of the family was so obscure and had lived in Jamaica for so long. But he had taken the trouble to make inquiries. I told him exactly how much I was worth and said that an encumbered estate and a worthless title meant nothing to me. I explained that I was settled in my life, or at least in my financial affairs, that I had no interest in the Ashton estate. He believed me, and we had a good laugh over a few too many drinks. He was murdered on his way home."

Anya looked at him aghast. "But—but Lord Budleigh won't know all that, will he?"

"He seems to know about the meeting. He mentioned it today. He'd never mentioned it before. He did today."

She sat silently for some time, then said in a voice that had lost some of its conviction, "It still doesn't prove anything. It still doesn't mean that you killed him."

"No," he said, and his voice didn't have much conviction in it either.

She sat up straighter. This wouldn't do. They couldn't have escaped the threat to her only to land Damian in this mess. The only reason Lord and Lady Budleigh were doing this at all was—"Why, why are they doing it?" she said. "What are they hoping they'll get?"

"If they can't threaten you with prison or hanging for Charlie's death, they'll threaten me with—this."

"And get what from it?" She stood up again. She was pacing the room again.

"Think about it, Anya. If they can make this stick, this accusation, then I'm a murderer. Arnold Ashton's murderer. And if that's how I got my title, then I'm no earl either. I'm a murderer, and I can't even ask for clemency. They discredit me, and Preston could become the executor of Great-Aunt Griselda's will."

"They can't discredit you because they can't make it stick! You didn't murder Arnold Ashton!" He didn't answer. She sat down across from him again. She grasped his shoulders. "Did you? Did you do it?" He didn't answer. "Because if you did, then we still have to find a way to prove you didn't."

For the first time, his face lightened, and his usual amused glint appeared in his eyes. "And you, you don't care if I murdered the man?"

"One less Ashton in the world is neither here nor there to me, my lord."

He laughed now. She was thankful to see it. He talked about it more easily now, now that she'd made him laugh—she wondered if anyone else made him laugh like this. They talked about it at length, though it felt like they were going over and over the same ground.

Finally, she said, "There's only one thing for it. We have to find this highwayman who actually killed Arnold Ashton. What else can we do? That way Preston Budleigh can scream himself hoarse trying to discredit you, but he can't make anything stick."

"What, and hand this highwayman, who is just going about his life, over to the Runners?"

She made an impatient noise. "If you won't do that, then we can have the man shipped off to France *after* he's confessed. Who cares? We must find him, and then Preston Budleigh's blustering accusations can go hang!"

They were talking about it some more when another thought occurred to her. "So, you knew where Arnold Ashton was that night. You knew he'd be in Hampstead Heath, since he invited you there. Did anyone else know his whereabouts?"

"I have no idea. He came alone. He invited me. He might have talked about his plans."

He was quiet, and she was thinking about how they could find out if Arnold Ashton, two years ago, had told anyone about his plans on a particular date, at a particular time. She saw a frown shadow his brow.

"What?" she said. "You've thought of something. What is it?"

He shook his head. "I was just thinking that he came alone to the inn. And so did I. Linus knew where I was going. That's all."

She didn't say anything. She just looked at him.

It was his turn to make an impatient noise. "I know you don't like him, Anya—"

"I've never said anything like that."

"I see the way you look at him. I try to keep him away from you."

She looked crossly at him. "I don't know how anyone can relax around you if you keep trying to read their mind. I don't *not* like him. He's very loyal to you. *That's* what makes me wonder—"

"No, Anya. He's very loyal to me, it's true. But he wouldn't have murdered anyone for me. He wouldn't have murdered Arnold Ashton just so I could become a lord and inherit an estate." He waved his hand now. "He might—you don't need to say it. But he would have known better than anyone that I had no interest in a rotting estate and less in a title."

Anya pursed her lips. She knew the question of Linus's loyalty could become a sore topic between them. But she couldn't do nothing either. "I see what you're saying. But if someone is as loyal as you say—I mean, you told me he was a pickpocket when you met him. And now you said he regularly gets drunk at any local tavern he can find. What if his judgment wasn't clear?"

"He would have told me."

"Maybe he was so drunk—"

"So drunk he forgot he killed Arnold Ashton? No, Anya—"

"You seem sure he's innocent. You could at least consider—"

His headshake was firm. "Drop it, Anya. He didn't do it. Your dislike is clouding your judgment."

She wasn't convinced.

23

O ver the next week things got worse. Rumors about Damian's hand in Arnold Ashton's death were making their way around London like a wildfire.

Damian Ashton saw Arnold Ashton hours before he died. Not only was this apparently a suspicious circumstance, but the fact that it had not come to light for two years seemed even more suspicious. After all, if Damian Ashton had nothing to hide, why hadn't he spoken about this little tryst before? Why *had* the two men met? Had they even known each other? Wasn't it possible that it was a setup, that in fact Damian Ashton invited Arnold Ashton to Hampstead Heath on that night just so that the man could be ambushed later on? After all, Arnold Ashton was the last surviving Ashton. The only member of the family standing between the title and Damian Ashton. Wouldn't it be tempting to hurry things along if you were that close to getting everything you wanted? It was evident from his success in his business ventures that Damian Ashton was ambitious. Why just stop at earnings? Why not a title and an estate? After all, Damian Ashton was ambitious in Parliament too. And the Ashton title had come with a convenient peerage, a standing in Parliament.

Living in court, Anya usually heard all the latest rumors. Whatever the ladies of the chamber and the courtiers didn't know, it wasn't worth knowing—but if there *was* something they didn't know, it seemed that the palace employees could easily fill in the gaps. Damian Ashton's hand in Arnold Ashton's death managed to surpass the now-waning interest in Charlie Budleigh's death. After all, the man's death at the hands of some unknown creditor was foretold by many. And here was some ready gossip. No one really trusted Damian Ashton, did they? He was much too insular. Kept himself to himself. Didn't take his place in society like a normal peer would. Who would do that?

Only someone who had something to hide.

Anya couldn't help feeling that in saving herself, she had put first Jeremy and now Damian in a very dangerous position. It was because of her, because she refused Charlie Budleigh's offer of marriage, because she retrieved the incriminating objects from Clara Budleigh; those were the reasons that Jeremy was injured in the first place and now Damian was under suspicion. It wasn't just that he could lose the precarious standing he had in London society, he could be accused of murder and if he was convicted, he could lose his life. If things didn't go that far, he could lose the peerage and his standing. He often said that he didn't believe in titles, that he had seen what titles did to men. But she knew that the title gave him a chance to have his say in Parliament, to argue for and against causes he was passionate about. He might be flippant about all of that, but she had a feeling it meant something to him.

Her heart had never been less in her music. When she had musical engagements, she felt that half her mind was on other things. She was disconnected from her singing and her sitar. It made her feel like she was losing herself.

She fretted when she was in the palace, yet when she visited Damian in his house, she hardly felt any better. The guilt, if anything, was worse there. She tried to speak to him about how she felt, to express her guilt. To suggest that maybe the best idea, the only way to stop all this, was for her to marry and hand the money over to the Budleighs, but Damian had no sympathy for this view. The dowager meant for Anya to have the money. And he was damned if he would give in to bullying from Clara and Preston.

Damian and Anya didn't have a formal arrangement, but somehow on nights when she wasn't engaged to play music at the palace or elsewhere, she took to coming around to his house. It was lucky he didn't have much of a staff in his rented lodgings. She didn't think she had a reputation to maintain, though if it were spread about that she was spending time in an earl's lodgings, that would be a first, and she may become easier game for other men at court. But she felt protective of Damian's standing. London society might be forgiving of men who took mistresses, but they were generally more forgiving if the man also showed some future interest in marriage with a woman of society and standing. Given how precarious his current position was, his relationship with a court singer would only make it plummet further.

She tried speaking to him about Linus Temperance. "If you didn't kill Arnold Ashton," she said once or twice, "and you didn't tell anyone where he was going to be that night, and the only person who knew where you would both be is Linus, then isn't it possible that he may have had a hand in Arnold Ashton's death?"

Damian wasn't interested in this theory. "I know Linus, Anya. If you knew him, if you could look beyond the harsh exterior, you would know that he couldn't have done it."

"It isn't about how he looks!"

"What then, Anya? His background as a pickpocket, the fact that he has a tendency to get drunk? I shouldn't have told you about either of those things. It's pitched you against him, and they weren't my secrets to tell."

She couldn't let it rest. "Can't we let the Runners do their work? If you ask Linus to speak to them, let them question him, maybe it would shed some light on what actually happened to Arnold Ashton that night two years ago. Surely, we have to do everything we can to find out the truth."

But Damian was too loyal to the boy he had saved ten years ago to listen.

In the days that followed Damian's speech in Parliament, Anya felt like the world was closing in on her. That something was catching up with her that had always been waiting just around the corner. Why, why was she tempting fate with her relationship with Damian? It would only make things harder, that much worse, when everything fell apart, as it was sure to.

One night, Ivor Tristram, Lila's husband, invited Anya and Damian to a prizefight in Highgate Commons. Anya was surprised at the invitation. Lila herself came to the palace to deliver it, and the two women walked in the grounds. The grounds were still crisp with frost, but a watery sun was trying to peek through the clouds. Birds were unfreezing too and the pond was potted with melting spheres of ice.

"Oh, it's beautiful here," Lila said. She'd never been to the palace. She had of course never been presented. "A little too manicured, but still, peaceful in a way."

"You came to the palace to tell me how beautiful it was?" Anya asked, amused.

"Of course I didn't. Ivor wants to speak to you and Damian about the rumors surrounding Damian."

Anya turned to look at her sister. "And this conversation needs to take place in Highgate Commons on the night of a prizefight?" she asked ironically.

"You're not married, Anya. How do you expect Ivor and me to entertain you—you and Damian, together in our home?"

Anya looked at her sister. Lila was dressed in a perfectly fitted flame-colored pelisse. Her hair was dressed in flowing waves, and there was a glow about her. Marriage to Ivor Tristram suited her. Lila was all fire, but it was clear that Ivor could calm her. Anya wondered—a little evilly—if Ivor Tristram found marriage to Lila quite as soothing.

"I thought *you* didn't care about reputation," Anya couldn't help saying. "Didn't you always say reputation only mattered if you wanted to marry?"

"And you, you have no plans to marry?" Lila gave her one of her piercing looks.

Anya couldn't help bristling at the question, mild though it was. She wasn't used to anyone questioning her plans, or poking at what was her private business. Even Trixie didn't do that. And anyway, whatever her feelings for Damian, she was sure *he* at least had no thoughts of marriage.

"Damian and I have no thoughts of marriage," she said a little crossly.

"Damian?" asked Lila innocently. "Oh no, I wasn't talking about Damian. Don't you mean to marry someone or the other—Jeremy, was it?—so that you can claim your inheritance?" Lila was all big eyes and bland face. "Goodness, *is* there something between you and Damian? One would never have known."

Anya wondered if other people wanted to throttle Lila as

often as she did. "You know, I see now why Damian is always threatening Jeremy with violence. There is no one as infuriating as a sibling. I never said there was anything—I just meant that—" She abruptly stopped speaking. "I wish you wouldn't be so aggravating!"

"I'm your sister. I am designed to aggravate you. And to poke my head in your business. I'm going to be intensely provoking at every opportunity."

"You won't need to *try*," Anya retorted.

"If you mean to let me back into your life, then you'll have to put up with it." Now Lila was eyeing her sideways.

Anya tried to keep her eyes determinedly facing forward, but then she couldn't. "Do you mean to let me back into your life, Lila?" Here it was. The question. She hadn't meant to ask it. At least not yet. There was too much else that needed her attention.

They were silent for a moment or two. "I did invite you to my wedding, Anya," Lila said at last. "Why would I have done that if I didn't want you back in my life?"

"Why did you invite Mira and me?" Anya couldn't help asking. "Because we are your sisters?"

"You said something like it before," Lila said, glancing at her. "And no, I didn't do it because it was the proper thing to do." She made an impatient noise. "I suppose it isn't so much why am I trying to reconcile now, Anya, don't you see? It's more why I waited for so long. I should have done it years ago!"

Something was stuck in Anya's throat. It was hard to put it into words. She jerked her head. Her voice was softer when she spoke. Almost like she was speaking to herself. "It's like you know you should do something. Even that you want to. But doing it is much, much harder than not. And—"

"Time passes," Lila said.

Anya nodded. "Yes, time passes." Lila looked like she was going to say more, but Anya placed an urgent hand on her arm to forestall her. "Lila, I want to talk about this. I want to talk to you." She flicked her head. "No, that isn't quite true. I half want to and half dread it. Do you understand?"

Lila gave a short nod.

"But right now, right now I must focus on what is happening to Damian—to Lord Ashton. I have to sort this mess out. Or at least try to help. Do you understand?"

"I had no intention of speaking of it today," Lila said at once. "You are right. And I completely agree. We must sort out the other mess first." But she placed an urgent hand on Anya's arm. "But, Anya, promise me you won't disappear from my life before we've had a chance to talk."

Anya nodded. Her throat was impossibly tight, and she didn't feel like she could have said anything anyway. Nothing coherent, at any rate. But then she did say one thing. "Don't imagine that I'm not grateful to you."

Lila waved a hand. "I don't want your gratitude. Perhaps when this is all over, you could come and see me down in Sussex."

Lila's husband, Ivor, owned an estate near Rye in Sussex. Since her marriage to him, Lila had given up her gambling salon and opened a school for prostitutes there, to get education, to get training in a respectable profession, to have their children and give them up for adoption if they wanted, or to educate them and keep them if they preferred. Anya realized now that she would love to go down there and see it.

"Don't answer now," Lila said briskly. "Come to this prizefight tonight. It is out in the open fields; it will be cold as the devil. And you'll have to wrap up warm. It is rumored that Molyneaux is in the lineup. Despite his loss to Cribb last year, you know everyone still thinks he's the only true champion. It will be fun. But it will also give Ivor a chance to speak with you. He goes about society because of his businesses. He knows what people are saying. He wants to help. We both do. Say you'll come, Anya."

24

Later that day, before she left the palace to make her way to Damian's so they could head to the prizefight, she found Trixie sitting in a room off the kitchens and embroidering a cushion cover. Or rather, she was embroidering the cushion cover with her hands but had a book on something or the other propped up in front of her on a sturdy wooden table, held open with a heavy pestle-and-mortar set, and it was clear that her head wasn't really in the embroidery. Anya clucked her tongue when she saw her, and Trixie pricked her thumb. "Oh, heaven, Anya, you scared the life out of me!" She was sucking on the blood.

"What are you reading?"

"It's about newfangled machines in factories."

"I cannot imagine a subject more designed to put me to sleep!"

Trixie smiled. "But it's so interesting. They are planning to use them in farming and all kinds of other enterprises."

Anya watched her protégé in some amusement. Trixie had far surpassed her in learning. And Anya knew she had to accept that she herself would be able to do little for the young woman.

Not in a material sense, anyway. "Trixie, you know my sister Lila? Or at least I have told you about her."

Trixie looked a little surprised but nodded.

"I've told you she used to run a gaming salon?"

"It sounds exciting. Better than living in the palace. But it sounds even more wonderful to be your own person, to have the independence to do what you please."

"Yes, exactly! And you see, Trixie, the thing is, she gave up the salon when she married. Her husband and she live half the time in London now and half the time in his home in Sussex, and she's opened up some kind of school there for prostitutes and other women down on their luck so she can train them for some or the other respectable profession. If they want it. And for their children, if they have any."

"I see." Trixie still sounded like she didn't know where this was going. But she was listening.

"Look, I haven't spoken to Lila about this, and I can't make any promises. And I wanted to speak to you first. But I can't help thinking about it, Trixie. All your learning is wasted here. If you stay here, you'll have to become a palace servant, and no amount of learning will help you overcome your lack of social standing. And as for the prospect of my marriage, it is starting to seem like it was always a hopeless project." She hesitated, not sure how Trixie would take it. And it was still a half-formed thought in her own mind. "Thing is, I was wondering, shall I speak to Lila about you? You know so much. You could help in her school. You could learn." She stopped abruptly. She had hardly articulated the thought to herself properly, and here she was, blurting it out. The idea had come to her when she was speaking to Lila earlier.

Trixie had put down the embroidery. Her eyebrows were raised. "Then I won't be anywhere near you," she said now.

Anya looked guiltily at her. Trixie was so knowledgeable and so pragmatic it was easy to forget she was only sixteen. "Trixie, what if I can't bring myself to marry any of them? Not Darren Greenwood, not anyone else. What then?"

"I don't want you to marry just for me," Trixie said, a frown on her brow. "But to be sent away—"

Anya grabbed her protégé's arms. "To be sent away! What a goose you are! That is not what I meant at all. I just meant that—oh, I've made a hash of it by speaking too soon. But I worry about you here, and you are very young. And look at how clever you are. You think I can teach you anything more? Your books can, I know that, so you don't need to say it, but what then? What will happen to all your book learning? Tell me you'll give it some thought. And use your brain and not some misbegotten sense of loyalty to me!"

She managed to elicit a nod out of Trixie and had to be satisfied with that. Trixie looked not excited but a little forlorn at the idea, and Anya knew she'd have to give Trixie time to think about it. If Trixie did take her up on the offer, not to mention if Lila was agreeable, then that would at least solve one problem. Of course, Anya would have no one left in the palace who was her friend or supporter. But that was a selfish, selfish thought.

Later in the evening, Anya found herself sitting next to Damian in an open carriage, wrapped in her greatcoat and scarves, her breath puckering the air, watching two men fighting bare-chested and bare-knuckled in a cordoned-off ring in the open fields.

In the carriage next to them were Lila and Ivor, and it was hard to say which of the two was enjoying the brutal fight between Molyneaux the famous boxer and his opponent, Power, more. Even Anya had to admit that there was something thrilling about it. The men had little fear, and punches were flying at all the sensitive parts of the body. Their faces were already bloody and swelling. They had moments of quiet, when they held each other close, almost intimately, bare hands about each other's necks, sweat mingling, breath merging, and then the blows would land again and the skirmishes would be too fast to capture properly.

The crowd was suffering from collective hysterics. The ring was surrounded by carriages. Not only did carriages clot thickly around the cordoned area where the men were in combat, but in fact there were carriages behind those, and more behind *those*, and many people were standing up on their carriages to look over the crowd in front of them. There was a lot of shouting and screaming and women threatening to faint and men promising to join the fight, not to mention quite a lot of booing. There were people of all social classes. People in spanking-new carriages. People in rented vehicles. Farm workers standing where they could or climbing up behind a carriage if its owner didn't mind. There were women too, farm workers *and* sisters and daughters and wives of men of society. Prizefights like these weren't allowed in the city. But here, there was no one to stop it.

Lila's face was glowing, and she was yelling like the best of them. And Anya, though gasping when something especially gory happened—or if one of the fighters landed hard on the ground, which seemed to happen every minute or so—couldn't help thinking that this was nice.

It was strangely normal. To be sitting here on the open carriage with Damian, who had put several guineas on the chances of Molyneaux winning, next to her sister and her husband, as if they were just a normal couple, she and Damian, and like Lila and she were just normal sisters.

It was cold, and she was watching two men apparently trying

to kill each other, but still—it was a moment she would cherish once this was all over. A moment she could revisit for years. A moment when everything felt normal. A shiver went through her at the thought. A shiver, she thought, of foreboding.

If Anya had thought that they would watch the fighting for a short while and spend the rest of the evening talking about Damian's predicament, she was sadly mistaken. There was no getting Lila and Ivor to focus on anything while the bouts were going on, and Damian didn't have a thought for anything but the punishing rights and the bruising lefts being thrown in the ring either. Men and women all around them were shouting encouragement and advice. The men who were helping the boxers recover between the rounds were offering their boxer a knee to sit on. The men weren't even freezing. There was sweat flying everywhere.

It was only after all the rounds were over that Anya found herself walking in the grounds with her three companions. There were still crowds of people in the grounds, many spectators lingering after the boxing was over, still in a fever of excitement after the matches, wanting to discuss everything they'd seen in great detail.

Lila walked with her hand snugly entwined in the crook of Ivor's arm, but Anya didn't feel like she could do that with Damian. It made her shy, this sudden public domain in which she had never spent time with Damian before. She realized she'd never so much as touched his hand outside the confines of his house before, not where other people could see it. The novelty of it was stunning. He seemed unconcerned by it. He had been looking grim ever since that day in Parliament and with all the news of the growing rumors, but tonight was the first time he'd looked relaxed. She could only be thankful.

"I wanted to meet you and discuss some things with you," Ivor said, breaking into her thoughts.

And just like that, the grim look was back on Damian's face, and Anya wished Lila's husband hadn't ruined the moment. Ivor was powerful-looking. Taller than average, but also built almost like one of the pugilists they had just been watching. Not quite as broad and muscular, but very strong-looking. He had dark hair and a serious face, and he looked like he was used to taking charge, yet Anya couldn't help noticing the warm glow with which he looked at Lila, how his eyes rarely strayed far from his wife, how he noticed when she was getting bored, yet wasn't afraid to fight his corner when he needed to—which was a lucky thing if you were Lila's husband.

"Do you have to go and spoil the evening, Ivor?" Lila said. Lila was one of those women, Anya thought, who looked even more beautiful when she was freezing, her cheeks pink, her nose pinched, her eyes sparkling, making her midnight dress even darker and more mysterious.

"Yes, darling," Ivor said.

"It's very boring of you," Lila complained. "I was hoping for a lengthy session of deep analysis of the fights we just watched."

"I'll give you a lengthy session when we're back home, if you wish," Ivor murmured.

Lila went a bright pink.

A look passed between husband and wife that was almost too intimate to witness.

It sent a sudden and unexpected pang through Anya. It wasn't the promise that silently passed between Lila and Ivor, but how comfortable they were with each other, how together. How they sometimes seemed not like two people but two parts of a whole.

She was wondering if it was ever possible to see other people's closeness without feeling horribly alone yourself when she felt a hand on her back. It was Damian. She turned her head to look at him and he gave her a little smile. A little smile that seemed to understand how she felt, being here with Lila and Ivor.

She should have felt infinitely reassured. But instead it made her feel lonelier than ever. Because she knew it was temporary, what she had with Damian. He didn't care for anyone but Jeremy. He never pretended he did. He didn't make a home in London. He had no interest in society life. He would leave for Folkestone soon. And then the gap in her life would be harder to bear because he had temporarily filled it. He was looking at her questioningly now, but she couldn't smile back. The night suddenly felt unbearably cold. And Anya wished she was back home. Not in the dream she had with Damian, but back in the palace, back to her real life. Why had she forgotten it so easily, thrown it off like a cloak as soon as he came into her life? How had she forgotten what her life was really like?

Ivor broke the silence. "You must know that the rumors about your hand in Arnold Ashton's death have grown exponentially in the last two weeks."

"Yes," Damian said. "I do know. I could hardly help knowing." He was looking straight ahead as they walked, not turning to look at Ivor. "As it happens, I didn't do it."

"That's none of my business," Ivor said. "Do you have any idea what to do about it?"

Damian was silent, a frown creasing his brow, and Anya suddenly thought how exceptional it must be for him to be offered help of any kind. She realized suddenly that though *he* said he cared for and looked out for Jeremy, there was no one to do the same for him. It hadn't occurred to her before, not like this.

"I can't imagine why you'd have any thoughts on this at all, Tristram," he said, with that aloof tone of his. He sounded a little stiff. No, not a man who easily accepted help.

His words were mild enough, but the tone was clear. This was no one's business but his own. Anya looked at Ivor out the corners of her eyes, wondering what Lila's husband would say now.

To her surprise, instead of taking offense, Ivor nodded. "I understand that. And respect it. But my wife and I think, given that you are Anya's—trustee—that your reputation is important to us."

Trustee! Anya nearly laughed out loud.

As if that's what Lila was most concerned about. If *that* was Lila or Ivor's real concern, Anya would take off her muff and eat it. It wasn't that particular relationship between Anya and Damian that her sister was mainly concerned about. Really, this was too much. If Damian told them to go to the devil, it would be exactly what the two deserved. What right had they to poke into her and Damian's relationship? She waited for Damian to give some horribly ironic response.

"You're right," Damian said, somewhat to her shock. "Perhaps it is your concern, then."

She turned to look at him in surprise, but he wasn't looking at her. She turned to look at the couple walking on the other side of her.

Ivor spoke again. "I'm glad you think so."

Was she imagining it, or was there a new note of respect in his voice? Almost as if this had been a test of some kind and Damian had passed it. Almost as if Ivor had dared Damian to acknowledge his relationship with Anya. And Damian had—what? Acknowledged it? Anya didn't think she'd ever understand men.

"The thing is," Ivor said, breaking into her thoughts, "I've looked into it and the report always said that Arnold Ashton was murdered by a highwayman."

"Yes," Damian responded.

"If you didn't do it, and no one you know did it for you, then it could be that a highwayman was in fact responsible."

Damian frowned. "Yes."

"Then we must find this highwayman!" Lila said. "It's obvious, isn't it? Ivor and I have been talking about it. The Runners gave up at the time. But then, that is *exactly* what I expect of Runners. They are a shockingly useless breed."

"If there is such a highwayman, when he knew he had killed someone, he may have changed turfs," Ivor added. "Maybe that's why no one has found him."

"But we think now that two years have passed, there's always the chance he could have come back to his old turf, or not have gone too far in the first place. Highwaymen like their turfs," Lila said, as if she had personally done a detailed study on the habits of highwaymen.

Even Damian looked amused. "And you know this—how?"

Ivor looked a little sheepish. "I'm afraid Hector—my man— and I didn't spend an innocent youth. This is the kind of thing you pick up when you know all kinds of people."

"Do you think we can find this highwayman?" Anya asked— torn between excitement and skepticism. Now that Damian wasn't taking offense at Ivor and Lila's interference, she found herself getting caught up in the discussion too. And this—this search for the highwayman—this had been on her mind too.

"We can try," Ivor said. "But I didn't want to make any inquiries without consulting with you first, and without getting a more detailed account of your movements on that night."

Anya wondered again if Damian would answer Ivor's question. Or if he would go all Damian again. But he again surprised her. He again went over his final—and in fact, only—meeting with Arnold Ashton. Anya noticed that he didn't mention that Linus was the one other person who knew about the meeting. She dithered, feeling like it was wrong to leave out this detail. How could they look into what really happened to Arnold Ashton, unless they had all the facts?

"Did anyone else know about this meeting?" Ivor asked. "Or did Ashton bring anyone with him? A valet, a groom?"

Damian didn't answer at once. Then said, "He brought no one with him."

He was avoiding her eyes. Anya gritted her teeth. His loyalty to Linus went too far. What did she have to say or do to convince him to look squarely at all the facts? Ivor too was giving Damian a sharp look. He had noticed that only one of his questions had been answered. A sharp man, Ivor Tristram. But he didn't pursue it. Sharp *and* intuitive.

They discussed the question some more. Damian and Ivor discussed some of the inquiries each could make, and Anya was at least relieved to see that making plans with Ivor Tristram seemed to be having a positive effect on Damian. That was something at least. She couldn't help thinking how lucky Lila was to be with this man. And Ivor, he looked like he believed he was the luckiest man in the world to be with Lila.

At the end of the evening, Lila and Ivor said that they would drive to Damian's house first because Lila wanted to write a note for Jeremy—he was out of town to visit friends—to invite him and Kenneth Laudsley to something or the other.

The drive wasn't a short one, and Anya was all but asleep by the time they pulled up outside Damian's rented house. The carriages were parked, and the four walked up to Damian's house.

It was a good couple of hours after midnight. A group of five laughing people had also just got out of their carriages and were walking up to the house next to Damian's. Anya recognized them as Damian's neighbors, the Pembrokes, and their friends who were renting the house next door for the season. Damian stopped to exchange a word or two with the party, made up of two colorfully dressed women and three men, all of whom seemed to be in a very good mood. They had apparently been to the pleasure gardens and had clearly danced and drunk too much. Everyone was in a very good mood. Lila was telling the party about the fights they had watched. They were listening raptly to her detailed description.

They were talking and walking in the direction of the two houses, and were next to Damian's house, when a shadow peeled itself off the wall and Anya, whose head was woolly from the lateness of the hour and the long ride, almost screamed.

"Lord Ashton, is it?" the man asked. The man was thin and pale-looking, and not tall, and he had curiously light gray eyes. He introduced himself as Mr. Sowerby.

"Have the Bow Street Runners started accosting people in the middle of the night outside their homes?" Damian asked mildly.

"Had a few run-ins with the law before, have you, my lord?" Sowerby asked.

"How can I help you?"

"You can find your man Linus Temperance, my lord, and hand him over to us."

Anya's heart started thudding. Linus. So Clara Budleigh had reported the theft of her reticule. That must be it. Why else would the Runners be looking for Linus? The party of five—the Pembrokes and their friends—were giving one another curious glances, and Anya noticed they were staying where they were and not giving her group privacy.

"And why would I do that?" Damian asked, still in that mild way.

"Do we have to do this in the middle of the night, man?" Ivor asked Sowerby.

"When it's freezing and our noses are about to fall off," Lila added.

Anya wondered how they could all keep their voices so calm. She was going numb with fear.

The women in the other party were giggling. A man said, "Come on, man. Let us get these women inside or we'll never hear the end of it."

Sowerby ignored them. "I've been waiting here for hours, and no one will let me into your lodgings, Lord Ashton. They say Linus Temperance isn't here."

"There's your answer, then," Damian said.

"There, that's your answer," one of the young men repeated.

"I'd like to search the property," the Runner said.

"That won't be possible," Damian said. "Though I'm mildly interested in knowing what you want my man for."

"For the murder of Arnold Ashton, my lord, that would be. At your instruction or not, remains to be seen."

Anya gasped. There was a palpable shift in mood. The women in the other party stopped giggling. Uncomfortable looks were exchanged. Ivor and Lila looked frozen too.

"What the devil would make you say that?" Damian asked, his brow dark.

"We've been given information, my lord, if you must know."

"By whom?" Damian demanded.

"Now, that's not for me to say, my lord. I can hardly give you his—or *her*—name. That's what they call confidential information."

Anya was staring at the Runner. Ivor Tristram was frowning. Lila looked like she was already trying to figure a way out. It was Damian, though. His face. He frowned at first, like he couldn't decipher the man's words. He was looking curiously at the Runner. But then his face changed. The creases of confusion left him. Suddenly and completely. His face went strangely blank. He wasn't looking at the Runner now, or at anyone else. He was looking only at Anya.

Anya almost jerked back at that look on his face. Not aggressive, not violent, never that. But completely and utterly faraway. It was like something had frozen in the depths of his eyes. She stared at him. She couldn't understand what the look meant. What had happened that she had missed? Her brain was numb and couldn't make sense of it. It took her some moments to realize that Damian thought that it was she who had informed against Linus Temperance. She instinctively reached out a hand.

But he looked away and spoke to the Runner. "Linus isn't here like my staff have already informed you. But perhaps you might like to come back at a more civilized hour?"

Her heart was beating painfully. Damian, after that first look, was not looking at her at all. It took the combined persuasion of Damian and Ivor to get the Runner to leave, which he did reluctantly. The Pembrokes finally took their leave, but Anya could see the wary looks they were giving Damian. Did they already believe he was guilty? That his man had killed Arnold Ashton, at his instruction? She cursed their luck at bumping into the Pembrokes. She wondered how quickly the news would get around town.

After the Runner left, Ivor said seriously to Damian, "This has suddenly got worse. If they think your man did it, they will think that you instructed him."

But Damian wasn't looking at any of them. Gone was the way he had confided in Ivor. "It's too late to do anything about it right now," he said, a little coolly. "I'll have to look into it in the morning."

Lila and Ivor glanced at each other at the sudden, cool tone. Anya knew it well. Oh, she knew that aloof tone. Her heart was freezing more at every moment that passed.

"We can take Anya back to the palace," Lila offered, watching Damian warily.

She'd caught on quickly, her sister, and noticed the shift in mood. Damian didn't answer. He still wasn't looking at Anya.

"Thank you," Anya said, her voice seemingly coming from a long way away. She felt it was strange, talking in this way about who would escort her home, when her heart was freezing with every moment that passed.

Lila and Ivor retreated to their carriage to give Anya a moment to say goodbye. She looked at Damian. It took some moments, but when he did finally look at her, the remote look in his eyes may as well have been a punch in the guts. "You could at least have told me," he said, in a voice she hadn't heard before. It wasn't his aloof or ironic voice. Not his warm one that was only for Anya. It was something else. Something so cold and so unforgiving that she had no words. But behind the cold, there was hurt. Yet behind that was something even worse. Almost like he had been proven right, that she couldn't be trusted. Like he had known all along that she would turn out to be like everyone else.

She turned the ring on her finger round and round. She should speak, say something, tell him she'd never do something like that. However much she wanted him to talk to Linus, perhaps let the Runners talk to him, she'd never go behind his back. All she had to do was tell him. But what was the point? He believed that she could. What else could possibly matter?

"I'll take your leave, Lord Ashton," she said.

Her voice was cold. There was a crack in it that she thought would never heal. She'd said the words. But she wanted, more than anything, for him to say, *Of course not, come inside, let's talk about it.* But he didn't. He didn't say anything at all.

She made herself turn and walk away in the direction of Lila and Ivor's carriage, knowing all of a sudden clearly and surely that he wouldn't call and stop her from leaving. Even though she knew, she *knew,* if she left now, there would be something final and irrevocable about it.

25

There was no rest for Damian, not that night and not on the ones that followed.

The first thing to do was to get Linus out of the country. Tuppence had shut Linus in the basement when the Runner had come calling. That's where Damian found him when he walked back into the house and Tuppence came to him nearly in tears, saying they were all going to be strung up in the gallows if anyone found out that Linus was in fact still in the house. Damian made his way to the cellars. Linus was lying on the floor of the basement, no doubt covered in the dust and cobwebs of decades, staring at the ceiling and singing a bawdy song.

Damian rolled up a keg and sat on it, feeling a little resigned. "Do you have to be drunk right now, Linus? There isn't much time to be lost if we are to get you to France."

Linus sat up and swayed ominously. Damian couldn't help thinking that when Linus was drunk and singing a stupid song, he wasn't that different from the fourteen-year-old urchin who had stolen from him outside a shop on Oxford Street. He'd taken Damian's money but also a silk handkerchief. Damian let him keep the handkerchief, and Linus still sometimes wore it tied around his wrist.

"I didn't murder that man, sir, Mr. Ashton, my lord," he said and hiccupped. "Whatever they're saying 'bout me. I didn't do it."

Damian sighed. He had managed to teach some sense of cleanliness and certainly loyalty to Linus, but his drinking habit only seemed to have gotten worse over the years. "I know that. But there might be no way to prove it. They could hang you one way or another. And if they think I put you up to it, then I won't be able to save you. We have to get you across the border."

"I don't speak no heathen tongue, sir, Mr. Ashton, my lord. What will I do in France with those Frenchies?"

Damian had to admit it was hard to imagine Linus anywhere but here. For a few short years of his life, he'd lived up north. But Linus was firmly a London man now. It was nearly impossible to imagine him in a different country. "I'll send you to some friends who'll find you work. Now get up, drink something that will sober you up, get clean, and we'll have you to Dover as soon as we can. You might have to lie low for a day or two, but I'll book you passage to France."

Damian stood up. There was no time to be lost, but still he might not be able to get passage right way. And the Runner would be back tomorrow and insist on searching the house. He would insist on turning the place inside out, in fact. Linus would have to go somewhere else before he could be shipped off to Dover.

"Tuppence has an uncle who runs a taproom not far from Tothill Fields, doesn't she? Can you stay there for a day or two?"

Linus nodded and hiccupped loudly. Damian turned to leave the cellar.

"Sir, what makes the Runner think it were me that did that bloke Arnold Ashton in?"

Damian turned reluctantly. He had been hoping Linus was too drunk to ask that question. "I trusted in the wrong person. You'll have to forgive me. I told someone that you knew about my appointment with Arnold Ashton that night."

"Who, sir, if I may be so bold as to ask?"

Damian hesitated. "Miss Marleigh," he said shortly.

Linus looked impassively at him. Then said, "Not like you to let a pretty face bamboozle you, sir."

Damian felt a sliver of irritation at Linus calling Anya a pretty face in that insolent way. Anya didn't like Linus, didn't trust him, but Damian was sure it was a mutual feeling. Yet Linus was right. Damian hadn't ever let a face, pretty or not, betray him like this before. He had always been so careful about whom he let in. He felt cold, just cold. He felt nothing, in fact. There was a blank where there had been his feelings for Anya.

He was about to walk out again when Linus said, "What if I did tell someone where the geezer was going to be, sir, that night?" His voice was uncharacteristically hesitant. "What if I blurted it out to someone when I was in me cups, sir, and then later forgot I did it?"

Damian turned again. "Well, did you?"

Linus shook his head. "I can't remember. Not fully. You know how I am."

Damian considered him. "I know how you are. And to tell you the truth, Linus, if you *did* tell someone where Arnold Ashton would be that night, what of it? You didn't know he was going to get murdered. But the truth is, it doesn't matter at this point. I doubt that *you* murdered the man and then forgot all about it. But the Runners won't care about that. They could still hang you, whether you did it or not. Let's not stand about wasting time, Linus. Let's find a way to get you out of here first."

Not an hour later, Linus was smuggled out of the house and packed off to Tuppence's uncle's taproom, where he was instructed to lie low for a day or two, until a passage could be booked to Calais and he could be sent off to Dover without attracting too much attention.

It was funny, Damian thought a couple of days later, after he finally managed to book Linus passage on a ship that was to leave Dover in three days, that the numbness of the first night had gone.

In fact, right now, everything was proving infernally aggravating.

The booking of the passage took far longer than it needed. The clerk was bored, the passage dates and times uncertain, and the whole transaction was carried out in a musty, airless office that seemed to have forgotten to leave the eighteenth century behind. The number of forms that had to be filled surely were only designed to make you die a slow death. Then his carriage broke an axle as he was heading back home. And the traffic coming up to his house was stalled for what felt like hours.

He was in a foul mood as he walked briskly up the steps to his rented house in Mayfair. Even the door and the knocker seemed hopelessly worn and the paint peeling. Why was he renting this decrepit old place? Didn't he have any standards? Didn't he have staff that should remind him he had standards? He walked in through the door and flung his gloves on the side table in the foyer.

He was about to call to Linus when he remembered the man wasn't there and was still in Tothill Fields, at Tuppence's uncle's place, waiting for word from Damian. He frowned, looking irritably about him. He shrugged off his coat and tried to hang it up, but it kept falling off. He cursed heavily. It was time to go home to Folkestone. As soon as possible. It wouldn't do to travel to Dover with Linus. He had to send him off anonymously, ideally on a stagecoach. Or stowed away with someone he could trust. Once Linus was safely out of the country, it was time for Damian to head back to Folkestone. Maybe the rumors about Damian's hand in Arnold Ashton's death would die down when he was no longer in town. Or maybe they wouldn't. He didn't know if he cared. Maybe he should just sell the estate in Folkestone and live somewhere different. None of it mattered anyway.

He called to Mrs. Garner, who came up from the kitchen, and before he could ask her if he could have some coffee brought up, she started telling him about all the things he needed to pay attention to. The hot tap in the bath wasn't working. There was no chicken in the house for his dinner because the one they had was old and dried up. Tuppence was distracted from her duties these last two days. Jane Simmonds, who was an excellent housemaid, had made off back to Folkestone willy-nilly several days ago. Couldn't she stay in London instead of minding an empty house in Folkestone? Oh, and Linus was nowhere to be found.

Mrs. Garner was very round and very muscular and had a heavy and habitual frown at the best of times. This was apparently not the best of times. She was practically glaring murderously at him.

Damian's irritation went up several notches. He said impatiently, "Mrs. Garner, can't you solve these problems yourself? Isn't that what I employ you for?"

She was taken aback at his tone. His voice was irritable and his words rude. He was never rude to his employees. He gritted his teeth. Really, was this the time for faulty taps and aging chickens?

She drew herself up to full height. "Well, my lord, if I am not giving you adequate service, you will of course let me know."

He bristled some more. "Of course, *you* will let me know if you can no longer carry out your normal duties," he found himself saying. Good god, what was wrong with him? He never said things like that to his staff.

Jeremy walked in through the front door as he was saying the words and he and Mrs. Garner were in the middle of a heavy staring contest. Mrs. Garner was bristling, and probably on the verge of handing in her notice, but then withdrew to the kitchens, muttering that there were other more congenial households and there she wouldn't have to put up with broken taps and distracted housemaids and employers who didn't like her work. Moreover, *there* she wouldn't have to deal with the man of the house.

"Everything all right, brother?" Jeremy said, his voice casual enough, but with a keen look in his eyes that Damian knew very well.

So he hadn't missed the uncharacteristic rudeness. Jeremy wouldn't. He didn't miss much. He had a mud-spattered, wind-blown look, but still that fresh-faced Jeremy look that should have been soothing. But instead, the keen, discerning look was irritating. Did Jeremy have to look at him like that? "Where have you been?" Damian snapped. "I could have done with some help these last couple of days. But of course you are nowhere to be found when you're needed. I suppose you had a good time with your friends in Oxfordshire?"

Jeremy took his coat and gloves off and looked squarely at Damian. "What's happened?"

Damian led the way into the front parlor and in a few short

words filled Jeremy in on the events of the last two days since the Runner Sowerby had turned up at the house in the middle of the night, looking for Linus.

"Linus?" Jeremy frowned. "What makes them think he had anything to do with Arnold Ashton's death?"

"I suppose because they want to pin it on me. It must seem like a good, solid bet to accuse a man who's too low in social standing to defend himself. The Runner has come back and searched the house twice since then. He's convinced I'm harboring Linus."

"But what's made the Runners suspect Linus at all?"

Damian hesitated. Then jerked his head impatiently. "Miss Marleigh gave them information."

Jeremy was sitting on one of the armchairs and now he leaned forward. "Anya? That's not possible."

Damian turned away and started looking through some correspondence. "She didn't deny it. And she had been trying to convince me to let the Runners speak to Linus. She knew— I told her that I had spoken to Linus about Arnold Ashton's movements on that night two years ago. She's the only one that knew."

"But a casual highwayman could have murdered Arnold Ashton. Why does it have to be someone who knew exactly where he was?"

"Because nothing was stolen. A casual highwayman doesn't bother shooting someone and then not even taking the man's watch or money. And I suppose the worst of it is that I arranged to meet Ashton there. That's the most suspicious thing of all. And people *want* to pin it on me."

Jeremy didn't speak for a few moments. Then said, "It doesn't sound like Anya."

"I'm sure she was just trying to protect me."

"And is that such a bad thing to do?"

Damian could feel Jeremy's eyes looking steadily at him. He kept his own turned away. He was staring unseeingly at the correspondence in his hands. "It doesn't matter."

"Doesn't it?"

"It's done. And it teaches me a much-needed lesson."

A pause again. "And what is that, brother?"

Damian turned to walk out of the room. "Oh, simply whom to trust."

"Is that what it is?" Jeremy asked, his voice deceptively soft behind him.

Damian didn't have time for this. He stopped and turned to look impatiently at his brother. "If you have something to say to me, just say it, Jeremy."

Jeremy came to his feet. "Nothing much, brother. But it looks a lot to me like you're putting a barrier between yourself and Anya."

"Don't be ridiculous. If anything, she's the one that's wedged a barrier between us by what she did."

Jeremy looked uncharacteristically serious. Even grim. "Damian, I never interfere in your life. I certainly would never interfere with anyone—any woman—you chose to have in your life or not. We've never done anything like that to each other. And your understanding in—in my relationship with—I'm eternally grateful."

Damian looked at him. Waiting for it. And here it was.

"If you think Anya did this, that she informed against Linus behind your back—if you really believe that—then speak to her. By cutting her off you're only—"

"What?" Damian demanded.

"You're only protecting yourself, Damian."

Damian's face was like thunder now. "As I should have done from the start. I opened up to her in a way that I've never let myself open to anyone. And I made a mistake. I didn't just tell her my secrets. I told her something about Linus. That he was a thief when I met him. That he was—and is—a drunk. She's never trusted him. And to tell you the truth, I don't need her to trust him. But she could have trusted me." He jerked his head. "There's nothing more to say. There are things I need to do. And I need to head back to Folkestone. If you want to stay in London, then I'll hold on to these lodgings for you." He turned to leave the room again.

But Jeremy wasn't done. His tone was still gentle when he spoke. Almost casual. "You know, I don't hold it against you, Damian."

Damian really shouldn't ask. He didn't *want* to ask. He knew his brother very well, and that deceptively casual tone. He *wouldn't* ask. He ground his teeth as he turned to face Jeremy again. "What exactly don't you hold against me?"

"That you're terrified of your feelings. I suppose it's only because you're not used to having any."

Damian stared at his little brother. "Are you saying I'm a cold-hearted bastard?"

"Oh no, nothing of the sort. All I'm saying is you're a coward."

Thus saying, his little brother brushed past him and left the room. Leaving Damian frozen to the spot.

26

All Anya would have liked to do after that night in Highgate Commons was avoid her sister Lila.

It was bad enough what happened with Damian—though Anya was determined to think as little about it as she could—but to have to dissect it with Lila, which was exactly what Lila would want, no, that was unthinkable. This, *this* was the kind of thing where it would be much better not to have a sister in your life at all. They had the tendency to know an uncomfortable amount about you, about the way your mind and heart worked, and they had no qualms about using the information against you.

Anya felt that she had armed herself against whatever Lila could throw at her. When the messenger brought the summons that Anya had a guest, she had a good mind to get him to tell Lila that she was busy, but here Lila was, a couple of days after Highgate Commons, ostensibly helping Anya thread ribbons through some baskets Trixie had been weaving, but really watching her carefully from under her eyelashes. Anya avoided looking back at her for as long as she could, by keeping her eyes focused on her threading. And really, it was only after a *lot* of staring from Lila that Anya couldn't hold it in.

"What?" she said. They were sitting in one of the orangeries at the back of the palace. Not the one in which Charlie Budleigh had died, but another one in which lived potfuls of bougainvillea from British trading posts around the world. White, bright purple, and a vivid orange, it made the orangery look like it was full of exploding fountains.

Lila looked innocently at her. "What?"

"You know, maybe those big innocent eyes of yours work with Ivor, who has less experience of you. You can't fool me."

"Oh no, not at all," Lila said, smoothing out a bit of green ribbon she had just threaded into one of the baskets. "He finds it infuriating too. Just as much as you. And *you* don't have to live with it every day like he does."

"Poor man," Anya said with feeling.

"I feel bad for him too. But in the end, it's good for him. Now, do not distract me." Lila looked squarely at her with those owl eyes of hers. "Will you speak to me about what happened with Damian Ashton the other night? You know my Hannah, don't you? She would call herself my lady's maid, but I would call her my manager. She has a sister, and they don't see one another a lot, but whenever her sister Lucy, who lives in Somerset, comes around to visit, they disappear for hours into some corner of the house where no one can find them and only come out when they have shared every single detail of their lives with each other at great length." Lila smiled. "I always think that's the right way to go for sisters."

"Oh, you do, do you?" Anya said with asperity. "Lovely. So, tell me, dear sister, how is it that you and Ivor are not already on the way to becoming parents?" Take that, Lila. Two could play at this game. "Since we are sharing intensely private details that need not concern anyone but ourselves, perhaps you could enlighten me on this point."

But Lila, as usual, looked unruffled. "We are actively prevent-ing it. Don't look so shocked. It is only for some time, until we are ready. In my work, I am surrounded by young prostitutes—most of them no older than your Trixie, some considerably younger—whose insides are in danger of being torn apart when they give birth. It does make one cautious. And, let me tell you, despite the condition they are in, there is no one as good as a prostitute at knowing how to delay pregnancy. The *things* they know. And not just about pregnancy. About all kinds of interesting things. Ask me anytime. It will make your eyes pop."

"You're not going to shock me, you know. So I wouldn't bother trying. I am not completely gauche and inexperienced." Anya couldn't help feeling torn between annoyance at her sister's nosiness and amusement that Lila, as usual, wanted to power through things, not dwell on difficulties, act as if the sisters were already close and not that they had to work at it. But here was a chance to talk about one thing, at least. "Lila, while we are on the subject of your work, I would very much like to come down to Sussex and see the work you do."

"I would like nothing better," Lila said at once. "Once all this mess is sorted out."

"Once it is sorted out, I would like to talk to you about Trixie." Anya embarked on the subject but then seemed to feel constrained, for some reason. "You see, I've taken her up and tried to educate her over the last few years. And she is clever and intelligent and so knowledgeable. And this opportunity to marry someone and claim my inheritance meant that she and I could both have some independence. But I wondered if—well, if it wouldn't be better if . . ." Anya stopped abruptly. She couldn't help feeling a little cross at how unsure she sounded.

"You know, I could do with someone like Trixie in my school," Lila said musingly. "Someone knowledgeable and young and intelligent, who wants more education, but can also help out."

Anya let out an exasperated sigh. "How like you to do me a favor and make it sound like it's me doing you one."

Lila's owl eyes looked at Anya. "I want to be back in your life, have I not made that clear? You are the one hesitating. I am merely trying to make things easier."

Anya gave a jerk of her head. "Lila, you can't make it seem like it's easy and uncomplicated, because it isn't."

"I am not asking to make it uncomplicated. I simply want to help. Something happened between you and Damian Ashton the other night. I think you care about each other—"

"No, no, we don't," Anya said. She came to her feet. "Yes, there was something between us. But it was—it was nothing. It clearly meant nothing to him and—and—"

Lila stayed where she was, one of Trixie's baskets in her lap, a length of purple silk ribbon in her hands. "It clearly meant something to both of you."

Anya looked at her sister in annoyance. "You know, Lila, you were always the nosy one. Mira had the grace to leave you alone. She knew when not to probe or fuss. *You* never did. Nothing has changed in all these years."

Lila sat there, looking up at her, and now—*drat the woman!*— there were large tears in those enormous eyes, and Anya quickly sat down again and grabbed her hands. "Lila, I don't mean it. You *know* I don't mean it. Of course, you are endlessly infuriating. But of course I want you back in my life." Lila, the wretch. How someone could put you in such a rage and then turn you to mush two seconds later was a mystery. And here she was, Anya, saying that she wanted Lila back in her life. She hadn't meant to touch on this subject yet. But how like Lila to rush.

Lila quickly batted her tears away. That was another thing about Lila. Anya had never known her to dwell on things or make someone who was apologizing feel worse. "Do you?" The tears were gone, but the hesitation in her voice was real.

Anya couldn't help but feel a little surprised. Even though she, of all people, knew how vulnerable Lila could be. "I do, Lila," she said. "I do want you back in my life—"

"But?"

Anya flicked her head.

Lila looked hesitantly at her. "I feel I have forced myself into your life. And though some of the time I think you want me there, and Ivor says he thinks so too, and that I must persist, at other times, I really wonder if you'd rather I left you alone. If Kenneth hadn't called me, if he hadn't told me you were in trouble, I wonder if you would ever have got in touch."

This was so unlike Lila that Anya sat more firmly down on the floor. And gripped those hands harder. The hands that were not like Anya's long fingers, but were a lot like their father's, strong and determined. "You *have* forced your way back into my life. Because that's just like you, Lila. It is exactly the kind of thing anyone that knows you and loves you would expect you to do. And you are nosy and confounding. *And*—well—you have no idea how much I've missed you."

Lila looked at her, her eyes large. "Have you?"

"Like a hole in my heart, Lila." The thing in her throat that was in danger of choking her was back. "I might not *want* to tell you every damn detail of my life. Yet, in my head, I turn to you when I have things to tell. I always know exactly the kind of thing you'll say back to me too. Most of it is enraging, but still."

Lila chuckled, wiped her nose with the back of her hand, and took a deep breath. "It wasn't just that we were sent off to schools in different parts of the country. Me in Yorkshire, you in Bath."

Anya quickly shook her head. "No, it wasn't just that. We've—we were hurt and separated before you went to school. You know, I was relieved when Sarah sent me off to Bath instead of to Yorkshire. I was actually *relieved*."

"As was I. I am desperate to be close to you and Mira again. I won't deny it. But many times in my life, I was relieved not to have to see you. Because—because—"

"Because it would mean being confronted with your own guilt. Don't think I don't know it, Lila. I *know*."

The relief in Lila's face was palpable. And Anya felt it course through her own veins. Yes, of course. The fact was simple. No one could know how she'd felt all these years, no one but Lila. And perhaps Mira. No one else knew the walls of guilt. The walls they'd built against each other. That had kept them out of each other's lives, and yet had always been no more than gaping holes. That guilt would have to be confronted. They would have to talk about the triplets. They would have to talk about the fact that the three of them had left the little toddlers behind, abandoned them. They would have to talk about how the three of them had allowed Sarah and Jonathan Marleigh to come between them, to wedge them apart.

"Lila, I know we must talk about it all. But right now—"

"Right now, we have to sort out the mess Damian Ashton is in. I know it."

Anya came to her feet again. "Right now," she said firmly, "I have to get dressed for a musical evening. It's a small gathering, but I must do my vocal practices. And I didn't get much sleep last night."

Lila came to her feet too and flounced out her skirts. "I won't press you now. I know you have other things you must deal with first. I know we have to talk about us—and our sisters. I know that too. I am not planning on breezing through it. I know you think it's what I'll do."

They walked out of the orangery, and Anya coursed around the palace to take Lila back to the front to drop her off.

Lila's tears were long gone, and now she was back to making light conversation again. "I shall look forward to seeing Trixie soon and speaking to her," she said.

Anya nodded.

"And your musical evening—will there be many people you know there?"

"Not many that I know. And even when there are, they see me as akin to the wallpaper, so even if I have met them before, it's not like I know them or they know me."

"Do you have many appointments these days?"

"One or two."

"And what happened with Damian the other night?"

Anya leaned forward and gave her sister a kiss on the cheek. "Nice try, Lila. But do go away before I throttle you, darling."

Lila hugged her back. "I suppose it was worth another shot," she said philosophically, before turning around and walking out toward the road.

27

The next night, Anya found herself walking near Tothill Fields with Jeremy Ashton at her side. The streets were mud-splattered after a morning of rain. The walls of the dwellings were soot-colored, and even though it was late afternoon and dark, and the fog was thick, there were still people lurking at street corners and calling out to them as they passed.

"Hot pie for sale, mister and missus, if you step inside wi' me, that is," someone called. "Juicy hot pie like ye've never tasted this side of the river."

"Room for the night, sir, or just for the hour, if it suits ye' better. Clean sheets for an extra penny!" said someone else.

"Oye, you're a beautiful bugger, ain't you?" called a woman. She placed sooty fingers between her lips and whistled.

"Was that woman soliciting you?" Anya inquired, holding her skirts up carefully against the worst of the mud and looking all about her like she'd entered a foreign country. Gone were the neat, pretty houses of the wealthy that were often arranged around perfectly maintained squares. In their place were dwellings nudging up to one another and often filthy and grubby and crumbling. They weren't far from the place people called the Devil's Acre, one of the foulest slums of the city.

"I thought she was soliciting you," Jeremy answered.

They were both dressed simply and unostentatiously for this outing, but Anya couldn't help feeling they stuck out by a mile. Out from the fog, men with missing teeth emerged, leering at Anya and asking if the pair of them wanted to come in and have a drink. Anya was sure it would be a very, very bad idea.

"You know, I shouldn't have let you convince me to come here. We are a hairbreadth from the Almonry, the worst slum in the city, and I've heard men disappear there, never to be found again."

"I'm surprised anyone returns from this place without all their hair turning white," Anya said. "But I have to speak to Linus Temperance, and this is my last opportunity. Once your brother has shipped him off, we will never know the truth." Jeremy had come around to the palace to tell her that Damian had told him what had happened and that Damian had managed to book a passage for Linus to France.

"Linus may know nothing more than Damian does," Jeremy cautioned, for the tenth time.

"Then we will be no worse off than we are now. Your brother may never want to speak to me again—and that is his choice!—but I can't simply turn my back and pretend everything is fine. That just because I am safe, I need not move another finger to help."

Thankfully, Tuppence's uncle's taproom turned out to be in a slightly better neighborhood. Still soot-covered but not as seedy as the other streets they had just passed.

They stared at the building. It was built on two floors, the windows were clouded over with fog, and the roof slanted as if trying to hide what was going on inside it. There was a cry and bustle coming from inside, noises of music and jolly dancing. But even here, there was a prostitute or two hanging near the door.

"It could look worse, I suppose," Anya said uncertainly.

"Tuppence's uncle will never tell us about Linus. Damian has given the man clear instructions—on pain of death—to not tell a soul he's harboring Linus."

They stared at the building. People went in and out of it. There seemed to be farmers and laborers and housemaids and men and women who had spent all day selling things and were now ready to let their hair down. Anya had the strange impulse to follow people in and pretend to be someone else, just for one night. But there was no point going in. No one was going to hand over Linus on a platter. Damian would have made sure of that.

They circled the building. It was clear that the kitchens were at the back. They debated the merits of smuggling themselves in through the kitchens and back doors and then searching the whole building. Neither one was too keen on the plan. And it was unlikely to work. They would undoubtedly be recognized as strangers and chucked out on their arses.

Surely, if Linus was living here, he'd be living upstairs? Before Jeremy could stop her, Anya stooped low, found a few pebbles, and hurled one to an upstairs window.

"What are you doing?" Jeremy hissed.

Anya hurled another one.

"Anya!" Jeremy said in an urgent whisper. "He may not be here at all!"

"Then it's just as well if we find out for sure."

She hurled another pebble. This one struck gold. A head poked out. Definitely not Linus's. It was a young girl, looking bored. She was pale, but clean enough. "What in hell d'ye think ye're doing?" she asked.

"Are you Mary?" Anya improvised. "My—uh—brother here wants a word with Mary."

She was leaning casually out of the window. Anya could see she had two pretty brown braids. "And why might your brother want a word with this Mary? Sounds shifty, if you ask me. Did he get her with child, yer brother?" She was picking her teeth with a spiky piece of wood.

"That is what he must speak to Mary about," Anya said.

"What is the *matter* with you?" Jeremy was whispering urgently. "Will you stop throwing me under the wheels of the nearest stagecoach?" He looked up at the girl. "Sorry to disturb you, Miss—uh—"

She sniggered. "Been a mighty long time since I saw such a juicy one as you, my lord. If Mary don't want you, there might be others who do, if you catch my drift."

Anya giggled. The girl giggled back. Jeremy looked thunderous. "I'm not a lord. Now—"

"You look like a lord. You sound like a lord. I say you're a lord."

Anya giggled again. Jeremy made an impatient noise. "It's not you we're here to see. And as for Mary, I will speak to her later," he said in a lofty voice. "It's the other bloke we're here to see. The one with the scar."

The girl's face became impassive. "No one here of that description." She was staring down at her fingernails.

"I bet you there are many men here of that description," Anya said. "What's your name?"

"Janet, miss."

"Janet, he's here, isn't he? The very tall, very skinny man with the scar running all down his face?"

"No, miss, no one like that. Now, you're keeping me from my duties—"

"He's really nice, isn't he, the man with the scar?" Anya tried. "Helpful in the taproom and around the house, I'm sure."

This struck gold too.

"That he is not! He's drunk half the time. Doesn't help out. Father doesn't like having him." She leaned forward conspiratorially. "But he can't afford to turn him out now, can he?"

"Can't he?"

"He's getting paid, Father. So he can't turn it down and throw the geezer out, can he?"

"Can we speak to him? Please?"

The girl turned mum again. Anya looked beseechingly at Jeremy. Looking resigned, he searched in his pockets and came up with coins.

The girl grinned. "Why didn't you say so in the first place, my lord? I'd produce my granny for a handful of that. Unless you want to come upstairs, that is. There's other things you could do for me, I reckon, and then I wouldn't even ask for those coins of yours."

Jeremy went a bright red. Anya grinned at Janet. "The coins are yours. My brother is—uh—promised to Mary, or I'm sure he would take you up on your kind offer. But we have to speak to this man with the scar."

At Anya's behest, Jeremy tossed up a coin or two that Janet caught with practiced ease. The girl disappeared and was gone for so long Anya was sure she was gone for good. Twenty minutes passed, and so many shady-looking men ventured by, some stopping to speak to them, some asking them for money, others looking strangely at them that Anya was sure they'd get murdered before they so much as discovered where Linus was hiding. She was about to say that they needed to think of something else when there was another noise. Someone appeared at the window, and this time it was Linus.

"Mr. Ashton, sir. Miss Marleigh," he said.

It was difficult to say which one he was less excited to see. Jeremy had warned her that Linus didn't trust anyone close to Damian. Anya didn't find this hard to believe. She sighed. "Linus, I wish you would come down and speak to us. We can't speak to you standing down here and you up there."

He was leaning on the sill now, not unlike the way Janet had been. He was also chewing on a thin stalk, hopefully not the same one as Janet. "What about, miss?" Linus asked.

"Can't you come down here, Linus?"

"What's the mad rush?"

"The rush!" Anya wanted to throttle the man, just because of how infuriatingly calm he sounded. "Aren't you imminently about to be shipped off to France?"

"And whose door shall I lay *that* at, miss?"

Anya clucked impatiently, but it was Jeremy who answered. "Linus, you and I have never been friends. I expect you will never be friends with any of Damian's friends. But I know you're loyal to him. I know you wouldn't have done anything that you thought could hurt him."

"That I wouldn't," Linus said.

"Arnold Ashton's murder *is* hurting him."

Anya was very impressed by the tack Jeremy was taking. It was obviously the right one. Asking Linus to help them—to help Anya and Jeremy—clearly would have been the wrong way to go. But asking him to help Damian out of a fix—that was the right approach. Anya knew she wouldn't have come up with so much smooth diplomacy.

"I didn't do it, believe me or don't," Linus said, looking as unemotional as he always did.

"But you knew where Arnold Ashton would be that night," Anya said.

Linus disappeared.

Anya nearly screamed after him. She growled in impatience instead. "What the devil is wrong with that man?"

"Hold on. I don't think he's done a bunk on us," Jeremy said.

And he was right. Because Linus appeared again. This time he climbed—with some difficulty—out of the tiny window frame and then agilely down the brick wall. Anya remembered he had enjoyed a varied career as a chimney sweep and a pickpocket.

Linus jumped down onto street level, and Anya remembered how tall and thin he was. He towered over her, and she had to crane her neck to look at his face. She noticed how light his eyes were, how hard to look into. She hadn't tried before. They'd been skirting around one another ever since they'd met.

"If we stand about here," he said, "someone will murder us. Me they'll murder just for the crime of standing with the two of you shiny pennies. Let's keep walking. Do you know how much you stick out, Mr. Ashton, Miss Marleigh, and did you think of maybe coming in disguise?"

Anya and Jeremy fell into step like obedient children. Anya had thought the plain brown wool dress she was wearing *was* a disguise.

"I did know where my lord was meeting Arnold Ashton," Linus said, as soon as the three of them were walking.

Anya couldn't help noticing that even though he didn't like her, Linus was keeping her shepherded between himself and Jeremy. She was strangely touched.

"Lord Ashton told me himself, but he didn't want me going with him. There was no call to. I wasn't his groom, just his valet." His eyes were shifting about. "The thing is, I've been giving it a lot of thought. Haven't had anything to do for the last four days. Holed up like I am. Tuppence's uncle don't want me anywhere near the taproom. Says if anyone sees me, I'm a goner. *And* they'll say he was harboring a murderer. And that won't be so good for him. Though the characters I see here, one more or less murderer is neither here nor there is my way of thinking. But I've been thinking about it, see?" He looked a little guilty now.

Anya could hardly keep herself from prodding him. But she had a feeling it was better to let Jeremy do the talking. There was a chance Linus was a smidge less disdainful of Jeremy.

"And?" Jeremy said.

"I've tried to talk to Lord Ashton about it, it's not like I've not. But he's in no mind to listen. And it's not my fault."

Anya's heart was pounding. What was Linus about to say? Then she couldn't contain herself. "You did it? You killed Arnold Ashton?"

He couldn't have looked more scornful if she were a worm under his shoe. "Miss Marleigh," he said in a bored-sounding voice, "like I said, I *didn't* kill the bloke. Didn't I say that?" he asked Jeremy.

Jeremy glanced once at Anya, then back at Linus, and nodded. "You did."

"Exactly. I did, sir, Mr. Ashton. As I was saying, I've been giving the matter some thought—"

"Dear god, and *what?*"

Linus looked cross now. "Miss Marleigh, if you'll stop jumping down a bloke's throat."

She was about to scream with impatience, but Jeremy clamped a warning hand around her wrist.

"The thing is, you might not have noticed it, but I like a wee drink now and again," Linus said.

The pressure around her wrist increased substantially. She made a small choking noise but didn't comment.

"When I have a drink or two," Linus continued, "I sometimes don't remember what I did or said or who I said it to the next day. And I've been wondering and wondering who I might have spoken to about that night."

"And?" Anya was nearly crawling out of her skin with impatience.

"And nothing," Linus said, unperturbed. "I've thought about it and thought about it, and I didn't tell anyone."

Anya looked at him, completely flabbergasted. "You've been building up to this for half an hour, to tell us that *you didn't tell anyone?*"

Linus actually looked a little surprised. "But it is important, Miss Marleigh," he said. "It's important that you know that I didn't tell anyone. I didn't betray Lord Ashton."

"Oh, dear god," Anya moaned. "After all this."

They walked in silence for a minute or two. They had circled the streets—at least Linus had; Jeremy and Anya had meekly followed—and were now back at the taproom. The noise and bustle in the taproom seemed to have doubled in the time they'd been walking. Clearly, this building was the place to be.

"But I do happen to know Neesy Elliot's new turf."

The man had clearly gone mad. Before Anya could clobber him, Jeremy intervened. "What are you talking about, Linus?"

"Mr. Ashton, I might not have been allowed down in the taproom, but as you can see, they don't always know when I'm not in my room. I haven't been completely idle."

Anya looked at the man. "And?"

"I've been making some inquiries. The man—the highwayman—you're likely after is Neesy Elliot. I'm not sure, mind, but he's the one that fits the bill best. The place near the Heath where this Arnold Ashton died was known to be his turf round about that time. I haven't been able to get my hands on him or I'd have got him to cough it up. And Lord Ashton will have me shipped off before I can pursue it. But Elliot acts near the Heath now too; he hasn't gone far. If you wanted to find him, I can draw you a map of the likely places. If he didn't do the bloke in, he'll know who did."

Anya stared at the man dumbfounded. "You found out all this?" She was impressed.

"There's no need to sound so surprised," Linus said, not at all grateful for how impressed she sounded. "You're not the only one with a brain around here."

"I never said I was," she said meekly. "I'm just surprised you went to the trouble."

This was apparently the wrong thing to say. Linus was bristling now. "And why is that? Because a bloke like me, why would he be loyal, is that it? The Runner might be looking for me, to put my neck in a noose, but everyone will say it was my lord who put me up to it. You think I don't want to help him?"

Anya was feeling duly chastised, but then Linus's eyelids flickered. "What?" she said.

He flicked his head. "It's just, like I said, I didn't tell anyone I knew where the bloke—Arnold Ashton—was that night. I wasn't responsible for what happened to him. See? But—"

"But?" Anya prodded.

"But, see, a few nights ago, roundabout the time I got that reticule off that horsy lady—"

Anya stifled a snort at this description of Lady Budleigh. "Yes? Did something happen?"

Linus looked sheepish. "See, it was the night after the

thievery. And I was in me cups. Like I said, I like a wee drink now and again. And I don't remember clearly, but there was this bloke who was chatting me up in a taproom. And there's a chance—"

"You told him about the reticule?" Anya looked aghast. She'd thought Lady Budleigh had simply recognized Linus. But had Linus spilled the beans too?

Linus shook his head. "No, miss. I didn't say nothing about the purse. I reckon Lady Budleigh just recognized me. She's met me once or twice down in Folkestone. But I don't know—I might have said something about how I knew my lord couldn't have done the bloke—Arnold Ashton—in because he didn't go after the bloke when he left the hostelry where they had a drink. See? I was only saying my lord *couldn't* have done it, but—"

"But you might have confirmed that Damian did in fact have a drink with Arnold Ashton that night," Jeremy finished, looking grim.

Linus dejectedly nodded.

"Do you know that *that* could be how the Budleighs know about that meeting between Damian and Arnold Ashton? That's how it might have come to light?" Jeremy said. He sounded uncharacteristically severe, and Linus looked even more downcast.

Anya couldn't help intervening. "I'm sure the man—whoever you spoke to a few nights ago—I'm sure the Budleighs sent him to get you drunk and then get information out of you," she said kindly. "I'm sure Clara Budleigh knows very well about your drinking problem." Anya was quite proud of herself for supporting him, given that he was never nice to her. There was no point berating him for what he had done now. What was done was done. The whole *ton* now knew that Damian had had a few drinks with Arnold Ashton on that fateful night.

But Linus wasn't impressed by her kindness. He frowned. "Are you saying I can't be trusted to hold my drink?" He was scowling now.

Anya bristled. For heaven's sake, couldn't the man stop taking offense at everything she said?

Jeremy wisely took hold of her wrist again. "Thanks, Linus, you've been a big help. We'll be on our way now. Safe passage to France, and I'm sure you'll let Damian know somehow when you've made your way there." He pulled her away before she could put Linus's back up some more.

28

For the next three nights, Jeremy and Anya stood vigil in deserted roads around the Heath, the ones Linus had mentioned as likely hot spots for the "gentlemen" of the trade, as highwaymen were called. They were waiting for the highwayman—for Neesy Elliot—to make an appearance. But they waited in vain.

Carriages passed. Not frequently, but there were one or two every hour. Some of them looked opulent and like they had wealthy passengers in them. Some of the carriage drivers even carried pistols quite openly, suggesting that this area was known to be a lure for highwaymen.

But nothing happened.

No carriages were stopped by pistol shots. No one attempted to rob the passengers. Nothing untoward happened to disturb the peace.

The nights were cold, Jeremy and Anya wrapped up to their eyeballs, and Anya was starting to think it was all in vain. For some reason, she'd felt hopeful after that chat with Linus Temperance. She'd felt they had a real, solid lead. An actual name. A new bit of information that had never come to light before. All they had to do now was track Neesy Elliot down. If he wasn't the right highwayman, after all, then he'd be able to give them other names. If he *was* the highwayman, then they would have to deal with the problem of how to get him to confess to Arnold Ashton's murder when they got to that point. She'd been feeling hopeful. After the first freezing night or two, this hope started to dwindle fast.

On the fourth night, a freezing night early in March, they had been whiling away the time watching a bunch of local children playing cricket, but even the children had now made their way indoors, leaving their bat and ball standing against the wall of a shed. Anya and Jeremy were sitting on some musty burlap, backs against the same wall, watching a road that was quiet and deserted and that curled around a small hill but had relatively regular carriages passing by. They were waiting for something—anything—to happen. Anya was so cold she was hugging her knees.

Jeremy yawned loudly for the fifth time. "Remind me again why we're doing this."

"I want to know what happened to Arnold Ashton, if you do not."

"What will it achieve, Anya? Linus is already in France."

She didn't answer at first. There was no moon tonight and the night was eerie. Shadows loomed large, and it was so dark it was hard to tell what was an object, like a tree or a wall, and what was a dark void. Her breath puffed in clouds. She was trying hard to stop her teeth from chattering. After each of the last three nights—four if you counted the one on which they spoke to Linus—she had returned to Lila's home in Berkeley Square since it was too late to return to the palace, feeling like she would never get warm again.

"'The *ton* will carry on thinking that Damian did it. That he either killed Arnold Ashton himself or that he instructed Linus to do it. Unless we prove them wrong."

"And you care what they think of him?"

The voice was gentle, almost casual. The eyes, she knew, would be compassionate, and so she kept her own carefully averted. Compassion was not what she needed right now. She didn't want his understanding eyes. "This is happening because of me. Don't you see, Jeremy? They're only going after your brother because they want *me* to hand over the dowager's wealth to them, and I've so far thwarted them. Of course, I can't let Damian pay the price."

He didn't say anything for a while. And she thought—gratefully—that they were done with the subject. When he spoke again, his voice was gentle. "You have to think about the future too, Anya. If we can prove that Damian had nothing to do with Arnold Ashton's death, then he can still be your executor and you can marry and claim Great-Auntie Griselda's money. You will marry me, won't you? So you can claim your inheritance? Great-Auntie meant for you to have it."

The question of marriage hadn't come up since the first time Jeremy had brought it up. She had forgotten about it. Or had always thought it was a joke. So much had happened since then. The weeks she'd spent with Damian, which already felt like a dream. Lila's return to her life. Lady Budleigh's reticule. The Runner. Linus's flight to Dover. The first time Jeremy had mentioned marriage, that seemed like a long time ago. She wondered if she would ever be able to look back on this time and not be thrown by how unreal it felt.

A sob, for some reason, rose in her throat. "I can't marry you," she said, swallowing hard so Jeremy wouldn't see the sparkle of tears in her eyes.

"And why is that?"

"I can't do that to you. You love Kenneth Laudsley."

He was crumbling a dry leaf in his hands. "You know I'm never sure if he loves me. Or if I'm just a passing distraction. Just when I start to think that he does love me, after all, even if it's in his own way, he goes all Kenneth on me again. And I'm never sure of my footing."

"Not everyone is good at showing how they feel. And not everyone loves in the same way," she said. Even though she felt like a fraud, talking about love like it was something she understood.

He started working on the next leaf. "That's neither here nor there, Anya." He looked up at her with those kind eyes of his, which also had the capacity to intuit much more than they let on. "The real reason you won't marry me—because you see there's no good reason not to, *I* am unlikely to marry anyone, and *you* need your inheritance for yourself and Trixie—the real reason is"—and his voice was even gentler now—"that you love my brother."

Her throat was all but closed now, and her chest hurt. "But you see, Jeremy, I'm sure he doesn't love me."

He was silent for some time. Then said, "He—the thing with Damian is that—Anya, he's very—"

"No," she said suddenly. "Don't. Don't make excuses for him. Because anytime you have to make excuses for someone's feelings for you, it's the same as saying that they don't love you. When—when he thought that I had betrayed him, he—he snatched at it like he *wanted* to believe it."

The air was still and cold around them. "Why are you helping him, then, Anya?"

"I have to help him because he wouldn't be in this mess if it weren't for me." She shook her head. "But that is the extent of it. How could I ever have anything more to do with someone who didn't trust me?"

"I could tell him that you had nothing to do with the information against Linus."

She looked fiercely at him. "No, Jeremy, don't you dare." She made an impatient sound. How could she explain? She looked beseechingly at him. "Don't you see? It's not whether or not he'd believe what you'd say. It's that he believed I'd betrayed him in the first place. No, it isn't just that. It's that he assumed it, didn't even talk to me about it. Didn't ask me. And he looked almost relieved that I had been caught out. Like he had expected all along that I wouldn't be trustworthy!"

Jeremy looked sad now. "Anya, I don't know that he trusts anyone. Not deep down in his heart. I've thought for years that he's shut himself off. Think of it, Anya. First our stepfather, the way he was. Then our mother died. And he's made his own way since then. I had him. He didn't really have anyone he could turn to."

She jerked her head. "Leave it be, Jeremy. It shouldn't be this hard, and it shouldn't need to be explained in this way. He's *decided* not to trust me and that's that. I just need to find out what happened to Arnold Ashton. Then I can move on with my life. It will all blow over. My twenty-fifth birthday will come and go in a few short months. And we can forget any of this . . ."

His hand whipped out and caught her wrist.

She abruptly stopped talking. And she heard it. Not a carriage—which was the only sound they had heard for hours—but the sounds of a horse. Not riding hard, as if trying to get somewhere, but almost meandering, punctuated by light snuffles and whinnying. They certainly hadn't heard anything like that for the last several hours. The rare rider did ride on this road, but only at great speed, and even one of those hadn't been by for hours. It was a bit late for someone grazing their horse. It was after midnight, and it was freezing.

Every sense was on high alert. Sure enough, a man, with a black cloth mask hanging about his chin, came around the corner of the hillock, whistling lightly to his horse. He paused in his whistling to say, "Now then, Merrily, my lad, let's see if we can cook up some fun tonight."

Before Jeremy could stop her, Anya was on her feet. Not only did she quickly come to standing, but she ran forward so she was a mere few feet from the horse and rider. The horse was startled, and it rose up on its hind legs, cried in alarm, and completely dislodged its rider. There was a dull thud and a cry as the man fell off his horse.

Anya's hand was at her mouth. Dear god, she'd killed Neesy Elliot, the famous highwayman of Hampstead Heath. She and Jeremy ran forward. The horse was neighing wildly and looked very nervous but at least it didn't gallop off. The man was not dead. He was sitting up, clutching his back, and cursing heavily.

"Are you all right, sir?" Anya asked, kneeling down beside him.

"Are you hurt?" Jeremy asked.

The man looked querulously at the pair of them. "Who the bloody hell are you two nincompoops? Do you have to loom out of the dark at a man like that, an innocent man just going about his work? You scared the living daylights out of Merrily there, and Merrily has seen some wild nights." He was rubbing his back. "If my back is broken, I'm sure you two numpties can tell me what I should do about it!"

Anya looked guiltily at the man. "I'm so sorry!"

"Sorry, man. We can get you to a doctor," Jeremy added.

"A doctor! No old sawbones for me, thanking you very

much," the man said. "Not letting one of them near me, not for love nor money. Though what do the two of you think you're doing? You nearly killed me—"

"It's just you startled us," Anya said quickly. "We weren't expecting you to come around the corner. Or at least, it's exactly what we were expecting, or hoping for, but you see we've been waiting for so many nights, and we didn't see anyone like you, so we had given up expecting—"

"Dear god, she talks!" the man moaned. He gingerly stood up, accepting Jeremy's hand at his elbow but then shrugging it off as soon as he was on his feet. "Why do I need to know any of this, miss?"

"Marleigh."

"I don't need to know your name! Now can you be so kind as to leave a man to his work?" He turned to his horse—Merrily—and spoke soothingly to it. "Now, now, come now, lad, it was just a young lass—I don't need to tell *you* what young lassies are like. Give one some rope, and she'll have it strung around your neck in a second. And then what'll she do? I'll tell you what she'll do. She'll—"

"It is surely your turn to introduce yourself," Anya said frostily, ruthlessly interrupting the man's most interesting observations on young women. "Your manners are atrocious."

The man turned his head and looked at her like he'd never seen anything like her before. "Good god almighty, who are you, the mistress of Almack's?"

"I'm no such thing. We just want to know your name, and then we'll be on our way. Or at least, after we've asked you some questions about your movements. Two years ago, that is. We're not concerned with your current movements," she added graciously. "You may go about those once you've answered our questions."

The man, short, squat, bandy-legged, and with a shrewd glint in his eye, was looking warily at her. "You know, this is why I never married a second time. Was a big mistake the first time. Shouldn't have done it. Never could stomach their chatter. But it's worse than that because you can't trust a single thing they say. My mam tried to poison me when I was just in my cradle, and my good wife who swore eternal loyalty ran off with a pastor. A prosy old bore he was too. Don't know what she saw in him. But that's women for you. Don't trust 'em, don't listen to their chatter. It's the only way to live. Now, if *she'll* get out of my way, I'll be gone in two winks."

"It's rude to talk about me like I'm not here," Anya declared. "I *am* right here. You can address your remarks to me, if you please."

"But I *don't* please! I don't want to talk to you at all. I do everything I can not to talk to women. They have a tendency to chew your ear off if you so much as glance in their direction. Now, I've asked a few times and I'll ask again. I'm just an honest man who prefers not to have any truck with the fairer sex. Leave me be, to get on with my work."

"And what work might that be, sir?" Jeremy asked.

The man rolled his eyes. "I am a clerk for His Majesty, the King. What d'you think?"

"I think we know who you are," Jeremy said.

The man looked bored.

"Are you Neesy Elliot?" Anya asked.

He started like a gun had gone off right next to his ear. Now he looked warier than ever. He crossed himself. "She knows my name! How does she know my name? Can she read my mind too?"

"Two years ago, on a dark night just before Christmas, did you happen to stop a carriage? It was someone you didn't steal anything from." Anya had her arms crossed over her chest and couldn't help thinking she sounded like Neesy Elliot's executioner. "The man died, perhaps in the altercation."

He was looking crossly at her now. "I don't know who you are or what your business is. I have nothing—"

Just as he said the words, they all heard it: the distant sound of a carriage.

The man turned to the pair of them. Now he was talking briskly and the bored tone was gone. "Now then, my lad, you take this woman of yours off—haul her over your shoulder, if you must, and you take yourself off and make yourselves scarce. I have work to get on with. A man's got to eat. And you're in my way. Mighty inconvenient it is too."

"Tell us if you killed that man two years ago and we will leave you alone!" Anya said desperately.

"Get her away from me," the man said, suddenly pulling out a pistol and waving it about. "Or I won't answer for the consequences."

"Now, Mr. Elliot," Jeremy said, "there's no need to wave that gun about. We are all rational here—"

The man held the gun, unwaveringly now, straight at Anya's head. "Off with the pair of you. Now. I won't ask again. And like you said, if I've done murder before, I'll surely have no qualms about doing it again, see?" Neesy Elliot pulled his cloth mask to cover the lower half of his face. His hat was pulled down over his eyes. Now you couldn't make out his features. The pistol in his hand was still pointing directly at Anya's head, though.

Anya was willing to stand her ground. If they let him waylay that carriage and steal from the passengers, he would be off immediately after on his horse and who knew when they'd find him again. She was going to protest loudly and physically if she had to, but Jeremy was holding her arm in a tight grip. "Come on," he hissed.

She let herself be practically dragged away. They retreated to the wall of the barn. They had taken a hackney cab to the Heath and had no way of chasing the highwayman if he took off. Anya was seething with impatience. "Do you expect me to just stand here?" she hissed. "The man is just there. We can't let him slip through our fingers!"

"Do you really think he's going to stand about answering your questions about whether or not he killed someone two years ago?" Jeremy hissed.

"What do you think I should have done?" Anya demanded. "Asked him around to tea a few times to get to know him better, *then* asked him if he killed someone? Isn't that why we've been sitting around freezing our arses off, so we can ask him this very question? What is wrong with you? I have to go back to him."

"He has a gun, Anya, and I don't think he'd hesitate to use it."

"He'll make off as soon as he's robbed the poor people in that carriage," Anya complained. "And we'll never find him again. *And* are you telling me, *Captain* Ashton, that you are just going to stand there and let that man rob those poor people? Because I am not!"

Thus saying, she picked up the bat and ball that were still propped against the wall of the barn. The carriage was almost upon them now. She had seconds. The ball wasn't made of cork. Which was a good thing. Because she might not have been able to risk it with a cork ball. A cork ball could kill someone. But with this lighter one made for children she was willing to try. The carriage was nearly upon them now and would be coming around the bend any moment. Once Neesy Elliot stopped the carriage, it would be too late. She had to stop him before he stopped the travelers.

The carriage came around the bend. She registered that not only did Elliot have his pistol still in his hands and his mask covering his face and hat pulled down low, but the driver of the carriage also already had a pistol in his hands. The corner must be known to attract gentlemen of the trade. She bounced the ball up, and on its way down thwacked it with all her might. It went off like a gunshot, rose in a neat arc, curved in a perfectly executed parabola, and whacked the pistol right out of Neesy Elliot's hand. She couldn't help whooping slightly at the perfect delivery. Take *that*, Lord Damian Ashton!

Just as Neesy Elliot cried out, they heard a gunshot. A real one this time.

The carriage didn't pause, not even for a second. It didn't even seem to slow down. It was gone around the curve of the hill in a flash.

But Neesy Elliot fell a second time. Not off his horse this time. He in fact slumped forward on his horse. And lay there like he was dead.

"I think he's been shot!" Jeremy cried.

Anya quickly dropped the bat. They both ran up to the horse, who was whinnying wildly and moving restlessly in circles, and the highwayman who was still slumped forward.

"Mr. Elliot!" Anya cried as they reached him. "Mr. Elliot, are you all right?"

He lifted himself up—he wasn't dead, but there was a clear and freely bleeding gunshot wound on his rib cage. Anya gasped.

"You!" he said, when he saw her. He was looking down at them. "You did this! You did this to me, you cursed woman."

"No, no, I mean, no, I didn't! It was the driver. He was ready for you. Didn't you see? You should have ducked! Why didn't you duck? Please come down from the horse. We have to put pressure on the wound. And we—Jeremy could take Merrily and get a doctor."

But the man was not coming off the horse. He was bleeding profusely. "Deliver myself into your clutches, ye'd like that, wouldn't ye'?" he was muttering.

The man was going to bleed to death at this rate. He was showing no signs of getting off the horse, yet he didn't seem strong enough to stay on it for long either, much less ride it anywhere.

"I have to put pressure on the wound," Anya said urgently, "or the man will die. He is already losing precious seconds. Jeremy, give me a hand up. Perhaps I can bind it and then we can get him down off the horse between us."

Jeremy helped, and she climbed up behind the highwayman. As soon as she did, and before she had even found a stable seat behind the man or reached for his wound to help him put pressure on it, the horse finally gave up the fight to be brave and took off like a gunshot, carrying Anya and the highwayman with him.

29

Anya screamed and tried to get the runaway horse under control, but the highwayman was in the way. He had slumped forward again and she had no idea if he was conscious or not. She couldn't stop the bleeding, and she couldn't stop the horse. She couldn't give in to the wild panic that was building inside her.

All she could do was somehow try to hold on for dear life to the highwayman, with all her strength, so that neither she nor he fell off the horse. The horse was galloping so wildly and lurching so much that she knew she was in danger of falling and breaking her neck at any moment. And so was Neesy Elliot. The terrain was rough, and though there was mud everywhere and it may have made the ground softer, the speed at which they were going and the rocks that were everywhere meant that if either of them came off the horse they would crack their heads open.

Wild countryside flashed past. Mud flew. Hills around them were a blur. They were riding so fast, it was impossible to keep track of where they were going. The thought that the horse's flight would be brief, that Merrily would get tired of the wild, panicked run, was short-lived. The horse, which had stood its ground by the highwayman for such a long time, had completely lost its head and showed no signs of stopping or even slowing down.

She lost track of time as hills, trees, and the odd cottage in the middle of nowhere flashed past. She had tried to wake Neesy Elliot at first, tried to get him conscious so he could get the horse under control or even just so he could support himself a little and not fall off the runaway horse, but she was wasting her breath, and with every wasted effort, she would lose the strength to hold on to the horse with her thighs and to the highwayman with all the strength of her hands. She had to save her breath. She had to stay focused or she would fall off and no one would even know where to find her broken body.

She had no idea how long they rode. Was it half an hour, an hour? But finally, when she was sure she would crash to her death and die, because her hands and thighs could no longer hold her, and long after she had given up hope, the horse miraculously slowed down. He was still cantering, but he was exhausted and was panting hard. He had simply run out of steam, she thought.

The countryside looked farther out of the city even than the Heath, but she didn't know how far she was from where she had left Jeremy. The horse came to a standstill outside what looked like a derelict cottage.

She practically fell off the horse, and Elliot slid off the horse after her. He fell to the ground again, for the second time that evening. She was numb with shock and cold, her ears and hands had no sensation, and her legs were throbbing with pain, but she had the presence of mind to realize she had to try to bind the highwayman's wound or he would die. Although he had been bleeding heavily for so long he would probably die anyway.

"Mr. Elliot," she said urgently, crouching next to him.

But the fall had miraculously brought him back to consciousness. He was tight about the mouth and looked green, though it was hard to tell for sure in the darkness. She tried to bind her scarf on his wound, but he grabbed it from her. She clucked impatiently, told him he needed help, and stood up to retrieve the scarf.

And then, she didn't know how it happened, or how he moved so quickly, but Elliot was on his feet, he had a length of rope in his hands, and he had drawn her wrists together and bound them together tightly before she could struggle out of reach. Maybe she hadn't been able to stop him because she didn't seriously think that this was what he was trying to do.

She made an impatient noise. She held up her wrists, which were now bound tightly in front of her with rope. "Are you mad? I am your only chance of surviving your gunshot wound. *Why* are you binding me up?" She was almost screaming in frustration. "Untie me at once. You're being unbelievably dense, Mr. Elliot. Not to mention unbelievably rude!"

The man could hardly stand upright. He was swaying ominously. "You, this is all your doing. I never have anything to do with women. Because this is what happens when I do! Never want to have anything to do with a woman if I can help it." He was lurching now from the blood loss, and his face looked even more green and drawn, but he managed to grab the rope that hung from her wrists and dragged her by it. She struggled and pulled against him, but weak though he was, he was still strong enough to drag her to the railing that ran around the cottage and tie the other end of the rope to it.

She was too tired to even protest. The man was harmless. He was simply out of his mind with blood loss. She slumped down on the low wooden bench that sat outside the railing, her wrists bound at an awkward angle. "Are you going to untie me, Mr. Elliot? This is very, *very* rude, you know. And you will die of blood loss if you don't let me help you."

But he had slumped again and slid to the ground. There was blood everywhere. And more pouring from him. He lay lifelessly on the ground, looking ashen.

"Mr. Elliot, Mr. Elliot," she said urgently, "you are bleeding to death. You must let me help you."

He came to again and sat up. He looked like he was barely alive by this point. He was clutching the wound, which was so near to his chest.

"Please, Mr. Elliot," she tried again. "Untie me so I can help you."

"I told ye', I don't trust women. And I don't listen to their chatter. It's always a mistake to listen to them. Always! Never have I once listened to a woman and *not* lived to regret it."

"You will die."

"Be that as it may," he said weakly.

They both sat there now. She on the bench, her hands tied in front of her and held at an awkward angle against the strain of the rope, which was tied to the fence. He, slumped on the ground, patching himself up weakly with her scarf, but too weak to do a good job of it. Within seconds, the scarf was soaked. She wondered if the two of them were going to die of the cold. She at least was wearing a coat lined with fur. His was frayed and patched. And he was shivering from shock and cold.

They sat there silently. His bleeding had slowed. She had no idea if this was because of the makeshift bandage or because there was not much blood left to leak. He looked like he had fallen into a faint again.

"I did kill that bloke," the man suddenly said. His head was lolling now. And his voice slurred. But he lifted his head all of a sudden. He looked incredibly uncomfortable and in pain, slumped like that, but coming to every now and again with a jerk.

"What man?" She was numb with cold, but she tried to shake herself awake to hear what he had to say. "What man?"

He didn't answer for so long that she thought he had fainted again.

"Mr. Elliot. Mr. Elliot," she called.

After many more minutes of silence, he jerked awake. "That man two years ago. I did kill him, if you must know. Though I don't know why I should be telling you."

"Why, why did you kill him and then not take anything? Why?"

"He was wearing a tidy little watch," he said thickly. "And had a money bag on him that looked fat and juicy. I wanted to take them, don't get me wrong. It wasn't like me to leave things behind that I had earned, see? But I have my code. I had more coming to me. I couldn't take that *and* take what he had on him."

She frowned, wondering if he was delirious. "What do you mean you had more coming to you?"

She was afraid he would fall silent again, but he was speaking quickly now, like he needed to get it all out. Like he knew he didn't have much time. "I was promised money, a lot of it, for doing the man in."

Her blood froze. Her heart was pounding. She hardly dared ask. "By whom, Mr. Elliot?"

"See, I didn't know who it was. It was just a woman. A horse-faced woman. In a veil and everything. Posh as a shiny penny. You know the kind, the kind that's always looking down on you for being poor and not as high and mighty as she. I know the kind. But it was only after I saw her again some months later, just by chance, on a street in the West End, and I put two and two together. I asked around in the shop she was in, and that was when I knew who she was. Didn't know at the time, mind, only later on."

Horse-faced. Better than everyone else. Anya knew who it was. "Clara. Clara Budleigh. She paid you to kill Arnold Ashton."

"See, I never did kill anyone else." His voice was hoarse now. A whisper that sounded painful. A rasping breath was coming from him. A nasty gurgling sound was coming from his chest every time he tried to draw a breath in. Every breath was a struggle. "Never in all my career. I never killed anyone but that bloke. That wasn't my way. Scare 'em and all. But I never killed them. That money she promised me was cursed. I never should have done it. Had nothing but bad luck since then. And to tell you the truth, I always thought she'd come back for me. Always thought if I don't tell someone about what she got me to do, she's going to do me in, or hand me over to them Runners. She looked like the kind who wouldn't like loose ends."

He was silent after that, and really there was nothing more to say. He fainted again for so long that she thought he was dead. She stared at him, willing him to wake up.

When he did finally wake up again, she spoke urgently. Because she knew now he had moments left to live. "Mr. Elliot, you have to untie me. You must!"

"Never should have done it," he kept muttering, so low that she could hardly hear him now. "Always knew I should've stuck to my code. Never hurt 'em or kill 'em. Just do the job. Just . . ." He heaved a great sigh and fell into a faint so deep she knew he wouldn't wake up again.

She sat there, holding a macabre kind of vigil over the man.

She didn't know the exact moment his breath stopped. But it was near enough because the cloud in front of his face evaporated and there was no more breath there.

She sat there helplessly, mourning the man at first, and then realizing, suddenly and without a shadow of a doubt, that she was going to die of cold if she couldn't get herself free. Because he could no longer do it for her. There was no one who could free her.

The sudden realization brought her to her feet. She was going to die of the cold if she couldn't get herself free. The one person who could have freed her was dead. No one else knew where she was. Jeremy could keep looking for hours, but by the time he found her she could be dead of the cold or thirst, whichever took her first. As it was, it was hours since she had had a sip of anything to drink. She mentally repeated these simple facts to herself so that she could wake up her slow brain. So that she couldn't forget. She didn't have time to waste.

She was numb and aching. She jumped up and down a few times to get the blood pumping through her veins. She tried to wrench herself free. She pulled and pulled at the rope, but it seemed to only get tighter. It burned into her flesh, and the more she pulled the more it dug into her wrists.

She pulled at the rope, girded herself against the fence, and pulled. Her wrists were bleeding so profusely that she was crying from it. From it, or from frustration at the stupid predicament she was in, which was becoming more urgent by the minute, or from the growing realization that she would die like this, in the middle of nowhere and no one would find her, she didn't know.

When her wrists could take no more battering, she tried to pull instead at the fence posts. Maybe she could dislodge those from the ground. But though the house looked derelict, the fence posts were sturdy, and Anya wondered if this was where Neesy Elliot had lived and the fence was where he had tied his horse. There were water troughs nearby, she saw now, for the horse. In fact, she vaguely remembered, Merrily had made his way straight to one of them when he had first offloaded his riders. She was too busy trying to wake Elliot up to have noticed.

Merrily had taken off at first but was back now.

"You couldn't untie me, could you?" she said to the horse. She was strangely comforted by the horse's presence. Merrily was skinny but also muscly at the same time. He was brown but had a white patch near his nose. He had mellow eyes. Yet he was no help at all. It was a false comfort.

She started kicking at the fence posts. This made the horse whinny nervously. She kicked and kicked, but the fence posts weren't budging. At least she wasn't as cold as she had been. She was bleeding at her wrists and now thirstier than ever, but warmer. At least she was warmer.

She sat down on the bench and cried. Cried she didn't even know for what. Maybe she was crying for Trixie. Because who else would mourn her if she died? Not one person had passed by in the hours since she had been tied to the post. How long was it? An hour? Two? Or even more?

Lila would mourn her. Lila, who was just back in her life. Anya cried for Lila. Lila had Ivor. She would mourn Anya. So would Mira in her own way. But they would get over it. There was so little communication between the sisters that they would get over it; they wouldn't lose anything real. Trixie, she hoped, would find a way to escape the lecherous men of the palace. She would mourn Anya. But she was young. She could have a better life. She could use the education Anya had tried to give her. She would be resourceful. Perhaps Lila would still take her in. Yes, Lila would do that.

How stupid, Anya thought. How stupid to have wanted one opportunity all these years to heal things with her sisters, and now Lila was trying to get back into her life, trying to make up for lost time, and Anya had been resisting it, or at least trying to slow things down. How stupid! How stupid was she? *One more chance*, she thought. *Could I have one more chance?*

"No, damn it, no, I won't give in!" She got up again, but now her wrists were so sore that after a few more times pulling at the rope she gave up. Her feet were too numb to kick the posts.

She sank down on the bench again and cried even more. This, this was the way she would die. This was no way to die! How, how had she let herself be in such a stupid predicament? Why hadn't she fought when she could have? Why did she let him tie her? She sat down and watched a line of ants making their way to where something, a mouse or something, lay near the blackberry bush. She watched the ants in a daze, feeling small and helpless. Why did ants always travel in strange curves? They were trotting down from the fence to which she was tied but taking an absurd angle to get to the bush. Really, ants were strange creatures. Why wouldn't you take the most direct path? The ants were taking a direct line to her reticule and then veering off at an angle to get to the bush.

Her reticule.

She straightened. She had to get to her reticule. She had to get it before she gave in to the cold, her thirst, and her extreme tiredness, and fell asleep. If she fell asleep there was always the chance she wouldn't wake up. Or she would linger on for another couple of days and die a slow and tortured death. The house was tucked away behind a copse of trees. It wasn't visible from the road. If it could be called a road and not just a worn mud path. Even if someone passed by, they wouldn't see her. And she wouldn't be able to keep fighting or shouting for even another day, let alone more.

She eyed the reticule that had fallen just out of reach when Elliot dragged her over to the fence. The horse was now sniffing about the highwayman and making moaning noises that were horrible to hear.

"It's okay," she whispered. "It's okay, Merrily."

The horse carried on sniffing around Elliot and making those terrible noises. She could hardly bear the horse's mourning. She was exhausted, sleep-deprived from the last few sleepless nights, cold and numb. She slid as far down as she could and stretched out her leg. Even at maximum stretch, she was only able to gently tap the reticule with the tip of her boot. She couldn't even nudge it, couldn't move it. She could just give it a tap. She tried over and over again. Finally, it moved a little. But just sideways. Not closer. At least she could move it. She stretched to her breaking point. The rope didn't have much give, and she was basically straining at the fence posts. Every part of her body was hurting.

It took a long time to budge the reticule with her foot. It took even longer to draw the reticule, bit by slow, tortured bit, toward her, instead of driving it farther away. She cursed and swore and cried some more. The whole thing was plain torture. She was sure her strength would give out before she could draw it closer.

She finally managed to get it close enough that she could stoop and pick it up. Getting it open was another matter. Her hands were numb with cold, and she kept on dropping the damned thing as she tried to pull at the string and get the mouth open. She finally, *finally* managed to get her cold, shaking hand on the sheathed blade that she kept in there for protection. Getting the blade out didn't take so much time. Once she had a grip around the blade, she simply had to slip her hand out and let the reticule fall to the ground. But now she had to hold it in her cold, numb fingers and try to cut the ropes around her wrists without nicking herself and bleeding to death, before even the cold or the thirst could kill her.

She started hacking.

30

━━◆━━

I t took Damian a good few days after he took Linus to Tuppence's uncle's taproom to realize that he loved Anya.

She betrayed him, she went behind his back. Not only did she betray him, but she betrayed a secret that was not even his. That he should never have confided in her. She justified everything he thought and felt about his fellow human beings, validated every barrier he had ever erected between himself and others. That was the plain truth. He couldn't shy away from it.

And yet he still loved her. That was the truth too. It was deeply lowering.

For some reason, in the numbness that followed Sowerby's appearance at his door and the fury at the world that followed after that, he thought that he was cured of any feeling for her. He was sure it would never come back. It was a schism, not a gradual withdrawal. He would not love Anya again, and if he was really sensible he would keep himself protected from that infernal feeling forever.

And he was relieved. Relieved that he was free of her. Relieved that he no longer had to wait for her to betray him. He didn't have to watch and wait because she had already done it.

But it seemed that the relief was as temporary as the numbness and the fury. Because after the relief was over, what flooded inside him was nothing he had experienced before. It wasn't love. It was pure pain.

He didn't know if the pain was for his mother, or his father, or his stepfather, or Jeremy, or what. Or in fact for Anya, because it was all mixed together now. All of his pain became one humongous thing, and its threads couldn't be separated, nor could they be cut out from him like a sore. It was a physical, tortured pain that he felt had been hiding inside him all his life. Just waiting to come out and consume him. To annihilate him. He felt like he had been running from it all his life, and now it had caught up with him.

It was pain for his father, whose life ambitions and plans had all died too young. It was pain at being left alone to fend for himself and Jeremy. At having to protect himself and Jeremy from an uncouth stepfather who shouldn't have been in their mother's life in the first place. Pain he hadn't allowed himself to feel when he left his mother behind, knowing what her life would be like with his stepfather, or even when she died. He had sealed it away inside himself, never to be looked at again. But now it was out. And it was such a monster that he was sure he would never be able to bottle it up again. He was sure that it would destroy him. He couldn't cry. He wanted to, but it was like the pain was too big, too much bigger than him, to give him the relief of tears. It simply wanted to eat him and destroy him. It didn't want to let him have any relief.

Getting thoroughly drunk was the only way to tackle something like this.

Of course, it turned out that neither Jeremy nor Linus were there when you needed them. This was the worst of it.

He was in love with Anya, or in pain with her. That was it, he was in *pain* with Anya Marleigh. It was thoroughly demeaning and pointless and hopeless and he had no idea how he had let himself get in this state. But that wasn't the main problem. The biggest problem was that even the two people he could generally turn to—if not for sympathy or to confide secrets, at least for companionship—were completely absent. He knew where one was, having sent him off to Dover by stagecoach and then hopefully France on a ship himself. Where the hell was the other one? Really, what was the point of a brother if that brother didn't help you get drunk when you needed to?

He tried to remain drunk for as long as possible and was in fact soaked in brandy late one night and staring moodily at the blaze in his fireplace, his shirtsleeves rolled up, his collar askew, when his housekeeper, Mrs. Garner, came to tell him that some street urchin was at the door. It was the early hours of the morning and the child would not leave, and what was more, the child had Mr. Jeremy's glove.

Damian was sure the woman was losing her mind. "Jeremy's glove?" he said, staring at her. "Have you gone mad? Because if you have, come and drink with me. I have been asking you to for *days*, and you keep refusing me," he added petulantly. What did she mean, "urchin," anyway? Linus? Maybe she meant Linus. "Linus?" he asked. In case that's who she meant.

She looked thoroughly disgusted. "It's Mrs. Garner, sir. I'm not Mr. Temperance, as you can well see. Now, I want to send this mite about his business. He has no business to come calling at a gentleman's abode in the early hours of the morning asking to see the master. But I don't like him having Mr. Jeremy's glove, sir, and he says he has a letter from your brother inside it. *I* have not seen this missive, so I cannot verify that such a letter exists or if it is in fact a sorry tale. I am merely telling you what the mite said."

He tried to make sense of this and couldn't. "What's Jeremy going and writing letters to me for? Can't he just talk to me? Where is he?" he asked querulously. Jeremy was never where you wanted him. In fact, Damian hadn't seen him for days. "I suppose he's gone off to see some friends again and didn't even have the decency to tell me?"

"It doesn't sound like it, sir. I swear the lad said something about how Miss Anya was in trouble and that Mr. Jeremy was looking for her."

This penetrated the fog, and he stared at his housekeeper. What was this about Anya being in trouble? Wasn't she at the palace? He hadn't been thinking about her, why should he, except when he did think of her, in his mind she was always safely tucked away in the palace, singing or some such thing. Something safe and happy. *He* wasn't safe or happy. But at least—in his head—she was.

He was about to ask his housekeeper to bring this urchin to him, though he was almost certain the whole thing was a hallucination, when a child appeared from behind the woman. Dear god, was he real or part of the hallucination? It was a skinny child, dressed in somewhat shabby clothing, but clean for all that. Not exactly a street urchin. He wished Mrs. Garner would get her facts right.

"That's not a street urchin," he declared.

"That he is, sir," Mrs. Garner said.

"He is not. He is much too clean. And doesn't look under-nourished."

"An urchin is as urchin does." Mrs. Garner stuck to her guns.

"Have you any experience of urchins? Because I can tell you they don't look like that." This was obviously a point that needed to be cleared up before anything else could happen.

"I am happy to inform you," Mrs. Garner said loftily, "that I do not have much truck with street urchins, them not coming into my general purview normally. Sir."

"Then how can you possibly know what they look like?" *Take that, Mrs. Garner.* The point was now dealt with to his satisfaction. Damian looked at the boy, who had been happy to leave the adults to debate his antecedents and didn't seem to have anything to add to the question. "Who the devil are you?"

"Benny, sir, my lord. Your brother, sir, my lord, he asked me to give you this." The child was holding out a glove and a letter. Or at least a piece of paper.

Damian took it. Trying to clear his vision, he stared down at what was unmistakably Jeremy's lavish handwriting. "Brother, Anya has disappeared. There's no time to tell you all of it, but she's in trouble. I'm looking for her, but I need your help. Benny will tell you where to go. Please. Come quick as you can."

Damian stood up so quickly he reeled. He grabbed the back of a chair for support. He realized all at once and blindingly that this was the wrong time to be drunk. Why, why the hell was he drunk? There was only one thing to do.

He took up the flower vase that stood on the coffee table and emptied it all over himself.

The urchin—Benny, that is—grinned, and Mrs. Garner looked at him warily. Damian stood there, dripping on the carpet.

"We must go right now. I will take my carriage. Mrs. Garner, I need Wallerby to get my curricle ready, and at once. Come now, Benny, you must tell me where to go."

He was brisk now. He had no idea what Jeremy was talking about, but this was a time for action, not debate.

Out in the foyer, Mrs. Garner gave him a towel to wipe himself. She wanted him to change his sopping clothes, but there was no time. She helped him shrug into his coat and boots. It seemed to take an age.

Once outside, the carriage was ready for him. His groom, Wallerby, wanted to know if he should come with him. But Damian shook his head. It was only a curricle, and he needed Benny to sit next to him and give him directions.

"How the devil did you get here from the Heath?" he asked, as this question struck him with some force.

"My nag, sir. My pa's nag, that is. She's a bit lame, and it took a long time."

Damian yelled to Wallerby to feed and water the nag. Wallerby looked disgusted at this idea, feeling no doubt that anything that went by the description "nag" was beneath his notice. But Damian didn't have time to mend ruffled feathers.

He drove fast, but it still took nearly an hour to get to the Heath and wind his way to where the boy said he lived, and where Jeremy had apparently found him. Once at the boy's cottage, the boy told him what Jeremy had told him. That Jeremy would start traveling in the direction he thought Anya had gone—on another nag borrowed from the boy's father's farm—and that Damian must follow in that direction too.

Damian thanked Benny's father, a grumpy farmer who looked just as grumpy after Damian compensated him—generously—for his time and nags. He dithered for a second, wondering if he should park the curricle here and travel just on his horse. It would be faster. But he had to find Anya, and Anya would then need transport too. He held on to the curricle.

Damian started out, completely sober now, but having little idea what he was doing. It took another hour, and by that time he was starting to wonder if this was his brother's idea of an elaborate prank when he finally came upon Jeremy. It took only one look at his brother's face to realize that this was no prank. He was riding a sorry-looking, skinny horse.

"It's been three hours," were Jeremy's first words. "And I can't find her. I have no idea where Elliot's taken her."

His face was so grim it made Damian go cold. They started moving, Damian in his curricle and Jeremy on the nag, in the direction Jeremy indicated.

Jeremy tried to tell him what had happened. But the story was so convoluted that it took some unraveling. It seemed to involve Tuppence's father's uncle and his daughter Janet, someone called Mary, Linus himself, a highwayman called Neesy Elliot, another someone for some reason called Merrily, the boy Benny, his father, and his nags.

Damian felt a cold fury pooling inside him as the story became clearer. He couldn't believe what he was hearing. This, this was it. This was exactly why you couldn't put someone like Jeremy with someone like Anya and hope that the outcome would be a good one. And what was his brother going on about a cricket ball for? A *cricket* ball? "You just let the man ride off with her?"

"Yes, I did! It's all my fault; I am saying as much, aren't I? I couldn't stop the horse. And I had no vehicle. I walked around for a long time before I came upon Benny's house. It was the first sniff I had of a horse all night. I dashed off the note to you and since then I've been searching, going in circles, calling. But I can't find her. I can't find her, and she could be dead!"

Apparently, pain wasn't the last thing he was going to feel

either, like he had thought in the last few days. That wasn't his final feeling. Because it seemed that a cold terror could replace the pain. A new and sudden and devastating fear that he would lose her.

And he realized in that moment that if Anya died there would be no point in anything. His estate, his business ventures, his efforts in Parliament to bring about a more just society, even Jeremy—none of it would matter anymore. And in fact, he realized that it had been hollow all along, this life he thought he had made for himself in which he kept himself at a safe distance from just about everything and everyone. Without Anya, it would all be pointless. Without her, it always *had* been pointless. He just hadn't known it.

They rode in hopeless semicircles. Jeremy had ridden in the direction Anya had disappeared. But when paths went off the road, it was impossible to know which one, if any, the highwayman might have taken. The paths were muddy, and there were marks everywhere. It was impossible to know which ones might have been made by the horse that Jeremy was calling Merrily.

In the end, when Damian was frantic with fear, Jeremy spotted the horse, the highwayman's horse. When he heard Jeremy's cry, Damian wasn't far from him. They had been meeting and separating as they rode, trying to cover ground more efficiently. He rode the curricle quickly in the direction of the cry. Jeremy was sliding off the nag when Damian pulled up in the curricle. The horse—it must be Merrily—was whinnying nervously. It was standing restlessly on the outside of a dense copse of trees, but as they got nearer, it turned and made its way through the copse. They followed through the trees, and it came to a halt on the other side.

At the horse's feet was a body, and at first Damian thought

that his worst nightmare had come true and she was dead. But Jeremy recognized the body as the highwayman. Jeremy stooped quickly and checked the man's pulse, though there was no need to. The man was covered in his own blood. Jeremy shook his head grimly as he stood up.

But Damian had no head for him or the highwayman. Because there she was. She was on the ground by the fence that ran around the house. She was kneeling forward, her chest slumped on her thighs. He walked slowly up to her because he couldn't bear it. He couldn't bear that he would find her dead. Dead of the cold. Dead from something the highwayman had done to her. Dead from thirst. There were any number of reasons she could have died before he got to her.

But as he got closer he heard the sound that felt like a miracle to him. She was slumped over, and—dear god—there was blood everywhere. Next to her on the ground was a tattered, blood-covered rope and a bloody and very sharp blade. Blood was flowing from her wrists still, and it looked like she had only just managed to free herself and now didn't have an ounce of strength left to get up again.

She was sobbing. Sobbing her heart out. Lying there, bent double over her thighs. And he had no idea if she had the strength to get up, to get on a horse, or if she was too tired, too hurt, too cold to come to her feet.

He knelt down next to her and put his arms around her.

"Anya," he said, "Anya."

And he sobbed too.

31

Two weeks later, as Damian made his way to the palace, he had time to reflect on the conversation he had had with dear Preston and Clara a few days ago.

He and Jeremy had gone back to the highwayman's derelict cottage—or rather, the derelict cottage that the highwayman had used as his lodgings (it was unclear who it actually belonged to), the day after they found Anya there, sobbing and bleeding. They searched it. Found it to be crumbling into ruins inside and overgrown with weeds that were climbing in through the walls. It was in ruins except for one room that the highwayman must have used for his own. A quick search found stolen trinkets and small stashes of money. Some remains of food. Tattered blankets. A horseshoe with *M* carved into it. They were meager belongings, and while there was something self-contained about them, something that might have had some dignity when Elliot was alive, they now looked lonely and forlorn. It had been difficult to look at them.

But more importantly, tucked away under a floorboard was something Damian had desperately hoped he would find, but had hardly dared expect. Anya had briefly told them on the ride back into town that Neesy Elliot had confessed to the murder of Arnold Ashton. Not only that, but he had told her that Clara Budleigh had paid him to kill the man.

Damian was almost certain that the Budleighs had not known that Arnold Ashton was not the last remaining man standing between them and the Ashton estate. They had not known that Damian Ashton, grandson of a native Jamaican woman and great-grandson of an Ashton that had long abandoned his country for the warmer climate of the Caribbean, was set to inherit the Ashton estate. He had no idea if they did away with any of the other Ashtons standing in the way of their inheriting the title and estate, but it seemed now that they had done away with Arnold Ashton. Damian was shocked to hear it, yet, was he surprised? Yes, he thought, damn it, he *was* surprised. It was one thing to try all kinds of strategies to get at the Ashton acres and title. But he hadn't imagined that murder was one of them.

The problem was proof.

With Neesy Elliot dead, how would they ever go about proving what had happened? If they couldn't prove it, then rumors of Damian's hand in the death would linger. The Runner Sowerby had not stopped sniffing around and threatening that he would bring the truth to light. He would probably keep on trying his best to stick the murder on Damian. The *ton* would keep feeding the scandal too. For as long as it had legs.

But Damian found something in Elliot's cottage that gave him some hope. Jeremy had told him how the man did not trust women, not for a second. Damian had hoped that this lack of trust in women had stretched far enough to include Clara Budleigh.

He was right.

Under the floorboards was a note that Elliot had written in

a hand that looked both painstaking and painful. The letters were awkward, some big, some small, the words misspelled. But in it, Elliot wrote what had happened to Arnold Ashton. His guilt hadn't gone so far that he had confessed all to a solicitor or Runner, but it had plagued him enough that he managed somehow to write down the bare facts on a slip of paper. In it he said that he hadn't known the woman's name at the time, but had later discovered that it was Clara, Lady Budleigh. She had paid him to lie in wait for a certain Arnold Ashton on a lone road in Hampstead Heath on a given evening and to shoot the man in the head.

Elliot had gone as far as to get the note witnessed and signed by someone else. Given that this other man's name had no job title next to it, Damian guessed that it was probably another highwayman rather than a man of the law. Anya had mentioned that Elliot had been afraid for his life. He had wondered if Clara Budleigh was the kind of woman who would not leave loose ends and would put an end to Neesy Elliot's existence at the earliest opportunity. As a precaution, he had changed his turf and, it seemed, had written this note.

The note wasn't much as evidence went. Anyone could have concocted it, and the witness's name counted for less than nothing. The whole thing could be discounted. He doubted it would stand up in a court of law. His only hope was that it would count, not with Clara, perhaps, but with Preston, who was definitely the weak link in the chain.

He and Jeremy buried Neesy Elliot in his back garden, with a little wood placard that read *Neesy Elliot*. Jeremy said he hoped the man would enjoy the view of the stars and the night sky that had been his friend for so many years. Damian made a present of Merrily to Benny and his father. Benny whooped in joy, and his father stared moodily at the horse but didn't say no to the present of yet another nag for his motley collection. Damian left them some more coins, some food, and the horseshoe for Merrily.

Damian then made his way down to Folkestone and presented his dear cousin Preston with a copy of the note that he had found buried under Neesy Elliot's floorboard. And told him that the note would be published any day now unless Preston made it clear to the *ton* that Damian had no hand in Arnold Ashton's death. *And* the Budleighs promised to stop trying to get their hands on the Ashton estate, and in fact, on the dowager's money, which would belong to Anya Marleigh in a few weeks.

Damian thought it wise to lay these simple facts in front of Preston and not Clara. Preston didn't have much sense, but he *was* practical, and Damian hoped that he would see the danger the note posed to his wife. More importantly, Preston didn't have any backbone and was likely to crumble at the first post. Damian was also banking on the idea that Preston would feel some sense of guilt, even if Clara didn't. He held his breath, though he tried to look relaxed, when he presented a copy to Preston.

Damian expected some dithering, but it did not come. Preston slumped when he had had a quick read of the note. "That's that, then," he said.

They sat in the parlor in which the dowager's will had been read a few months ago. "That, as you say, is indeed that, Preston," Damian said, not entirely unkindly.

"You think this'll stand up in a court of law?"

Damian hesitated, but only for one second. "You know, I don't know. But I bet you, society will love it if I publish it and taken with the fact that it is a dying man's declaration, the *ton* might take it somewhat seriously, might they not?" Not to mention that Clara Budleigh was hardly popular in the *ton*. She was too stuck-up and frigid in her manner to be popular. Preston likely knew that too.

Preston didn't dither for long. "If I retract all my accusations, will you hand the original back to me?"

"I won't. I will hold on to it. As insurance, you might say. Because, you see, I don't trust you or Clara one little bit, Preston. But you have my word for it. I will only ever use it if I must. Not otherwise."

Preston wiped his mouth with his handkerchief. "And why this largesse? Why so generous, Damian?" He sounded tired. "You could still publish this note."

"It's not generosity. You are a peer. The law will likely do nothing. I am merely practical. And, you know, the strange thing is, Preston, I'm almost convinced that you had little to do with this."

Preston didn't argue. There was something to be said about his loyalty to Clara, however misplaced it was, thought Damian. He didn't try to justify or defend her, but didn't condemn her either. It was like he accepted her for who she was. Perhaps that was the only way he could live with her. Damian would almost feel sorry for Preston, except that one way or another Preston had allowed it all to happen—he hadn't stopped it. He hadn't stopped Arnold Ashton's death. Or the campaign against Anya. And in Damian's eyes, that made him as guilty as his wife. From things that Preston said, it seemed that Charlie had known about how Arnold Ashton had died too. Apparently, he hadn't wanted any part of it. Damian should have some sympathy for Charlie, but no, nothing could replace the rage he felt whenever he thought of what the man had tried to do to Anya. If he had been haunted by his family's collective guilt, then it was less than he deserved to suffer.

As Damian was getting ready to take his leave, dear Clara walked into the room. She was dressed in a severely high-cut dress, this one a putrid green, that looked like it was trying to strangle her. Her hands tightened on thin air at the sight of Damian. Surprise and displeasure seemed to be fighting for supremacy on her face. "Damian," she said, her tone dripping with loathing. "To what do we owe this visit? You know, I really don't think we should entertain you, given what the *ton* thinks of your hand in Arnold Ashton's death. We have our reputation to think of. And the man was a distant relative."

Damian smiled. Clara looked at him with hatred. Preston mutely held out the copy of Neesy Elliot's note. She read it quickly. Nothing changed on her face. She didn't look at her husband but handed the note back to him. "I should have known the man couldn't be trusted," she said.

"I have to hand it to you, dear Cousin Clara," Damian said, full of admiration. "Not a bat of an eyelid. Not a grimace. Not a twitch. Not a protest that the note means nothing."

She actually looked surprised. "Why should there be?" She looked at Damian. "The Budleigh money belongs to us. I had every right—in fact, a duty—to try to claim it back."

"A duty?"

"*You* may not understand duty. Your family did a bunk, if I may be so crude, generations ago. What would you understand about duty? *I* do have a duty. And so does Preston. We must do everything we can to preserve the name, the lands. It is a sacred job, and only the worthy can do it. Only the ones that can handle the burden of it."

Damian knew he was looking at her like she was an animal in the zoo. "You know, I really think you believe that."

"I do believe it. If you had any lineage to think about, anything at all that gave you a sense of who you are or your place in the world . . ." She curled her lip.

Preston sat down heavily on the edge of a chair and looked despondently at the floor. Neesy Elliot's note hung limply in his hands.

"Thank you," Damian said to Clara. "I now understand why you had to go after Anya Marleigh, why you feel no remorse at the death of Charlie Budleigh, why you were willing to use him as a pawn in your games, why you were willing to marry Anya off to some decaying old Budleigh. You have made it admirably clear. And if I feel I must wash my brain out with chlorine after this little chat, that is of course my problem, not yours. The question is, though, dear cousin, why did you go after the Ashton land and title? That is not Budleigh money."

She still looked surprised. "The Budleighs and Ashtons are cousins. The title and estate *would* have come to Preston if you hadn't stood in the way. It was meant to come to us. Why else did a lot of Ashtons and Budleighs die? Why would there have been such an unlikely series of accidents and deaths if fate did not see Preston and me as the rightful custodians?"

"Why, indeed?" Damian said faintly.

"But to tell you the truth, Damian, we only needed the Ashton estate and title to help us buffer and support the Budleigh estate. I had no personal interest in the Ashton estate. We had to have it so that we could preserve the Budleigh estate. *That* must come before anything."

Damian looked at Preston, who looked defeated. "Before *anything*, Clara?" he said, almost feeling sorry for Preston.

"What could be more important?" Clara answered.

Damian couldn't help glancing at the copy of Elliot's letter that was still dangling in Preston's hands.

Clara looked a little frozen for the first time. "Now that you have ruined it all, I suppose I shall have to think of a different way."

Damian left the Budleighs feeling like he had entered a different realm, in which logic was all twisted and people spoke a different language. Clara was a hundred percent sure that she was right and that he was wrong. And not only was he wrong but he was so stupid he could never be made to understand what was obvious to superior mortals. That he could never have the moral purpose that she did. There was no room for doubt or remorse. He couldn't help feeling that he would have more luck in explaining culpability to an orangutan.

Damian received a note not long after his visit saying that Preston would publicly apologize for his "mistake" in thinking that Damian had a hand in Arnold Ashton's death. And that Preston and Clara were planning on making their way to the Continent and spending some years there, for Preston's health, which was apparently precarious. Damian had no idea if Preston had prevailed on his wife to undertake these actions, or in fact if she was prosaic enough to accept the inevitable.

Damian hoped that it would be a good long time before he had to look at his dear cousins Preston and Clara again. This outcome wasn't justice for Arnold Ashton or for poor Neesy Elliot, but Damian was enough of a realist to know that it was as good as he was going to get. In fact, it was better than he had hoped.

He was at the palace now. He had been so preoccupied with

his thoughts that he had barely noticed the journey. He handed over his carriage to be parked. And waited to be ushered in. This, he thought, *this* meeting with Anya was surely the thing he had been preparing for all his life. He tugged at his unruly hair. Why, then, did he feel so woefully unprepared?

32

As he watched the musicians prepare for the evening's festivities, Damian felt more like a schoolboy than he had ever felt in his life. He was dressed for court. Or as much as he ever did. Black satin and sapphire velvet. His boots were shining—Mrs. Garner had appointed a new valet, someone trained and qualified, and apparently it made a huge difference to a man's comfort and appearance to have a trained valet. Who knew? He'd have to find another job for Linus when he came back from France. He might have to hold on to the new valet.

His hair was less untidy than usual—he hoped. He tried to look completely at his ease. But he felt like a schoolboy.

Anya hadn't seen him yet. She was tuning her sitar and chatting with the other two musicians, the violinist and pianist. The violinist—Serena Mercurio—looked as severe in her black clothes as ever. But she did have a humorous light in her eye when they landed on Anya and the women exchanged some or the other comment. Mary Drummond—who was wearing enormous hoops under her bright yellow skirt—was as usual chiding and chivvying the younger women. They looked at peace, the three women, in their easy camaraderie. They even looked happy.

Wasn't that great? After all that she and he had been through, after the days he had waited to see her, she looked happy. Wasn't that wonderful.

He would wait until she had finished for the evening. He had things he wished to say to her.

He had things he had wished to say to her for the two weeks since he and Jeremy had taken her, cold, crying, and bleeding, to her sister's house in Berkeley Square in the early hours of the morning. He had left her there that morning.

He hadn't wanted to be parted from her. He'd wanted more than anything to never let her out of his sight again. But cold and sobbing as she was, she'd insisted on being taken to the Tristrams' house. She wouldn't hear of going to Damian's. She was sobbing in his arms, but he couldn't help noticing, even then, that she never once put her arms around him. She never rested her head on his shoulder or his chest. She didn't fight him or resist him, but she didn't draw closer. It was the early hours of the morning, and Lila took one look at her broken sister, took her in her arms, and didn't even look back at Damian Ashton, who was standing forlornly at the door, or at Jeremy, who looked pale with tiredness and worry. The butler—a forbidding man named Walsham—suggested that the men come back another day. At a more suitable hour. That, half past seven in the morning, not being a very suitable hour. He had tried to argue, knowing that it was foolish. You couldn't just stand outside a gentleman's house and beg or demand to be let in. Apparently, Walsham felt the same. He didn't exactly argue with Damian, but he didn't budge from his position. Jeremy finally squeezed Damian's arm and suggested that they leave. He and Jeremy made their way back to their lodgings.

Later in the morning, he would have made his way back to Lila and Ivor's house. But a note from Lila was delivered, saying that Anya wished for privacy to recover. And could they postpone their visit? She wanted to assure the brothers that Anya was well taken care of. The doctor had seen her, and though she was nearly frozen to the bone and had various cuts and injuries, she would recover soon enough. The doctor was not too worried. Would they wait for Lila to let them know when it was convenient to visit?

The note was polite, but it was also final. There was no room for quarrel. And Damian wondered how he had ever let it get this way, where he had no claim on her at all. Where her sister, or really anyone in her life, could tell him what he could or could not do, when he could or could not see her.

Lila did not get back to him to let him know that it was convenient to visit. He chafed at the bit for days, unable to sleep or eat or make civil conversation, knowing that Jeremy was holding the fort with his housekeeper, Mrs. Garner, and even with Damian's new valet. He did what he had to do about Neesy Elliot and the Budleighs, but his mind was on Anya.

He sent notes to Lila's place. He even—uninvited—showed up at Lila Tristram's door one afternoon and stood on the doorstep for nearly an hour. But Walsham said that the women were not taking visitors. Short of breaking down the door, there was nothing he could do.

So here he was. In the palace. Just like any of the other guests at this soiree. Waiting to hear her sing and play her sitar like he was a stranger to her and she was a stranger to him, no different from anyone else. Damn and blast Lila Tristram. Damn and blast all of them. To not let him see her, speak to her, explain to her. Ask her what he needed to ask her. What he should have asked her a long time ago, maybe as soon as they met. If he had asked her, then she would be his and he could protect her. He wouldn't need anyone's permission to see her and hold her.

He was planning to find a quiet spot near a wall and lose himself in the music and wait the evening out. Then, when she was done with her work, he would ask if he could have a word. And if that thought made him feel like an awkward schoolboy, so be it.

As he stood by a wall and watched, the musicians took their places.

There was a moment, just a breath of a moment, as Anya sat herself down and placed the instrument ready to be played across her lap, when she caught sight of him.

She froze. Just for a second. So brief that anyone else would have missed it. She froze in that second and blinked. Her fingers completely still on her strings. He watched her chest rise and fall. He watched those lashes of hers as she blinked.

But then she started plucking. Like she was barely breathing. Like she could hardly think. But she was plucking. The soulful strains of the sitar filled the room, made the air itself vibrate. The others took her cue. She looked away from him and she started singing. The voice didn't waver. It wasn't frozen or stilted. It was just her usual voice.

And she didn't look at him even one more time for the entire hour that the musicians were entertaining the assembled guests. Not even one more time. It was like he didn't exist. In fact, even that spot in the room where he was standing didn't exist. Not once did her eyes so much as flicker in his direction.

It was excruciating. He found he couldn't breathe. He could barely look at her and he couldn't look away.

The music was enchanting. The company was small—made

of only about thirty or forty guests—and very appreciative of the music. But he couldn't bear standing there, waiting to speak to her. Time was stretching to the breaking point. And it was like a physical ache. Even her music hurt today.

The music finally came to an end. There was the usual breathless silence for a second that always followed her music, before the crescendo of an applause.

The musicians put away their instruments, and many of the guests wanted to speak to them. She was listening to the people complimenting her, smiling, nodding, thanking them, accepting some champagne, and gulping it down as he had seen her do when she had been singing. She looked delicious. The gown she wore was made of the filmiest gauze. It was so beige it was almost not there, but it was embroidered in red and yellow and bronze. It suited her perfectly.

She was still not looking at him. She was drinking her champagne and accepting the thanks of the guests.

It took a long time for the crowd around the musicians to thin. He was about to get up his courage and go to her, hoping that it wouldn't show that he felt like a bumbling child, that just the sight of those eyes of hers could do that to him, but another man made it to her first.

Dear god. It was that man—Darren Greenwood.

Damian froze. This couldn't be happening. He hadn't even noticed Greenwood in the company. Where had the man sprung from? Was he just waiting for his chance? He watched in agony as the man bowed to her and she smiled back at him. They seemed to talk for about an hour, though realistically it was probably no more than about ten or so minutes—Darren Greenwood was exactly the kind of boring man who would be polite and not take up more time than was seemly. Still, did she have to be so marked in her attentions? Did she have to talk to him for that long? People would think she liked the man, talking with him in that smiling way for such a long time!

Damian was already restless when he got to the palace. Actually he was already restless *before* he was anywhere near the palace. But now he was practically climbing out of his skin. Did the man have to look so solid and steady? Did she have to smile at him in that way? Why were they talking for so long? Greenwood finally walked away. And Damian had his path clear.

Except then she turned and stared directly at him. How she knew where exactly he was standing was not clear. All he knew was he couldn't breathe.

And then before he could start breathing again or make his way to her, she—dear god—started walking toward him. He had the strange and completely discombobulating feeling that he had turned to stone or ice, that he was glued to the spot.

He stood his ground. Hardly breathing.

She got to him and made him a little curtsy. He bowed. It was a wonder he didn't fall on his face. He couldn't feel his limbs.

"Lord Ashton, I have not had the chance to thank you."

His heart was beating so fast there was a good chance he was going to faint. She was so beautiful. So incredibly beautiful. But more importantly, she was alive. She was alive and he never wanted to let her out of his sight again. He never wanted to live through another few hours, or even another hour, when he was not sure if she was dead or alive or if he would ever see her again. How he had thought he could live apart from her wasn't clear. It was obvious he must have been mad. She was looking at him like he was nothing more than a stranger.

"Thank me?" he said stupidly.

"You and Jeremy saved my life."

"You saved your life," he said. "You got yourself free."

"I don't know if I had it in me to get up again. It had taken every ounce of strength just to cut myself free. I had no legs to get up again, much less try to find my way home. So thank you."

Now, now was his chance. To say everything he wanted to say. Everything he'd been storing up for days and weeks. Admittedly she couldn't look more coldly at him if he were the innards of a rat decapitated by the palace cats. But still, she was here. Right here. He could see her and speak to her. And he could say what he had been dying to say for the last two weeks. He had practiced it too. He'd made a botch of it.

"You don't need to marry Greenwood. You have other options," he blurted out.

If she looked cold before, now her eyes were like steel. "Do I now?" she said, her eyes glinting.

Had he seen her eyes glint like that before?

"You don't need to marry him for the inheritance. You could marry me and that would solve your problem."

Oh, dear lord. *What* was he saying? He meant to propose, of course he did. What on earth was he going on about the inheritance for? *That's* not what he meant to say at all.

"Indeed," she said, sounding as frozen as she looked. Her lip curled. Not just frozen, but also disdainful. "How kind of you. How helpful to point out my options. But I could not ask you to make such a sacrifice."

"It wouldn't be a sacrifice at all, I can assure you!"

She was grinding her teeth now. "How kind."

"It isn't at all. Not when *you* did so much to help me. With Neesy Elliot, with—with—" What was he *saying*?

"Oh, I see. You're *grateful*."

"No, not at all. Never. I—"

"Mr. Greenwood cares for me. I am sure he would make a delightful husband."

He was talking fast now. This conversation had gone completely wrong. He had to try to salvage it. "Great-Auntie Griselda wanted us to be together. I am sure of it. There's no other reason she could have left the money like she did. She left it to you, but with me as executor. She mentioned you to me a few times. She admired you. She wanted us to meet, but I rarely visited the Budleighs if I could help it, and so I never got to meet you before it was too late and she was gone. She wanted us to be together. I am sure of it."

Her lips were a tight line. "How kind of you to try to do what your great-aunt wanted," she said coldly. "I am sure she would have appreciated it. I don't see why I should do what the dowager wanted, however."

She was turning away, and he knew he had botched it, made a royal mess of it, and he reached out a desperate hand. "Anya, don't go. I know I'm doing a very bad job of it. Of course it isn't about the inheritance. Or about Great-Auntie Griselda. I love you. You know I do. And I love you so much that I don't even care anymore if you had a hand in what happened to Linus or not."

He stopped abruptly. Wondering how it was that she had gone from coldness through disdain straight to fury. Because now her eyes were blazing. He was half sure she was going to punch him. She was breathing hard. She took a step closer. "How incredibly kind," she said, her teeth clenched. "How forgiving, Lord Ashton. How lucky I am."

He was wondering if any man in the history of proposals had driven a woman to incandescent rage. But it wasn't the rage that broke him. Because along with the rage, maybe *because* of the rage, her eyes filled with tears. They were large and unblinking now, those eyes of hers.

"Anya," he said helplessly.

"Thank you for your time, Lord Ashton. Thank you for being so kind as to love me and not caring anymore if I can be trusted or not. I will always cherish . . ." But she couldn't say another word. Her eyes swam. She didn't brush away the tears or let them fall. She looked at him good and proper, her eyes large and fathomless. And his heart broke. For himself or for her, he wasn't sure. "I will always cherish the time we spent together," she said in a softer voice.

Without saying another word, she turned away. With her back perfectly straight, and quite calmly, she walked back to her place with the other musicians.

He stood there wondering if there was a more colossal idiot anywhere in the world. He stood there wondering how he'd managed to break two hearts—hers and his own—all in the space of a few careless minutes.

33

Anya's twenty-fifth birthday came and went without too much commotion. Lila and Ivor invited her, Trixie, Jeremy, and Kenneth for a small celebration. Kenneth was such easy company, even Trixie had a lovely time. He was full of cryptic sayings and most of the time seemed to be half asleep on the most comfortable piece of furniture he could find, but when he spoke to Trixie, she could also see his kindness. And he made Trixie giggle.

"Thank you for looking out for Trixie," she couldn't help saying to him, as he filled her glass with some sparkling champagne punch—one of Lila's special recipes, today with a hint of mango syrup in it, and a dash of lime, and some shaved pistachios on the side, to mimic Anya's favorite mango kulfi from their Delhi days.

"Good god," he said. "Do not say so. It would damage my reputation if people thought I was kind." He gave her a speaking glance before wandering off.

She couldn't help noticing that his eyes often watched Jeremy to make sure he wasn't feeling too exhausted or worn-out. She hoped Jeremy's doubts were misplaced, that Kenneth did care for him. But Kenneth wasn't one to wear his heart on his sleeve, and she supposed only time would tell.

Anya had the chance to speak to Jeremy for some moments in the garden, where the May sunshine was making the blue-bells sing and the blossoms unfurl their warmth.

"You know, you could still marry me today by special license and get your hands on Great-Auntie Griselda's fortune," Jeremy said. "She meant you to have it. We could do it before midnight by the speediest special license ever procured."

She shook her head and laughed. She had given up any hope she'd had of having independence. And it felt right. The dowager's wealth was never hers. Darren Greenwood had asked her to marry him, and she had gently turned him down. Trixie was taken care of, and so her main concern was over. Lila had promised that she would take Trixie on.

Lila and Trixie had spoken at some length and the fact that both Lila and Anya were in favor of the plan had finally swayed Trixie. Trixie wasn't old enough to be a teacher in Lila's school. Old or experienced enough. But Lila had promised to take her on as an assistant to the teachers, even an apprentice. They were always impoverished, she said. There was not enough money coming in from the Tristram estate to easily fund the school, so she relied on donations, but she could house and pay Trixie a small wage if the girl wanted. Anya could see that though Trixie was pulled by her loyalty to Anya and didn't want to leave her, the prospect of having some independence, but more importantly to be paid to do what she loved—to educate herself further, to read, to learn more, and, wonder of wonders, to teach—was something that brought a sparkle to Trixie's eyes. It was obvious too that Trixie had never imagined that such a life existed or was possible. Anya had instantly given her blessing and declared that she couldn't imagine giving Trixie over to anyone other than Lila. This had made Lila bark with sardonic laughter, but Anya couldn't help noticing that her sister's cheeks had gone a little pink. She had turned away quickly so people wouldn't notice something as dreadful as Lila blushing.

Amelia Canningford, Lord Budleigh and Charlie Budleigh's sister, had written to Anya. She told her that now that Preston and Clara were leaving for the Continent, Amelia and her husband would make their home at the Budleigh estate and raise their daughter, Laura, and Preston's three boys there. She hoped, said Amelia, that Anya didn't think that Amelia or her husband had anything to do with what Clara had done or tried to do to Anya. She assured her that she didn't grudge Anya her mother's money. Though if Anya was short of a suitor—and of course no one wanted the money to go to *that man*—Anya only had to say, and Amelia was sure she could find someone suitable. Not, she assured Anya, so that Anya would hand over the Budleigh money to the Canningfords, but only so that Anya would have a comfortable independence.

Anya couldn't bring herself to respond. But she thought that Amelia was telling the truth. She probably had no hand in Lady Budleigh's plans. Weak as Charlie was, she doubted that he had had much to do with it either, except to weakly go along with anything he thought would get him out of the financial hole he'd dug for himself.

"I don't need the money. I'm never short of work," she said to Jeremy now. Lila and Ivor's gardens were exquisite. They were large but divided into comfortable nooks. The one they were walking in had an archway dripping with wisteria. It was glorious. Anya wished she could make her home under that arch. "Lila will hardly let me starve when I'm old and not wanted at the palace. I can always teach music if I need to. Seminaries are always looking for tutors, or Lila might want one. I will be fine."

Jeremy was giving her his kind but discerning look. Really, she was coming to hate that look.

"Is that what you want?" he asked.

"I'm fine, Jeremy. Don't look at me like that."

"He knows he botched it, Anya."

She smiled brightly at him. "Oh, that. Don't worry about it for a minute. It was a passing thing. For him and for me. A lovely memory. It was never meant to be permanent." And she was coming to believe it. Whatever Damian had done at the end, she would still cherish the time they had spent together. Lila had found Ivor. But maybe Anya had to be satisfied with memories. It could be worse. Some people never even got to experience what she'd briefly had with Damian. She had her music. She had her life. Damian was perhaps never meant to be a permanent part of it. Perhaps love *and* a vocation were too much to ask, and she was lucky just to have one of those things. "Let's go inside or there will be no cake left," she said.

Luckily, Jeremy didn't press it, the subject of marriage, or the question of Damian Ashton. He asked hesitantly if she wouldn't let him explain to Damian that she had no hand in what happened to Linus. He even said that he didn't think Damian believed her guilty anymore. But she tossed her head and said that Damian had believed it, whether he did now or not, hadn't even stopped to ask her about it, that she didn't think he would ever truly let anyone in. What was the point of such a half-hearted love?

It was after the other guests left and Trixie was escorted back to the palace that the sisters sat in the swings in the garden. "I must get back to Sussex for a bit," Lila said. "See how the school is getting on. I have good teachers, but the young women need help staying motivated sometimes. You wouldn't think it, but many of them think it's easier to carry on plying their trade than try to learn figures." She looked at Anya. "You know, if you didn't want to live in the palace, you can always use this house. Ivor and I aren't always here. And even when we are, it's far larger than we need. You'd always have a home here."

Anya rocked back and forth on the swing. "I have to stay in London because that's where my work is. I might try to save up for a little cottage, so I don't have to live in the palace. It'll be lonely without Trixie when she moves to your school in Sussex. But thank you," she said, knowing she sounded stiff, and not wanting to. It was a kind and generous offer. And it was exactly like Lila to make it. But Anya couldn't imagine it. Taking her sister up on it. Staying on at Lila and Ivor's house. Never really making it her own. Always being a third wheel. Always being a bystander to Lila and Ivor's easy intimacy.

"You can't get me out of your life, Anya. You know it. You can do what you like. You can turn me down when I offer you things. You can be cold if you like. But you won't get rid of me. Not now that we're back together."

Something burned in Anya's chest. It was important to her that Lila was back in her life. Even her interference and nosiness (and making no bones about it, the way she ordered everyone around), even that was something Anya wanted and needed. But telling her how she felt was something else entirely. Her throat was closed. She wanted to say more. But words were difficult sometimes. "When I was tied up by Neesy Elliot," she began, her throat tight, "and I thought—perhaps melodramatically—that I might die, one of the things I re-

gretted the most was—well, it was that I'd kept you shut out."
She stopped abruptly.

Lila looked at her with understanding. "We were all responsible for the lost years, Anya. We all left the triplets behind.
We were all not exactly complicit in our guilt, we were too
young, but perhaps equally complicit in our shame. If we had
banded together, we could at least have had an easier time of
it with Sarah and Jonathan. But we didn't. All three of us did
that, not just you."

Anya flicked her head. "No, it isn't that that I regretted.
You're right. All three of us did that. Kept a barrier erected
between us. But we've had the time as adults to make amends.
You tried to take the first step by inviting us to your wedding.
And Mira and I said no. And now you've been trying to come
back into my life and I haven't been able to take you up on it.
Not fully or wholeheartedly." She looked at Lila, her eyes full.
"I do want to, Lila. Sometimes, it's like I don't know how."

Lila's face was still. Then she said, "You know, I don't know
either. I know I look like I do. But I don't. I'm the queen of
looking strong and confident, especially when I don't feel it. I
don't know how to go about it at all."

"You don't?"

"Half the time, I don't know what I should do with you.
Come closer, give you space, share something, keep something
a secret, talk more, talk less. I don't know. Because there's no
map or guide."

Anya looked at Lila, feeling a little torn between amusement
and exasperation. "So what do you do, then?"

"I fake it," Lila said. "I ask myself, what would I do if I
weren't terrified? What would I do if we were normal sisters?
And then I just do it."

Anya stared at Lila, then went off into a peal of laughter that took even her by surprise. Lila smiled complacently for some moments and then started laughing too. They were hiccupping, half crying, several minutes later.

"Now we just have to win Mira over, and we are on our way," Lila said when they finally stopped spluttering.

Anya laughed. Her throat was hurting. But Lila could still make her laugh. It wasn't just Lila's words but the determined look on her face. But there was something else that needed to be said. "The triplets," she said.

"We must find them. But I want to thaw Mira first. It's something the three of us have to do: work together to find the triplets. I'm sure of it."

Anya hesitated. This was unchartered territory. And she didn't know if she had the courage for it. Why even bother? Why not let things remain unsaid? Yet perhaps Lila's approach was best. Act as if you do know what you're doing. Act as if you're not terrified. "Lila," she said gently, "they aren't our sisters. You know that, don't you?"

Lila's face blazed. "How can you say that? Of course they are! We let them down in the worst possible way, and it's true, they didn't grow up with us. But they are our sisters!"

Anya looked quietly at her for a long time, hoping that she didn't have to spell it out, hoping that Lila would come around to it herself. After all, deep down, Lila must know. Didn't she? But no understanding showed on Lila's face.

"Lila, they're our half sisters," she tried again, gentler still.

"What are you talking about?"

Anya stared a little helplessly at her sister. "Mama disappeared. Don't you remember? I barely remember it; we were very little. She was gone for almost a year. Papa was out of his mind. Lila, when she came back, she was pregnant. She gave birth to the triplets soon after."

Lila swung off her swing so fast she nearly fell over. She stood there, chest heaving, face blazing, staring at Anya. "Maybe it was less than a year. Less than nine months. She must have been pregnant before she left! It was a long time ago. How would you know how long she was gone? You were a child!"

Anya didn't speak. She stayed sitting on her swing. She kept looking at her sister.

It took a long time for the fire to leave Lila's face. It took a long time, but she finally sat down on her swing again. "They're not our sisters. Or at least, they will *always* be our sisters. But they are not Papa's children. How is it you remember this and I don't? I'm older. How could you have understood something like that?"

"I've only pieced it together over the years. It's not like it would have made sense then. But you remember Papa hated the triplets. So did we. And he never stopped us from hating them. He never told us off or told us we could do better. He hated them as much as we did."

Lila batted away tears. "Oh, those poor, poor little things. How, how could we have left them like that? We were all they had. So many times, *so* many times, Anya, I dream of being given that choice again. And in the dream, the three of us, we say it's all six or none at all. Why did Sarah Marleigh want us anyway, the evil, *evil* witch!"

"Because it was more cruel that way," Anya said. "It was cruel to separate us. To bind the three of us with this guilt that we can never shake. To punish us for being our father's children. To punish us for the fact that our father chose to be with Mama and us and not her and Jonathan. To separate the triplets in the cruelest possible way."

But Lila shook her head. "I've thought about it and thought about it. Sarah was an evil witch, without a doubt. She was cruel and she liked being cruel. But I don't believe she adopted us just out of cruelty."

Anya frowned. "What, then?"

"I have no idea. But I'm going to try to find out. She must have had some other reason. I can't imagine that Sarah would do something to put herself out, even just to be cruel."

They sat silently on their swings for a long time.

Finally, Anya said, "Let's find the triplets."

"Yes, we must find them. But first, Mira."

"Do you have any ideas how to bring her around?" Mira was definitely the hardest nut to crack.

Anya was happy to see the sparkle return to Lila's eyes. "Not yet," she said and grinned. "But something will come along, I'm sure of it. And if nothing else, then perhaps something terrible will happen to her that will deliver her right to our door and we will welcome her with open arms. She will *hate* that."

Anya couldn't help grinning back. "You have no idea how much I love you," she said, before she could stop herself.

But, Lila being Lila, she didn't make too much of the moment. She didn't dwell on it or make Anya uncomfortable. "Oh, I know that," she said lightly. "You can't live without me."

Anya laughed. "I didn't say that."

Lila waved a hand. "What are mere words?" But then she stopped grinning and looked hesitantly at Anya.

"What?" Anya asked. Were there any more difficult revelations?

"Now, don't bite my head off. It's just that Jeremy told me Damian proposed and you turned him down."

Anya bent down to pluck a few daisies. She started threading them to make a chain. "He still isn't sure if I betrayed him or not. He says he no longer cares if I did or not. It's why I couldn't bear to return to his house, and I came back to you that night when Neesy Elliot died. There's no point."

"He sounds like a very stupid man. But have you told him you didn't betray him?"

Anya jerked her head. "Why should I? Why should I need to? He should understand it himself, without me spelling it out."

Lila looked thoughtfully into space for some time. "You know, I don't know any man—any man worth knowing, that is—who isn't terrified of love. Poor things, it must seem to them like it comes out of nowhere. Like a lightning strike or something designed to hurt them. And then it's *there* and they don't know what to do with it." She sounded sympathetic. "I once told Ivor to his face that he was a coward. That he was afraid of loving me."

"And how did that go?"

"Never mind that," Lila said, waving a cool hand. "That's neither here nor there. What I mean is, Anya, maybe Damian thinks he needs you to be perfect, to never hurt him, to never terrify him. Maybe he thinks he needs that so that he can feel safe enough to love you, even though there *is* no safety in love. But—"

"But?" Anya couldn't help asking.

"Darling, aren't you looking for him to be the same? For his love to be perfect? To never hurt you or misunderstand you, to be able to read what's in your heart and your mind, even though you guard it so carefully? Aren't you looking for a perfect love too? Maybe, Anya, there's no such thing."

Anya had no idea how Lila could at the same time make her laugh and put her in a rage, and then when she thought that's all Lila would ever do, here she was and it turned out she could make her weep. Not that she was weeping. She wasn't weeping.

Luckily, she was saved by the bell.

Walsham came out to the garden, looking grim. But then Walsham always looked grim whenever Lila had visitors. He seemed to take them as something of a personal affront. His back was rigid and his knuckles curled with arthritis, but his eyebrow was just as disapproving as ever. He was holding his head up like there was a bad smell he was trying to avoid.

"Mrs. Lila," he said, "there is a *person* at the door."

"Oh dear, how dare someone come to our door?" Lila said at once, looking blandly up at Walsham. "We must write a notice to inform the world that we do *not*, under any circumstances, like visitors."

Walsham did not blink. "The person says he is a lawyer looking for Miss Anya."

"I'm so sorry, Walsham," Lila said. "Did I forget to add lawyers to the long list of people who are not allowed to visit me? How careless of me."

"If such a class of person would understand that a gentleman's dwelling is a gentleman's dwelling, not a place for lowly transactions—"

"Were you or were you not my butler when I ran a gambling den, Walsham?"

"I prefer not to remember such times, Mrs. Lila."

"A lawyer is better than a gambler . . ." Lila murmured.

"Gambling is only a hobby, even if a vile one. The other is the person's chosen profession," Walsham said.

"What about a stray mongrel? Is a lawyer better or a stray mongrel?"

"*One* of them can't help being what they are," Walsham said with great dignity.

Lila winked at Anya. Walsham held his head high as he left the garden to walk indoors. The lawyer was reluctantly shown in, and Walsham made sure with his deep sniffs that everyone knew that he was not happy with this, not happy at all.

It was Mr. Prism.

He looked as long and lanky and neat as ever, not a hair out of place, not a wrinkle in his neat clothing. He apologized profusely for disturbing the sisters, bowed to Lila several times—he seemed a little struck by her flaming beauty—then turned to Anya and said that he had bumped into her protégé at the palace and Miss Cleaver said that he would find her here, at her sister's house. He hoped Miss Marleigh—and Mrs. Tristram—didn't mind that he took the liberty of making his way here. He thought it best to get his business over with instead of waiting for a different day. But of course he would come back another day if he was in the way.

"Thank you, Mr. Prism," Anya said. "I'm sorry to put you to all this trouble. Do I need to do some paperwork now that I am twenty-five? To give up all claims to the dowager's money or something?" Lawyers loved paperwork. That was no doubt why the man was here. Everything would have to be said, read, and signed five times over. She may as well have a fortifying drink. She would offer him a cup of tea. "Can we offer Mr. Prism some tea?" she asked Lila. "Or will this give Walsham an apoplexy?"

"Walsham has one of those at least once a day. His day wouldn't be complete if he didn't. We must give the lovely Mr. Prism some cake too."

The lovely Mr. Prism went a bright pink. "Thank you—I—you are heavenly—that is to say, so kind."

Lila graciously inclined her head and then turned and half winked at her sister, who was trying not to laugh.

Mr. Prism was having great trouble concentrating, but he conscientiously turned to Anya. "Your sister—"

"Is divine."

"Yes. That is to say—too kind."

"Isn't she just?"

He cleared his throat. "As to your question about paperwork, Miss Marleigh, it is something to do with why I am here. As we know, the dowager simply wanted the money to go to you on your twenty-fifth birthday if you married, and if your executor gave his consent to said marriage. If you didn't marry, the money automatically reverted to the executor. There's no more paperwork in that regard."

"Yes," Anya said, wondering why lawyers felt like they needed to repeat tedious details quite so many times. "I know all this."

"Since you are not married and it is your twenty-fifth birthday today, the money would revert to Lord Ashton."

"Yes. I know," she said, slightly impatiently.

"Now that the money is his, Lord Ashton has signed over the dowager's money to you, Miss Marleigh, and it is entirely, without condition, at your disposal. With immediate effect."

Anya nearly fell off the swing.

34

Anya stood behind Laura, her hands guiding Laura's skinny little arms, waiting for Toby's delivery. The delivery came—a neat one at that; he must have been practicing—and with Anya's help, Laura swung the bat wide and thwacked the ball good and hard so that it gave her and Anya time to pack in a solid run as the three boys ran to retrieve the ball. Laura was jumping up and down, her red braids swinging about, her face red from excitement and from the bright June sunshine. "Look, Anya, look, we got another run, we got another run!"

The boys returned with the ball. Trevor and Brendan were grinning and wiping their foreheads. Toby was frowning. "It isn't right if you're helping her, you know," he said to Anya. "How can that be right? No one's helping us."

Now Anya was at the crease, and the next few swings went for fours. Laura was nearly out of her mind with excitement. "That's more than one run! It's more than two runs!" she was screaming. "It's more than six! Oh, wait, Anya, is it more than six?" She was trying to count up to four on her fingers.

The boys and Laura were sweaty and disheveled by the time

they stopped for a drink. Laura was clinging to her skirts and asking when she would leave. "Will you leave tomorrow, Anya? The day after? In three hundred weeks? Oh, please leave in three hundred weeks!"

The boys were busy recounting all the wonderful things they were doing in school, but especially how phenomenal they were at cricket, and how they were by far better than any of their friends. Trevor and Brendan had apparently never lost a match. They seemed to feel that they had to demonstrate to Anya all the great deliveries and shots they had made in recent history. Laura was telling Anya that now she lived here, with the cousins, and so she would always find her here. Always and always and always, Anya!

Amelia Canningford and her husband, Geoffrey, stepped out of the house, where they were now making their home while acting as guardians to the three boys when their parents were "traveling on the Continent" for the sake of Preston Budleigh's health.

Amelia Canningford, while she could make herself understood in a letter, looked just as nervous as always in person. "Geoffrey says that perhaps I didn't convey our thanks graciously enough just now," she said, her face pink. She was wearing a blue floral dress. A little insipidly cut but more relaxed than anything Anya had ever seen Lady Budleigh wear.

"There's no 'perhaps' about it, old chap," her husband said, smacking her on the back and making her shake. He looked at Anya. "My wife gets flustered when there are financial things to discuss. Don't you, old chap?" he asked Amelia.

"Yes, yes, I do. Mama always said I had no more sense than a sparrow, probably less. You must forgive me. I am eternally grateful to you for what you have done, Anya. Mr. Prism makes me nervous when he repeats things. It makes me worry I'm missing important details. Or that I am too stupid to understand plain English."

"That wouldn't surprise me at all," said Geoffrey.

"You're welcome," Anya said, uncomfortable at the effusion.

Amelia was batting her eyelids.

"Out with it, chum," her husband helpfully said. "No point letting it curdle."

"Yes, yes," Amelia said. "I do hope you won't hold it against *us* what—what—I mean, my brother, he has no backbone. Mama always said a man with no backbone always ends up with a horse-faced . . ." She stopped abruptly and blotted her mouth with a handkerchief.

"I never think there's any harm in calling a spade a spade," Geoffrey Canningford elaborated. "The woman *is* sour-faced. She could make milk curdle just by looking at it. And Charlie, Charlie got what was coming to him. He was always going to end that way. I said it often enough. Didn't I say it?"

Amelia nodded. "You did say it. If there's anything we can ever do—I mean you, being in your situation, at court like that, I mean, I suppose no one will marry you—"

Her husband thumped her on the back so hard she nearly fell over. "Always stop while you're ahead, I always say."

Amelia blushed. "These are of course not my views, Anya, just society's. Thank you for what you did. A lesser woman wouldn't have done it. We will always be grateful."

Anya shook her head quickly. She had done nothing. She had conferred with Mr. Prism, asked him if the Budleigh grandchildren were comfortably placed, and when he assured her they were, she asked him what kind of amount the Canningfords would need to be able to hold on to the Budleigh estate and not end in a debtors' prison. He named a sum. It was half of what the dowager had left her. She would still have a very comfortable independence if she handed half of the dowager's money over to the Canningfords, to be used for maintaining the Budleigh estate and its tenants. The estate, of course, belonged to Lord Budleigh, but nothing could be done about that.

Mr. Prism had all but rolled his eyes when she said that's what she wanted to do. It seemed, he couldn't help saying, that *no one* wished to hold on to Dowager Countess Budleigh's generous bequest.

She came today to Folkestone, to the Budleigh house, to complete the formalities and make sure the paperwork was in order. It took a tediously long time, with Amelia expressing broken thanks, Geoffrey egging her on to say the right things, and Mr. Prism repeating everything eleven times.

When it was done and she was done with the Canningfords, she would look for a little cottage in London. Somewhere that was hers. Within easy reach of Lila's home, if possible, but somewhere she had her own space and her own life. Really, it was all she had ever wanted or hoped for. More than she expected. It would be enough.

The thought of looking for a respectable female companion was more daunting. When she had reluctantly told the Queen of her plans, the Queen had been having a difficult morning with her husband. She frowned heavily at Anya and said querulously, "I suppose since you *can* get your independence, why shouldn't you get it? Why should you care about anyone else or whether or not *they* are allowed to have any independence?"

Anya apologized. She said she would make herself scarce before she enraged the Queen more. To which the Queen said, "If you do not *instantly* show yourself when I summon you for a musical evening, you can expect to find yourself housed in the Tower. I hope that is clear. I will find a female companion for you. And I hope she is a termagant who restricts your independence to such a degree that you have the shame to regret all your impertinences to me!"

Anya murmured that the Queen would have become bored of her long ago *but* for her many impertinences. To which the Queen snorted and waved her on her way. "Out of my sight before I have you cuffed to a pillar and make it so that you are not allowed to leave."

Now, standing outside in the sunshine, on the Budleigh estate, Anya listened as patiently as she could to all the thanks Amelia and Geoffrey wanted to give her. When they finally retreated back into the house, she played some more overs with Laura and the boys. The children made her promise that she would come back at Christmas, and though she said that would depend on whether or not she was invited, she thought there was little chance of her coming back to Folkestone again.

She made her way, on foot, down the lane that led toward the Swann Inn, from where she could get the stagecoach back to London. The walk would take half an hour and Amelia had nearly swooned at the thought of so much walking and in such warm weather, and the housekeeper, Mrs. Winsome, pronounced that Anya would inevitably die of the heat if she walked and her corpse would have to be peeled off the road, where it would lie melting, but Anya resolutely said no to a carriage ride to the Swann Inn.

It was a perfectly beautiful day for a walk. Wisteria clung to the old oaks and pollen floated on the air. Ducks waddled ungracefully around the duck pond that stood at the border of the Budleigh estate, with little yellow fluff balls in tow.

Dragonflies feathered the water and little darting fish-colored shadows under the surface. It was nearly perfect, Anya thought, and wondered why she was sighing so wistfully when it was all so perfect or why there was an ache in her heart where there should only have been sunshine. She watched the ducks for a little while, waddling with their three fuzzy ducklings.

She could still hear the laughter and shouts coming from the four children, though she couldn't see them anymore. She'd made her way to the Budleigh estate reluctantly. She wanted the Canningfords to have the money, but she didn't want to speak to them. She didn't think it would be a happy visit. But now that it was over, the formalities dealt with, cricket played, she was strangely reluctant to leave. Amelia had offered her a bed for the night, or for some nights if she chose (Laura had begged her to stay), but she had turned it down. She could hardly go back now and ask if she could stay after all. She started on her way again.

In the lane, she bumped into Jane Simmonds, the Budleighs' former housemaid. "Jane!"

"Miss Marleigh." Jane made her a curtsy. Jane was older than Anya by a few years and very pretty, her brown hair tied back neatly and pretty freckles around her nose and cheekbones, though there were also faint lines of tiredness around her eyes. At the moment, there were twin spots of color in her cheeks. "Miss Marleigh, I never got to thank you. Not properly. And I would like to have. But I was barely in London for a day or two. I never had the chance."

Anya was astonished. "What on earth for?"

"For standing up for me over the thing with the oil, miss. No one ever sticks up for a servant. And I have my boy. He's only five. And he's ever so clever. I want him to be educated. I want him to have a good life. I depend on my income. It's not easy for me to find other employment, miss. I can't just pick and choose like some can."

"You are employed now, though, aren't you?" Anya said quickly so that Jane couldn't carry on thanking her. There was too much thanks going around today for comfort. And she certainly hadn't done anything for Jane. "I mean, I should thank you for everything you did for me in London with the Budleigh staff. Not the other way round."

"Oh no, miss. I was glad to do it. Lady Budleigh was never nice to me. Though to be fair, she was never nice to anyone. But it wasn't a chore to help you. I would do anything to help you. You just have to name it." The twin spots of color deepened.

Anya was embarrassed. "You're comfortably placed now?"

"Oh yes, miss. Mrs. Canningford offered me my job back. She knew I didn't do anything with the oil, not even by mistake. I cherish what work I get. And I would do anything to hold on to it. I'm a good worker, dependable, and Mrs. Canningford knows it. But I'm comfortable in Lord Ashton's household, so I said no. And anyway"—the color in her cheeks was bordering on scarlet now—"there's a gardener on Lord Ashton's estate who likes me and who doesn't mind that I have a child." She smiled shyly.

"Good, that's good. I'm glad you're well. I'm happy for you." Anya looked into the distance. "And Lord Ashton? I hope he's well too?"

"Oh yes, miss. I mean, I don't know, miss. He's in London."

Yes, Jeremy had assured her Damian was in London. That's why she had chosen to come and finish her business with the Canningfords now. She was relieved that he was in London. She didn't know why the ache in her heart was growing, then. "That's good, that he's well. And you're well. Your child is well. The gardener is well too. Everyone is well." Now she was blabbering.

She took her leave of Jane Simmonds. She kept walking down the lane. Her footsteps for some reason were slowing down. She didn't know why her treacherous footsteps were slowing down. She stood uncertainly. She checked in her pockets. There wasn't much. But there were two carrots that Laura had given her to feed the horses, but then they hadn't gone to feed the horses, after all. And she had forgotten to give the carrots back.

She found her footsteps turning toward the Ashton estate. Even though she knew he wasn't there, for some reason, her heart was still pounding. *Treacherous*, she thought. Her heart was treacherous. There was no good reason for it to be trying to climb up her throat.

It took her another ten minutes to get to the goat pen.

There they were, Sally and Prinny. Sally, the gray one with the cheeky eyes, instantly came over and started sniffing at her hand and butting her leg. Anya gave her velvet ears a rub and handed her a carrot. Prinny, the black-and-white one, walked over too and rubbed himself on her leg. She grinned and handed him a carrot also. She rubbed his ears, and he rubbed himself against her skirt and made soft snuffling noises.

"I suppose you can be nice to everyone in the world but not me."

Anya's heart nearly exploded.

So, not in London, after all.

She kept her face turned to the goats. She was having trouble breathing. "Would you like your ears tickled too, Lord Ashton?" she said, her voice remarkably steady.

"I was talking to Prinny. He hates me. But apparently he is

just lovely to complete strangers. Traitor, I tell you. You'd think he'd be grateful I haven't roasted him."

She turned to look at him. There he was. Hair as untidy as ever. Clothes scruffy. Leaning on the fence. Not in London. Still talking to goats. "You're not in London."

"Neatly observed. I am not."

"And Jeremy thought you were, did he?"

"I told him I'd be in London."

She looked severely at him. "You have no problems lying to your own brother?"

"None whatsoever."

"And I suppose Jane Simmonds got it all wrong too? She also thought you were in London?"

"Oh no, I asked her to tell you I was in London."

She stared at him dumbfounded. "You get your staff to lie for you regularly, my lord?"

"She didn't lie for me. She lied for *you*. She is a great fan of yours. She told me in clear terms that generally she hates lying."

She bent and picked up a sprig of lavender and started crumbling it in her fingers. "And Jane Simmonds thought that it would be very good for me to know that you were in London? Perhaps so I could come to the goat pen if I had a burning desire to do so?"

He took the fence in a neat jump, and she gasped. Because suddenly he was quite near. Though he didn't quite complete the distance between them. He wasn't touching her. He was standing some feet away. It was just that she could see the green flecks in his brown eyes.

"She thought it might be," he said. "She thought it might be good for you to hear what I have to say."

"She was wrong. I—I don't need to—there is no need to—"

"Anya." His voice was different now. Not mocking or teasing. Something else. "I am an idiot."

"It's taken you long enough to figure that out," she said, slightly breathlessly.

"I'm used to taking care of myself. And maybe Jeremy, when he lets me. But no one else. And trusting no one else. This is new for me, Anya. I'm not proud of it. I made a complete hash of things."

She was barely breathing now. Not looking at him. Looking at the ground, frowning. He walked closer. She still didn't look at him. She wondered if she would crack in two if she looked at him. Curse Jane Simmonds for saying that he was in London. He was near her now. Nearly touching. And then he lifted his hand. And he brought it close to hers. And touched hers with the back of his. Lightly. "Anya."

"You'll mistrust me again. I'll do something, or I won't do something, and you'll hold it against me again," she said quickly. She was looking at him now. Willing him to understand that it wouldn't work.

He didn't speak for some time, then finally said, "That's not unlikely. And you'll get annoyed at me. And you'll tell me I'm an idiot. And Jeremy will tell me I'm an idiot. Your sister will probably murder me. I know all that. But I love you. I can't live without you. And so you can't leave me. Even though I'm imperfect. And might hurt you again."

She glared at him. "You know this innocent act won't work on me."

He moved closer, so that she could feel his warmth. So that she couldn't breathe at all. Couldn't think. His fingers were touching hers now. Not quite holding them. He leaned forward to kiss her earlobe. "What did you say?" he murmured.

"I said," she said breathlessly, "that this innocent—that this innocent—"

She *meant* to say that this act of his wouldn't work at all. It was all a sham. She knew him too well. Except instead now she was kissing him, for some reason as hungrily as he was kissing her. Holding on to his face, his dear, familiar face. And she was wondering why it felt like she would rather have died than not kiss him again. When she broke the kiss, he was panting as hard as she was. They stood for a long time, faces touching, breathing each other in.

"I will not live in Folkestone," she said as she pulled away.

"No?"

"I have my work. If you expect me to give up my work—"

He kissed her again. Then he just held her close. "I would never ask you to do that."

"No."

"No, your sister would kill me."

She couldn't help laughing. "You're scared of her."

"Terrified."

"I must live in London so I can work."

"To tell you the truth, I'm sick of Folkestone."

He kissed her again and time seemed to stop. Something shifted. She held his face. He kissed her forehead and held her close. When they finally broke apart, he took her hand and they started walking. She had no idea where they were going. To the house, away from the house, to see his other animals? She realized she didn't care.

"But this is your life," she tried again. One may as well make one more attempt to talk sense.

He looked sideways at her and gave her his lazy smile. "You know, Anya, I thought so, before I met you. I thought this was my life and that it was more than enough. But it turns out that you are my life."

She smiled and he grinned back. And she chuckled. Then she got serious again. "The goats will go where we go."

"But we will, of course, cook them."

She gasped. "We are not going to cook them!"

He put an arm around her. "No, darling. Of course we aren't going to cook them. I say let them live and let them make lots of little babies. Would you like to see the grounds? They are especially beautiful in early summer."

She shook her head.

"The orangery? The gardeners are always singing odes to the orangery."

She shook her head again.

"We could walk up the lane and admire the countryside?"

She looked at him a little shyly, her heart thudding against her chest. "I was wondering, Lord Ashton," she murmured, "if you would take me to the house instead."

The words were innocuous enough, but the look in her eyes and the way she said them were enough for him to take his arm from her waist, grab hold of her hand, entwine his fingers with hers, and say, "I would like nothing better." He kissed her hand. "And I wish you'd call me Damian."

ACKNOWLEDGMENTS

I'm writing these acknowledgments a few months after my book launch for *Unladylike Lessons in Love*. Before the launch, I was terrified of doing a launch. Now I'm terrified that no matter how many book events I do, nothing will match that launch. The book seems small when faced with such a sea of people. *The people*, on the other hand, seem *huge*. This is thanks from someone who's always felt like a misfit, to all the people who keep showing me that there are a whole bunch of misfits out there, and when you put us all together in a room, it seems we fit quite nicely together.

Priya Doraswamy, thanks for understanding me. You're the perfect friend and agent for my restless soul.

To the HarperCollins team. Kate Bradley, thank you for your professional eye on my manuscripts and your moving speech at the launch. Maud Davies, for reading and supporting what I write. And I deeply appreciated your fuchsia dress on launch day! Thank you for all your creative and hard work, Meg Le Huquet, Ellie Game, Sarah Foster, Dawn Cooper, Penelope Isaac, and Kati Nicholls and team. To the Avon team. Allie Roche, very excited to work with you. Thank you to Asanté

Simons, DJ DeSmyter, Lucia Macro, Erika Tsang, and Kerry Rubenstein and team.

Waterstones Clapham Junction and Laura, how wonderful that you supported me and opened your doors and said yes to every strange idea I had, like Regency dancing, filling the store over capacity, the raffle, and all the rest. Really sorry for setting the alarm off so many times . . .

To the friends who supported me at the launch. Your words and presence meant more than you can imagine. Rosa Temple, you rocked the Q&A. Ciara Flood, wow, that bookmark, and just your beautiful, creative self. Charlotte, what are the chances that you were in the country. I am so lucky! Grainne and Tam, I'm eternally grateful you're in my life. Mei, let's never stop talking about changing the world. Jheni, you came up and whispered some very precious words in my ear. Liz, let's find some new charity shops and cafés to talk in. Friendred, always love seeing your glorious, fabulous self. Karen and Mark, Jane and Matt, and your amazing, intelligent kids. Dympna and Rebecca, how wonderful that you made it. Jane, Tara, Nicole, Dom, Michelle (my dancing partner, I would have been lost without you!). Agata, Melody, and Sarah, your support means a lot. Teek, Liz, and Jim, Gwen, thanks for always being there. Amelia Walker, Tashmia Owen, Lisa Turner, how great that I'm getting to know you.

To friends and authors Helen Holmes, Stella Oni, Harkiran Dhindsa, Elizabeth Chakrabarty, Stacey Thomas, Jessica Bull, Kate Morrison, Estella Rua, you made the evening extra special with your sparkling presence and your creativity and books. Bloggers Mia, Clair, Elsa and Evie, how *amazing* that you made it. Mia, there's no doubt why you're creative blogger of the year in 2023. (Long live the Book Party, Vic Hyde and A.J. West.)

Shani Akilah, Kirsty White, Jess Davies, Monica Germana, Pam Percy, Fiona Goh, would love to see more of you all. Vic Hyde, can't wait to explore more in this journey with your glorious self.

You wonderous people I work with. Siobhan, Danielle, Terry, Jo, Carole, Susi, Tanveer, Hilary, Joy, Nabihah and The Reading Cafe, Cath, Gem, Katharine, Sarah, Adrienne, Annie. Zarifah and Katie, and Nieves, how phenomenal that you were there. Royce, we rocked that panel!

Mrs. Bennet's Ballroom, we had *such* a good time giggling, laughing, and trying to dance. How wonderful you were. I'll keep quiet about the back room where we all got changed amongst the cardboard boxes and without a mirror . . .

People who couldn't make it but who mean a lot to me. Hannah Marriott, I'm so grateful you're in my life, with your warmth, generosity, and creativity. Ananda Breed and Jamilah Ahmad, Ruth MacDonald, Arun Sood, Katy Moran, Michelle Birkby, Maz Evans, Jenni Fletcher, Felicity George, Misky, Winnie Li, Sophie Page, Sophie Irwin, Jane Dunn, Marianne Ratcliffe, Hannah Copley, Susmita Bhattacharya, Aiysha Jahan, Vaseem Khan, Abir Mukherjee, Hamish Morjaria, always enjoy our conversations. Harry Kerr, your genuine appreciation of Arya means a lot to me. Angie Kirwin, what a wonderful, wonderful chat we had the first time we connected.

So many book lovers, bloggers, reviewers, all-around book people, thanks for your support. Thank you to Margaret James, Cathie Hartigan, Linda Hill, Nils Shukla, Jane Wickenden, bookaholicbecky, Angela Lam, Insta Tours, Random Things Tours, Luisa Jones, acottagefullofbooks, Joanne at Portobello, and others.

Authors like William Dalrymple, Sven Beckert, Shashi

Tharoor, Georgette Heyer, Julia Cameron, Elizabeth Gilbert, Julia Quinn, Mary Balogh, and more, thank you for your work.

My partner, for always supporting me and teaching me about the creative life. For never giving up. My kids for helping me find a place in the world. My sister, for never saying no when I request a read, and for knowing way too much about me and still giving me your love and support.

DISCOVER MORE OF
THE MARLEIGH SISTERS

Amita Murray takes us on a journey from the pleasure gardens of society to the dangerous streets of 19th-century London in this spectacular romantic debut by an unforgettable new voice.

"Sizzling romance with a splash of intrigue." —Julia Quinn

"Lila Marleigh is a smart, unconventional, and independent English-Indian beauty who controls what's allowed into her iced champagne punch, her gaming establishment, and her life . . . till Ivor Tristram turns up, and yes, it's a romance and mystery and Lila is charming, but it's the painful secret at the heart of her family that leaves me wanting even more. Are the Marleighs going to be the next Bridgertons? I can only hope!"
—Ovidia Yu, author of the Crown Colony Series and *Aunty Lee's Delights*

"This romantic adventure bolts from the first page while following professional hostess Lila Marleigh as she untangles a crime and finds lust—or is it love? You'll have to finish this in one sitting—call in sick!"
—Sumi Hahn, author of *The Mermaid from Jeju*